# SLEEP
# TIGHT

# SLEEP TIGHT

## JEFF JACOBSON

**PINNACLE BOOKS**
Kensington Publishing Corp.
www.kensingtonbooks.com

Kensington Publishing Corp.
119 West 40th Street
New York, NY 10018

All Kensington titles, imprints, and distributed lines are available at special quantity discounts for bulk purchases for sales promotions, premiums, fund-raising, educational, or institutional use.

Special book excerpts or customized printings can also be created to fit specific needs. For details, write or phone the office of the Kensington special sales manager: Kensington Publishing Corp., 119 West 40th Street, New York, NY 10018, attn: Special Sales Department; phone 1-800-221-2647.

This book is a work of fiction. Names, characters, businesses, organizations, places, events, and incidents either are the product of the author's imagination or are used fictitiously. Any resemblance to actual persons, living or dead, events, or locales is entirely coincidental.

PINNACLE BOOKS and the Pinnacle logo are Reg. U.S. Pat. & TM Off.

ISBN-13: 978-0-7860-3078-1
ISBN-10: 0-7860-3078-X

First printing: August 2013

10 9 8 7 6 5 4 3 2 1

Printed in the United States of America

First electronic edition: August 2013

eISBN-13: 978-0-7860-3079-8
eISBN-10: 0-7860-3079-8

*For Mads, Saw, and Deb—my everything*

# ACKNOWLEDGMENTS

The author would like to thank
Gus and Jennifer Alagna, David and Joyce Boyd,
Jen and House Domonkos, all good pals,
the amazing faculty, students, and staff at
the Fiction Department at CCC,
Gary Goldstein, 'cause this book wouldn't exist
without him, the wisdom and guidance of Doug Grad,
the man, the myth, the legend, "Hell" Owen LaMay,
Mom and Dad,
Karrie and John O'Donnell,
Lou and Sandra Phillips—always and forever,
Mary Reid, my guide to the south side,
Jon and Laura Wojtalik, for the babysitting and sanity,
Arlene Wojtalik, the best mother-in-law in the whole world,
and the best five-string banjo player in his height, weight,
and age group,
the one and only Mort Castle.

# Table C-1: Summary of WHO Global Pandemic Phases (WHO Global Influenza Preparedness Plan, 2005)*

## Interpandemic Period

**Phase 1.** No new influenza virus subtypes have been detected in humans. An influenza virus subtype that has caused human infection may be present in animals. If present in animals, the risk of human infection or disease is considered to be low.

**Phase 2.** No new influenza virus subtypes have been detected in humans. However, a circulating animal influenza virus subtype poses a substantial risk of human disease.

## Pandemic Alert Period

**Phase 3.** Human infection(s) with a new subtype but no human-to-human spread or at most rare instances of spread to a close contact.

**Phase 4.** Small cluster(s) with limited human-to-human transmission but spread is highly localized, suggesting that the virus is not well adapted to humans.

**Phase 5.** Larger cluster(s) but human-to-human spread is still localized, suggesting that the virus is becoming increasingly better adapted to humans but may not yet be fully transmissible (substantial pandemic risk).

## Pandemic Period

**Phase 6.** Pandemic phase: increased and sustained transmission in the general population.

*Taken from the World Health Organization website.

# PHASE 1

PHASE 1

# CHAPTER 1

7:13 PM
*December 27*

The change in cabin pressure squeezed Viktor's skull mercilessly, yanking him out of a dreamless void and thrusting him into cold, hard reality as his international flight out of the Koltsovo Airport in Yekaterinburg descended into Chicago. He blinked; the rows of seats ahead of him floated, drifting from side to side in his blurred vision. His heart raced. Saliva filled his mouth and his stomach threatened to erupt. He didn't think he had eaten anything since a rushed breakfast before the flight.

If that was true, he hadn't eaten in over eighteen hours. Had he been asleep the entire flight?

*Not sleep*, his body insisted. *Something worse.*

Viktor swallowed. Carefully. Something was very, very wrong. Under everything, even beneath the shakily controlled panic, there was something else.

He *itched*.

The sensation was insidious. Awful. Excruciating. He froze. He couldn't put his finger on where he could scratch. It seemed to appear all over and nowhere at once, as if the horrible sensation slithered throughout his body with the speed of thought, stretching out its jagged fingernails to caress just under the skin of his armpit, his face, the center of his back, his scrotum. He reached a trembling hand out and took hold of his water bottle.

The thought of the tepid liquid triggered an eruption of nausea and he let go.

Across the aisle, a middle-aged man in a rumpled suit tucked a paper cross into a Bible and gathered his belongings. Viktor slowly turned to the right. It felt like the bones at the base of his skull were grinding glass between them as he moved his head. The seat next to him was empty, and in the seat nearest the window, an older woman studied her crash-landing instructions, working hard to avoid his stare.

The captain's voice clicked over the whispered hum of air rushing past the fuselage. He spoke for a while in a southern Russian accent. After the announcement, one of the flight attendants translated his announcement into German and then still another gave her best shot at an English version. "This is Captain speaking. Continuation of final approach is fast approaching. If everyone please can sit still, putting seating belt on, remaining calm, we will be landing in Chicago in few short minutes. Home of Cubs footballs and Blackhawk hockey. Ha. Ha. Ha. Also Al Capone."

Viktor unbuckled his seat belt. Struggled to his feet. He hoped he could make it to the bathroom before one of the flight attendants tried to stop him. He wasn't sure what would happen then.

Sweat collected under the illicit cargo hidden carefully along both sides of his chest and stomach. Acutely aware of these small lumps, he knew he had to look truly awful as he found his feet and stood, hitting his head on the overhead bin.

The nice leather jacket, the new jeans, the crisp white shirt were all supposed to convey that he was the lazy son of someone rich. But the new clothes couldn't hide how he felt. He was tall and underfed, and he lurched up the aisle like a scarecrow running from a storm. Passengers flinched when they saw him.

Viktor made it inside the restroom before any of the flight attendants said anything. He sagged inside the plastic door, trying to slow his breathing. He turned on the light above the mirror and saw that he was much worse than he had feared.

His eyes were red and began to weep in the light. His skin had gotten frighteningly pale. It didn't make sense. His heart raced; his face should be red from all the blood surging through his body. He fumbled with the buttons to his crisp white shirt, and lifted the heavy T-shirt underneath.

The cargo was still there. Still quiet. Still unmoving.


"Don't worry. They won't get loose. No. It's the squeaks that will get you caught," Roman had said in his native language. Roman was a man full of nervous laughter and nicotine.

When Viktor stepped into the back room of the vet office outside of Yekaterinburg, he found the tiny cages, each no bigger than a toaster, on the operating table in a neat line. His passport, student visa, two credit cards, a driver's license, and just over three hundred dollars in U.S. currency had been stacked in the opposite corner. Down there, some of the metal surface was still smeared with congealed blood.

Roman held up a wisp of a vest, made from flesh-colored nylon pantyhose. He laughed. "I know, I know. It looks like something a prostitute would wear."

Viktor stripped to his underwear and stepped into it. He slid the straps into place, stretching the nylon from underneath his crotch, knotted it together at the hips, and ran it up the sides of his stomach and chest until it ended in a loop around each shoulder. Roman tied these across his shoulders.

"Trust me, they all wear these. I know a man who carried twenty-four lizards and snakes into Los Angeles not four years ago."

Viktor held up his arms and turned in a slow circle.

Roman said, "These animals? They will have it easier than you, my friend. Nineteen hours without a cigarette! Put on your pants. Walk around. We have . . ." He checked his watch. "Forty-three minutes."

"Until the flight?" Viktor asked, confused, trying not to let any panic show.

"No. Until we leave this office." Timing was everything. A difference of an hour in the international flight time could mean life or death for the cargo.


Viktor went to splash water on his face in the cramped airplane bathroom, but the sound of the trickling water wormed into his head and he suddenly spewed bile onto the mirror. His legs buckled and he dropped to his knees, dry-heaving into the metal sink. He hoped the gagging sounds couldn't be heard outside of the bathroom. Reaching up, he managed to pull one of the paper towels out of the dispenser and laid it on the damp bottom of the sink. Using that, he wiped some of the sweat off his face.

It made no sense. Why was he so sick?

One of the pouches along his left side twitched and squirmed. Another, on the right side, started to move. And yet another.

They were waking up.


He clearly remembered the rest of the preparation in the veterinarian hospital, watching closely as the vet placed a syringe on top of each cage. Each syringe held such little medicine they looked almost empty. The man waited patiently, until Roman, checking his watch, gave him a nod. The vet put a heavy leather glove on his left hand and opened the first cage.

He gave an injection every five minutes. Then they would squeeze each animal into yet another nylon pantyhose, twisting the material to trap it. The ends were then tied to straps in the vest. In the end, Viktor carried six on each side, each lump no bigger than a computer mouse.

"Good! Good! You look good!" Roman said, once Viktor had put his shirt back on. "Turn around. Good!" Viktor walked around the tiny operating room, experimentally swinging his arms.

"Try not to sweat," Roman offered.

The vet remained still the entire time, until he spotted movement. It was a tiny bug, venturing out of the sixth cage. The thing was no bigger than the head of the eagle on the old American coins they had given Viktor. The vet squashed it with his thumb and flicked it away.

Viktor could remember the ride to the airport, the perfunctory bribe in customs, a quick toast of ice-cold vodka in the airport bar, then the long walk to the plane. He found his seat, flirted unenthusiastically with one of the ugly attendants, and tried not to think about landing in Chicago.

After that, absolutely nothing.

A sharp rap at the door. "Sir! Sir! We are landing very soon. You must take your seat."

Viktor tried to respond; his voice came out garbled as if his tongue had forgotten how to create words. It must have worked for a moment because the knocking stopped.

He stared at himself in the mirror again. *Just land, get through customs, and then outside, where a van is waiting.* He sucked in a deep breath and blew it out through his nose.

Everything was going to be fine.

A thin trickle of blood slid out of his left nostril.

Viktor swore and wiped it away. More blood collected on his upper lip. He realized he could use this to his advantage and wound toilet paper around his fist, then pressed it to his nose. He was now just a passenger with a bloody nose because of the dry air in the cabin. That was all.

Something tickled his stomach.

At first, he thought it was just that maddening phantom itch. But this felt different. Something was moving across his skin. He pulled his shirt up, and there, crawling along the sparse black hairs around his belly button, was a tiny bug. Without hesitation, he pinched it between his thumb and forefinger and felt an insignificant, unsatisfying crunch. Examining his fingertips, he found a faint smear of blood.

The attendant knocked on the door again. Louder this time. "Sir! I insist, sir!"

Viktor wiped the remains of the bug on his new jeans, jammed the blood soaked tissue back to his nose, and opened the door. He glared at the attendant over the tissue. The phantom itch crawled across his scalp.

When the plane finally landed, Viktor was afraid he couldn't stand. He waited in his seat until nearly all the passengers had disembarked, effectively trapping the older woman next to him. She didn't make a move to get up, gripping her purse in two tight fists, staring unwaveringly at the perky young starlet skipping through warm surf on the cover of the in-flight magazine stuffed in the pouch on the back of the seat in front.

Viktor didn't care. He wedged his hands under his thighs, anything to hide the shaking. He couldn't stop licking his lips. The vibrations in his head threatened to spin out of control and he fought against the seizures that echoed throughout his body. The shaking built. His feet thrummed against his carry-on bag. Drool spilled from quivering lips. A distant burst of his heartbeat.

Abruptly, everything slowed down.

He stopped shaking. Wiped his mouth. The sounds of muttered conversations as the passengers filed past and pulled bags out of the overhead compartments seemed to be coming from underwater.

Viktor took a deep breath. Sweet relief flooded through his body, leaving him dazed and warm. His eyelids slowly slid shut. His breathing slowed.

Now the woman next to him really didn't know what to do. She thought he was asleep. The last of the passengers filed out. She hit the button for one of the attendants. Down at the front of the plane, the group looked back at her. When they saw Viktor, the attendant who had kicked him out of the lavatory started up the aisle, shaking her head.

She stopped a few seats away. "Sir. Please, sir. You are to leave now."

Viktor didn't move. Neither did the woman next to him.

"Sir. Sir." A little louder.

The attendant looked back at her group and shrugged.

Viktor gasped and jolted awake. The woman next to him flinched and let out a hushed yip.

The pain was back with a vengeance, drilling into the nerve cells in his stomach and behind his eyes, sparking agony as it burrowed deeper. He scrambled to his feet, spun, and almost fell back into the seat.

He licked his lips and grabbed his bag as tremors shook his limbs. Despite the loss of control, he still managed to hang on to the handle in one hand and pull himself along with the other. The attendants backed away as he staggered down the aisle.

Someone at the far end of the tunnel spoke into a phone. Viktor didn't like that.

When he got within four feet, he bared his teeth and growled at the flight attendant on the phone.

She flinched and dropped it.

He leaned away and stumbled up the ramp, out into the bright lights of customs, and took three hitching breaths. A bewildering labyrinth of lines that looked like they had been laid out by a couple of drunk government employees waited impatiently, all strung together with fake velvet ropes. Thirty or so passengers stood in line, sneaking glances back at him.

Their eyes crawled across his skin.

One of the pouches squirmed against his left hip and just like that, that furtive *itch* scrabbled across his back and Viktor couldn't take it anymore. He finally simply surrendered and let the shrieking in his head blot out everything else.

# CHAPTER 2

"Those flowers really bring out the color of your eyes," Sam told his partner.

"Damn. Can't tell you how touched I am that you noticed," Ed said. "Keeps me up at night sometimes, worrying if I'm handsome enough."

Sam tried not to smile and sipped his coffee instead. A snowstorm out over the Rockies had delayed Ed's girlfriend's flight, and the coffee had gotten cold and bitter while they waited.

It was late, and O'Hare was quiet. Bleary-eyed travellers trickled down the escalators from customs upstairs. Below, in the baggage claim area, most of the benches were empty; a few people sat along the snaking conveyer belts, waiting impatiently for the airlines to track down missing bags.

Sam looked back through the double set of glass doors at their unmarked Crown Vic. Calling it unmarked was a joke. Everybody in Chicago knew damn well that nobody drove Crown Vics except cops and those poor deluded schmucks who bought them used for God knew what reason at police auctions. Sam had left it parked illegally right in front of the doors on the lower level, where arriving passengers spilled out of O'Hare. It had been out there long enough to collect a halfhearted, thin layer of snow from a minor snow earlier. He wasn't worried about any tickets though; O'Hare's security, like everybody else, knew enough to leave it alone.

Technically, they were supposed to be supporting the anti-gang units in one of the pointless sweeps of one of the Chicago Housing Authority's worst buildings on the South Side. But that was like spraying a wasp's nest with water. All it did was piss everybody off.

Ed and Sam decided their time was better spent picking up Carolina.

Sam caught sight of his reflection. A wiry guy in his fifties with thinning gray hair glared back at him. The expression on his face caught him off guard. He looked like he might kick a dog for the hell of it. This surprised Sam; he was actually in a decent mood. As decent as his moods could get, anyway.

Ed, a heavyset black man the same age as Sam, waited for his girlfriend with a deep well of patience born of decades of endless stakeouts and too much fast food etched in his crinkled eyes. He held his flowers upright, not upside down, against his leg, like some guys. Not sideways either, held with indifference in crossed arms. Ed stood in a wide, relaxed stance, yet held those flowers as if they were growing out of a northern Illinois meadow at high noon.

Sam checked his watch. 11:47. Carolina's flight was nearly two hours late. They had been hoping to pick her up, drop her off, and be at the sweep for all the paperwork at the end. He was pouring the coffee into the water fountain and thinking of something to tell Commander Mendoza when he heard gunshots at the top of the escalator.

* * *

Ed left the flowers on the floor between the escalators and they stormed up two and three steps at a time. Ed glided into customs, his old .38 Special held with both hands, elbows loose. It carried six hand-loaded .357 caliber shells. Technically, he wasn't supposed to be carrying anything that powerful, but the big revolver had been grandfathered in when they changed the rules.

Sam, on the other hand, preferred a more modern Glock, with a nine-shot clip. He wasn't so much concerned with power as quantity. He'd rather spray lead all over the place than chose his shots carefully. If he had to shoot, then chances were he'd empty the clip, and probably the next one too.

Sam popped up a few steps behind and went right as Ed broke left.

They saw a tall, rail-thin male, standing at the far end of the hall, on the other side of the maze of blue rope lines. The man had a semiautomatic pistol jammed into the soft tissue under his chin.

A security guard, bleeding from his hip, crawled slowly away. The rest of the tourists and passengers huddled against the booths and examination tables.

Viktor's eyes were closed. His shoulders quivered, as if low, vicious jolts of electricity shot along his backbone every few seconds.

It was clear that he had disarmed the guard and fired a few rounds. But that didn't explain why the tall man was bleeding too. Ed and Sam got closer. He appeared to have ragged slashes across his face and neck. Blood collected in the crotch of his jeans.

The detectives got close enough to see the blood seeping into the industrial carpet as it spilled down his shoe.

Sam said, "Put that fucking gun down."

A sob burst out of Viktor. A low, guttural cry.

Sam tried again. "Put—"

Underneath the fresh blood, muscles under Viktor's arm twitched. The pistol started to come down, and the darkness of the muzzle grew larger every second as the detectives came within range.

Ed fired.

Viktor's left eye disappeared and his head flopped to one shoulder. His long frame sagged and collapsed. One of the passengers uttered a short, sharp scream, but that was all.

Silence bloomed as gun smoke drifted toward the ceiling.

Sam held up his star and addressed the witnesses. "Chicago PD. Everybody relax. It's over. Now, is anyone else hurt?" He bent to examine the bullet wound in the guard and winced. It looked like the bullet had gone through the bone, only an inch away from the outside of his hip. The man's face was knotted in pain. Sam patted his shoulder. "Hang in there. Must hurt like a sonofabitch. Didn't hit any arteries or anything though. You'll live."

Ed flipped open his cell phone and began to speak, giving the dispatcher a quick summary of dry, emotionless facts.

Sam stood. "Any doctors in here?"

An older woman raised her hand. "I am nurse," she said with a heavy Russian accent.

"Great," Sam said. "Can you help him out? You employees, does anybody have a first aid kit around here?"

Somebody brought out a kit and Sam gave it to the nurse. He stepped back, letting the nurse get to work. He waited until Ed got off the phone, and they approached the body together.

Viktor looked like he was still in as much agony in death as in life. His mouth was open, upper lip curled up, baring his teeth. He had landed on his back, one leg curled awkwardly under the other. There was a fist-sized hole in the back of his skull.

"Shit," Ed said.

Sam nodded, looking around at customs. "That's exactly what we just stepped in, brother. You got any ideas?"

"Not right now."

"Me, neither."

Sam squatted next to the corpse, pulled out a pen, and used it to gently lift Viktor's leather jacket. He couldn't see any passport inside, and guessed that the ID must be in his back pocket. But he didn't want to turn the body over. No point in messing up the evidence any more than necessary. He understood only too well they were facing a serious political shitstorm and blizzard of paperwork. The realization made him very, very tired.

He peered closely at Viktor's fingernails. They were full of crinkled strips of skin and clotted blood. "Lacerations," he said quietly, indicating the slashes across the corpse's face, neck, and arms.

Something moved under Viktor's shirt.

Sam dropped the pen and stood quickly. Ed already had his gun back out. "Fuck is that?" Sam asked.

Under the shirt, a small lump wriggled along Viktor's stomach. It paused, as if resting a moment, then continued, heading for his waist.

"Goddamnit. I don't want to put another hole in this sonofabitch," Ed said.

Sam retrieved his pen and used it to lift the shirttail, revealing more deep gouges sliced across Viktor's abdomen.

Something dark and furry burst into his face in an eruption of brown wings.

"Oh, fuck!" Sam blurted and fell back.

The animal flitted away, rising and dipping as it whirled throughout the hall.

"It's a goddamn bat," Ed said with a shaky laugh. They

ignored the fluttering bat overhead for a moment and turned their attention back to Viktor. Sam lifted the shirt again, this time peeling it back to expose the nylon straps and pouches strapped to Viktor's torso.

More of the pouches were moving. Sam said, "Better let animal control know."

# CHAPTER 3

Airport security showed up first, cordoning the area off and hustling the witnesses to a series of rooms for statements. Then the paramedics hauled off the bleeding security guard. Chicago PD wasn't long after, and soon customs flickered with popping flashbulbs. The FBI was informed, and two sleepy guys in blue suits showed up and looked like they expected somebody to bring them coffee. Another couple of guys in darker suits showed some official-looking credentials to get inside, but would neither confirm nor deny they were from the CIA. The boys from Homeland Security barged in and started barking orders. Nobody paid much attention. Some poor bastard from the FAA rushed around, looking lost and unable to answer any questions.

The word "terrorist" hung in the air like the gunpowder from Ed's .38.

The bat had disappeared.

Once they'd given their statements to everybody, Ed and Sam sat back and enjoyed the circus. They knew damn well they were in for one hell of an ass-chewing from Commander Mendoza in the morning, but for now, it was fun to just watch

the show as the various departments and agencies fought
for jurisdiction. Apparently, the man had come from one of
the more interesting countries in Eastern Europe, as far as
the government was concerned. And no, they would only
share information with the local Chicago cops if the situation
demanded it, and only if they deemed the public health to be
at risk.

But when three astronauts in blue plastic suits with the ini-
tials CDC stenciled in no-nonsense letters a foot high on their
backs appeared at the top of the escalators, the arguing trickled into silence. The men from the CDC conferred briefly
with the FBI agents, then moved on to investigate the body.

A squad of soldiers followed and formed a seven-man
perimeter around the body. The rest took posts at various
points throughout the room. They wore air filter masks, plastic covers over their fatigues, rubber boots sealed with duct
tape, and surgical rubber gloves. Two more carried supplies
for the guys in charge.

The FBI agents started moving everyone back. It wasn't
hard. All of the fight had gone out of the various agencies. It
was clear that the CDC was now in charge, and nobody was
protesting. Nobody wanted to go to war with the CDC.

Germs didn't fight fair.

Once someone was dead, you could stop worrying. Get
him somewhere cold where the medical guys could cut him
open and figure out what killed him and you were good to go.
But when that particular agency got involved . . . all bets were
off. If you could catch some kind of god-awful flesh-rotting
disease from a corpse, then nobody wanted to fuck around.
Everybody started to look for excuses to get the hell out of
there.

One of the FBI agents addressed the crowd. "Need your
attention for a quick moment, folks, make sure everybody is
up to speed. As of now, the body of the suspect will be handed
off to the custody of the CDC."

The guys from the CDC ignored all this and used long

tongs to place the remaining bats in small jars with lids connected to a complicated air filtration machine. One stood back and instructed the others. His voice was inaudible as he leaned over the body. He stepped back and unfolded one of the thickest body bags Sam had ever seen.

"So we'd like to turn the scene over to them," the FBI agent continued. "If we can have everyone file out in an orderly fashion, we'll finish up the debriefing and a few other things in no time."

Ed said out of the side of his mouth, "What 'other things'?"

"My money's on some kind of decontamination song and dance."

They wandered over to the edge of the escalators and saw the CDC guys spraying everything down with foam that expanded over every surface with sea-green bubbles. Behind that was more air-filtration equipment. Buckets to step in. Collapsible rooms to march through.

"Fuck that. I paid sixty bucks for these shoes," Ed said. "They ain't hosing 'em down. And Carolina's flight still hasn't landed."

"So much for your flowers."

They walked away from the escalators. Sam acted like he was retrieving his briefcase, picking up a thin one abandoned in the shooting. He made a show of checking his watch as everyone crowded around the escalators. While he appeared to be merging into an organized line, he joined his partner in the far corner and they slipped through one of the employee-only doors.

# CHAPTER 4

Tommy Krazinsky kissed his daughter Grace good night, tucked the blanket tighter around her shoulders, and arranged Grace's stuffed animals so they formed a protective wall around her. He made sure to slip her favorite, some kind of puppy with butterfly wings, under the blanket, so that Grace could cradle it in the crook of her small arm.

"I'd hate to forget Princess . . . who's this again?"

"Princess Tianna Fuzzycakes, Daddy." She watched him with a four-year-old's solemn eyes.

"Of course. She'll keep you safe, okay?"

Until tonight, Tommy had been able to stay with his daughter until she fell asleep on Sunday nights, but tonight was his first night at his new job. His best guess was that it would take just under an hour to get downtown. He didn't own a car and would have to rely on Chicago's rather unreliable public transportation. At least he didn't have to catch a bus. Tommy could walk to the Red Line and catch an El straight downtown.

He was about to start work for the Department of Streets and Sanitation. Although he would normally start his shift at the division headquarters on the West Side, tonight he'd been summoned downtown.

He kissed Grace's forehead again. "Sorry, baby. Daddy loves you, little one." He kissed her forehead once more and stood. Shrugging into his coat, he said, "I'll see you soon, okay? Don't worry about anything. Daddy's gonna fix it. I'll straighten things out with Mommy. I promise." He patted her bed and left before his voice cracked.

Mommy was Kimmy. Kimmy was Tommy's ex-wife. They had been high school sweethearts. Their relationship had gone slowly but steadily south when Kimmy had finally discovered why men were so gosh darn nice to her.

Tommy had loved her before she had blossomed into a knockout: long black hair, the grin and eyes of an angel, and the body of a lustful demon. Her father had been a complete and utter drunken wreck, and she had fallen hard for the only boy who showed her kindness. Throughout high school, Tommy was the only man who had mattered in her life. In her mind, their lives were predestined. The two were going to spend their lives living in Bridgeport, barbecuing on weekends, cheering for the Sox, raising kids, attending St. Mary of Perpetual Help on West Thirty-second Street every Sunday and holiday, and pretty much living within the nexus of the Stevenson and Dan Ryan expressways for the rest of their lives.

That didn't work out.

But by then, she'd already had Grace, and Tommy was sleeping on the couch. Four years later, she was living with Grace in a three-room flat in Wrigleyville. Her mom, Florence, owned the building, and lived downstairs.

While Tommy was able to spend weekends with Grace, he and Kimmy didn't talk much if they could help it. Grace wasn't in school yet, but Tommy could see a whole new set of issues clouding up on the horizon when that happened next year.

He gently closed Grace's bedroom door. He stood for a

moment in the middle of the long hall. The living room and front door in the shotgun apartment were off to the left. Kimmy was in the kitchen off to the right. Tommy knew better. He knew he should turn left and leave quietly.

But his daughter's fear made him angry. He turned to the right.

"What do you want?" The words hit him before he'd stepped into the kitchen.

Tommy shook his head, held his palms up, like he was surrendering. "I don't have time to argue. She's four years old, for Chrissakes. Why in the hell would you tell her there's goddamn monsters in the closet and under the bed?"

"You don't have to take care of her five days a week. You don't know what it's like. She's an angel, I'm sure, when she's with you. She's not like that here. No. Here, she won't stay in her goddamn bed. You go be Father of the Year somewhere else. I'm her mom. I'll take care of it. I'm sorry, but you don't know what the fuck you're talking about." She flipped the page of her magazine.

"I shoulda known better than—"

"You're going to be late. Do you know what that means?"

Tommy nodded, slowly. He couldn't resist getting the last word in and said, "Shoulda known better," and left.

Tommy had had an assault charge filed against him last year.

Kimmy had taken Tommy to the mall, forcing him to buy new clothes. She sent him into a store, waiting with Grace in the food court. When Tommy got back, he found Kimmy openly flirting with a group of college dipshits. Grace was a few seats over, sitting next to some stranger, telling him what crayons to use in her coloring book.

Tommy immediately sensed some seriously unpleasant vibes from the guy. Tommy stepped up to the table and told Grace to go sit by her mother. Kimmy turned and finally noticed Grace sitting so close to the guy. She was as surprised as Tommy, but not anywhere near as angry. The college boys eventually figured out that the husband was pissed and faded back into the mall.

"Take Grace home," Tommy said, never taking his eyes off the guy. "I'll catch up later."

The guy decided it was time to go as well and went to lift his food tray. Tommy slammed it back to the table. Sweet and sour chicken and white rice flew up and scattered across the table. Tommy leaned in close. "Do you know my wife? Do you know my daughter? Do you know me?"

"What are you, some kinda nut? Fuck you," the guy said.

Tommy snatched the tray and jabbed it into the guy's throat. The guy made a gagging noise and fell backwards. Tommy swung the tray over his head and bashed it into the guy's face. He was still pounding the man when mall security showed up and tackled him.

The guy decided to push his luck and press charges. When it went to trial, the guy's lawyer managed to show only the beating from the surveillance video, not how close he had been sitting to Grace, not where his hand may have been.

Tommy was found guilty, and since he had no previous record of any consequence, he had to perform a few hundred hours of community service. But the blot on his record prohibited him from gaining any kind of custody. He only got to see Grace on the weekends and that was only because Kimmy wanted some time to herself.

Sometimes Tommy wondered if he'd ever find anybody else, maybe get married again someday, but he tried not to dwell on it. He knew a part of him would never be able to let go of Kimmy completely. He didn't like it, but wasn't going to kid himself. If she ever woke up and realized that he had always been the only one for her, he'd take her back in a heartbeat, no matter what she had said or done.

Still, he didn't think that was likely. He knew she'd moved on, even if she did still show him affection once in a while.

But that affection was probably closer to pity, like the feeling a supermodel might get when she sees a puppy in the rain.

Tommy kicked at the thin layer of slush as he headed for the Addison El stop. At least the snow was keeping most people inside. Tommy hated Wrigleyville. The muscleheads who crowded the sidewalks, the entire frat-house-row feel, the fake lovable losers posturing. And the whole upper-class thing irritated him.

He hurried across the street, dodging cabs and SUVs. It wasn't much of a storm, but you never knew when a little snow could throw the CTA into chaos. The last thing he needed was to be late.

Tonight especially. Kimmy had arranged the whole thing. When Tommy had finally found out that she was seeing some mover and shaker down at City Hall, the wheels had already been set in motion, and he could either remain quiet like a good little cog or get ground up in the machine, crushed by the merciless juggernaut of Chicago politics.

So, for his daughter, he kept quiet. He was determined to be a good little cog, even if it killed him.

# CHAPTER 5

**9:04 PM**
**December 27**

Ed and Sam marched through the blowing snow, looking for an unlocked door. If Ed was mad about his shoes, he didn't say anything. To complain about the weather would go against all code of ethics if you grew up in the Midwest. You joked about the conditions, sure, loved to brag about it, of course, but you never, ever whined about it. The worse the weather got, the more superior you could feel over the punks in New York and the space cadet pussies in L.A.

They finally gave up and started out to the runways to flag down one of the luggage carriers. They flashed their badges. The woman didn't even take off her ear protection, just jerked her head and the empty line of luggage cars she was towing. Ed and Sam hopped on. Ed's phone beeped. He checked it and said, "Well, it's official. This night has gone to shit. Carolina's flight was cancelled. She won't be in until tomorrow. Maybe."

Sam shrugged. "Guess we should head for home. Get a good night's sleep, be fresh for all the paperwork in the morning."

They cracked up.

The baggage handlers showed them how to find their way through the winding conveyor belts and out into the terminal.

The place was full of bright lights and plenty of law enforcement. Most of the local cops were in charge of keeping the reporters out of the terminal. They slipped under the yellow tape and found their Crown Vic blocked by a dizzying array of police cruisers, somber government sedans, and tech vans.

Sam shook his head. "Moses himself couldn't part all that shit."

"We need new wheels, that's for damn sure."

They hiked out in the snow again, until they found a young cop standing in front of his cruiser, diverting traffic into the parking garages, where drivers would be forced back onto the O'Hare Expressway, heading back into the city.

"Officer . . ." Sam squinted at the cop's badge. "Reid? I'm afraid I've got some bad news for you. My partner and I have an emergency, and we need this car. Immediately. You will continue your assignment, and you're doing fine work, by the way, but when you are relieved, you will take our car back to Division One. Eleventh Street, you understand?"

"But . . ." The cop looked like he'd been ordered to suck his thumb in front of all the traffic.

"You questioning orders? Seriously?" Sam glared at Ed. "Can you fucking believe this?" He turned back to the cop, getting uncomfortably close. "You mean to tell me you're actually going to interfere with superior officers when they are attempting to deal with an honest-to-God homicide emergency?"

"Son," Ed said patiently, long accustomed to playing the good cop. "Do yourself a favor. Turn your keys over to this man. You do not want to piss him off."

Officer Reid thought about it for a few more seconds and said, "The keys are in the ignition." Ed climbed into the driver's seat while Sam stretched out in the passenger's. The cop tapped on the driver's window. Ed hit the button and the window slid down. Officer Reid leaned in, trying to be as intimidating as possible, like he had pulled them over for some traffic violation. "You can't just take a cruiser whenever you feel like it. I'm calling this in."

"You better," Ed said. "You damn well better follow procedure." He sent the window back up, hit the lights and the siren too just for the hell of it, and sent cars scattering as they tore off down the crowded highway.

"Thought it was long overdue you and I sat down, face to face, without all the goddamn lawyers between us." Lee leaned back, crossing his alligator-skin dress shoes on the corner of his desk and lacing his fingers behind his head. He had a face chiseled for politics. Strong. Handsome. Reassuring. Tonight he wore his concerned, caring look. "Wanted to make sure you understood how this deal works."

Tommy knew how the deal worked.

Lee didn't wait for Tommy. "You grew up here. You know how things happen in this city. You're either scratching somebody's back or you're out on your ass."

Tommy nodded, let his gaze wander around Lee's office. Cornelius Shea, "Lee" to friends and enemies alike, was the youngest commissioner of Streets and Sanitation in the history of the city of Chicago. He had enough muscle to snag an office on the second-to-top floor of City Hall. A large photograph of Lee and then Mayor Daley Jr. hung directly behind his desk. More photos of Lee shaking hands with VIPs were hung around the opulent office. Most citizens wouldn't have gotten this far, and Tommy understood why Lee hadn't taken down the pictures of himself with former Illinois governors, considering three out of the last four were currently behind bars for corruption. Lee preferred instead to conduct press conferences out in front, with City Hall itself serving as a dramatic backdrop, or give interviews as he walked the streets of one of the quieter neighborhoods, proving he was just a man of the people.

And of course, he had a framed print of goddamned Wrigley Field at night. It figured.

Lee arched one thick black eyebrow. "You hearing me, or is this some kinda big joke to you?"

"I hear you."

"I sure as hell hope so. You play by my rules, everybody's happy. You got yourself a cushy job until you retire and get to be a dad to your little girl. Fuck it up, and I promise you you'll never see her again. Hell, you'll be lucky you don't end up in prison. Your job is to keep me happy. That's all you gotta worry about. And keeping me happy means steering clear of any goddamn nosy social workers, or anybody else that gets curious, especially any cock-sucking reporters."

He lit a cigarette, blew smoke at the ceiling. He was dressed in a tux, with the bow tie rakishly open and hanging on either side of the unbuttoned collar. He probably thought he looked like James Bond after a casual night gambling in Monaco. There was some heavy-duty charity dinner with all the heavyweights in town at the brand-spanking-new Serenity Hotel, with proceeds supposedly going to help needy children. Maybe get his picture in the *Trib*'s *RedEye*.

The boys with the real power, and the true recipients of most of the money, wouldn't show up in the paper. They wouldn't get within ten feet of a camera.

Politics in Chicago.

Lee took another drag. Tommy guessed that the city ban on indoor smoking in public buildings didn't apply to this particular office. "Shit. It's not a bad deal, when you stop and think about it. Let's cut through the bullshit. A piece of ass like Kimmy . . . fuck me, you didn't think she'd stick with you forever, did you? Jesus Christ. I hope not. No friggin' way. Hell, I can't believe she stuck with you for this long."

Tommy had been shocked when a whole army of lawyers accompanied Kimmy to the divorce proceedings. He'd figured they'd sign some papers, agree to share custody of Grace, and it would be all simple and clean. He hadn't even thought to bring a lawyer.

It hadn't taken long for Tommy to get a queasy feeling, like he was the only one at a party who didn't know anybody and all the guests were starting to lick their lips and look at him like he was going to be the main course for dinner. It had been obvious that the lawyers and the judge were all good friends and golfing buddies. There had been no one else in the courtroom, so they hadn't even tried to pretend.

The judge had awarded Kimmy sole custody of Grace, and hit Tommy with an absurdly high child-support bill. There was no way he could afford to pay, not with his old job. Everybody knew this, and Tommy felt stupid for not figuring out the deal sooner. Not a day later, a job offer had come through, an offer to work for the City of Chicago, as an employee for the Department of Streets and Sanitation. His salary had seemed suspiciously high, until he'd realized that most of his pay would be taken out for child support and various other contributions to the union and the city.

"So." Lee stubbed out his cigarette. "I'm going to assume we have an understanding."

"Sure."

"Then I suggest you get moving. Don't want to be late clocking in your first night."

Tommy stood and headed for the door.

"I hope we don't need to talk ever again." Lee said. "Fact is, I don't want to look at you. Makes me a little sick, thinking about you and Kimmy. Tell Ray down at the desk I said you didn't have to sign out. Let's keep this meeting off the books."

# CHAPTER 6

The bat wheeled through the freezing night air, senses reeling. Once free of the nylon pouch, it had flitted about the terminal, keeping to the shadows. The giant Christmas trees erected throughout the terminal offered no clear openings, and the lights confused it, so the bat rose higher and eventually squeezed into a crack between one of the futuristic struts and the ceiling. It tried eating a spider, but found the taste to be bitter and alien. The brief respite allowed the bat to catch its breath, but it couldn't remain hidden much longer. It needed warmth and water.

The six-year-old female sheath-tailed bat was one of the most endangered animals in the world. Experts estimated the total population to be less than a hundred mature individuals. She had been caught with a fishing net strung over the fissure where the colony lived on the Seychelles Island, just north of Madagascar. She weighed close to ten grams, and wasn't much bigger than a young mouse.

She was sick.

She was having trouble swallowing, and she had scraped bloody furrows in her pelt with her claws and teeth in response to the infuriating parasites that crawled through her fur. Arching her back, she tried to scrape the invaders off on the sharp edge of the angled ceiling, but they just flattened themselves against her pale skin or took refuge under her wings. A growing restlessness drove her from her perch, and she fluttered through the terminal once more. She had known fear for so long, it was simply a part of her now, but the disorienting panic kept her moving.

She found a sliver of a crack near the top of the vast wall of windows that faced north, and tasted unfamiliar air. Wanting only to leave the stale, dry atmosphere of the terminal behind, she squeezed through and immediately panicked. The temperature hovered around twenty-eight degrees, and she had never been this cold. She beat her wings harder, swooping through the hurricane of flashing red and blue lights that covered the inner drive of O'Hare.

She rose higher, soaring out over the parking lot. She could sense the tectonic vibrations emanating from the city below, urging her higher and higher. The bat had never encountered snow before, and the drifting flakes wreaked havoc with her echolocation organs. A roaring filled her ears, and the horrible, shrieking engines of an incoming jet drove her away from the airport.

She turned east, instinctively drawn to the vast stillness of Lake Michigan. For a while, she simply glided, surfing the bitter winds that pushed her to the southeast. The adrenaline that had surged through her compact body began to ebb. Her tiny heart hitched twice, her wings folded, and she dropped, tumbling through snowy skies into the vast forest of concrete and steel and harsh lights of downtown.

The free fall squeezed the last dregs of adrenaline into her system and she found the power to spread her wings and soar, whirling in an ever-downward spiral. She smacked into a frost-covered window, bounced off, and plummeted to the street. She found her wings once again, and tried to aim for the darkness along the Chicago River, but the draft from a passing El train sent her spinning into the girders that held up Upper Wacker Drive.

She fell like a stone into the frozen gutter along the edge of Lower Wacker.

Her heart convulsed again, and she pulled her wings close. Headlights splashed over her and moved on, leaving her bathed in the sickly yellow light from the irregular fluorescent bulbs. The panic and sickness had driven her consciousness deep into the recesses of her mind, and she was only dimly aware of the icy concrete.

She was still alive when the first of the rats emerged from the sewer drain and scurried along the gutter. It was soon followed by several more. Farther down the street, even more rats appeared in another drain. Waiting for the relative darkness between the passing headlights, they crept along toward the bat.

The first rat seized her in his huge incisors and scurried back into the darkness of the sewers, leaving nothing but splayed footprints and long, wormlike tracks from their tails in the gray slush.

The parasites, commonly known as bat bugs, sensed the life slipping out of their host and crawled off of her body as it was ripped apart and the pieces grew cold. They smelled the carbon dioxide exhaled by the rats and crept onto their new hosts. The rats, eyes bright with hunger and muzzles wet with the bat's blood, felt nothing as the bat bugs wriggled through their coarse hair and gorged themselves.

# CHAPTER 7

**10:44 PM**
**December 27**

Tommy's first night on the job started in a bar, a dim hole in the wall on the West Side. It wasn't anything fancy. A few flat screens hung around the place, tuned to sports. A dozen tables were spread out over a greasy linoleum floor. A thick haze of smoke hung throughout the bar; these guys didn't pay much attention to the no-smoking ordinance either. It didn't even look like the place had a name. The only notable attribute was an extremely large parking lot in the back, with at least three exits leading to major avenues and expressways.

The parking lot was full of city vehicles. CTA vans. Dark blue electrician trucks. Sewer behemoths, with the huge tubes draped over the cab. Tommy counted at least thirteen Streets and Sans trucks. Some were garbage trucks, others were heavy-duty work vans, fellow rat control workers.

Don, his partner, led Tommy through the tables and sat near the grimy front windows, filled with neon beer signs and dead flies. Don lit a cigarette and shoved a sticky menu at Tommy. There was a narrow kitchen behind the bar, where, apparently, they'd make pretty much anything you wanted as long as it was deep fried and covered in plastic melted cheese.

"First night, my treat." Don's mustache and wide nose made him look a lot like an easygoing walrus. When he first climbed in the cab, Tommy wasn't sure what to make of his new partner. Don's bulk made it difficult for him to even fit behind the wheel. He'd fixed Tommy with a cold stare and nodded at Tommy's ragged Sox cap. "You a fan, or is that for show, just to fit in with the guys here?"

"I grew up in Bridgeport," Tommy answered, getting pissed.

"Thank Christ." Don grinned. "Last guy I had to break in, fucking douche bag coulda cared less about sports. Jesus humpin' Christ, can you imagine? Fucking living in Chicago, and you don't like sports? Give me a fucking break. The only thing worse woulda been if he'd a been a Cubs fan."

So they talked baseball as Don headed west. Both clubs had new managers, so there was plenty to discuss. They really didn't hate the Cubs, but it was more fun to make fun of the struggling north-side club. As south-side fans, neither one missed Ozzy, but they were heartbroken that both Buehrle and Pierzynski were gone. It wouldn't be the same without them. And before Tommy knew it, they were pulling into the parking lot.

Don ordered a double cheeseburger and cheese fries with a Diet Coke. "Don't drink booze anymore," he said. "Doc says it's not a good idea. But hell, you feel like a beer, knock yourself out." Tommy got the chicken sandwich and potato chips. He thought about it for a moment, decided fuck it, and ordered a beer with it. He had to admit, so far, his first night on the job wasn't so bad.

"I'm not gonna bullshit you. Day shift has the cushy end of the job. Hell, all they do is ride around all day and look busy. Put out some poison, a few traps, hang some signs, quote, 'make their presence known in the neighborhoods.'" Don shrugged. "You and me, we get the shit end of the stick. We're the ones getting our hands dirty, out collecting the dead rats."

Don stabbed a cheese fry into a lake of ketchup and fixed

Tommy with a grin that straightened out his mustache. "But you, my friend, you stick with me and I'll show you some things you never seen. Things that make this job of ours a sweet deal. But first, you gotta answer me this. Who's upstairs pulling strings for you? Guy like you doesn't just fall into a job like this. I got ten guys on the garbage detail fighting for this spot. What makes you special?"

Tommy had known this was coming. Hell, he'd be pissed if he'd worked for a job for a long time only to watch some young punk jump ahead of him. "Believe it or not, Lee Shea got me this job."

"No shit?"

"No shit."

"He a friend of yours?"

"Hell, no. You?"

"Fuck, no. I hate that slimy little bastard."

"Me, too. So let's just say he's got my balls in a vise. Says to be here and be ready for work, and well, here I am."

"You ain't the only one in town. Motherfucker's got his hands in a lot of places around town. Yours ain't the only balls that sonofabitch is squeezing." Don sat back, absentmindedly wiping ketchup and cheese out of the corners of his mustache. "What the hell are you gonna do? Fuckin' Chicago. Might as well make the best of it. Have another beer. We're gonna be here a while. Take a nap, you feel like it. We'll head out later. I got a place where we can find all the rats we need."

# CHAPTER 8

**11:44 PM**
*December 27*

Ed followed the Kennedy into the city and got off at Addison, heading east.

"Jesus. I'd forgotten how much I hate cruisers," Sam said, struggling to find a comfortable position for his long legs among all the electronic crap and extra gear in the front seat. He unscrewed his flask, offered it to Ed. Ed shook his head. Sam took a deep pull. He mostly hated the police cars because they didn't have a radio. Oh sure, every car had plenty of law communication equipment, but not an honest-to-goodness AM/FM radio. Not that the radio stations played much that they liked anyway.

Ed and Sam couldn't stand most current popular music. R and B? Please. That used to mean something more than grunting and cooing "baby" a thousand times. Once in a while, they'd get lucky, and hear an old Sam and Dave song, maybe even some Muddy Waters, and they'd sing along, Ed in an unnaturally deep baritone, and Sam in a strangled, off-key cry. Outside the car, it probably sounded like shit, but inside, he figured they harmonized just fine.

Hearing a good song was rare. They stayed away from the

popular stations. Sometimes the local college kids got tired of playing songs in which the musicians had apparently fallen asleep on their keyboards staring into the unfathomable depths of their belly buttons, and went retro and played some good stuff. You'd be surprised how hard it was to hear legendary local blues folks like Junior Wells, Magic Sam, Koko Taylor, or even Howlin' Wolf on the radio.

Jazz? Sure, there was enough jazz to make your ears bleed. Problem was, Sam thought most of it sounded like somebody recorded a toddler with ADHD attacking a piano with a hammer while somebody else threw a drum set down the stairs.

They pulled up in front of one of the grand old dames that lined Lake Shore Drive, colossal, ornate buildings decades beyond their glory years. Ed hit the siren, jolting the night doorman out of a nap. Ed left the spinning lights on, splashing the front of the building with a blinking blue light show.

The night doorman watched them with bleary eyes and unlocked the door. Sam flashed his star but didn't explain as they strode through the marble foyer and stepped inside the elevator.

Sam rolled his head around, easing the kinks in his neck. He eyed the numbers clicking past. "Soft or hard?" he asked.

Ed considered it for a moment. "How long's it been?"

"Seven months. At least."

"Last time, we kick in the door, go in hard?"

"Think so. We've broken the chain at least twice."

"Soft then. I've already shot somebody tonight. Got it out of my system."

The elevator doors opened on the top floor. They stepped out onto plush red carpet and followed the hall to the end. Sam checked his watch. Three in the morning. If their past visits were any indication, David Thatcher should be just about partied out by now, and they would be catching him either unconscious or just about to pass out.

Ed rapped briskly on the door and held his star up to the

peephole, blocking them from sight. No answer. Ed knocked again. "Mr. Thatcher? Chicago PD. Open up, sir."

From behind the door, a groggy voice said, "What, what do you want?"

"Please open the door, Mr. Thatcher."

The door opened, but only a crack. David's eye appeared. "What the hell is going on?" Acting tough.

Sam threw his shoulder into the door, forcing it to open the length of the chain. "Hey, David. How ya doing?"

"Oh, fuck. Not you two." He tried to shut the door, but Sam's foot was in the way.

Sam laughed. "Miss us? I hate to break it to ya, pal, but did you know there's a warrant out for your arrest? Got two boys in a squad car downstairs, waiting for your ass. Go look, see if you don't believe me." Sam withdrew his foot.

David slammed the door.

They gave him a minute. Sam knocked on the door, said loudly, "You can either talk to us, or we'll just kick the door down again and those boys downstairs will be happy to slap some cuffs on you. Your call." Sam gave it a second to sink in, then said, "My patience is getting a little thin."

They heard the click and tinkle as the chain was unlatched. The door swung open, and David stood in the doorway, arms crossed, scowling. He was young, maybe mid-twenties, dressed in a blue satin robe and not much else. His blond dreadlocks were smashed flat on the left side of his head, giving him a lopsided appearance. "I didn't do nothin'."

Sam pushed past him and stood in the middle of the apartment. It was a hell of a lot nicer than Sam's place. Hardwood floors. Leather couches. Marble coffee table. Recessed lighting. A giant poster of Pacino's *Scarface*. An artistic black and white poster of two blondes making out. Pizza boxes and greasy fast food bags spoiled the cultured effect, though.

"Your mommy still paying the rent?"

"Fuck you. Fuck you both."

"David, David, David." Ed shook his head, shut the door behind him, and leaned against it. "You really should be glad to see us. If we hadn't heard about you, and intercepted those officers downstairs, you'd be in a real pickle right now."

Sam checked his watch. "We told 'em five minutes. You got two minutes left."

"So what?" David put his hands on his hips. "I ain't done nothin'."

Ed shrugged. "You pissed somebody off, that's all I can say. Word is, they got you dealing on tape. Digital video, five-point-one stereo surround, all the bells and whistles. It's truly astonishing where they can put a camera these days."

"Let's cut to the chase, for your sake," Sam said. "We're offering to take care of any evidence. That way, the boys downstairs can't take you in. Make us happy, and who knows, that tape might just get lost. Happens all the time."

"I got nothing. I don't deal anymore. I'm clean."

"Sure you are. You got . . . thirty seconds to convince yourself that it's true."

David lasted twenty seconds before muttering, "You guys are such motherfuckers." He turned over the giant subwoofer and pulled out three baggies of pot, at least five pounds each.

Sam tossed two bags to Ed, who stashed them in his overcoat. "You sure that's it?"

David shook his head, finally said, "Fuck. Fuck!" He went to the empty aquarium and pulled out a baggie of fine white powder.

Sam took that as well. "Now, tell me the truth. Don't you feel better?"

Back in the car, Ed took the passenger seat and chuckled. "That kid." He split open a Swisher Sweet with his pocket knife, scooped out the sweet smelling tobacco, and sprinkled

some of the weed in its place as Sam pulled out onto the
Drive. "He gets any dumber, we're gonna have to call Social
Services."

"Well, I suppose there's a good reason they call it dope,"
Sam said, weaving the cruiser through traffic. He rolled down
the driver's window as Ed lit the blunt. Ed passed it to him,
but Sam shook his head and laughed. "You fucking hippies.
I'm driving, dammit."

Ed took another hit.

Sam pulled a flask out of his jacket and took a long sip. He
hit the lights and the gas and sped south through the blowing
snow on Lake Shore Drive.

# CHAPTER 9

**2:14 AM**
*December 28*

"Rule number one. Get yourself some decent boots. Those, they go to what, the top of your ankle?" Don asked as the truck rolled down West Ogden, passing three buildings, liquor stores, and vacant lots filled with nothing but snow. The avenue was nearly deserted at three-thirty in the morning. Parts of the West Side looked abandoned at the best of times; tonight it looked damn near apocalyptic.

They'd been at the bar close to five hours, shooting the shit, watching basketball and hockey. Don introduced Tommy around to most of the regulars. When Don mentioned Lee's name, guys would invariably wince and offer their condolences. Then they changed the subject. Quickly.

Tommy lifted his foot to his knee and peered at it skeptically. He'd had the boots for nearly five years. Heavy-duty leather with thick soles, he couldn't see what was wrong with them.

"Nah. They're no good," Don said. "You want something that'll go up to your knees. Like some snake hunting boots, you know? Might have to hit some of the motorcycle stores, or the farm and hunting stores down in Indiana. I'll see if I can dig up an extra pair of pads for now. When you get 'em, make sure they're big enough that they'll fit over your jeans. Had a rat run up inside my work pants once. Whoo boy, lemme tell ya, that was fun."

The crossed Cermak, then South Pulaski.

"Rule number two. Don't waste your time chasin' rats with bait. Mr. Rat, he's too goddamn smart. And there's just too many of 'em. So you find a colony, and you poison the living shit out of it."

"We're heading for a colony?"

"We're heading for the biggest, baddest colony you ever seen. Just you wait. We could kill rats until Christ comes back, and we wouldn't make a goddamn dent in their population."

Tommy considered this for a moment. "You ever been to Palmisano Park in Bridgeport?"

Don shook his head.

"It's a nature park, got a lake, some paths and shit. Used to be the Stearns Limestone Quarry."

"Oh sure, sure."

"My dad told me, back in the day, when they were done hauling limestone out, somebody had the bright idea to fill half of it up with garbage, then make a park out of it."

Don laughed. "Bet they got more than they bargained for."

"Dad told me that the rats got so bad, they had to burn the garbage. Guess they had to stand around the place, killing rats as it all burned. Heard they switched to construction junk to fill it in."

"Where we're headed, it's a little off the beaten path," Don said with a sly grin. "Like everything else our esteemed commissioner has got his fingers in, it's in that gray area in between of not exactly legal and a fuckin' war crime."

Don turned off into an industrial wasteland. "Take a deep breath. Just south of here, there's the biggest raw sewage treatment plant you've ever seen. You ever hear of the Deep Tunnel?"

"Storm runoff?"

"Yeah. It's so all the water has somewhere to go, so all our shit, and I mean that literally, understand, doesn't wash out into the lake." He turned into an industrial section, followed a few of the smaller streets that wove through the warehouses and deserted factories until they came to a shipping yard. Don nodded to the gate's watchmen and followed a gravel road that wound around the trucks and down into a surprisingly deep quarry.

Down at the far end was a tunnel.

A set of narrow gauge train tracks that hadn't felt steel wheels in decades, nearly obliterated in dirt and gravel, stretched into the darkness. Don didn't even slow down and before Tommy could say anything, they were hurtling into the tunnel. Rough-hewn rock whipped past his window.

"Huh." Tommy swallowed. "Didn't realize we were actually headed underground."

"Well, you wanna catch rats, you ain't gonna catch 'em sipping cocktails at the Drake." Don considered this for a moment. "Well, that's a different kinda rat now, isn't it?" He caught sight of Tommy's wide eyes. "Relax. We got a ways to go. You'll get used to it."

The Streets and Sans truck shuddered as it rumbled down the tunnel. The headlights trembled, throwing crazy, flickering shadows across the uneven surfaces. The tunnel was big enough that two medium trucks could drive along side by side. Don kept the needle at a steady thirty-five miles an hour. "Believe it or not, we make better time down here than up top. No goddamn stoplights." He laughed.

"How far are we going?"

"All the way back to downtown. 'Course, we'll be a half-mile under the streets, at least. Some of the old-timers claim there's tunnels that go down damn near a mile or more. See, the whole thing's like goddamn Swiss cheese. You wouldn't believe how many abandoned rail lines, storm drains, and God knows what else crisscross under the city. The Deep Tunnel engineers, they knew this, and they connected a bunch, so when it rains the lake doesn't turn into a goddamn Porta-Potty."

They passed a few intersections, and Tommy caught a quick glimpse of smaller tunnels before they were swallowed in the gloom. "You sure we shouldn't be leaving a trail of breadcrumbs or something?"

"I wouldn't want to be down here without a flashlight, that's for goddamn sure. But I been coming down here, once a week or more, for, let's see now, over two years now. Something like that."

After about fifteen minutes, the tunnel opened up. There were no lights save the headlights, so Tommy couldn't tell how large it was. But he couldn't see the ceiling, and the place was full of rusting El cars. The truck bounced over a dozen sets of tracks, then followed the road as it ran down between the long lines of derelict hulks. The spill of the headlights briefly illuminated the dusty, opaque windows, reflecting distorted, ghostly images of the truck. It gave Tommy a skittish feeling.

He found he was having a hard time taking a deep breath. The thought of all that rock above, the weight of the entire city pressing down, down . . . He dried the palms of his hands on his jeans. The motion led him to his boots and he remembered that he wasn't wearing the right kind of boots and that made things worse.

The El train corpses passed out of sight and the walls swallowed them up again. This one was shorter though, before long they came to a circular area, with a number of smaller tunnels branching off. It was clear which tunnel to use; the tire tracks had crushed the gravel into two easy-to-follow paths. Don pulled off to the side of the tire tracks and shifted into park. He pointed to an empty ring on the wall next to the tunnel. "Flag's gone. That means somebody's down in there. Tunnel isn't wide enough for two vehicles. 'Specially garbage trucks."

"Garbage trucks?"

"Sure. Why do you think we're here? You want to find rats, you go looking for garbage."

"Wait, there's a dump down here?'

"Oh, yeah. An awful damn big one."

"Why go to the trouble of driving all the way down here?"

Don spread his hands. "Landfills are big business. Nobody wants a garbage dump in their backyard, so these places, they can get away with charging an arm and a leg. 'Specially if it's Uncle Sam picking up the bill. Your pal and mine, friend of the people Mr. Cornelius Shea, when he found out about this place, he had about a third of his drivers start dumping their loads down here. See, then he charges the city for the regular landfill costs, and pockets the surplus."

Tommy was quiet for a while. "Jesus Christ. All I can think about are the assholes in my neighborhood, these wannabe crooks and gangbangers. They'll bust open the back window of somebody's piece-of-shit car, crawl in, see what they can steal. If they get a stereo, they'll take off down the block, hoopin' and hollerin', thinkin' they hit the jackpot. What a score." He shook his head. "Those douche bags got nothing on these goddamn politicians."

"What, you saying our elected officials aren't going into politics to serve their fellow man?" Don laughed. "It's the Machine, kid. Don't look so shocked. And it ain't just regular garbage down there. Shit, you think a landfill costs money? Try finding somewhere legal to dump toxic waste. If I were you, I wouldn't linger when we're getting the rats. I try to breathe through my shirt, you know?"

A bobbing light appeared in the darkness, growing in intensity by the second. Don flashed his brights. The approaching lights flashed back. A pale blue garbage truck filled the entrance, with only a foot or two between metal and rock. It rumbled out of the tunnel and pulled abreast of their van.

The driver's window rolled down and a hairy arm held out a red flag on a three-foot PVC pipe to Don. Don said, "Working late."

The garbage truck driver spit. "Boss got spooked. Heard a rumor that somebody was watchin'. Wanted the times we came dumping staggered even more. Wants at least an hour between each truck, you believe that shit?"

Don shrugged. "Be seein' ya."

The driver saluted, and headed back toward the surface. Don put the van in drive and they entered the tunnel. Their van was smaller than the garbage truck, but the walls were still uncomfortably close. Tommy never thought he would ever worry about claustrophobia, but this shit was getting old.

"What's above us?" Tommy asked. "I mean, where in the Loop?"

"Dunno exactly. All I know is that we're far enough down, you can't even hear the subway."

The right wall fell away into nothingness.

"And here we are," Don said, turning the van off the road. The headlights illuminated a vast chasm. Fifteen yards out, the ground dropped steeply and disappeared, leaving hulking mountains of rotting garbage. Metal and plastic gleamed dully through the blackened ooze like bone as flesh decayed around it. The smell slithered through the air vents and cracks around the doorframes and sizzled in their nostrils. Tommy had expected it to smell like a bad Dumpster in the summer, but this didn't have that revolting element that made your gorge rise. It had a burnt, chemical smell, like pepper spray steeped in bleach.

Don wrapped a bandanna around his nose and mouth and tied it in the back. He hefted a Maglite, saying, "Time to earn our keep," and climbed out. Tommy followed, still stunned at the amount of garbage. The cavern stretched as far as the headlights shined; the place must have been as large as a football field. Probably bigger.

Don whipped the flashlight around. "Shut your door. Don't need to come back and find any surprises." He didn't have to say it twice. Tommy slammed the door and the sound echoed across the immense cave. He flinched at the noise, feeling as if he'd just woken something dark and massive. Something that could seal off the tunnel before they got out.

He hurried to catch up to Don. Don said, "Watch your head," and shined the light at the cave roof, revealing a slab of rock that sloped down at nearly a forty-five-degree angle. Don squatted under this and turned the flashlight at clusters of rat corpses. "Anywhere else, you try and lay out some poisoned bait, the rats laugh at you. They're too damn smart. And there's plenty of food. But down here, I dunno. Maybe the toxic fumes scramble their brains. There's always plenty of dead ones. Anyway, this is where you find 'em."

He led Tommy back to the van and they put on heavy leather gloves first, then disposable rubber gloves to cover the leather. Don took a box of blue plastic bags back to the rats. Tommy would hold each bag open while Don reached under the ledge and grabbed a rat by its tail. When the rat was in the bag, Tommy twisted the top and sealed it with yellow tape stamped with the three incomplete rings over a full circle, the sphincter-tightening symbol of biological hazardous material.

When they had collected fifty rats, they put them in a metal bin in the back of the van and laid out more poisoned bait. The entire process didn't take longer than half an hour. They stripped off their rubber gloves and left them in the bin with the rats. Back in the cab, they sat for a moment, pulling off the leather gloves.

Tommy surveyed the rolling mounds of refuse. "Fifty rats. This doesn't make a damn bit of difference, does it?"

"Not one damn bit." Don turned off the headlights.

Darkness settled over the van with a totality that made

Tommy feel as if someone had just pulled a thick rubber bag over his head.

"Check this out," Don said. "Give your eyes a sec."

Tommy's other senses exploded into awareness. He clutched the door handle, just to triple-check the door was closed. Far off, he could hear a quiet skittering. The sound got closer.

Don turned on the parking lights. Countless red pinpricks out in the distant darkness froze and watched the van silently. "Holy shit," Tommy breathed.

Don started the van, turned on the headlights. The rats vanished. "No. Not one damn bit," he repeated. "Still, this is what we get paid for. Rats will always breed faster'n we can kill 'em. But it keeps Lee happy. And that, my friend, is the secret to a successful career in Streets and Sans."

# CHAPTER 10

**3:57 AM**
**December 28**

Dr. Reischtal was down on his knees on the smooth, polished stone floor, under the window at the end of the hallway. His back was bowed, forehead resting on his clasped hands, and he was halfway through whispering his morning prayers when the phone rang.

At first, he wasn't sure how to react. His first instinct was simply to ignore the shrill bleating. One did not put God on hold while one answered a paltry phone call. Yet, this was the department phone. His staff was under strict orders only to call this phone under precise circumstances.

He felt his concentration vacillate. He clenched his hands tighter, raising his voice from a whisper to almost a hoarse shout. Work could wait. Everything could wait. His time with the Lord was precious. Sacred. In fact, his devotion to his Lord was what made him so effective at his profession.

Dr. Reischtal was the director of special operations for the special pathogens branch in the Center for Disease Control and Prevention. With the exception of Dr. Reischtal himself, no one was entirely sure what these special responsibilities entailed, only that he was the man to contact if certain parameters were exceeded when a suspicious death was reported.

Dr. Reischtal knew. He understood the exacting nature of his responsibilities, and why striving to maintain a clear line of communication with his Lord was so vitally important.

Unlike the traditional priests and the wishy-washy New Age pastors who spoke of the devil as if he were some sort of harmless metaphor, Dr. Reischtal knew Satan was real. The idiotic fire-and-brimstone born-again evangelists were closer to the truth, but they howled about the devil as if he strode through the cornfields on cloven feet, slinging fire at all true believers with his pitchfork and seducing everybody else down into the pits of hell.

Dr. Reischtal knew better. He knew that Satan existed in the tiniest of organisms, patiently waiting for a chance to turn this paradise mankind had been given into a hellish wasteland. It was only fitting then, that the ancient one lurked in the primordial ooze.

Hell was not a place separate from paradise, and the devil strived to turn paradise into hell. He knew this because he had seen the devil, pinned under glass, as he watched him carefully with own two eyes through a microscope.

Pieces of Satan were kept frozen, locked away deep in the cavernous levels of the CDC. Dr. Reischtal had filed a memo that these samples be destroyed, but the suggestion was quietly rebuked. The samples were vital, in case further vaccines needed to be developed.

He said nothing else. In his professional life, he was smart enough not to refer to Satan by name, or even suggest that they were all dealing with mankind's oldest and deadliest foe. But he knew. He knew. And his job, his holy mission, was to maintain a vigil, watching and waiting for any signs of where Satan may be trying to force his way through a crack into this world.

The phone continued to ring. There was no answering

machine, no voice mail. It would continue to ring until he answered.

Dr. Reischtal's prayers faltered and stopped. He pushed himself to his feet, placating his discomfort at leaving the prayers unfinished with the promise that he would start over when he finished with the phone call.

"Yes," he said into the receiver. Only the knowledge that punishment would be severe for the voice on the other end of the line made him feel a little better. He listened for a moment, then said, "Chicago. I would have thought New York." He exhaled. "No matter. Assemble the components. I want a plane ready within the hour. I will expect a car at my door in precisely thirty minutes." He remembered his prayers. "No. Make that sixty. Please remind the liaison in Chicago that they are to follow the strictest isolation procedures. Any—I repeat, any—deviation from my written protocol will be dealt with in the harshest possible manner." He replaced the receiver.

God did not tell him whether they were false alarms or if true battles were about to begin when the calls came in. So he made sure he was ready. "I pledge my allegiance, oh Lord, in this endless war. In this life and the next," he said, then went back down the hall, knelt under the round window that looked out to the stars, and began to pray again.

# CHAPTER 11

**5:16 AM**
**December 28**

Lee was not happy. His head felt like it was going to crack open any moment, spilling his throbbing brain onto the slate tile of the suite's bathroom. The sun was creeping over the far edge of Lake Michigan, slicing through the air and boiling his eyes. He could handle the sun though; he'd find the damn switch that lowered the blinds later. Although he couldn't, for the life of him, understand what he'd been thinking last night when he'd demanded a view of the lake.

No, what Lee needed right fucking now was a goddamn drink of water.

Problem was, he couldn't figure out how to turn the faucet on.

There were no handles. Just curving horns of pure, smooth onyx that jutted boldly over two shallow black sinks. He tried waving his hands under what he thought might be the faucet, hoping for a motion sensor, but nothing happened. He squinted around the gleaming, ultra-modern bathroom. Everything was gray and black, with brilliant white starburst accents. Even the toilet and bidet, elevated on two steps like thrones, were jet black. He tried the second sink and got the same result. Behind him, across a space larger than most living rooms, waited both a tub big enough to fit four people and a shower that could easily fit another four, with a bewildering array of nozzles that sprayed you from every conceivable angle. Lee honestly couldn't remember if he'd even used them last night or not.

The morning sun still sizzled through the bare windows, ricocheting off the mirrors that covered every inch of wall space. Even the ceiling was one solid mirror. Lee wasn't sure why. Who in the hell would want to look up and watch themselves taking a dump?

He swept the chic complimentary perfumes and toiletries off the counter in disgust. It didn't help his head, but it reminded him not to let his rage slip out of control. He took a deep breath, releasing it slowly through his nose like the anger-management counselor had coached. It didn't work. It felt like he still had barbed wire wrapped around his skull, and some giggling evil bastard kept twisting it tighter. He idly scratched at his right ass cheek. Fresh itching erupting up his torso, and he attacked it, ending with a furious scratching in his right armpit.

What kind of shit had he gotten into last night? His head hadn't hurt like this since . . . well, right now he couldn't remember. He was going to have a serious chat with Jamal when he felt better, and if the dealer wasn't forthcoming about his party favors, Lee would only be too happy to call on a couple of large, mean boys he kept employed down at the motor pool for just such occasions.

Maybe the hooker had some aspirin. Or maybe even something stronger. He couldn't remember her name. He'd left her sprawled facedown on the bed, still passed out. The thought of digging through the wreckage of their suite for aspirin sounded exhausting, and so he simply squatted, holding on to his pounding head. Plus there was always the chance he might take the wrong pill, and he couldn't be seen acting irrationally in public.

The itching spread to his groin and he took a moment to

rake his nails through his pubic hair. For a moment, the scratching felt so good it almost eclipsed the pain his skull. He wondered if a shower might help. Maybe he could try and get some of the spray in his mouth, get a drink of water that way.

He stood, feeling the sunlight wash over his body. He caught sight of himself in the mirror. Instinctively, his gaze went to his abs. Still flat and tight. Then to the skin under his jaw. Still firm. Good. But too many nights like—

Wait a goddamn minute. He turned sideways, so the sunlight illuminated the right side of his body. Tiny red blotches covered his skin, from his ass to up under his armpit. He looked down at his groin in horror. More red bumps.

That BITCH.

He stormed into the suite and grabbed the hooker by the ankle and dragged her off the bed. "Get up. GET UP! Get up, you filthy, diseased cunt." The girl struggled to open her eyes through a mass of blond curls and landed in an awkward tangle of long limbs and heavy breasts. She couldn't have been more than nineteen.

"Baby, what's—"

"You fuckin' whore. Shut your fucking mouth." He paced around the bed, clenching and unclenching his fists.

"Baby, I—"

Lee sprang at her. He grabbed a fistful of blond curls and punched her twice in the face. Grabbing her hair with both hands, he head-butted her, and felt the satisfying crunch as her nose shattered. She collapsed on the floor. He straddled her chest and took his time, using both fists in swinging, roundhouse arcs. After the fifth or six blow, she stopped struggling under him and tried to wrap her skinny arms over her head.

He was still hitting her when somebody knocked on the door.

* * *

Lee sat back, panting. He glanced quickly around the room, as if to make sure there were no cameras aimed at him. He stood, collecting himself for a moment, paused long enough to spit on her, then crossed the room and opened the door. "What?"

His uncle was at the door. Short, with a bad back. Dead eyes that wouldn't blink at a night fire at an orphanage. "Jesus Christ, Lee, you want to bother answering your cell?"

"I got busy."

"Do we, or do we not, have an agreement that you will keep it with you at all times? I have been calling you all morning. And when I call, you answer. It does not get any more simple than that." This was Lee's uncle Phil. He was an alderman, and although Lee was the star, nobody was kidding anybody.

Phil ran the show.

Phil, with his hunched figure, sunken eyes, and gray hair, would never rise beyond an alderman. He was, however, a very skillful Chicago alderman. As a Chicago alderman, as long as you weren't a convicted child molester or a member of the NRA, you could get away with most anything. But he had gotten his fingers too dirty for the kind of scrutiny that comes with the elections for a higher office.

Lee, however, was handsome and charming enough for the business. Phil found all possibilities of opportunities as far as Lee was concerned. Lee wasn't going to be just a Streets and Sans commissioner forever. No, he was being groomed. Whispers floated through the elevators and walls in City Hall. "Congressman. Maybe even a senator. After that, who knows?"

And Phil would be the man behind the throne. The only one Lee trusted utterly. Phil was looking forward to all the new pies he'd be able to dip into.

This morning, however, made the job difficult. "You some kinda run-of-the-mill, bought-and-paid-for politician who puts his dick before the job? Is that it? Is that who you are? Somebody who'd rather fuck some coked-up whore than take care of himself?"

Lee stammered out, "No . . . no . . . I . . ."

"'I' what?" What's that? What are you trying to say for yourself?"

"I just found out."

"Oh. You just. Found. Out. I see."

"I'm taking care of this situation."

"I see."

They listened to the whore trying to cry through a shattered face.

Lee said, "I'll deal with it. I promise."

Phil pushed past him and shut the door softly. He locked it. Tested it. Took a deep breath. He turned on Lee. "What kind of fucking hotel did you set us up with here? Jesus Christ, did my sister beat you in the head with a frying pan when you were a child?"

"What the fuck are you talking about?"

"You aren't the only one that's been bit, dickhead."

Phil waited until Lee met his eyes, making sure that Lee understood that he was talking about the businessmen who worked so adeptly behind the scenes to make sure the Machine was well-oiled in their favor. "Nobody's blaming you. Not yet. This goddamn hotel—it's got fucking bugs, Lee."

"Bugs?" The beating had quickened Lee's pulse, but his head was still foggy.

"Yeah, you fucking idiot. Our friends, they're all bit up. So am I. Itches like a sonofabitch."

Puzzle pieces finally started snapping together for Lee.

Phil saw the light of understanding finally dawn on Lee's face. "First, get on the phone with the manager. I want eggs and oysters and Bloody Marys in their rooms five minutes ago. Make sure those guys are taken care of. Next, get Dr. Preston up here immediately. I'll be there in ten minutes. I gotta go back and get some ointment on these rashes. Tell the manager to meet me in the lobby in fifteen minutes, but I'll stop by the rooms first, see if I can't calm the old bastards down."

"Okay." Lee looked back at his whore. "Call that pimp. He needs to escort his property from my room. Stupid bitch got drunk and fell out of the tub."

# CHAPTER 12

*9:10 AM*
*December 28*

Two men and a dog moved in a halting shuffle along the wide corridor. The beagle, Daisy, padded silently along and stopped at the sixth doorway. The two men froze and held their breath. The dog nosed the door open and pushed inside. They followed her inside. Daisy sniffed and pawed at the crumpled sheets that lay at the foot of the bed in the vast suite, gave one short bark, and promptly sat down.

"What does that mean?" Mr. Ullman, the general manager asked. He was a sweating, pallid man in his mid-fifties who demanded that the employees call him Mr. Ullman, never by his first name. He looked like he might be sick any minute.

Daisy's handler, Roger Bickle, was a round little man dressed in a white uniform with a red bow tie. He knelt down and peeled up the fitted sheet from the mattress. Using a pen flashlight, he lifted the edge of the mattress and examined the seams. Daisy barked again.

"What does that mean?" Mr. Ullman asked again, impatience cracking his voice. "Why is he doing that?"

"It's a 'she,' sir, and it means that we have a positive result."

"Positive? So that is . . ." Mr. Ullman was clearly over-whelmed and confused. He refused to give up the hope that a positive result meant that his rooms were pest-free.

The exterminator shook his head. "It's not a good thing, sir. I'm sorry." He stood, grim and apologetic, hoping his pro-fessional appearance would reassure the general manager. Roger secretly liked wearing his company's uniform. He went along with the usual bitching and moaning about the ridicu-lous outfit in the locker room, but every morning, he felt proud to clip on the bow tie. He believed the uniform carried authority, and had a calming effect on clients.

He circled the bed, pulling up the fitted sheet as he went. "I'm afraid to inform you that Daisy has given us a positive sign. And what that means, sir, is that you have an infestation of bedbugs." He swept the pen light along the seams in the mattress and focused on a spot near the headboard. "Yes. Here we are. You can clearly see a physical presence right here."

Mr. Ullman got closer, put on his glasses, and stooped over, peering at the circle of light. He saw brown spots dot-ting the fabric and what looked like tiny, finely crumbled scabs. "What is it?" he finally asked.

"Bedbug fecal matter," Roger said with no small amount of satisfaction. For a moment, he thought the general manager might actually vomit. "See, what happens is—"

"Please, I don't need to know." Mr. Ullman sank back onto the leather couch. "All I want to know is how to get rid of them. Quickly and quietly."

"They might be in the couch too," Roger pointed out help-fully.

Mr. Ullman leapt to his feet and swatted at the tail of his suit coat. He looked like he was about to cry. Instead, he fingered his tie.

Roger grunted and pulled the mattress sideways about a

foot. Lying on the floor, he shone the pen light on the underside of the mattress. "Yes, sir. There is most definitely an infestation of bedbugs here." He pinched something tiny between his thumb and forefinger. It looked like the husk of some foreign fruit seed. "Here we have an exoskeleton."

He swung his flashlight back to the wall. "And like any bug, when there's one, there's a ton." He held the exoskeleton out.

Mr. Ullman waved it away. Now that the harsh reality had settled in, he only wanted to know one thing. "How do we get rid of them?"

Roger struggled to his feet. "That, sir, is not an easy question."

"Surely you must have some kind of pesticide for these things."

"Yes and no," Roger said while checking the other side of the bed. "DDT nearly wiped them out fifty years ago, but of course, to the benefit of humanity"——he had a quiet laugh with himself—"that's been banned. Most of the bugs they've tested show signs of immunity anyway. Bedbugs are awfully . . . resilient. The main problem with pesticides is that even if you find one that works, all you're doing in a building like this is driving them from one room to another, or one floor to another. They can fit anywhere."

"A building like this? Are you kidding? This floor was just completed two weeks ago! This entire building is brand new!" Mr. Ullman was starting to take the infestation personally.

The Serenity was Chicago's latest luxury hotel, inhabiting an entire city block, stretching from Washington to the south to Randolph on the North Side, and Dearborn to State, west to east. Much of the space near the streets had been carefully landscaped, layered with reflection pools and birch trees. The building itself was triangle shaped, both in footprint and profile. It rose one hundred and thirty-four floors above the city, culminating in a great sweeping point at the top. The leading edge of the building faced the lake, flanked on both sides by curving slabs of gray windows. The locals had immediately dubbed it "The Fin," as in a shark's dorsal fin, to the dismay of the owners and Mr. Ullman.

Mr. Ullman kept trying to get the exterminator to understand the true significance of the hotel. "We have been in the news practically every day for weeks now. It has all been carefully orchestrated, I can assure you. Surely, you heard about the charity ball last night? Everyone in town was here."

Roger considered this. He spread his hands apart in a helpless gesture. "If this building is so new, then why would it have so many bugs?"

Mr. Ullman licked his lips, then pressed them together so tightly they almost disappeared. He did not want to discuss the matter. "I think you will understand our need for discretion. We had a . . . situation, where we discovered that a group of homeless people had been hiding in the unfinished sections near the roof, and using these rooms to sleep in at night. We scrubbed and fumigated everything, of course."

"Of course."

"I can only assume . . ." Mr. Ullman gestured helplessly.

They contemplated the room in silence, until finally Roger felt compelled to say something, anything. "Yes, well. The problem is that once they are established, it can be very difficult to eradicate them. The females lay an average of up to five eggs per day when they've had a good meal. That's over two hundred eggs in their lifetime. And the babies are ravenous. That's what I'm assuming we have here. Bedbugs molt five times before reaching adulthood. That's why I'm finding so many exoskeletons."

Roger slid the entire bed away from the wall and shined his light behind the headboard. "Aha! Here we go." He produced a pair of tweezers and held it up for the manager. Up close, it wasn't exactly menacing. The little bug was about the size of an apple seed. Six feeble legs waved about helplessly.

"Yes, yes," Mr. Ullman said. "Fine. But now what do we do?"

Roger dropped the bug in a specimen vial and secured it in the chest pocket of his uniform. "To be absolutely sure, I would recommend clearing out every piece of furniture in these rooms and destroying them. Start over. At the very least, dispose of all the mattresses, the couches, the easy chairs. Anything with padding and fabric."

Mr. Ullman was aghast. "Are you joking? Do you have any idea of what this couch cost? More than your annual salary, I'm guessing. That chair? Hand built in Italy. The mattress alone cost over fourteen thousand dollars for God's sake. Are you seriously saying there is no chemical that we can use to kill these things?"

Roger shook his head. "The amount you'd have to use would destroy the furniture. Heat can kill these things, but again, you'd risk ruining the furniture." He thought for a moment. "Bedbugs can live up to a year without eating. But they have very weak jaws. They're just tubes, really, one for injecting you with their saliva, which contains both an anesthetic and an anticoagulant, and the second one sucks out your blood. Fascinating stuff, really when you—"

"I'm sure it is. You were saying."

"Well, they can't chew through much of anything. Not like your cockroach, let me tell you. It's not hard to trap them. If you could get by without all this furniture for some time . . . some considerable time . . . you could seal everything in plastic sheeting. Then we could go through the rooms, sealing every crack and crevice with clear silicone."

"Would that solve the problem?"

"You would have to store them for over a year."

"So I could theoretically not dispose of these, and claim it on insurance?"

"If you have bedbug insurance."

Mr. Ullman studied his spotless shoes. "It was overlooked."

"I don't know if your insurance will pay for it or not, but if you seal this furniture and this mattress and box springs, the rest of the bed too, just to be sure, then, yes, I think it would take care of the problem."

"As soon as possible, get it done."

The furniture was encased with industrial-strength plastic wrap and sealed with clear plastic sheets, to be on the safe side. All of it, the couches, the chairs, the mattresses, were triple sealed in duct tape. The workmen rolled it away to the freight elevators while more exterminators arrived to seal the cracks between the floors and the walls, all electrical outlets, light fixtures, and anywhere else a dime could fit sideways. The carpets were steam cleaned again and again, and inch-wide double-sided tape encircled the inside of every vent.

The furniture was taken to the basement, where it was wheeled past the massive clothes washers and dryers, then carried down the stairs through the narrow walkways between massive pipes and various industrial machines, down into the third level of the sub-basement. The concrete here had been slapped against the crumbling walls that linked tunnels under the Washington and Lake train stations. They pried open a steel door at the far end, and packed the furniture inside a room the size of small church. The door was padlocked, sealed with duct tape, and promptly forgotten by the staff.

It took only a few seconds for the noise from the workers to diminish and disappear completely. Thirty minutes later, the first rat squirmed into the room from a crack in the far wall and sniffed the furniture. In three days, the rats began to build a nest. They tore through the plastic like a toddler going after a sliver of cake wrapped in Saran Wrap, digging into the soft underbelly of the cushions and mattresses.

The bedbugs grew aware of the new blood and crawled out to feed on the sleeping rats. As the rat nest grew, so did the bug population. The bedbugs encountered the bat bugs inside of the second week.

Bedbugs and bat bugs are so similar that each species can only be distinguished by microscopic examination. Inevitably, some of the male bedbugs attempted to mate with the bat bugs. The males crawled over the bat bugs, stabbing the females in the abdomen with their hypodermic genitalia, filling the body cavity with sperm. All but one of the traumatic inseminations produced sterile offspring. This one female found a quiet spot inside one of the expensive mattresses and laid three sticky white eggs. Fourteen days later, the eggs hatched.

All three bugs carried the virus.

# PHASE 2

PHASE 2

# CHAPTER 13

When the seasons change in Chicago, the transformation can be startling. Bare branches become lush and vibrant; trees seem to appear out of nowhere. Bushes flourish like a happy cancer, hiding garbage and cracked foundations. Grass turns green overnight. Even the air smells different, as if it were being piped in from somewhere down south.

During these first few weeks of true warmth, the city's denizens peel off layers of clothing, like snakes shedding their skin, and emerge from the darkness of winter hibernation with pale skin and an insatiable lust for the sun. A collective sigh of relief can be heard, and just like the plants and trees, the abandoned sidewalks erupt with life.

Louis W. Holtzfelder liked to take a midmorning break from his tax law office in the upper floors of 845 North Michigan and stroll across the bridge to the Starbucks on the other side of the Chicago River in the Trib building. In the winter, he parked in the heated underground garage, and rode the elevator up to his office. Same thing in the deep summer. There was no point in suffering the extremes of Chicago's

weather like some common laborer when his status afforded
him twenty-four-hour climate control.

When the weather was mild, a Goldilocks blend of spring
warmth and refreshing breezes without summer's oppressive
heat, he gladly left the sedate hum of fluorescent lights taste-
fully hidden behind soothing smoked glass, and ventured onto
Michigan Avenue on foot. No doubt the attire of the office
girls that suddenly appeared on streets had something to do
with this decision, but he would never admit this, not even to
himself. Still, he couldn't help but notice the annual baring of
shocking amounts of female flesh and he tried not to stare as
he made his way through corporate workers and throngs of
tourists to get his soy chai latte espresso.

Sometimes he would even take the time to sit on one of the
benches along the river if the stench from the polluted water
wasn't too bad. Today, though, he needed to get back to the
office as soon as possible. He shouldn't have even left, because the temp's lack of intelligence was staggering, but by
eleven in the morning, Holtzfelder hadn't been able to resist
the sunlight and smells of tree blossoms and snatches of in-
toxicating, exotic perfume he occasionally could catch as he
passed the girls on the street.

He was on his way back when he saw the homeless
woman, approaching the bridge on the far side. At least, he
thought it was a woman. She was black, of course.

He'd seen her before, shambling along the sidewalks like
some great sluggish buffalo, pushing a shopping cart. He had
had the misfortune of having to wait for her as she took hours
to cross in front of his Jaguar. Holtzfelder believed there
should be some kind of ordinance that banned the homeless
from the city. Or at least kept them in the South Loop, well
away from where the decent people worked. This was the price
he paid for venturing onto public streets on such a beautiful
day he reasoned, and tried not to let her presence interfere with
his pleasant stroll.

She stopped at the edge of the bridge, nearly completely

blocking the sidewalk with her overloaded cart. Tourists kept a wide berth, pushing their children out in traffic on the Michigan Avenue Bridge to shield their delicate sensibilities from an honest-to-God street vagrant.

No matter the weather, she wore layers upon layers of tattered, rotten scavenged clothing. A pair of oversized black Chuck Taylor shoes could be seen under the frayed plaid bell-bottoms. Holtzfelder knew the brand because his son had begged for a pair for his thirteenth birthday many years ago. Holtzfelder had refused. No son of his was ever going to look "punk."

Most curious of all though, the homeless woman wore some kind of plastic Halloween novelty Viking helmet. The cartoonish horns pushed their way through holes in the brown hood attached to a brown cloak that draped her bulky frame. A circle of graying, waxy hair encircled a dark face with the texture of an old walnut. She could have been anywhere from a beaten forty-year-old to a still spry eighty-year-old.

Holtzfelder just knew she was going to accost him as he drew closer. He curled his free hand into a fist and focused his gaze firmly on the blinking DON'T WALK sign on the far corner. The lights were not going to help him. He would be stuck on the corner while the traffic sped along Upper Wacker and he feared that he would be exposed and vulnerable. Well, that was ridiculous. He was Louis W. Holtzfelder; some of his clients were among the most important people in the city. He set his jaw.

He was all ready to give her a piece of his mind when he got within five feet, but she wasn't even looking at him. Instead, she was intently watching the promenade down by the water. Unable to stop himself, as if he was passing a gruesome traffic accident, he followed her gaze.

Down on the walkway that ran along the river, between the wrought-iron benches and cement flowerbeds, was a rat. Holtzfelder's lips pursed. Rats had no more a right to be in the city than the homeless did. Still, it wasn't natural to see a rat out in the direct sunlight, moving so slowly.

In fact, the rat wasn't acting right at all. It stumbled from the shadows, staggering slightly as if drunk. He needed his glasses, because there seemed to be something wrong with the rat's hair. It looked almost as if it was crumbling away, leaving a trail of dirt behind it. It hobbled to the edge of the river, and simply fell in. There was no jump, no grace, nothing natural. It looked like it was dying.

The homeless woman spoke, so suddenly and so close that Holtzfelder jumped. "Rats be sicker than a motherfucker. All over the place. This town, it be in all kindsa trouble. You watch."

Holtzfelder edged around her and the cart, with no idea of what to say. The lights changed, and he hurried across the street, leaving the woman still staring at the empty space where the rat had fallen.

# CHAPTER 14

**8:45 PM**
**April 17**

Those first months on the job, Tommy learned the habits of *rattus norvegicus*. Don would lead him down into the labyrinth of tunnels and subways and fissures, leaving behind the vicious winter winds that howled through the streets above. Tommy found it fascinating. He felt privileged somehow, exploring this forbidden perspective, as if buried deep beneath the skyscrapers where the city anchored itself into the earth, he could actually see the hidden corners and abrupt angles where the city crashed against itself, grinding the cement, buckling the sidewalks, cracking the bricks.

They would start each night by hitting the alleys behind restaurants and bars, restocking bait and checking holes. Then they'd creep into ancient basements or slip into abandoned buildings, carrying long poles with loops at the ends, swaddled in heavy leather. Tommy began to understand and follow the maze of tunnels under the Loop. They could enter the subway system at Harrison and climb out at Washington avoiding the train lines altogether.

Tommy could squirm into places where Don could only shine a flashlight. Thanks to his relatively small size and strength that hadn't faded since his glory days as an energetic human vacuum cleaner shortstop on the De La Salle Meteors, Don had come to rely on Tommy to crawl into holes and cracks, baiting and catching rats in places that had been previously inaccessible. They'd leave bait, and days later, return to collect dead rats to keep the people that read the paperwork happy. Along with his new boots, Tommy carried his high school aluminum bat, a Louisville Slugger Exogrid, in a sling across his back, in case any of the rats weren't quite dead.

The last stop of the night was always the incinerators on the West Side.

The work was filthy, choking, and dangerous. Still, Tommy enjoyed it, relished the rush as adrenaline pulsed through his body as he crawled through the dust, always facing the possibility of running into rats ready to defend their territory. It forced him to concentrate and kept his mind off of Kimmy and Grace, at least for those hours underground. Then, when they stopped at the bar after dropping off the dead rats at the end of the night, he felt as if he'd earned a beer, and could relax.

Don, though, was relaxed all the time. He moved in one speed and never got in much of a hurry. The way he saw it, the rats would always be around. Why rush? "Besides man, rats are the most successful mammal on the planet. They're everywhere. And they're gonna be too, long after we're gone. That's what I call job security. Long as you stay outta the boss's way, you got yourself a job for life. Nobody sane wants it, I'll tell you that much."

Then, that night in April, a couple of big guys were waiting in the locker room. They wore irritated scowls and name tags that claimed they were union reps. One said, "We understand you two have the highest numbers of dead rats in Streets and Sans."

The other one said with a flat smile, "Couple stone-cold killers."

The situation was a little dicey, because it was considered bad form to always be outshining your fellow employees, so most nights they took it easy, hanging out in the city employee bar. Still, Don said, "So what? We're doing our job. Any problems with that?"

The first union rep spread his hands and shook his head. "No. No problems. But things have changed, at least for the time being. We were sent down here to talk to everybody, explain the situation."

The second said, "No more dead rats. The little fuckers got a phone call from the governor. Let 'em be. Until further notice."

"Says who?" Don asked.

"Do we really have to spell it out for you? And does it matter?"

"Guess not," Don said.

"And it should go without saying, but we want to make this perfectly clear that this is to be kept between us. The wrong person hears that the rats aren't on the city's hit list anymore, they might jump to the wrong conclusions."

"Look at it as a reward for a job well done," the second one said.

There was no point in arguing. The message had been received loud and clear. From that night on, Don and Tommy made a show of putting out traps for the first hour or so, despite the fact that there was no bait in them. Then they would head to the bar and never leave until morning. The instructions were that simple. They would spend the night drinking beer, watching CSN, unless it was golf, then they would begrudgingly switch over to ESPN and that was the cue for everybody in the bar to argue loudly about all the other cities and sports besides Chicago.

Most everybody who worked in vermin control in

Streets and Sans knew that Lee was out there, pulling strings, fucking with their jobs, but nobody wanted to talk about it much. Tommy thought it was a hell of a way to earn a paycheck, but so far, Kimmy had kept her end of the bargain, and had not blocked his visits.

# CHAPTER 15

**9:13 PM**
**April 17**

"Now what do you suppose these fucking idiots are doing?" Ed asked, taking a thoughtful sip from Sam's flask.

Sam took the flask, leaned back, and got a better angle in the side mirror. Two blocks behind them, a Chicago Police cruiser jerked to a stop at the corner of Garfield and Halsted. They had the flashers on, sending jittery blue lights across the entire intersection. No sirens though. Two uniformed patrolmen burst out of the car.

The guy Ed and Sam had been watching didn't even bother to run. The cops slammed him on the pavement, cuffed his hands behind his back, and threw him in the back of the cruiser. They jumped into the front and took off. The traffic began to move again, and people ventured away from the buildings and started back across the street.

The whole thing took less than thirty seconds. It was as if a rock had been dropped into a puddle. For a moment, the waves splashed out, disturbing the surface, but before long the water slid back into place, obliterating all traces of the rock.

"Goddamnit," Ed said.

"We aren't the only ones picking forbidden fruit, brother."

"He's not holding." Every cop knew this. Very few drug dealers were dumb enough to stand out in the open and conduct business. They just arranged the deal, and sent the customers to the right spot for the actual transaction.

"Doesn't matter. Gotta be payback for something."

"If those pricks are working for the Latin Kings, we gotta think of something halfway clever."

The cruiser headed west down Garfield.

"Fifty bucks says they're headed into LK territory."

Ed whipped the Crown Vic in a tight U-turn. Horns echoed up and down Halsted. "Out of the way, hammerhead," he yelled at a Cadillac that blocked the street.

"Thank God we're keeping a low profile here," Sam said.

"Those two are so jacked up from nabbing somebody off the street without calling for backup, they aren't watching their mirrors. Don't sweat it."

The Cadillac finally got out of its own way and Ed sped past it. He squinted at the lights ahead. "Forgot my glasses. They still got their lights on?"

"Can't tell."

At the next side street, Ed yanked the wheel to the right, racing west along Fifty-fourth, so they were parallel to Garfield. They rushed through the summer darkness, blowing through stop signs.

"Easy," Sam said. "Last thing we need is to hit a kid."

"Yes, Miss Daisy."

Ed knew that Fifty-fourth Street dead-ended into train tracks so he turned south on Damen. Ed coasted along as Garfield got closer.

"There!" Sam pointed. The cruiser flashed past, running with just headlights. "You owe me fifty bucks."

Ed ignored this. "That boy is gonna be in a big hurt if they drop him off on the Latin Kings' turf." The guy was known on the streets as Ducey and known to the Justice Department as Darryl Adams. He'd grown up in the Blackstones, and now was one of the top lieutenants. Ed and Sam didn't give a damn about him, though. They were just keeping an eye on him on the off chance they might spot a certain Javier Delgado.

Delgado was wanted in connection with a suspicious murder-suicide in a crack house in Northern Indiana. Word was that Delgado was hiding out with family in Detroit, but Ed and Sam knew that Delgado and Ducey's sister had a three-year-old son together, so it was worth a shot. Commendations from both the narcotics squad and the homicide division certainly wouldn't hurt when they went looking for consulting gigs after retirement.

But now Ducey was about to be kicked into a rival gang's territory, a wolf tossed to the lions. The locals called it a "bitch drop," as in you got dropped off and then ran like a bitch. Ed and Sam didn't particularly give a rat's ass about a gangbanger like Ducey, but it was the principle of the thing.

Ed jumped into traffic on Garfield, cutting into traffic in a storm of horns and brake lights. He pulled up next to the cruiser and Sam locked eyes with the cop driving. Sam held up his badge and pointed to the curb.

The driver nodded and gave a mock salute. He didn't pull over to the side of Garfield. Instead, he turned the next corner and parked on a quiet side street, away from the eyes of passing cars.

"Let me do the talking," Sam said.

"Don't piss 'em off."

"Let me do the talking."

Ed eased to a stop behind the cruiser. The patrolmen didn't wait in the car like citizens. Instead, they met Ed and Sam in the wash of headlights in front of the Crown Vic.

"What can we do to help you out, detectives?" the driver asked with a fawning sincerity that was almost real enough to mask his irritation.

"Officer . . . Falwell, is it?" Sam asked.

"Yes, sir. Again, how can we help you, Detective . . . ?"

"I'm Detective Tackleberry. This is Detective Hightower." Sam hoped the patrolmen were too young to have bothered watching the movie *Police Academy*. "We're actually working with IA." Sam paused for dramatic emphasis, as if he was about to tell someone a loved one had been killed in the line of duty. "Officer Falwell, we need to speak with you in private, I'm afraid."

Officer Falwell and his partner exchanged glances. "Look, whatever you need to tell me, you can tell me in front of my partner."

Now it was Sam's turn to glance at Ed. Ed shrugged. Sam assumed a concerned expression. "Son, I hate to have to tell you this. It's why we flagged you down, didn't want to use the radio." He folded his arms, looked at the ground. "Somebody in IA has a real hard-on for you. Whatever you did, you pissed somebody off. Big time." He took a deep breath. "Apparently, they've got you targeted as an officer that picks men up on minor drug charges, then forces them to perform oral sex on you in exchange for kicking them loose."

Officer Falwell's mouth opened and snapped shut. Rage crawled over his face.

"That's a fucking lie," his partner shouted, and took a step forward.

Sam raised his hands. "Don't shoot me. I'm just the messenger. Why do you think we're talking to you out here?"

"That doesn't make any sense," Officer Falwell managed to croak.

"I know. I know." Sam nodded sympathetically. "That's department politics for you. How long have you been on the force? Year? Two years?"

"Five."

"Then this shouldn't be any surprise. You pissed on somebody's shoes. From here on, assume somebody's got their eye on you. Like him." Sam indicated Ducey, still in the back seat of the cruiser. "He legit, or are you using him for something else?"

"This is bullshit," the partner said. "Bullshit." He looked

like he wanted to punch something. Sam felt sorry for whoever got in the officer's way tonight.

Officer Falwell said, "I'm gonna fucking find who did this. Gonna fucking put their head through a fucking wall." He went to the back of the cruiser, yanked the door open, and dragged Ducey out. He unlocked the cuffs and said, "Get the fuck out of here. I see you again, you're fucking dead."

Ducey didn't need to be told twice. He'd been around enough to know that whatever was going down didn't involve him, and hauled ass toward Garfield.

Officer Falwell slammed the cruiser's back door and moved back around to the driver's side.

"You're welcome," Sam said.

"Fuck you," Officer Falwell shouted back, got in, and took off.

"You'd think he'd show a bit more gratitude," Ed said.

They found Ducey a few minutes later, moving quickly along the south side of Garfield. Ed pulled over and Sam stuck his arm out of the window and waved him closer.

It was clear Ducey wanted nothing to do with the Crown Vic, but he finally shook his head and sidled up to the car, not looking at the detectives. He kept his eyes flicking up and down the street instead.

"The fuck y'all want now?"

"Goddamn. Nobody's appreciating anything tonight," Sam told Ed. He looked back up at Ducey. "You know exactly what those boys were planning. My partner and I, we just spared you one hell of an ass-whupping or worse. You're lucky to be walking around right now."

"Yeah, yeah. Whatcha want?"

"Take a good look at us, kid. Memorize our faces. See, you owe us. Big time. And here's the thing. Nobody knows. Not your gangbanging buddies, not those cops back there.

Nobody. Not yet anyway. You piss me off, everybody on the South Side is gonna know you're a snitch. Here's my card."

Ducey took the card. He looked like he wanted to spit on it and drop it in the gutter, but he slipped it into his jeans. "Yeah, I'm shakin'. Cut the bullshit. Whatcha want?"

"Looking for Javier Delgado. You know why. If he's around, you let me know. I find out he's in town and I haven't heard from you, I know cops a thousand times worse than those two fuckheads back there."

Tommy and Don were discussing an upcoming three game series with the hated Twinkies with a couple of electricians, also employed by Streets and Sans. Both the Sox and the Cubs were off to shaky starts, but hey, it was early. Plenty of time left before the do-or-die days of September.

On TV over the bar, the anchor was wrapping up their lead story, "More details about this tragic death as they become available. In other news, Streets and Sanitation Commissioner Lee Shea today answered some tough questions about the rat population. Cecilia Palmers was on the scene at City Hall earlier today." The camera cut away to a shot of the east side of City Hall. Lee always conducted press conferences on the county side in the morning, because the light was better.

One of the Streets and Sans guys pointed at the TV. "Our fearless leader."

Don and Tommy turned to watch the news.

Lee was out in front of City Hall again, wearing his earnest, concerned expression. "I can assure you that everyone in my department is doing their absolute best with their limited resources. It is unfortunate that the rest of City Hall does not share my concern for the well-being of the citizens of Chicago. Nevertheless, you have my un-wavering promise that Streets and Sans is doing everything within its power to control the population of vermin. I can only ask that if anyone is concerned about pests in their neighborhoods, to not only call us, but to call their aldermen as well, and ask them why it was decided that Streets and Sans would not receive sufficient funds to do this job properly."

# CHAPTER 16

*8:07 AM*
*April 18*

"Oh, and by the way, the files are in the basement."

Martin kept going over that last sentence that Chad had tossed off so casually. That prick.

When Martin had volunteered, all he'd wanted was a chance to pitch in, make the partners notice his enthusiasm. Here was a man who got things done. Martin, despite his law degree, had worked in the same office job for the last eight years, and it was time to make his move. The firm was gearing up for a huge class-action lawsuit, so sure he'd absolutely volunteer for a thankless job of going through the hard copies of old files that nobody had gotten around to scanning yet for the name of an obscure subsidiary holdings company or something that no one could quite definitively tell him. Sure. He'd do that. He thought he'd at least be able to use an office, instead of the table in the cafeteria. And he certainly hadn't expected the files to be in the basement.

Thirty-two years old. Worked in the same job for over eight years. Two promotions. Family and a house in the far suburbs. A wife, two kids. Michael was in preschool and

Jonathan was a babe in his mother's arms. He'd be happy to show you pictures of both of 'em.

And so, every morning, for the last four days, he had gone down to the vast basement. Martin had no interest in lingering as he skirted through the blank, slate-gray walls and the endless locked doors. Usually, he had to use a key to access his firm's storage room, but this morning the door was still unlocked. Good. It was unlikely anyone had bothered to come down to check on the room.

He opened the door to darkness and waved his hand around for the light chain.

Yesterday, he'd run out of the room, leaving it unlocked. He'd been hearing squeaking all week, and while it made him uncomfortable, it was tolerable, but yesterday morning he had heard an awful squalling from something, then a whole bunch of hissing from things all over. He'd grabbed his files, slammed the door, not bothering locking it, and had run down to the elevator. Upstairs, in the cafeteria, he'd wiped the sweat from his face, put the files on the table and his lunch in the employee fridge. He thought about telling someone, but didn't want anyone to think he was being weak.

He stepped into the darkness, not wanting to linger.

A click. The jittering bulb cast a pallid orange light over the banks of filing cabinets, stacked wall to wall and two high, leaving a single walkway down the middle, about a foot and half across. He saw the dead rat immediately.

Martin yanked on the chain, plunging the room into darkness. He couldn't explain why; it was more of a nervous reaction. Maybe the rat would disappear when he turned the light on again, even though he knew perfectly well the rat was stone dead, lying against the cabinets on the left side of the room. Another click.

The rat hadn't gone anywhere. Martin's first impulse was to just shut the door and tell someone, but that would eat up too much of his time. He had to get home. God knew he had to get home. His poor wife was at the end of her rope with the two boys.

So instead, he used the toe of his right shoe to prod and flip the rat out into the hall. He'd have to use some kind of spray and disinfect his shoe later, and just hoped it wouldn't hurt the cheap leather. He squatted, opened a drawer, and pulled out a fistful of files. He did not see the tiny bugs scattered across the floor, all of them about the size of apple seeds, hiding amongst the dust and scraps of paper.

As he straightened, flipping through the files, five of the closest bugs crawled up the heel of his left shoe, paused at the top, stretched out, and caught hold of his black sock. They pulled themselves across the gap and nestled inside the ribs of the fabric. Some ancient instinct compelled them to hide, tucked away, unmoving, until hours later, as they felt the rhythm of his motions grow slow, when Martin fell asleep on the train. The ride out to Crystal Lake lasted an hour and twenty minutes, and Martin rarely stayed awake for the entire trip.

Hidden by his khakis, the bugs emerged and moved swiftly up his sock, pulled by the irresistible lure of warm, bare flesh. Each unfolded a narrow tube from its segmented body and sank it into his skin. The tube was actually split into two chambers; the larger one was hollow and was used for sucking out the beautiful red blood. The second, smaller tube was used for bathing the skin in an anti-coagulant and a numbing secretion, so the host wouldn't feel anything as microscopic teeth chewed through the layers of skin until hitting a blood vessel.

Ten minutes later, the bugs were full and swollen to almost twice their original size. They trundled back down to their hiding places in Martin's sock, where they tucked themselves away and quietly digested their meal.

The conductor woke Martin up at the end of the line and Martin walked tiredly out through the sea of cars in the parking lot, wondering why his leg had started itching.

* * *

"I'm hearing some confusing rumors, Lee."

Lee tried not to jump. His uncle Phil had an inherent distrust of phones, and had a habit of appearing out of nowhere in the massive corridors in City Hall, conferring quietly, then slipping away when his business was finished, disappearing into the cool marble. More than once, Lee had wondered if Phil knew about some kind of secret passages or something in the building.

Lee decided to play dumb and kept walking. He was heading downstairs; his personal trainer was waiting for a quick jog along the lakefront. If nothing else, Lee knew the steady movement would tire Phil out and the conversation would be short. "Oh yeah? How can I help?"

"You know damn well what I'm talking about. And don't think that people aren't noticing. You are treading on some very thin ice here. It's just a matter of time before some scumbag reporter gets one of your employees drunk and they spill their guts." Phil sighed. "Do you really think nobody is smart enough to put two and two together? How stupid do you think people are in this city? Or do you have some fantasy that you are untouchable? I'm praying that you didn't just torpedo your career before it even got started. This goes bad, you'll be lucky to end up picking up garbage in Peoria."

Lee rubbed his eyes. "Give it a fucking rest, will ya? They'll figure out a way to increase my budget. You'll see. You and your pals pull this crap all the time. The one time I try playing hardball, everybody shits their pants. I mean, seriously, what's the fucking difference?"

"If you can't tell the difference, then you're too stupid for this business. And that's exactly what this is, a fucking business. You can't get any more blood from a stone. Thought you understood that." Phil was silent for a moment. "Get your boys back to work. Tonight."

"Soon as your pals see things my way. You tell them that I

will see those extra zeroes in the budget, or everybody is going to be up to their eyeballs in rats. You tell them that, and you tell them that I'm serious as a fucking heart attack. I'm not kidding. You tell them—"

Lee stopped, just to make sure Phil understood, but Phil was gone.

# CHAPTER 17

Friday night in Tommy's house. "Sox game or Svengoolie?"

"S'gooleeee!"

Tommy laughed. "It's not too scary?" He knew the answer though; Svengoolie was never too scary. Occasionally he might show a classic from the thirties, but most of the time it was grade-D dreck from the fifties and sixties. Tonight it was *Beginning of the End*, in which Peter Graves squared off against giant grasshoppers that crawled over photos of buildings. Grace barely followed the plots anyway, and waited instead for the moments when crew members threw rubber chickens at Svengoolie. The jokes were so corny and so bad that Grace usually understood them, and she would gleefully zero in on one and ask Tommy the setup question all night, then endlessly repeat the punch line in a flurry of giggles.

Tommy loved being with her so much he didn't even mind missing the game. "All right then. You go set up the tent, and I'll get the popcorn." Grace ran down the hall to the living room to arrange the couch cushions and a blanket so they could lie on the floor, safely ensconced in their "tent."

In the easy chairs behind the "tent," Tommy's parents, Sidney and Francine, snored away.

Tommy hadn't been able to afford the mortgage payments on their house, so he'd sold that. All of the profits had gone to Kimmy. Now he lived with his parents. It wasn't so bad. They understood his predicament, and gave him as much time as he needed. He slept in his old room, and since he slept during the day, the constant, thrumming rush of the nearby Dan Ryan Expressway blocked out most of the noise. It was reassuring, like a mother's heartbeat to a baby.

The divorce had settled into a dull ache that he could ignore most of the time, like a cavity in a back molar. It didn't bother him much, unless he pushed on it. Things were easier if he just focused on what was right in front of him. He still got to be with Grace on the weekends.

Tommy was enough of a realist to know that this peace couldn't last forever. Some other shoe would drop eventually. And when it did, life had taught him that it would most likely be in the form of a steel-toed boot, aimed squarely at his head.

Before the movie started, he asked, "How's Uncle Lee?"

"Good," Grace said through a mouthful of popcorn.

"Do you see him a lot?"

"Sometimes."

Sometimes. That could mean anything. Sometimes trying to get an answer with some kind of useful information out of a four-year-old was like trying to track down an honest alderman. Every once in a while, though, they might surprise you.

"Mommy says we're going to see a lot more of him, 'cause we're moving downtown. Mommy says he might be my new daddy. You'll still be my old daddy though."

Tommy managed to get out, "Sure, honey. Sure." He swallowed, and said carefully, "Always, okay? I'll always be your daddy. No matter what."

# CHAPTER 18

Martin knew something was terribly, terribly wrong.

Since he'd gotten home last night, he hadn't been able to sleep because of the itching and pain. He'd been in the bathroom for an hour, standing under warm water, but that made the itching moan in hunger. The heat had unfurled a wave of skeletal fingers that went tickling up across his back. He turned and cranked the handle to cold, hoping to stun the itch, to numb his skin, to shock his system. As the brilliantly cold water hit his skull, agony seethed inside his brainpan. He fell out of the tub and curled into a fetal position on a dirty towel dropped on the filthy tiles.

His wife had knocked on the door. "Hon, I could use you downstairs, like *now*." Somewhere in the haze, he heard his oldest screaming about watching *SpongeBob*. The youngest cried nearby. Of course. The youngest couldn't go five minutes without crying unless he was in his mother's arms.

And his wife. She was always picking up the baby. Soothing it. Never teaching him a lesson. Never teaching him anything and saving him from everything. She'd rattled the door. "Martin! Martin! What the hell is wrong with you?"

Martin croaked, "Be there in a minute," and didn't know why. Maybe to make her go away.

She said, "You better not have been drinking again, buster. I'm coming back up in five minutes, and you better be out of there. If you've been drinking, so help me God . . ." Her voice trailed off as she stomped down the stairs.

Martin clasped his hands between his legs and squeezed as he rode out the waves of torment. Eventually he managed to rise to a kneeling position, then used the sink to prop himself up. He pawed through the medicine cabinet, spilling children's cough syrup and tampons into the sink. He found nothing that might help.

Nothing stronger than Tylenol or Advil and the symptoms were getting worse.

The next thing he knew, he was waking up on the floor next to the bed, but all he really noticed for the briefest dreamlike moment was the way everything glowed in the early morning sunlight. He tried to raise his head.

The sunlight started to burn.

He blinked.

He felt, or rather sensed the presence of his wife above him, yelling at him, bouncing a baby boy wearing soiled diapers. His other son was wailing from his room down the hall. None of this really concerned him as much as the way the sunlight cut into the room.

He clutched the blanket on the bed, pulled himself to his feet, and tottered out of the bedroom, down the stairs and into the kitchen. All he knew at that moment was that he was very thirsty. He grabbed a glass and stuck it under the faucet. Water hit the bottom of the glass and for some reason, the image and sound revolted him. Martin gave a surprised urking sound as thin, yellowish bile jumped out of his mouth and into the sink. He backed away, still dry-heaving.

Pushing past his wife, he moved in a hunched shuffle down the hall.

She was on the phone with her sister. "I don't know what

to do, that's what I'm telling you. No, no. He promised me. He promised. Yeah, no more drinking. That's the problem. He's acting, I don't even know anymore. . . . He's never been this hungover. What?" A quick pause, then, "No. No. No. He's not like that. I told you. He's not like that."

Martin shut the basement door and locked it.

He found his Marlboros sealed in a sandwich baggie with a lighter hidden away in the ceiling tiles. Just one cigarette. He'd given up drinking for his wife and the boys, and really, just one cigarette wasn't hurting anybody. He couldn't think of anything else that might offer some kind of relief, no matter how slight, from the convulsions that were wracking his body.

He inhaled, and the taste made him gag. The cigarette fell from his fingers and smoldered on the floor. He coughed and hacked. He could swear the smoke made his lungs themselves itch. The sensation spread throughout his chest, as if something had cracked inside and was now leaking. The dreadful sensation seeped out to his skin, and the prickling feeling became unbearable.

Martin cried out and frantically raked his fingernails across his scalp, down his neck, his shoulders. He might as well have been trying to extinguish a volcano with a Slurpee. He clawed deep furrows in his skin. It didn't help.

He reached up to the shelf of old sponges, toothbrushes, and household chemicals, desperate to find something abrasive like steel wool, something that could match the intensity of the itching, something that didn't screw around. His gaze slipped past the Lysol spray, the cold-water washing machine detergent, landing on the industrial jug of Drano Max Gel. He knew it was full, because he'd bought it just last week.

His wife pounded on the basement door. "Martin! Martin! If you don't open this goddamn door right now, I'm taking the boys and leaving for good! I promised you a divorce if you started drinking again and I mean it!"

He unscrewed the cap from the Drano and popped the foil

seal with his thumb. The itching grew worse, as if a thousand bees were vibrating under his skin, and they were excited at the sight of the drain cleaner. He upended the jug and held it over his head.

Soothing fire dripped from his skull.

He fell to his knees. Lighting flashed through the bloody furrows in his skin, but it wasn't enough. The Drano sizzled into his eyes and he gasped in sweet torture. He sank against the cool linoleum and put his palm on the lit cigarette. The burning finally got his attention.

His wife started kicking at the door. The boys kept screaming.

Fire. That was the answer. So elegant. So simple. He dragged the can of Raid from under the sink and crawled over to one of the plastic bins, piled haphazardly with a ton of other cardboard boxes. The bin was stuffed with old baby clothes his wife refused to throw out. He ripped off the lid and soaked the clothes with the insecticide. One click of his lighter and the fabric ignited with a solid pop.

He felt the heat lick his face and almost smiled.

Then he thrust his hands into the fire.

His wife kept kicking the door. The boys howling became even louder.

The sounds drilled into his head and within seconds, they blotted out everything else. It filled him with fury. He scrabbled to his feet, grabbing at the cardboard boxes full of old photos and tax returns and other useless crap his wife had insisted on hanging on to for God knows what reason, spilling them down over the fire.

He shook his head as if to clear the shrieking. The sudden movement made the noise even worse, so he staggered back, searching for something to quiet the sounds from upstairs so he could find some peace and return to the bliss in the flames.

He kicked over a children's toy box, spilling Tonka trucks, rubber balls, and Thomas the Tank Engine trains across the floor. He spotted a Cubby blue toy souvenir bat, three feet long and solid wood. It felt good in his hand. It felt right.

He carried it up the stairs and unlocked the door.

His wife had enough time to say, "What is wrong—" before the bat came down. She shrieked, "My baby!" as the infant's wail was silenced with a sudden crunch. He stopped her screaming next, then went upstairs to find his oldest son, stomping and complaining in his room.

In the basement, the flames melted the plastic bin and spread to the discarded can of Raid. It exploded, spreading burning shrapnel into the stacked cardboard boxes. Within minutes, the entire basement was on fire, and the flames rushed up the walls and across the ceiling.

Upstairs, the cries and screaming stopped.

# CHAPTER 19

*10:41 PM*
*April 19*

Dr. Reischtal found that he was unable to pray. He peered out at the night through the floor-to-ceiling windows on the top floor of the Cook County General Hospital. From dusk until dawn, the stars and sky were extinguished, blown out by the lights of the city, revealing nothing but a dull orange haze and the occasional landing lights of aircraft preparing to land as they approached O'Hare from the east. Light pollution. What an innocuous name for something so subtly sinister.

Without stars, he found the words to his Lord fell uselessly back to earth, unable to bridge the vastness of the universe. He felt trapped, smothered with the sick light. The idea that this may be a sign, that this shroud of false light could herald the end of days had occurred to him more than once.

The body in the freezer two floors down made this idea a frightening possibility.

Viktor's trail, as far as the bats were concerned, had gone cold in Yekaterinburg. They knew he was a poor student and his father was an unemployed laborer, crippled with debts. The motive for smuggling animals was easy enough to understand. Whether he would have returned to Russia or simply stayed in the U.S. was unclear.

The bats had come from all over the world. The bodies of the bats, including the parasites, had been dissected in the laboratories at Quantico. They had recovered eleven bats, nearly all from the critically endangered list, and thirty-seven internal and external parasites that ranged over four different species, including three from Viktor's own body.

All showed the beginning stages of the disease.

Eleven bats. One empty pouch.

And so, despite protests from his colleagues in the CDC who were more interested in saving a few pennies for their precious budgets, Dr. Reischtal had convinced the board that Viktor was just the beginning.

The virus would reappear.

And when it did, it would explode with a vengeance.

The special pathogens branch had quietly moved into the top three floors of the Cook County General Hospital, displacing patients and staff alike. It wasn't difficult. Cook County General had one of the worst reputations of not only Chicago but the country. The big joke in Chicago was that if you were taken to General, you were lucky to leave with all your organs. A few years back, there had been a huge scandal. Several top administrators had been convicted on providing kickback bribes to ambulance companies in return for bringing accident victims to the General, even if other hospitals were closer. The place was crowded, understaffed, and most of all, underfunded.

Other hospitals may have been better suited to Dr. Reischtal's requirements, but despite better facilities and more specialized doctors, Cook County General had one element that the others did not. Location. The only hospital located near the absolute center of the city, it filled an entire city block between Madison to the north, Wacker to the east, and Monroe to the south. To the west was the Chicago River; it

had been built next to the river in the aftermath of the Great
Fire in 1871.

The original building had been torn down in the late sixties,
and in the same spirit that would echo some of the progres-
sive architecture designed to serve the public throughout
Chicago, the building was designed as a squat, segmented
cylinder, twelve stories tall. The floors were staggered, spinning out from a central radius, providing decks shaped like
stingy slices of pie, like a tight circular staircase, outlined in
flowers shrubs, and small trees when the building was young.
The trees died within two years, and ivy had taken over. Leafy
strings hung from every surface in the summer and fall, as if
the pie slices had gone rancid and mold had crept over every
surface.

At first, the administrators were reluctant to simply hand
over control of their hospital to the CDC. However, a large
donation from the federal government had bought enthusiastic cooperation. The top floor consisted primarily of conference rooms and offices. The next two floors contained various
oncology wards. The patients had been moved without explanation or warning to either Northwestern Memorial or Rush
University Medical Center on the West Side.

Most of the equipment had been moved to other parts of
the hospital, leaving empty, sterile rooms. Dr. Reischtal's precise footsteps echoed though the bare halls and rooms as he
paced, waiting. He could not sleep because he could not pray.

So he paced.

And waited.


The walk to the CTA Red Line subway station at Balboa
only took six minutes for LaRissa Devine, from leaving her
classroom seat to thrumming down the subway steps. If she
was lucky, and the train was running late, she could catch
the 10:37 and get home to her mom, grandmom, and three
siblings and be in bed by 11:30. She needed all the sleep she

could get. The manager at the El Taco Loco branch knew damn well that she was one of the few employees he could trust completely, and needed her to get there early to start the prep work.

When she wasn't selling tacos and burritos that made a mockery out of Mexican cuisine, LaRissa was a student at Harold Washington City College, and her night class had just finished. She carried a heavy backpack; she always took every assigned book to every class. Her notebooks were filled with nearly every word out of her teachers' mouths, and color-coded with neon highlighters. Post-it notes stuck out of the pages like some kind of medieval defensive castle architecture. She never missed a class.

She knew that some of her classmates whispered among themselves, wondering if she had some kind of obsessive-compulsive disorder. She didn't care.

She slipped her card through the automated gate in the subway station and pushed on through. It was late, and no one was in the booth. She went down another flight of stairs. The escalator that rolled upstairs was frozen. It had been broken for almost two weeks.

She walked to the center of the station and sat on a bench, taking off her backpack and sinking gratefully against the wall. She was exhausted, but kept her eyes open. This time of night, it was better to sit where you could see anyone approaching you. The Balbo and Roosevelt subway stations were the end of the line for the whites, and the beginning of the line for a lot of blacks. This borderland effect could sometimes lead to trouble.

Anybody who said that Chicago wasn't segregated wasn't paying attention, or they were full of horse manure. They'd never ridden the Red Line south of Jackson, that was for sure.

Another reason her backpack was so heavy was because LaRissa carried her cousin's U-shaped bike lock in the outside pouch. And it wasn't just for looks. She had no problem jerking it out and using it if any fool was dumb enough to try and mess with a studious black girl. Tonight, though, was quiet. She thought for a moment about whether she could take out her biology homework, and thought tonight it might be okay. Sometimes she worried if she looked vulnerable if someone saw her with her face in a book. Since most of the shooting and problems took place when the weather turned much hotter, she thought it would be okay. She wanted to get a head start on her homework.

She did not put in her earbuds. She wanted to keep her ears wide open, and looked up from the text often to make sure she was alone. She did not, however, check under the bench.

The bugs came bubbling through the cracks where the concrete floor met the tiled wall like clotted oil escaping from a pressurized pipe. They had smelled her breath from inside the wall, and it was nearing time for another molt. Obeying an instinct older than man itself, they surged up the wall, looking for a chance to feed. Their excitement released pheromones that signaled a food source, and more bugs flooded to the surface.

LaRissa scratched her ear absentmindedly. She couldn't wrap her head around how these protein chains were supposed to function, but her report was due next week, and she would just as soon start stripping than wait until the last minute to start the paper.

By the time she looked back down at the book, it was too late.

The bugs were already flowing up her legs like some sticky, viscous liquid. They poured over her shoulders from the wall, slipping inside her collar. She screamed then, and her cry bounced off the concrete and tile of the subway station, but no one heard except the rats.

She jerked to her feet, hands flailing at the bugs, but it was like trying to swat snowflakes away in a blizzard. Her backpack fell on the concrete with a thud. She spun, slapping her chest, her neck, her hair. The bugs were everywhere.

LaRissa stumbled forward, feeling them invade her mouth as she kept screaming. The momentum carried her to the edge of the platform. Bugs crawled up into her nose, across her eye sockets, tiny legs struggling to find purchase on the slick surface of her eyeballs.

She kept spinning, flailing, until her left foot stepped off into space and she tumbled over the edge. She landed face-down, arms outstretched. Her right hand flopped against the third rail. Electricity rocketed through her, jerking and sizzling her small frame.

The lights in the subway station dimmed for a moment, then returned to normal.

Smoke curled gently from the body. The bugs that had survived the electricity dropped off and shuffled away, not liking the taste of cooked blood. The rats however, did not mind, and started gnawing at the body.

They had eaten most of her face and torn into her stomach, dragging her entrails across the wooden cross ties between the steel tracks when the next southbound train roared into the station. The driver was half asleep, and did not spot the body on the tracks until it was too late. He hit the brakes, but the train's momentum carried it across LaRissa's corpse. Over the scream of the brakes, he felt, rather than heard, the wet crunch that split the body into five pieces. He stared at a single drop of blood on the window and trembled for a moment, then vomited over the controls.

Within half an hour, the station was full of emergency personnel, cops, and equipment. The light and noise drove the bugs back into the darkness, back into the cracks in the wall, until it was as if they had never existed.

# PHASE 3

PHASE 3

# CHAPTER 20

**1:36 PM**
**August 11**

Qween Dorothy moved her great bulk ponderously up the sidewalk, using her shopping cart to split the relentless waves of people that flooded downtown at lunchtime. The bloom had worn off of summer, and now people wanted to get out, grab food, and retreat back into their air-conditioned offices as quickly as possible. The sticky heat even had people thinking back wistfully to the chill of winter.

Something moved in a canvas bag atop her cart.

Head down, she stared out at the scurrying workers through heavy-lidded eyes. They all seemed to be moving at accelerated speeds, like one of those chase scenes in old movies where the characters are all moving in fast motion. Sometimes, if she'd had enough gin, and she was feeling low enough, she wondered if somehow she inhabited a slightly different time and space than the rest of humanity. She lived in a world where time moved a half second slower, and her atoms vibrated to a slightly different rhythm, rendering her invisible to everyone that surrounded her.

But that was just pure foolishness, she would scold herself the next day. She had enough troubles and she didn't need to be adding bullshit science fiction yammering to her load. She sure as hell didn't want to end up like the babbling head cases that wandered along Lower Wacker, gibbering wildly and pointing to empty spaces in the air.

No, sir. Qween Dorothy might be a lot of things, like homeless, an unrepentant alcoholic, and a firm believer in Jesus Christ, but there was nothing wrong with her mental faculties, thank you very much.

Everybody went through bad times. You endure them. Got no other choice. 'Cause things will get better eventually. Just like the old blues songs said.

For the most part, she was quite content. She had freedom. Lot of folks couldn't say that. A clock told them where to be and when. Always rushing somewhere. She'd been in a few places where the people always pooh-poohed her ideas on being able to sit outside and breathe the fresh air. Those were the same people who assumed she wanted a damn bath. Even though Dorothy tried her best to follow the words of Christ, these people tried to shove their own version of religion down her throat. And of course, those were the same people who tried to take her bottles of gin away.

No, thank you.

No, *fucking* thank you.

The humid summers didn't bother her. She knew places to stay where the wind cooled her in the summer and where it was warm in the winter, places where skyscrapers vented billowing clouds of tropical heat. The rest of the time, the world was hers. And she had her friends, some in the regular world of nine-to-five jobs, mortgages, and clocks, and some who had fallen or jumped through the cracks and ended up living on the other side of that regular world.

The canvas bag moved again. It twitched.

Nobody noticed. Qween Dorothy knew it wasn't because she was invisible, as reassuring as that might be. The uncomfortable, real reason was that people simply didn't want to see her. Their gaze slid around her and her cart like oil over a light bulb.

She pushed her cart across Washington, ignoring the light. Brakes squealed and horns split the air. She paid little attention to all the racket. The last time a cab driver had gotten impatient and nudged her cart with his taxi, knocking it over and spilling her possessions into the street, she'd hauled the little bastard out of the car and kicked him until she got too tired.

Most of the homeless in the Loop didn't bother with a cart. It was easier to just leave their stuff under whatever ledge or overpass they'd claimed; pushing a cart across the wildly uneven asphalt and concrete of downtown was too much work. At least, this was the tendency of the folks that were truly homeless.

The Loop was also flooded with imposters jangling paper coffee and soda cups at passersby, pretending to be destitute, but they actually had a hot meal, a soft bed, and a family waiting for them after a day of panhandling in the streets. She didn't have much patience for the pretenders.

The frauds had learned the hard way to avoid Qween Dorothy at all costs.

She continued north on Clark, and the sidewalk that bordered City Hall grew wider. The crowds grew thinner. She left her cart near the revolving doors and unscrewed the bolts that secured the back wheels to the frame. She didn't like to leave it out on the street if she could help it, and taking off the hockey-puck-sized wheels seemed to deter most thieves. Without the wheels, to move the cart, you had to damn near carry the whole thing. You couldn't easily grab anything inside either. Everything was wrapped in two separate tarps and anchored with ropes and bungee cords. She told herself not to get her hopes up and tucked the wheels into her cloak.

She adjusted her plastic Viking helmet, grabbed the twitching canvas bag, and went into City Hall.

* * *

Qween Dorothy knew the eyes of the two policemen at the metal detectors, not to mention the cameras, were locked on her as soon as she pushed through the spinning doors into the cool darkness. The younger cop looked like he'd just as soon club her and dump her ass back on the street. She'd seen the older one before. He'd been patient with her requests, and even if his eyes betrayed his bemusement, at least he kept a patronizing tone out of his voice.

The corridor was crowded. City employees, young couples searching for the County Clerk for marriage licenses, a few listless protesters, and self important politicians who tried to look busy while casting glances around to see if anybody recognized them, clogged the metal detectors. She ignored everyone except the two cops and stepped up to the desk, surreptitiously depositing the bag on the floor, between her feet and desk.

"Afternoon, Qween," the older one said.

She clasped her hands and smiled. Without the cloak, the horns, and the All Stars, she might have been a kindly old lady on her way home from church. "Good afternoon"—she squinted—"Officer Nabor."

"What can we help you with today, Qween?"

"Well, sir, I'll tell you. You folks know me. You know I been here a long time. Seen lots a things. I'm telling you right now, there's some bad things going on."

"Bad things, Qween? Like last time, maybe the time before? When you were yelling about the city?"

Qween frowned. "I be lett—I *was* letting off some steam then." She found her smile. "Punks be stealing from me, moving into my spot. Fuck—*messing* with me. I was down here trying to get the city to do something different then."

Officer Nabor knew this. Today he understood Qween

Dorothy was trying very, very hard to be polite. "Okay. So what's different today?"

"Rats are dying, Officer Nabor."

The young cop snorted.

"And this is a problem . . . how again?" Officer Nabor said.

Qween tried to be patient. "Have you seen the river? I counted fourteen dead rats in it. Last week I saw over twenty-five in one day."

"Okay." It was almost a question.

"When's the last time you saw that many dead rats? Where you been? Ain't you seen the subways?"

"We drive to work," the young cop said. "Free parking."

"You need to go down there. See for yourselves what's happening."

Officer Nabor leaned on the desk. "I'm sorry, Qween, but I'm just not following you. Dead rats. So what?"

She stared at him for a moment. "If you ain't never seen this many dead rats before, why you suppose they be dying now? What you suppose is going on under this city?"

Officer Nabor shrugged.

"It's like a warning. A sign. I dunno, gotta be some scientific name for it."

"You mean like a portent?"

She considered this. "Maybe," she said slowly. It was hard to tell if he was mocking her or not. If she couldn't get them to understand that something was dead wrong, she wasn't sure how to convince them. The suspicion was creeping back. She'd come in here, trying to get the Man to listen. She should have known better. She realized she was being stupid. Must have been drunker than she thought earlier in the morning. The peace was beginning to wear off. Without thinking, she touched the side of her cloak, just enough to brush the bottle inside her down vest, just enough to double-check it was still there.

Both officers saw the change in her face. It was like

watching the side of an iceberg slough off. It started in almost slow motion, then caught speed, until gravity took over completely. The kindly old woman on her way home from church was gone. Qween Dorothy's street face was back with a vengeance. She tried to smile again, and the effect was chilling. This time the young cop touched his canister of pepper spray much the same way Qween had reassured herself.

"If you two dumbass dog dicks ain't smart enough to see that I be trying to *help* y'all, that ain't my problem. I got me a meeting with the mayor." She wrapped the cord that tied the bag shut around her wrist and moved briskly for the elevators.

The cops were in front of her in a heartbeat. Officer Nabor had his hands up, palms out, still trying to resolve things amicably.

"Now, Qween, let's not take this too far," Officer Nabor said. "The mayor's a very busy man, and I don't think they're gonna fit you into his schedule. I'm sorry, I don't know what to tell you."

"Well, I know what to tell *you*. You get the fuck outta my way."

"We can't do that, Qween. You know that." He moved to take her by the arm. "Let me help you back outside, get you on your way."

"Don't you fuckin' touch me." She jerked her arm back, dragging the bag with it.

"What's in the bag, Qween?" Officer Nabor asked. "Please tell me you don't have a rat in there. You can't bring that in here. Rats carry disease."

"No shit, you dumbass cracker."

The younger cop pulled the pepper spray loose, anxious to try it out.

By now, the confrontation had attracted a crowd. Behind Officer Nabor and his young partner, Qween could see more cops coming out of the elevator, no doubt sent by whoever was keeping an eye on the cameras. They were never going to listen. She hadn't really believed that she would have gotten in to see the mayor, but she had hoped that someone would have at least written her complaint down.

Well, if they weren't going to listen, then she was going to have to get their attention another way. She pulled the cord free in one smooth motion, and dumped the rat on the floor.

The young cop didn't hesitate. He brought up the pepper spray, and blasted Qween in the face. She stumbled back, and the cop stayed with her, arm extended, spray canister still inches from her face.

At her feet, the rat was still alive. It blinked and shuddered, confused in the sudden light. Officer Nabor jumped back, exhaling harshly. "Whoa, whoa there." The rat took off, scurrying into the shadows under the benches that lined the walls. Everyone screamed and scattered.

The young guard took his eyes off Qween for a half second to watch the rat get away, and Qween whipped her left arm over the cop's, trapping it in the long cloak. She drew back her right fist, fingers tight over the shopping-cart wheels, and clocked him square on the jaw. He tried to pull away, but she still had her cloak wrapped around his extended arm. She hit him again. His knees buckled.

Officer Nabor turned from the rat and tried to separate the old woman from his partner. By now, the rest of the cops had reached them, and together, they pulled Qween off the young cop.

Three men wrestled her to the floor. As she lay panting under their weight, she turned her head, feeling the cool marble against her cheek, and saw the rat, down at the far end of the hall, scuttle down the escalator and vanish.

# CHAPTER 21

**2:19 PM**
**August 11**

"Jesus fucking Christ." Commander Arturo Mendoza slumped back in his chair and clasped his hands across his chest. "Please tell me you aren't this goddamn stupid."

Sam shrugged and sat down across the desk. "We're not this goddamn stupid."

Ed took the other chair.

Commander Mendoza didn't appreciate the attempt to keep the meeting easy and quick. The bags under his eyes made it look he was peering out at them with a mixture of pity and resignation behind a mask that allowed no mercy. The rest of his face was frozen in permanent sour taste, as if he'd bitten into a rib and found that the bone had gone soft with rot. Only his narrow eyes showed any emotion.

The few photos and plaques on the wall in Mendoza's office felt obligatory. Mendoza, in varying ages, with three different mayors. There were no family photographs. Only Mendoza getting awards, and frames around grim images of nature, the ghostly line of birch trees in fog, water dripping from a bright red leaf, the knuckled bones of roots that crept across the dirt in arteries and veins that split off like the circulatory system of a mammal.

In the twenty-six years that Sam had been a friend of the Mendoza family, he'd never seen any personal photographs in the office. He'd gotten drunk at every family barbecue, every first communion, every *quinceañera*, and most birthdays that seemed to come along in an endless stream. Mendoza had six children whom he loved dearly. With the exception of a few friends, Commander Mendoza preferred to keep a wide chasm between his working life and his family.

"I have been telling you for years," Commander Mendoza said. "You need to listen to office politics. You need to know who's who. It's part of the job. Especially the way you two tend to irritate people. If you intend to relieve an officer of his suspect, who is already cuffed and in the backseat, I might add, you need to know who this officer's pal is upstairs. This officer, Officer Falwell, he's our deputy chief's second cousin's nephew or whatever. You needed to know this. But as usual, you couldn't give a flying fuck, and you had to go and humiliate the man."

"The man's a pompous asshole in a uniform." Sam couldn't help himself. "Everybody—included our esteemed Officer Falwell—knows he was taking the suspect into rival gang territory and kicking him out. That's not police work. That's just cold-blooded. He deserved a little humiliation."

"It *was* kinda funny," Ed said.

"Officer Falwell failed to see the joke. Guess he took it personally."

"It wasn't so long ago we didn't worry about some whining closet case," Sam said. "Motherfucker wants to shove his real feelings back down deep inside and then take it out on folks, fuck him. You know I'm right. Be a man, and come out and admit it. He'd feel better."

"Doesn't matter. It doesn't matter what makes him an asshole. You pushed his buttons and he made you his number-one priority. Once he found out your name, he went straight to Wilson. And believe me, he's got his head so far up Wilson's ass, the deputy chief should go ahead and charge him rent. Yesterday, I had a short yet extremely loud conversation with Deputy Chief Wilson. He's coming after you with both barrels this time. This is why you have suddenly found yourselves with clean desks and a workload that's wide open."

Ed and Sam said, "Aww, come on. Really?"

"Really. Everything has been dumped on Jackson and Ruiz. They were thrilled when I told them you two will be buying beers until those cases are closed." Mendoza sat up and put his forearms on the desk. "I honestly don't know this time. In the meantime, the union forbids me to park you at a desk somewhere and alphabetize parking tickets. So I will be sending you on official business missions. First off, you are going to escort a drunk homeless woman who caused a disturbance at City Hall this afternoon down to Twenty-sixth and California. On your way back, you are going to stop in Erickson's Butcher and get me and the wife a couple of nice New York strips. And make sure you tell Jens it's for me, not you two."

Dr. Reischtal was sitting in one of the empty patient rooms, back to the window, facing a blue wall broken only by the bland image of stylized sailboats scattered across a bright sea, when he got the call. He had been listening to the faint sounds of equipment being dismantled and hauled out of the floor below. Air purifiers, medical supplies, and computers carried out. All those massive rolls of plastic, a one-millimeter membrane of protection against the god of chaos and unreason beyond his faith, were being loaded into white vans with an obscure health industry uniform company on the side.

His team had been monitoring the police radios, as well as a few reporters' phones they had cloned. He was too busy trying not to focus on the systematic destruction of his wall of protection and he forgot about the phone. The sharp burst of noise made him flinch.

He snatched it. "Yes."

"Sir, this is Audio Specialist Castle. Sir, we're hearing some chatter about a rat loose in City Hall."

"And?"

"Sir, that's all we're hearing right now. No other details right now. If the police are talking, they're doing it with an unknown broadcast device."

"Check Streets and Sanitation."

"Yes, sir."

"Keep me posted, Audio Specialist Castle."

Dr. Reischtal hit END CALL and immediately hit SERGEANT REAVES.

"Yes, sir."

"We may have a situation relevant to our concerns occurring right now in City Hall. I would like an initial report, but quiet. A confirmation is all we need at this moment before proceeding further."

"Yes, sir."

Dr. Reischtal was silent for a moment. "And tell them to freeze the withdrawal. The next person that removes any object from this hospital will be taking blood samples of dying pigs in Nigeria. Make that understood."

# CHAPTER 22

"Don't they have, like, exterminators or something like that for this?"

"Shit, who do you think we are? You're looking at two of the finest rat exterminators in the city of Chicago."

"I'm looking at a couple of jagoffs," Tommy said, thinking of the equipment in the back. Along with the usual protective clothing and heavy-duty flashlights, extermination bags, and Tommy's aluminum baseball bat, this time they had long poles, four feet long, with choke ties at the end, a cage, evidence bags, evidence tags, and fishing nets, instead of the bait and traps. "I'm used to picking up dead ones."

Don used the van's size to crowd out cabs as he turned north onto LaSalle as the light turned yellow. The cab drivers didn't like it, and weren't shy about hitting their horns before ultimately backing off. The van was a clearly marked city vehicle and therefore if it was damaged in any way, whoever hit the van had to face the city of Chicago in traffic court.

Tommy enjoyed Don's casual command of traffic; he

could never drive with that much aggression, but it was fun when he was in the passenger seat.

Don parked out in front and put the yellow flashers on. They took their time getting equipment ready, because, as Don always pointed out, they weren't getting paid by the hour, and they had to match expectations established by the rest of their union brothers and sisters. Tommy pretended they were a couple of Ghostbusters as they headed inside.

A young, attractive woman met them inside and introduced herself as Tonya Shaw, a member of the public relations department. "Captain Harold Garnes is waiting downstairs. He's head of building security." She smiled a lot, her smooth caramel skin contrasting with teeth the color of fresh cream.

They followed her through the center of the building, along a cool marble floor and under a Baroque white ceiling that looked to Tommy like nothing more than white scoops of frosting.

"Wow." Don nudged Tommy. "A captain. Sounds serious. This rat, he carrying any weapons? Want to make sure we're prepared."

Tonya laughed, too quickly, and moved at almost a trot as she led them downstairs. Her heels trickled down the escalator with the grace of a tap dancer. The sound bounced around in the tight space like machine-gun fire. Don and Tommy couldn't help but admire the grace in such a tight skirt and followed at a slower speed.

At the bottom, the steel bars and clanking exit turnstiles of the Blue Line Washington Station waited off to the right. Except for a speck of a man on the left-hand wall who looked like he'd been behind that pile of newspapers and magazines since Daley Senior had taught those hippies an important life lesson, the place was empty.

"Where is everybody?" Don asked, his voice echoing around the relative quiet and glaring fluorescent lights.

"Captain Garnes has cordoned off the area. We don't want anyone getting bit, now do we?" She laughed again.

Definitely nervous, Tommy thought.

Don knew it too. "It's a good thing you move so fast in those heels," he said. "These rats, you never know where they might go. Quick too. Squirt around like they was flying."

"Captain Garnes is right here," Tonya said, stopping and gesturing at the cops down the hall as if the two Streets and Sans guys had just won a prize.

Captain Garnes looked like somebody had stuck a mustache and eyebrows on a bullet to try and give it a personality. Officer Nabor waited listlessly behind his boss along with several other cops. "It's down there," Captain Garnes said and didn't bother with introductions. That was all.

Don eventually nodded, and they continued along the hallway. Every door was closed, with the exception of the last door on the left. Tommy turned back to see Tonya and the policemen watching from a safe distance. He kept going, shining the flashlight under benches and plants, and feeling stupider by the second.

The last room opened into two long rows of cubicles. Tommy kneeled in the aisle and peered under the chairs and desks of the first pair of cubicles. No rat.

"Fuck this," Don said, and kicked one of the chairs down the aisle. It crashed into a cubicle wall and ricocheted across into more chairs. Nothing else moved. "It's not in here," he said in disgust. "We're gonna be here all night."

Tommy edged forward, still searching.

In the next to last cubicle, they found the rat curled into a tight ball in the corner. Don prodded the rat with the pole, but that was just a formality. He put on a rubber glove that went halfway to his elbow. Holding the tail, Don raised it and they gazed at it skeptically. It didn't look like most of the dead rats they had seen. Wild rats aren't much more than skin and bones to begin with, but this one was so emaciated it made them feel hungry just looking at it. The lips were peeled back in a grimace, exposing formidable teeth. Flecks of white froth were dotted along the gums and eyes.

"Fucked if I know," Don said finally. "We're done. Let's go get a beer." He'd fallen off the wagon for the third time that summer. He smiled around the rat. "Let's go see if I can't make Tonya move any quicker."

Neither saw the bug crawl from the rat and work its way up Don's glove.

Dr. Reischtal grew impatient. The phone had been silent for too long. He wanted to pace, but knew it could be seen as a weakness if anyone came in. He considered the possibilities of a sick rat. Perhaps he had been sitting in the center of this city for these long months, waiting for the occurrence of a virus outbreak among the wrong species.

He was tired of waiting. Tired of avoiding the potential for failure, that his conviction that this would be at least one of the final battles for his world was wrong. Tired of this stealthy battle with the enemy.

He called Audio Specialist Castle. "Any further information regarding the rodent in City Hall?"

"I have three confirmations that a homeless woman released a rat inside City Hall."

"Any logical reason why?"

"One report indicates that the woman may have wanted to display the rat for the mayor. No further explanation was available."

Dr. Reischtal hung up and called Sergeant Reaves again. "I want three men. One City of Chicago vehicle, equipped with two animal-remains kits, and appropriate identification, waiting out in one minute. Any vehicle will be fine. We're only going five blocks."

Don had it all planned out. He hid the rat behind his thigh as they walked up. When he got within ten feet he was going to hold it up and say, "Hey, does this rat match the description of the suspect?"

Instead, the rat twitched, then came violently alive. It thrashed and curled like a scorpion's tail, trying to slash Don's hand and arm with its oversized teeth.

Don flung the rat down. It thumped on the floor and immediately launched itself at his boots. It swarmed up his foot and clawed at his jeans. Don kicked and launched the rat forward. It slid about ten feet, incisors frantically clicking as it found purchase and scrabbled forward, its claws echoing the teeth as they scraped at the marble.

It ignored Tonya and the policemen and darted at Don again. This time, Tommy stepped in front of it. He pulled his aluminum bat out of the sling on his back as his feet found their sweet spot. He brought his hands down almost leisurely, the bat swinging in slow motion behind him. Until time sped up. The barrel whipped down and connected with the front shoulders of the rat the way a freight train connects with a stalled VW Bug.

The rat slapped into the wall with a soft crunch and a smear of red. The ballplayer in Tommy was still very much alive, as he elegantly followed through with the swing, eventually letting the right hand fall away, ending in the pose that had made Kimmy fall in love with him as she watched from the bleachers their sophomore year.

"You can put it on the board. . . . YES!" Don roared, mimicking the Sox play-by-play man Hawk Harrelson. He slapped Tommy on the back. He yelled down at Tonya and the policemen, "We weren't kidding when we said we don't fuck around." He hung his arm over Tommy's shoulders as they looked down at the rat. He called back to the group, "Uh, yeah. Clean-up on aisle fourteen. You're gonna need a big sponge and a bucket to clean this shit up."

Instead of Captain Garnes or Tonya though, they heard an icy voice behind them. "Do you realize that you've just destroyed an extremely valuable scientific specimen?"

# CHAPTER 23

Ed pulled up behind a uniform laundry van and a Streets and San truck. Sam eyeballed the two vehicles. "Any more and we could start a parade. Busy day in City Hall."

Inside, everyone was agitated, yelling into cell phones. There was one officer waiting at the front desk. Ed showed him his star and signed in, explaining, "We're here for a prisoner transfer."

The cop behind the desk looked skeptical. "They sent a couple of detectives for some old woman? It's not like she tried to shoot Derrick Rose or anything."

Ed nailed him with a dead-eyed stare.

Sam, still sore over the bullshit assignment, said, "Fuck you care?"

The cop shrugged. "Fine, whatever." He picked up the phone. "She's in the lockup on the county side."

Ed and Sam moved down the hall. The cop did a good job ignoring Sam's glare, so Sam stopped, until the cop didn't have a choice but to look over. Now Sam could be the one to shake his head first, as if dismissing the younger man.

Another cop standing at the top of the escalator stopped

Ed from going downstairs. "Sorry, buddy, this part of the building is temporarily closed."

Ed blinked. "Why?"

The cop hesitated. Ed oozed law enforcement from his pores, but the cop couldn't be sure. "I don't have any exact details at this time, sir."

Ed had to pull his star out again. "Unless there's some deranged fucknut down there with a gun, I'm going downstairs. Thank you, officer." He stepped onto the escalator.

Sam passed the second cop, still shaking his head.


They heard somebody with a deep Chicago accent arguing loudly with a thin, sharp voice. The argument got louder. Ed and Sam followed the clamoring voices and turned into a hallway. A knot of Chicago cops and an attractive woman in a tight suit blocked the view of the rest of the hallway.

They got closer, moved through the cops, and Sam got his first look at Dr. Reischtal.

A tall man, somewhere around his early fifties. Wearing a doctor's lab coat, buttoned to the top. Tiny round glasses, giving his eyes a perpetually narrow look, as if he was zeroing in wherever his gaze landed. Arms held loose, left hand clasped tightly over the right at his waist.

"—has absolutely no bearing on the fact you have just committed a serious felony crime."

The big guy in the Streets and Sans uniform snorted in disgust. "And I keep saying, we did our job."

Assistants in protective gear and surgical masks were placing a mangled dead rat into a container with its own air filter. Despite this, the soldiers took Sam's attention. Three of them, wearing National Guard uniforms. Sam squinted, wondering if he should start bringing his reading glasses with him on the job. He cursed himself for the thought, but something wasn't quite right with the soldiers. The uniforms were too new.

Ed and Sam got closer. All of the soldiers carried at least one sidearm, some kind of knife, and an assault rifle stowed on a sling behind them. Sam realized that they weren't AR-15s; he didn't even know what the hell these were. Something exotic. Fancy. Expensive. More details jumped out. They all wore knee pads. Sophisticated throat mikes. Wireless earbuds.

"Look pal, you're barking up the wrong tree here. You oughta be talkin' to my boss, you know, the guy who sent me here." The big guy in Streets and Sans uniform wasn't as tall as the doctor, but he might have weighed twice as much. Classic Chicago build. Mustache too. Hawks hat, the whole nine yards.

The other Streets and San guy was much younger. Clearly the quiet half of the pair. Maybe a couple of years out of high school. Didn't appear to be college material, except maybe on a sports scholarship. He had the build of a shortstop, low, lean, and quick. Cold eyes. The handle of an aluminum bat stuck up from behind his head in some harness.

Sam gave a small smile. It was always the quiet ones you had to watch out for.

"If you think you can hide behind your pathetic job, my dear friend, I can assure you that I will see to it that your bosses crucify you," Dr. Reischtal said. The guy was so cold Sam was surprised a hailstorm didn't accompany each word. "I will see to it."

Ed pushed through the knot of cops and said, "Perhaps I can be of assistance." He wearily pulled his star out for the third goddamn time in five minutes. "Detective Ed Jones. This is Detective Sam Johnson."

Dr. Reischtal tilted his head at the detectives. "Ah. I am . . . familiar with your work."

Sam glanced at the dead rat, Tommy's bat, and the blood on the wall. "Seems to me what we got here is a situation of a couple of Streets and San workers doing their job." He stared at Dr. Reischtal. "You got here late."

The techs glanced at Dr. Reischtal and showed him the

lights on the container. They glanced at the mess on the wall and more blood on the floor. Dr. Reischtal gave his head a short shake. "This mess is not ours. Leave it to them to clean it up."

As the techs headed for the escalator, Dr. Reischtal turned to the detectives and the Streets and San men and held his head so that the fluorescents caught his glasses. His eyes crackled with white energy. "Understand this. You will all be held responsible. I will see you again."

# CHAPTER 24

**3:19 PM**
**August 11**

The running joke among the cleaning women at the Clark Adams Building was that Herman Smith looked like a Muppet that belonged on *Barrio Sésamo*. His body was covered in short fur, and his face was all mustache and eyebrows. He wasn't a large man, but when he got to yelling at anybody he thought was underneath his position, he would puff his chest out and bounce on his toes, trying to make himself more physically intimidating.

The women had a pool going about his age; everybody had put in five bucks and given their best guess. Estimates of his age ran anywhere from thirty-five to fifty-eight. They knew he'd changed his name, as his former name was some unpronounceable jumble of consonants, but nobody had gotten a look at his records yet, so the pot was unclaimed. Apart from their curiosity about his age, they didn't like him much. He refused to help out upstairs, preferring instead to remain by himself in his basement.

He liked to think of it as *his* building; it took up an entire city block. He'd worked there for thirteen years and thirteen years was a long time. Long enough to see his three children old enough to attend college. It was dull, mindless work, but he didn't care, because it left him with time to find other ways to generate income.

He pushed through the employees' entrance. Paid his ten-dollar debt to the guy at the desk. His father had taught him the invaluable lesson of paying any debts immediately. Last night, the Cubs had surprised everyone and won two out of three against St. Louis. The security guard was a Cubs fan and bet with his heart. For once, he'd won. Herman, on the other hand, couldn't care less about one team or the other.

One level down, he followed the utility corridor all the way from the Clark side of the building to the east side. He always made sure to unlock a certain door the first level down as soon as he started his shift. This wasn't part of his regular job, but he had to uphold his end of the bargain. This provided access to the building from the relative privacy of the alley. He found the chain already unlocked.

Those rich pricks.

They had forgotten again. Or they were breaking another rule, going in or out during the daytime. It got dark back here, but not dark enough. It needed to be night; otherwise, someone passing on the street might see them. He locked the chain tight again, as a reminder to the bastards. If they were outside and needed in, well then, that was too damn bad.

He moved with an urgent purpose now, heading down another level to a forgotten storeroom that had been sealed off decades ago. Before retiring, Herman's predecessor had explained that the room had been repurposed and outlined the deal he'd struck. It served as a crash pad for a small group of stockbrokers and was a place for a quick snort of coke to get pumped for the trading floor and fuck girls from the downtown bars. Over the years, it had dwindled to just two brokers. Still, they paid Herman rent and everybody kept quiet.

But lately, they had been slacking off adhering to Herman's rules.

Vest-wearing ass-clowns.

He tried the door. It was locked.

He swore in Croatian, dug around his front pocket for the key. He stepped inside, and locked the door behind him. The place was dark and filled with furniture looted from the Chicago Board of Trade. A couple of desks with outdated computers, office chairs, a couple of leather couches. He switched on one of the lamps and the room grew a little brighter with the muddy light. They'd decorated the concrete walls with stolen street signs and abstract images taken from beer advertisements and horror movie posters.

Herman wrinkled his nose. The place smelled. Bad. The desks were covered in fast food containers and white Chinese food boxes. It didn't look like they used the half fridge in the corner for anything but beer. The garbage can was overflowing with old food. This was just the first room.

They had walled part of the room off using cubicle partitions, presumably for a bit of privacy. The first room was empty. Which meant they were probably outside, and Herman would be damned if he was going to clean this mess up himself. They would follow his rules or he would find someone else to rent the room.

He went to check the back room before he locked up the place for the night, just in case they were sleeping off an early drunk. Herman knew they had at least two couches behind the partitions. He just hoped they didn't have any girls back there. Girls didn't listen. Girls were loud. Girls were trouble.

There were no lights in the second room. If anything, it smelled worse back here. Something rotten. And something else too . . . something that smelled strangely like the bear claws he used to buy every morning, until he stopped because he couldn't shake the feeling he was wasting money on something frivolous.

He fished his penlight out of his pocket to check the couches.

Sure enough, there they were. Illuminated in the narrow, weak yellow beam, he could see one of the brokers still passed out on one of the couches. The other one had rolled off the second couch and lay facedown on the floor. He shook his head. Stupid, arrogant assholes.

"Hey," he said, kicking the frame of the closest couch. "Wake up. You forget the rules, hey?"

Neither man moved. In fact, they seemed unnaturally still.

Herman kicked the couch again. "Hey! Time to wake up. I'm talking to you!"

Still no movement.

He aimed the light straight into their faces and his gut knew before his brain figured out that the two brokers were dead. Something looked wrong with their skin, but it was hard to tell in the wavering light. They both seemed unnaturally pale, and the skin looked puffy almost, something akin to the texture of a rough sponge.

He backed out of the room, knees buckling. He dropped into an office chair and pushed himself across the room. He could not understand how they had died. For the first time in over six years, if he could have found a cigarette, he would have broken his solemn vow. He placed a trembling hand out to the desk to steady himself.

He switched the flashlight off. It wasn't much help in the first room anyway. He took several deep breaths, focusing on just inhaling and exhaling, long and slow. He needed to think this out. But the two corpses in the makeshift room, not ten feet from where he sat, kept getting in the way of making a decision. He felt paralyzed. He pulled his hands into fists and tried to just breathe.

The $CO_2$ he exhaled caught the attention of a dozen bugs dozing under the chair's seat. They set out to the edge of the fabric, thousands of years of instincts directing them to a large warm-blooded mammal.

To feed.

To spawn.

The bugs found Herman's slacks. Their jaws could not penetrate the fabric, so they latched onto the threads, wriggling along on six legs. They stopped when he moved, and just hung on, and when they felt the stillness, they worked their way closer to the warmth of bare flesh.

Herman couldn't feel them. The thought of fingerprints had just crossed his mind. He jerked his hand off the desk and wiped it with his rag. He stood up quickly and patted his pockets, making sure nothing had fallen out. His wife was always watching those police forensic TV shows, and it seemed like the cops would inevitably find some hair or some damn thing to discover the killer. He backed out of the room, hoping he hadn't touched anything else.

Outside, in the corridor, he locked the door and twisted the rag around the handle. He could always call 911 later, after he figured out what he would say. In the meantime, he would do his job and stick to his usual routine. He could always claim he found them later.

He started up the stairs, moving slow, and had to pause near the top to catch his breath.

The bugs crawled up under his shirt and over the waistband.

Herman opened the door to the basement and rubbed his sore back, rolled his shoulders, and made sure to lock to the door behind him. He still couldn't feel the bugs.

# CHAPTER 25

**3:21 PM**
**August 11**

Sam shook his head at the empty hallway. "What a fuckin' asshole." He called back to Captain Garnes, "You want to write this up?"

"Hell, no."

"Me, neither. He say who he's with?"

"CDC."

"Ahhh . . . shit."

"Shit is right. Listen, I'm sorry, but when this comes down, I'm passing this down to you, you know?"

"Yeah, yeah. I know."

"I got no time for the kind of shit that's gonna rain down, understand? What the hell are you doing here anyway?"

"Prisoner transfer. Some homeless woman."

Captain Garnes laughed. "I see. Assignment like that, you're already in trouble. What are you, a goddamn shit magnet or something? She's in the old jail. Get her and then get the fuck out of here."

Ed said, "Good seeing you again too, Harold," as Captain Garnes led the cops upstairs.

Sam gave Tommy his card. "That's us, your local shit collectors. You got problems, you let me know."

"Thanks," Don said and tilted his head at Tommy. "Fuck it. No more rat. We're done. Happy Hour isn't gonna last forever." He shook Ed and Sam's hands, doffed his Blackhawks cap at Tonya, and started upstairs.

Tommy grabbed the equipment, gave Tonya a nod, and followed.

Sam and Ed worked their way through City Hall, heading to the County side. The hallways were slowly beginning to fill up with people again. A deeply tanned, middle-aged guy came out of the sheriff's office. He was dressed like a tourist, baggy shorts, even looser loud Hawaiian shirt, but he was far too muscular for a regular tourist. He had a crew cut, and scars on his scalp. He tried not to limp, but something in his right knee was sore. He kept his gaze pointedly straight ahead and passed the detectives without a glance in their direction.

Something about the lack of expression on the guy's face set off Sam's radar, so he filed it away, and then focused on the job immediately in front of him. Inside, they saw an empty front area. Ed signed in. Sam stepped behind the front counter and knocked on the security door. It was unlocked. Behind it, the two rooms were empty, and the cell door stood open.

It didn't feel right. Something was off.

Sam unbuttoned his sport coat, keeping his hand near his shoulder holster. Ed sensed it too, and unsnapped his own holster.

Qween lay facedown inside the cell. Her hands were handcuffed behind her. When she heard Ed and Sam's footsteps, she rolled over and kicked out, yelling, "Dirty motherfucker."

"This is Detectives Ed Jones and Sam Johnson, ma'am," Ed said.

They got a look at her face. One eye was starting to puff

shut. Her bottom lip was cracked bloody. Somebody'd been using her as a punching bag. "Come git some, motherfuckers. That's right." She kicked out at them.

"Ma'am. We're here to pick you up. You promise to behave, we'll take those handcuffs off."

"You just want to get my back turned, fucker."

"We're serious, ma'am."

A pause while she thought about it. "Slide them keys over, then."

Ed sighed, slid the keys over to Qween, then stepped back and waited. When he was a rookie, he'd learned that ninety percent of being an effective patrol officer was being patient. Give people enough time to blow off steam and calm down, they would accept the situation, sometimes willingly follow him to the station. He didn't look at it as wasted time. It was worth going slow, instead of having some homeless prisoner puking or shitting in his car.

It took Qween a full minute to scoot over, grab the keys, and unlock herself. Ed thought she might be moving slowly on purpose; it felt like she might have done this before. She tried to pocket both the keys and the handcuffs but Ed made her give them back.

"Who did that to your face?" Sam asked.

"Who did that to yours?"

Ed tried not to laugh, but sometimes he couldn't help himself, like when his three-year-old grandson swore.

Sam said, "Ma'am, we're trying to help you out here. We don't much like it when someone decides to beat up a hand-cuffed prisoner. You want to tell us? We'll see to it that something is done." He kept seeing the guy in the Hawaiian shirt.

Qween squinted at them, then snorted. "The day I need some dumbass cracker and his Oreo partner to fight my battles is the day Jesus calls me home."

Ed brushed at some invisible lint on his suit jacket without meeting Sam's eyes. It was his signal that Sam should drop the questions. Patience was key here. Clearly, she'd rattled something near the top of the food chain if serious heavy-weights like Dr. Reischtal were taking an interest.

"You don't want to tell us, fine. Let's go," Sam said.

"Where we going?" she demanded.

"To Twenty-sixth and California," Ed said.

"Goddamnit." She rolled her eyes. "They gone sent an-other goddamn stupid dick licker."

"Excuse me?" Ed asked.

"Don't you people ever stop to think? Ain't nobody ever asked me why. Too busy thinking I just another crazy nigger lady. Stupid motherfuckers. Why you think I did it? Answer me that. Do this one thing, before hauling me off to another piss tank."

"Did what? Turn a rat loose?"

"No, take a dump on the sidewalk. 'Course the fucking rat."

"No idea."

"You did it to prove a point," Sam said.

"No shit. You be a regular Sherlock."

Sam started to like the homeless woman. "Okay. I'm lis-tening. You tell us."


Herman was halfway through cleaning his floors when an insistent sluggishness began to take hold. He couldn't believe it. He'd gotten nearly four hours of sleep last night, enough to keep him going at least until eleven, when he would start his second job as a cab driver, shuttling passengers back and forth to Midway. And tonight, panic had been flitting through his system because of the bodies in his secret rented room.

Still, there was no denying the exhaustion pulling at him. He finally gave up, and promised himself a short nap now, and finish the floors later. He switched off the floor buffer and went back to the desk in the maintenance room. Ever since he'd yelled at one of the cleaning women who had come down to ask for help one night, nobody ever came down here anymore during his shift, so he knew he wouldn't be disturbed.

Part of his mind knew something was wrong, but he ignored it, attributing it to the panic he'd felt earlier with the dead bodies. They didn't seem so important anymore. Nothing seemed important anymore. Only sleep. Shadows crowded at the edges of his vision and he had to feel around for the chair. He fell into it, but it rolled backwards and he slipped to the floor.

He didn't get up.

# CHAPTER 26

Qween took the detectives back to the Washington Blue Line Station under City Hall and made Sam pay for three tickets. Sam went first through the turnstile, followed by Qween. She took her time squeezing through, enjoying the tightness around her hips. "About the only action I get these days," she said with a lewd grin. Ed tried not to touch the bars any more than he had to. They descended into the subway down a wide set of smooth concrete stairs. The entire place needed to be repainted. The air was cool, but stale.

On the platform, they followed her through the crowd to the northbound edge and then along it. "You never see 'em in the light," Qween explained. They reached the end, where the platform simply stopped, dropping off to the darkness of the subway tunnel. One by one, they climbed down the utility ladder and walked along the tracks ten yards up the tunnel.

"Stop," Qween said. "Smell it?"

Sam shut his eyes and tested the air. She was right. Something thick clogged the atmosphere, stronger down in the shadows, almost enough to blot out the smell of human piss and burnt steel. He opened his eyes and found them fully adjusted to the dim light.

He saw dozens of rat corpses, curled up like pill bugs. The more his eyes adjusted to the dim light, the more rat corpses he could see. Hundreds of them. Something glinted in the wash from the fluorescents, then disappeared. Ed held up his smartphone, using a flashlight app. It was his favorite feature, once his oldest grandson had downloaded it and shown Ed how to use it. The light caught movement fifteen feet down the tunnel. It was the eyes of a living rat, which tugged at the shoulders of one of the corpses.

"Damn," Ed said. His voice echoed off the curving concrete.

The feeding rat flinched and hissed. Dozens of other answering hisses, as if they were tuned to the same radio static, erupted from the shadows all around them.

"Fuck me," Sam said, backing to the lights of the station. Ed splashed the light around, revealing square holes regularly spaced along both walls. These black tunnels were full of eyes. The closest rat squealed, whether in fury or terror Sam couldn't tell, and scuttled forward. Qween kicked at it and they scrambled back to the ladder. Ed and Sam pushed Qween up ahead of them, then pulled themselves over the ledge. They moved quickly into the light and stood for a moment, catching their breath, watching the edge for rats.

"Don't know about you, but I've seen enough," Sam said.

They decided a drink was necessary. After collecting Qween's cart, they found a quiet booth in the back of Monk's Pub a few blocks away. While the regulars laughed and shouted at the bar, plugging quarters into the jukebox, Ed, Sam, and Qween didn't talk. They concentrated on their shots of Jameson and slowly swirled the shot glasses in the condensation on the table that had collected from their beers.

Sam got tired of waiting for the waiter and went up to the

bar for another round. The bartender poured the shots and glanced over at their table. "I appreciate the business, but just so you know, the only reason she's allowed in here is 'cause she's with you."

"Fucking relax," Sam said. "You oughta worry about me instead. Tell you what. Give me six shots."

The bartender shrugged and didn't look at Sam again.

Sam popped another stick of nicotine gum and chewed on it ferociously. Some dipshit on the TV caught his eye. The evening news, interviewing some "witness" at City Hall. "Hey, turn that up," he said.

The bartender found the remote, and increased the volume.

"—crazy, you know. I heard people saying it was some kind of political statement, but I don't know." This was from the witness. They cut back to a perky reporter, wearing an elaborate outfit and about a gallon of hairspray to combat the humidity. The shot was live, outside of City Hall. "Some are calling it a sick joke, some are calling it a political prank that got out of control, and some are even saying it is part of some bizarre performance art piece."

The shot cut back to a prerecorded piece, shot inside City Hall. Tonya, looking cool and unflappable, smiled compassionately. "It's true that we experienced an unfortunate incident earlier today, yes. However, the important thing to remember here is that a mentally disturbed individual will be getting the help they need at this time."

Back to the reporter. "This is Cecilia Palmers, live from City Hall. Back to you, Barbara and Rob."

The smug, smiling face of a male anchor filled the screen. "Thanks, Cecilia. And now over to Tad Schilling, in Weather Center One. So tell me Tad, when are we going to get a break with this heat?"

Sam paid and borrowed a tray. He put all the shot glasses on it and carried it back to their table. "Just saw the news. They're brushing it under the rug as we speak. By tomorrow, it'll be forgotten." He passed out the first three shots and said, "Salute."

They downed the shots and sat in silence a while longer.

"So what now?" Ed asked. "We go back to Arturo. We tell him there's something going on with the rats. Some kind of disease. Shit. I can see the look on his face right now."

"No," Sam said. "We call the TV stations. Tell them what's going on. Get some footage of those dead rats."

"And you think they care about dead rats?" Ed asked. "Shit. They don't care about folks killing each other, as long as it stays on the South or West sides. What makes you think they gonna care about dead rats?"

"We need to pray to the good Lord for some guidance," Qween said.

Ed and Sam pretended they hadn't heard her suggestion.

Qween said, with a little more conviction, "I said, we need to pray."

"If that helps," Sam said, "go on ahead and pray."

"What's your religion, Mr. Sam Johnson?" Qween asked.

"I don't think that has any bearing on this case," Sam said.

"I think it has a whole lot to do with this case," Qween said. "Answer the question. If you want any more help from me, answer the question."

Sam took his second shot. "Okay. My folks were Jewish. I grew up in Skokie. Reform, I guess you'd say."

"Be straight. You Jews, you don't believe in the Lord Jesus Christ."

"Not in the way you believe, no."

"Okay, then. I ain't hold that against you."

"Good to hear it."

"But you ain't got any bearing on this, so shut the fuck up."

"Yes, ma'am."

"Edward Jones. What's your story? Don't break my heart. Tell me you're a Baptist from Down South. Please, boy. Please."

"Ma'am. Don't take this personally." Ed picked up his shot glass and held it, waiting until Qween held hers and they clinked the glass together. "I don't believe in God." He knocked his shot back. "Sorry. Your Bible, it's just myths and legends. No different from any other culture on Earth."

She surprised them and gave Ed a grin that displayed how few teeth she had left. "Don't you worry. Jesus Christ doesn't judge. He understands." Qween knocked back the Jameson, slammed the shot glass upside down on the wood. "You need to get yourself to church. Make sure it's Baptist. None of that Pentecostal foolishness. Shit, when I want to speak in tongues, I just drink Sambuca. Now, excuse me." She wriggled her bulk out of the booth. "All this quality whiskey goes right through me. I expect at least three more on the table when I get back."

When his cell phone rang, Lee was grateful for the interruption. He'd been sitting in a back room at a shithole of an Italian restaurant on the Near North Side and his throat hurt from all the laughing he was having to fake at all the stupid jokes. They kept shoving sausage and pasta on his plate; it wasn't like he could refuse to eat, so training tomorrow was going to be brutal. And it didn't help that he was sweating his balls off. Christ, what was it about these old fucking goombah types that they needed to keep the heat going in August?

Still, he was careful. The last goddamn thing he needed was for one of them to suspect he wasn't being sincere when he laughed. They'd turn on him like starving dogs. Forget his career. He'd be lucky not to end up as another "suicide" in the river.

Even though some of the older men frowned when his phone went off, he checked the number, saw that it was his uncle, and apologized profusely, saying, "It's Uncle Phil." The old men understood the importance of family, more specifically, the importance of getting a call from an elder in the business. Lee excused himself and slipped into the alley.

"What the fuck, Phil? These guys, they take it personally if you answer a phone in their presence."

"I know. I wouldn't have called, but we got bigger problems. You see the news? Hear about the rat loose in City Hall?"

"If this is your idea of an emergency, then I'm gonna have these guys cut your nuts off."

"Watch your mouth and listen close. Somebody's reaching out to you, and they've got enough juice to know to contact me first."

"So what?"

"Somebody from the CDC wants the names of the two employees that were in charge of catching the rat."

Lee's mind spun. "What the . . . why the fuck?"

"I have no idea. Only something big, bigger than us, is here, and they are serious.

"You need to find out who the fuck was downtown today and give them up quick. These people, they aren't fucking around. They got a hard-on for this rat and I don't want to know why."

# CHAPTER 27

**12:09 AM**
**August 12**

The owner kicked the detectives and the homeless woman out when closing time rolled around. Qween took her cart and disappeared in the shuddering roar and squealing sparks from an overhead El train. Ed and Sam barely noticed.

Ed said he'd walk home and Sam hailed a cab. Vague promises were made to follow up with Qween the next day, but they both knew it was bullshit. Sam fell into the cab and promptly fell asleep.

Ed told the cabbie Sam's address and knocked on the hood. He headed east, crossing Wacker, then the Chicago River. He lived in a condo on Clinton that overlooked the diesel-choked Metra and Amtrak train yard, the only reason he could afford the mortgage.

His girlfriend, Carolina, had been working the early-morning shift at a pancake place up on Belmont while Ed dropped her son off at his middle school. She would pick him up in the afternoon, spend time with him in evening, and if Ed was on duty, her mother would take over while Carolina went to law school at night. Ed whispered good night and gave

Grandma a peck on the cheek and slap on her ass as the grinning woman left.

His wife had died years earlier and his own children were grown with families of their own, scattered out around the suburbs. He grabbed a beer from the fridge and went to sit on the patio. At night, the train yard wasn't so bad. Only a couple of trains rolled by every half hour. He sat back, trying to focus on the reflections of the lights on the oily surface of the Chicago River—a dizzying array of spectral rainbows—and hoping he wouldn't have any dreams about the subway tunnels, he fell asleep.

The cabbie woke Sam up and said, "Eighteen-fifty, please."

Sam gave the guy a twenty and crawled out. He stood on the sidewalk and realized he didn't want to go inside and sit in the darkness and listen to the drip in the sink, the whine from the air-conditioning unit in the bedroom window, and nothing else. Around three, the dripping would be overshadowed by the muffled industrial noises from the dry-cleaning business downstairs.

He checked the time as the cab left. He knew of a liquor store about six or seven blocks away and set off. The night was cooling off and the air smelled decent. After walking a block, he felt good. The nap in the cab had really paid off. It was the first real sleep he'd had in a week, at least. He bought a pint of vodka, walked another half of a block, and ascended the Western Brown Line station. He sat in the shadows and cracked his bottle, drank deeply.

After a while, the next inbound El came along, so he stowed the bottle and boarded. He got off at Belmont and watched the traffic for a while. He took a few more pulls from the bottle. The next southbound train was nearly empty. In his car, there was only a Latino couple whispering and giggling and an older Asian guy trying not to fall asleep. Sam took a seat in the back. No one else got on at Fullerton.

Just past Armitage, the train descended into the tunnels under Chicago.

Sam pulled out the bottle and spent the night riding the subway, watching his reflection bounce and flicker against the rushing darkness beyond the window, wondering how many dead rats were out there.

# CHAPTER 28

The maintenance man in charge of the day shift found Herman curled up under his desk. He frowned. This was not like Herman. As long as he'd known the man, Herman had never slept through the night on the job. He knew for a fact that Herman sometimes took a nap, but only after he had finished his work, and needed rest before heading off to drive a cab. The day shift man didn't give a damn if Herman slept or not as long as the work was done, but he'd found the floor buffer in the middle of the hallway.

"Herman, Herman." He shook Herman's shoulder. "You can't sleep here, man. Come on."

Herman jolted awake and stared around, blinking rapidly, as if he didn't know where he was. He tried to swallow. His eyes finally focused on the day shift man. He croaked out a question.

The day shift man didn't understand him. "I don't know what the problem is, man, but you'd better get up and finish the floor before anybody else gets in, you know?" He held out his hand.

Herman smacked it away and scrambled out from under

the desk. He made a sound halfway between a whimper and a deep whine, and backed away from the other man.

"Herman, you okay? You want me to call somebody? A doctor, maybe?"

Herman spun and shuffled quickly down the corridor, disappearing into the shadows.

He raced up a utility staircase and burst into a corridor padded with thick carpet and bright fluorescent lights that burned his eyes. He stumbled along, hand slapping at door handles. They were all locked. He finally found a supply closet and fell inside. He crawled under the shelves to a dark corner and pressed his face into it, trying to quell the sobs threatening to erupt. The pain in his head was excruciating. The pain obliterated everything else, his job, his appearance, any rational thought. He couldn't even follow a logical sequence of ideas to try and understand what was wrong with him. He scraped his fingernails against the rough paint and pushed his forehead even harder into the corner.

Gradually, a new sensation crept up underneath the pain. Something bubbled mischievously under his skin. For the briefest moment, he almost felt relief, as this new feeling tipped the balance and he found that he could focus on something other than the agony spiking through his head.

But the sweet reprieve was gone in the time it took to exhale.

And then he wished he could have the pain back.

A sinister itch crawled up his back, starting just under his buttocks and snaking its way along his spine. He'd never felt anything like it before. It was maddening, as if a spider with feathers for legs was gently pulling itself along the inside of his skin.

He twisted his right arm back and frantically clawed at the whispering, teasing irritation. The second his fingers dragged the fabric of his shirt across the bare skin, disturbing the thick hair on his back, the itch got a thousand times worse. He heard something, something indistinct from a great distance, and didn't realize it was his own moan of despair.

He ripped his shirt over his head and dropped it. Twisting, he tried to reach the bad spots, his thick, stubby fingers failing to provide any relief. The blunt fingernails finally tore the surface of skin, and blood trickled down his back.

It made the itch worse.

He was openly sobbing now, slapping, clawing, raking his nails across the skin on his back as far as he could stretch. The itch, though, kept dancing away, waiting mockingly just out of reach. He struggled to his feet, pawing through the shelves for something, anything that he could use to scratch.

His fingers closed over a pair of industrial scissors with foot-long shears.

Without hesitation, he shoved the sharp points up into the spot between his shoulder blades. He rubbed them vigorously back and forth. A curious burning relief slowly spread along his spine and he closed his eyes. His breathing sounded unnaturally loud in the cramped closet.

The itching under his buttocks grew worse. He shifted his grip on the scissors, gripping them halfway up the shears. He stabbed the back of his right thigh, and raked the points from side to side. The blades tore through his pants and flesh like a fork sinking through the skin that forms on pudding as it cools. He paid no attention to blood seeping down the back of his legs, staining the khaki fabric a dark red.

The closet door opened.

A woman stood there. She gave a startled gasp at finding someone inside. She'd been working as an office administrator for over five years, and she'd never, ever been shocked like this at work before. She blushed and started to apologize. Then she saw the look in Herman's eyes. And when she saw the blood, she started screaming.

The scream pierced the insanity of itching, driving a bolt of fear directly into his skull, right between his eyes. The itching and pain from the headache cracked and fell away, leaving nothing but raw, naked panic. Adrenaline exploded throughout his system, and he lashed out with the scissors.

The two tips, spread slightly apart about an inch, like the jaws of a bored, not very hungry shark, sank into her side between the lower ribs, just under her left breast. Her scream caught and broke apart sharply as she struggled for another breath.

Herman yanked the tips of the scissors out, reversed his grip, curling his fingers through the round holes of the handles.

The woman found another breath as she stumbled backwards into a cubicle wall, and produced an even louder scream. Herman stayed close, raised his arm, and brought the scissors down across her face. The points slid through the plump tissue of her cheek, scraped along her jawbone, until finally plunging into the soft skin above her collarbone. He ripped them out and drove the blades into her skull again. This time, the shears sank four inches into her left eye, popping it like a squashed grape.

She kept screaming.

He did not relent, even as she fell to the floor. Again and again, he drove the scissors into her eyes. Her mouth. When she finally stopped making noise, her face looked like she'd fallen headfirst into a wood chipper.

He left her twitching in the hall and ran.

Herman burst out of the spinning doors into the August heat, full of sticky air and exhaust fumes. He stumbled, falling to his knees on the sidewalk in the midst of a throng of early-morning commuters. He had no comprehension that he was shirtless and covered in blood. Nothing existed for him except the liquid fear that was quickly hardening along his nerve endings into teeth clenching hate.

The roar from a northbound Orange Line train grew louder

as it passed, clattering along above Wells a block away. Herman clapped his hands to his ears and howled.

Most everyone approaching stopped once they saw all the blood. Except for one businessman, striding purposefully down the sidewalk, yammering into a cell phone. He wasn't paying attention and was nearly on top of Herman before he noticed anything. All he saw, though, was a shirtless man, which undoubtedly meant he was inebriated, rocking back and forth, hands on his head for some reason.

"Hang on, Bob. There's some kind of moron—"

Herman sprang at the man and stabbed him in the throat. The scissor blades hit the businessman's carotid artery, and when Herman yanked them out, blood erupted in a fine mist, spraying four feet across the sidewalk. The man took a step back, but something about his inner drive, his desire to dominate, remained in his posture, keeping him on his feet. His brain wouldn't let him drop his cell phone either.

Bob kept asking, "Hello? You still there? Hello?"

More screaming erupted around Herman. He threw himself into the crowd in a berserk frenzy, slashing and stabbing at anyone within reach. People fled in all directions. Behind him, the businessman's body finally gave up and sagged to the sidewalk.

Herman zeroed in on a shrieking woman in a gray suit. She darted into the empty street. Half a block away, the light had just changed, and the vehicles surged forward. All the drivers saw was some executive trying to beat the traffic.

Herman darted between a FedEx truck parked at the curb and a Streets and Sans van and chased her into the street. He focused solely on the running woman, utterly unaware of the giant black SUV that was racing up the street.

The driver was intent on beating a cab that had been irritating her for blocks, and when she saw the shirtless, hairy man dash out into the street, it was too late. The driver used her three-inch heels to stomp on the brakes, locking the tires up, rubber howling as it burned into the pavement, but the SUV had been travelling at nearly thirty-five miles an hour. All it did was slow down enough so that when the left headlight struck Herman, it knocked him forward a dozen feet, but then the fender caught him up and drove him into the pavement, grinding him along for a while. Eventually his legs drifted back and were caught under the front tire, and his entire body was ripped in half. Both halves tore loose and were crushed under the back tires.

Later, when they found his arm, his hand was still clutching the scissors.

# CHAPTER 29

*6:01 PM*
*August 12*

Don didn't show up for work. Tommy wasn't particularly surprised at first. They'd spent the night before drowning in beer. He figured Don would stumble in soon, so he clocked in, changed into his overalls and boots, and waited. At 6:30, Don was a half-hour late. He had never been this late since Tommy had started work at Streets and Sans. At 7:00, Tommy called him. Nobody answered.

They'd started the night before pounding Old Styles, sure, but it hadn't been any different than any of the other countless nights they'd spent at the bar with no name, except Don kept showing off the torn rubber glove, the marks on the leather gloves underneath, and finally, his unscathed hand. Everybody had wanted to hear the whole story as they came in, so Don and Tommy hadn't paid for one beer.

Around ten, Don had heard about some house party one of his nephews was throwing, so they drove down to Blue Island and found the place full of community college students. Don had tried to impress the girls, but somehow, tales of catching rats hadn't done much for them. Don's nephew heard the stories, and started bitching about a goddamn raccoon that had torn a hole in the roof and moved into the space above the attic. Full of a beer and fueled by the eyes of the coeds, Tommy had volunteered to climb up under the roof and catch the critter. He promised not hurt the poor animal, something he later regretted.

He'd found the raccoon, no problem, but the damn thing hissed at him and snapped at his grasping hands, slicing the shit out of his fingers and palm. Finally, a hour later, bleeding from both hands, Tommy gave up and crawled out from under the eaves. Don laughed, and told his nephew quietly that they'd leave some poisoned bait later in the week and the problem would be solved. Tommy wrapped his hands in paper towels soaked in hydrogen peroxide and waited for the girls to come and talk to him. It never happened. Don and Tommy didn't leave because there was still beer left in the keg, and hung out in the empty backyard, sitting in the cracked swing set for the rest of the night, until the beer was gone. The last Tommy had seen of Don was the man giving a drunken wave as he pulled into early morning traffic.

The supervisor couldn't have cared less if Don was late or not. He was caught up in a Sox game. Around 8:00, Tommy took the van and went for a ride. He'd been to Don's place just once, and wasn't sure he could recognize it.

The AM news stations were full of speculation about the motives behind a series of brutal attacks downtown that morning. Tommy, like most people who lived in a large city, shrugged off these tales of horror and tragedy, acknowledging that they lived in an insane, violent world, but if you dwelled on it too long, hopelessness might overtake you. It was better to pause a moment in silent reflection for the victims, then move on.

Don lived in a garden apartment off of Milwaukee near Roscoe; the "garden" part was bullshit for "basement." Don had an old little mutt, Rambo, that ran around like a berserk puppy for a while when he came home, then would find a spot and sleep for the next ten hours.

Tommy found the building, or at least what he thought might be the building, and double-parked, yellow flashers going. It was a brick three-flat that looked like a million others in the city. Don didn't answer his doorbell. Tommy leaned on the buzzer. Nothing. He went down the street and around to the alley and counted buildings as he walked. The night that Tommy had been there, Don had shown him how he didn't bother with the key to the garage; all he had to do was lift the loose door and pull the dead bolt free.

Tommy let himself into the garage and slipped through the inky blackness. He opened the inner door, crossed the backyard in two paces, and went down the cement steps to knock on Don's door. By now, Tommy didn't expect an answer. He heard Rambo's yips and paws on the other side. He tried the door.

It opened. Rambo was there, happy, as usual, to see somebody, anybody.

"Don? Don? You in here?" Tommy called. He took hold of the door and knocked again, louder. Rambo jumped at his legs and he picked up the dog. "Don?"

Still nothing. Tommy stepped into the kitchen, shut the door behind him, and scratched Rambo's ears. The layout was a shotgun shack, a straight shot down the hallway, with rooms and bathrooms on either side. The kitchen sat at the back end, the living room in the front.

"Don?" Down the dark hall, light seeped out of the crack around the bathroom door. Tommy found the light switch for the hall and flicked it on. He turned Rambo loose, and the dog went trotting down into the shadows of the living room. He opened the bathroom door and found it empty. Don's bedroom was also empty.

Tommy's shadow stretched across Rambo as the dog turned in slow circles on the couch before settling into another nap. Don's ancient thirteen-inch television flickered in the corner, sending dancing patterns of colors across the scuffed wooden floor.

Tommy crossed the darkness of the living room and was just about to twist the switch on the lamp when he stepped on something and realized it was Don's hand.


There was no music tonight. Sam and Ed weren't in the mood. They cruised up and down the one-way streets through the Loop, windows down, Sam driving and glaring at the tourists. By now, most of the secretaries in their gym shoes and the computer programmers in their wrinkled button-up short-sleeve shirts and all the rest of the suits had either gone home or hit the bars. Traffic was sparse.

"Brother, we don't find her, I don't see how we're gonna wriggle off this time," Ed said.

"You don't think Arturo'll bat for us?"

Ed shook his head. "Not this time. We fucked up. Should've taken her to lockup."

"No," Sam said flatly. "And let those fucks track her down inside? If they took a chance sweating her inside the goddamn sheriff's office in City Hall, no telling what would happen in County."

"Well, we shouldn't have turned her loose."

"Shoulda, woulda, coulda. Story of my fucking life," Sam said, spitting his nicotine gum out of the window.

"You got any ideas on how to fix this, I'm open to suggestions."

"Find her. Take her in. Make Arturo give her protective witness status."

"Arturo ain't gonna get within ten miles of this. You know that." Ed looked out the passenger window. "Maybe she should turn a rat loose in his office. Might get his attention then."

# CHAPTER 30

**8:20 PM**
**August 12**

The paramedics, Scott and Vince, weren't in a big hurry. They pulled up behind the Streets and Sans truck and took their time getting their bags ready, before sauntering up the sidewalk and ringing the buzzer. 911 had told them that the patient wasn't conscious, but was breathing steadily. That meant that there was no point in rushing. Some Polack kid was waiting impatiently in the foyer. He practically dragged them into the crappy little basement apartment.

All the lights were on. The patient, Don, another fucking Polack, was lying between the coffee table and the couch. He looked like he was just sleeping off a bad drunk.

Vince snapped on some purple surgical gloves and checked Don's vital signs. Scott sighed heavily and cornered Tommy. "You guys live here together?"

"What? Uh, no. No." Tommy caught the paramedic's leer. "It's not like that. We work together."

"Okay, fine. Sure. Whatever. Your name?"

"Tommy Krazinsky."

Vince spoke up. "What kind of drugs were you guys taking tonight?"

"What?" Tommy asked. "Drugs? No, no. Don never did any drugs."

"Look, I'm trying to find out what's wrong with your friend. It might mean the difference between life and death here. Now, what was your friend on?"

"I don't know what to tell you. As far as I know, he never took anything stronger than beer and aspirin."

There was a knock, and a Chicago cop stood in the front doorway. The cop was white, pushing forty. His mustache was in better shape than his body. "Who called it in?"

"I did." Tommy stepped forward.

The cop pulled out his notebook. "Name?" he asked, clicking his pen like he was cocking his handgun. Tommy gave his name and a statement. Scott poked around Don's apartment, looking for drugs, but came up empty. He held his hands up to the cop.

The cop walked over and got a better look at Don. Writing in his notebook, the cop said aloud, "Possible heart attack. Older white male. Drug angle looks less likely."

Vince finally decided that he didn't know what the hell was wrong with the patient, so they went back to the ambulance and brought back a collapsible gurney.

The kid, Tommy, asked if he could ride with them to the hospital.

Scott and Vince looked to the cop.

The cop asked the paramedics, "Where you taking him?"

Scott said, "Northwestern is closest."

The cop nodded, said to Tommy, "He'll be at Northwestern. You can drive your own vehicle slowly and safely there, and ask for him in the emergency room." He headed to his car, tilting his head, speaking in a bored tone into the mike on his shoulder.

The paramedics loaded Don into the ambulance. Vince

slammed the door shut and got in on the passenger side. Scott hit the lights and sirens and headed for Milwaukee Avenue.

The supervisor's voice came out of the phone, abrupt and out of breath. "Tommy? That you?"

"Yeah," he said as he clenched the phone against his shoulder, trying to buckle the seat belt with one hand and steer with the other. He picked up speed, following the ambulance.

"You know that Lee is looking for you guys? Is Don with you?"

"No. He's in the ambulance. He's sick."

"Sick? Sick how?"

"I don't know. He's unconscious."

There was a pause while the supervisor talked with somebody else. He came back on. "You say he's in an ambulance?"

"Yeah. They're taking him to the hospital right now."

"Which ambulance is this? What's the company?"

"I can't tell. A red and green one." Tommy weaved around vehicles that had pulled over for the ambulance, and were just starting to pull back into their lane again.

"Is there a number or a name on the side?"

"I don't know. They're taking him to Northwestern. Call there."

"Is there a number or a name on the side?"

Tommy hit SPEAKERPHONE and threw the phone on the dash. "I. Don't. Know," he yelled while scooting through an intersection against the light, trying to keep up with the ambulance. Other drivers hit their horns. To them, he was just another asshole trying to steal the road in the ambulance's wake.

Tommy followed as it turned left onto Division and crossed over the North Branch of the Chicago River. His phone was quiet for a minute. He heard the supervisor's voice, talking to someone else. "You got it? Okay. Fine. Better this way. Absolutely." Tommy hit his horn at drivers impatient to pull back into traffic, ignoring their rearview mirrors and his flashing yellow lights.

Tommy's phone flashed CALL ENDED.

The ambulance's brakes flickered uncertainly, and turned south on LaSalle. It seemed to Tommy they went slower, even though this was a four-lane street. The ambulance was far more cautious when it came to crossing streets. Tommy found it was easy to catch up. When they passed Chicago Ave, Tommy was confused. The ambulance continued going south on LaSalle, leaving Northwestern farther and farther behind.

He relaxed when he realized they were taking Don to Cook County General. Maybe they'd radioed ahead. Maybe they'd been told that Cook County General had better equipment for Don, with a team of specialists, ready and waiting for Don. Hell, maybe Cook County General dealt with this kind of thing everyday.

Maybe it was all going to be okay.

Sam pulled over to the curb and waved a homeless guy over.

The guy, a man in his thirties with wild hair, waved off imaginary insects. "Wasn't doing nothin', officer."

"What makes you think I'm an officer? Might be I'm just a tourist, trying to find my hotel."

"Whatever you says, officer."

Sam unwrapped more gum. "You seen Qween around?"

"Queen?" The man cocked his head, listening to phantom radio transmissions. "Of England?"

"Don't fuck with us, pal," Ed said, surprising Sam. Ed was usually happy playing the good cop. "I don't have much patience tonight. Got half a mind to come out and beat the living shit out of you for resisting arrest."

"Tell you what," Sam said, thinking it might be his turn to play good cop. "I got ten bucks if your memory improves."

The homeless man cocked his head the other direction, as

if receiving conflicting transmissions. "Well, now. Maybe I know, maybe I don't. Let's see the money."

Sam pulled out his wallet, found a ten-dollar bill. "You know who I'm talking about, right?"

The man looked offended. "Shit. Ever'body knows Qween." He took the ten. "Ain't seen her in two days."

"Know where she stays?"

The man shook his head. "Used to have a spot on Lower Wacker. Up and took everything somewheres else. Don't know where."

"You know why?"

"Have to ask her."

"You're not exactly earning your money here," Sam said.

The man shrugged. "Whatchu want? I don't know."

Ed leaned over, fixed the man with his dead eyes. "What's the story with the rats?"

The man didn't blink, didn't flinch, didn't hesitate. "The rats? They sick, man. Ever'body knows that. You stay away from 'em. Ever'body knows that."

# CHAPTER 31

*8:56 PM*
*August 12*

Tommy lost sight of the ambulance when it zoomed into the emergency driveway on Wacker Drive, where only medical or rescue vehicles were allowed. He pulled around the block and parked in the underground garage. He couldn't find the stairs and had to take the elevator instead.

While waiting for the doors to open, doubts started creeping into his head. Cook County General wasn't exactly known for its cutting-edge medical research. Cook County General wasn't exactly known for its quality medical care if you wanted to get down to it. He wasn't sure why Cook County General would have a team of specialists in whatever disease was keeping Don asleep.

The doors slid open and he stepped inside. He tried to stand still under pale fluorescents that hurt his eyes as the elevator lurched up the four stories to the lobby, but all those stories about Cook County General being a sick joke in the city knocked down the walls of his optimism.

The place was chronically underfunded, for one thing. Nobody knew who was really in charge, only that the city ran the place, so if you had no money left, no money at all, this was where you ended up. Sometimes, on a slow day for tragedy, the news would get all worked up over people literally crawling into the emergency room because they had no insurance and the ambulance companies wouldn't pick them up. The streets were full of horror stories about the emergency room, of waiting all day for a shot that turned out to be prepared with a dirty needle, of being forgotten, of people dying on the benches and being there all night before somebody called their name, gut-churning tales of malpractice, of doctors stealing drugs to feed their own habits, of AIDS-infected blood, of MRSA contaminating every doorknob, every water fountain, every surface imaginable, of rusty scalpels and dirty floors.

The emergency room wasn't as crowded as Tommy expected. He stood fifth or sixth in the line at the front desk, and overheard the nurse telling people with obvious injuries to go seek treatment at either Northwestern or Rush instead. Of course, most people, especially those bleeding on the tile floors, didn't take the news well. "Are you fucking kidding? What the hell is this? You call yourself a hospital?"

"We're undergoing a change of management," was all the nurse would say.

When it was Tommy's turn, he said, "I'm here to see Don Wycza. They just brought him in an ambulance."

The nurse, a black woman with a face that exhaustion had cut to the skull, checked the charts. "No, I'm sorry. There's nobody here by that name."

"Maybe he hasn't been added yet. I followed the ambulance here."

The nurse rechecked the clipboards on her desk, then stood and searched a few more places around her station. No luck. "What's his name again?" the nurse asked. "It's possible they didn't bring in the paperwork yet. I'll see if I can't find him. In the meantime, you have a seat. I'll call you if I hear about your friend."

"Okay, thanks." Tommy gave a little wave of gratitude,

then sank into a chair in the middle of a long line of plastic seats bolted to a long steel bar. He checked his phone. No calls. No texts. He snapped the phone shut and tucked it into his coveralls.

The patients in the emergency room could be divided into three categories. The first, and most popular, group was five people who held bloody towels around some limb, usually either a hand or foot. Summertime, and a lot of drunk people decide to fucking cut loose with a power tool while tackling some exterior home improvement project.

Tommy noticed that patients had their own groups of friends. The guys in the first group, and it seemed to be all guys, all had wives or girlfriends and sometimes young children. Sometimes, if the guys were old enough, the adult children would bring a parent in who'd had too much barbecue and beer and decided to prune the hedge with a chainsaw.

The second group was a little harder to define on its own, but the look of the friends helped. These were people who'd ingested too much alcohol or crack or meth or coke or something else. They had been brought in by one or two peers who desperately looked around for the best opportunity to slip away.

Everybody in the first and second group was being shuttled off to different hospitals.

The third group was only two people; one man and one woman. It was difficult to pinpoint the cause of their distress. Both were nearly catatonic. The man had been brought in by a cab driver who couldn't wake him up, and had driven halfway across the city to leave him at the only hospital that would take him because he didn't have an insurance card in his wallet.

The woman's husband had brought her in. He kept trying not to cry and squeezing her hand. She sagged against the plastic chair and gazed unseeing at the ceiling. A dark stain appeared at her crotch. Urine ran out of the bottom of her jeans and collected on the speckled tile floor. Tommy looked away.

"Tommy, Tommy Krazinsky?" the nurse at the head station called out.

Tommy bounded up. "Yeah? You got him?"

The nurse spoke into the phone, "Yes, he's here. Do you wish to speak—" After a moment, she hung up the phone. "Ahh, I'm sorry. I was just given a message to make sure you were at this location. I don't know who was asking."

"Probably my boss? I left a message at work telling them Don was coming here. Have you heard anything about him?"

"Sorry, not yet. I'll let you know."

Tommy sat back down, confused. He wasn't sure who would be looking for him. He kind of doubted his boss would try that hard to look for Don. He dug around in his overalls, pulled out a handful of business cards. He found the right one, dialed the number.

Two rings. A click. A voice. "This is Detective Johnson."

Tommy said, "Uh, hi. This is Tommy Krazinksy. Me and my partner met you yesterday at City Hall, the Streets and Sans guys. Don's at the CCG, but it's . . . Something's going on. See, he's—" There was a high-pitched squeal and the phone went dead.

Tommy tried to call again, but his phone wasn't working right.

Lee appeared and dropped into a seat across the aisle. "What the fuck is going on?"

Tommy jumped. He hadn't seen Lee come in.

Tommy was angled so that he could keep an eye on the front door, and looked up every time he heard the automatic doors swish, thinking that maybe Don might have woken up and been turned loose. Instead, he watched as injured people came in, and were sent almost immediately to another hospital. He hadn't seen the ambulance drivers either. They must have been busy shuttling people over to Northwestern.

Lee looked nervous. He was perfectly groomed, as always, snug in a tailored suit; the tie was color coordinated with his eyes. But something in his movements was off. Lee couldn't make eye contact, and this was his strength. Lee could maintain an almost supernatural eye contact with people, making them feel at ease, or intimidating the hell out of them. It was his most formidable method of communication, and he was acting as if he could catch some sort of venereal disease if he looked at Tommy. "What the fuck happened to Don?" he finally asked.

Tommy spread his hands helplessly. "I don't know. I went by his place because he didn't show up for work. Found him unconsciousness on the floor. They brought him here."

"You and Don are the two Streets and Sans guys that killed a rat in City Hall yesterday."

Tommy nodded. "I guess so. Unless there was another rat."

"Your partner told that story over a dozen times last night."

Tommy nodded.

"He claimed otherwise, but honestly now, did that rat bite him?"

Tommy shook his head.

"It's important. Did that rat draw blood in any way? The doctors need to know this."

"No. I saw his hands afterward. No scratches."

"His leg? Any bite anywhere?"

Tommy shook his head.

Lee's eyes flicked to the raccoon scratches on Tommy's hands. "You killed it with a baseball bat?"

"It's down in the van. I didn't break any rules that I know of."

Lee finally looked him dead in the face, blinking furiously. "No. No, of course not. Do you want to see him?"

"Hell, yeah."

"Let's go then." Lee got up and Tommy followed.

Four soldiers entered the emergency waiting room and

carried the two catatonic patients into triage. Curtains were drawn.

Lee led the way into the emergency center, past three or four nurses gathered at the work station in the center of the room, cubicle rooms along the outer walls, doors nothing but shower curtains. He didn't turn his back to Tommy. Nobody looked at them. Lee wound his way through the nearly empty emergency room to a restricted elevator. He punched in a code, and they waited for the doors to open.

"What's wrong with him?" Tommy asked.

Lee was quiet for a moment. "They're not sure. I was hoping you could shed some light on the situation." They stepped into the elevator. Lee hit the fifth-floor button.

"Well, is he going to be okay?"

"They're not sure. Nobody knows anything right now. Do you mind answering a few more questions from the doctors?"

"I'll do whatever I can to help Don."

"Good. That's what I like to hear in an employee. Loyalty and enthusiasm."

The doors opened on the fifth floor. The hallway was completely empty, and utterly enclosed in sheets of plastic, sealed shut with black Gorilla Tape. The ceiling and the floor were also covered. Each of the patients' rooms had its own plastic tunnel through the doorway. The sheeting was thick and opaque, and filtered the light into a shifting, flickering haze. Air drafts caught the plastic, giving the whole hallway a shimmering, fluid light, almost as if it were underwater.

"Don't worry about this," Lee said, tapping on the plastic with his shoe. "This is something else, entirely. Got nothing to do with you. They're painting or fumigating or some damn thing." Lee pointed at the first room off to the right. "You can wait in there. Doctors'll be along shortly."

Tommy stepped through the doorway and didn't see the men on either side of the door until it was too late. They took him down just inside the room, each grabbing an elbow, a shoulder, then sweeping his feet off the ground and slamming him to the floor. The breath exploded out of him and blackness swam in his eyes.

Something hot jabbed into his left butt cheek.

A moment later, wet concrete flowed through his veins, deadening any feeling; first his legs, then his back, his arms, and in three seconds he couldn't hold his head up. The darkness overwhelmed his eyes and he drifted into oblivion.

# CHAPTER 32

Sam parked in front of a fire hydrant and left the flashers going. They got out, looked up at the hospital. Lot of bad memories in this place. Too many late nights, waiting for a gunshot victim to make it through surgery and survive long enough to give a statement or for a suspect to sleep off a bad trip so they could haul them to the station. Too many late nights interviewing weeping family members. Too many late nights full of bad coffee and surreptitious visits down to the car park for a quick gulp at the flask. This place was a goddamn black hole, sucking them in if they got too close. Sam popped another stick of nicotine gum, threw the wrapper in the gutter, and followed Ed inside.

He'd never seen the emergency room so empty. It wasn't just lacking patients; the staff, the nurses, the doctors—all of them, except for a young white guy sitting behind the intake station—were gone. There were a few patients scattered around the room, either asleep or staring at the floor.

They got a better look at the young man in the intake station. He wore nurses' scrubs, but Sam decided that he'd eat his own shoe if this guy was a nurse. Clean shaven, closely cropped hair. Cold look in his eyes. No, this guy was military, Sam was positive.

"Evening," Ed said. He'd taken to simply leaving the star hanging outside his chest pocket. Made things easier. Sam had told him that Ed secretly just wanted to pretend he was a sheriff in the Old West.

"What can I do for you, officer?" the guy said.

"Looking for a witness. Heard the ambulance brought him in. Name's Don Wycza."

"Okay. Let me see what I can find," the guy said, tapping the keyboard.

"Kinda quiet tonight, huh?" Sam said, both detectives playing good cop.

"So they say," the guy said in an offhand way. "I wouldn't know. Just started."

Sam caught Ed's eye. Something wasn't right about this setup. Ed let a smile flicker at the edges of his mouth. He agreed. The kid hadn't asked how to spell the witness's name.

Sam wandered away from the desk while the guy put on a show of clicking the mouse around and hammering at the keyboard. Sam let his eyes flicker around the room and took note of the eyeballs in the ceiling, little half spheres of black glass. He wondered who was watching the empty emergency room.

He pulled out his phone and dialed Tommy. There was no ring, just an odd squeal. He held his phone up so Ed could listen. "You ever heard this before?"

Ed shook his massive gray head slowly. "It's not a bad signal." He didn't know much about cell phones, except that he had a cheap knockoff, and he had a lot of experience with lost calls. "Sounds like . . . interference."

"That's what I was thinking."

Sam headed back to the front desk. The need for two good cops was over; it was time to see if a bad cop could accomplish anything. "You track our witness down yet?" he asked the guy behind the desk.

The guy furrowed his brow and feigned confusion. "Not yet. Are you sure you've got the right hospital? We're sending a lot of patients over to Northwestern tonight."

"And why is that?"

The guy pretending to be a nurse frowned. "What's the nature of your business with Mr. Wycza, again?"

Sam fixed him with a dark stare. "What's your fucking name, asshole?"

The guy stared right back. The frown was gone, replaced with an echo of Ed's grin. Smooth and collected. Sam scared him about as much as the Tooth Fairy. "Why don't I get my supervisor on the phone. See if he can't help you more than I can."

"Wouldn't take much," Sam said, knowing intimidation wasn't going to work.

Ed popped Sam's shoulder with the back of his hand. "The fuck's he doing here?" he said, pointing with his chin at the elevators beyond the front desk, back in triage.

Lee Shea stepped through the elevator doors and headed for the back exit.

"Downright curious," Sam said. He and Ed stepped around the desk and followed Lee.

The guy behind the desk said loudly, "Gentlemen! You can't go back there."

Sam and Ed ignored him.

"I'm calling my supervisor," the guy threatened.

Sam called over his shoulder, "Please do. I'd like to have a word."

Ed and Sam moved briskly and caught up to Lee; they flanked him, matching him stride for stride. Ed said, "Evening. Well, well. Mr. Cornelieus Shea." A grin split his wide face.

Lee had had too much practice as a politician, with news cameras catching him at all hours of the day, to be caught looking guilty. A sincere, good-natured smile appeared, as easily as slipping on a pair of old socks. He stopped. "Hi, there. Can I help you?"

Sam bit his tongue, letting Ed do the talking.

Ed chuckled. "Us? No, no. Of course not. Just wanted to say hi. Seeing you here. How about that rat at City Hall yesterday, huh?".

Lee let puzzlement flash across his features. "I'm sorry, Mister . . . ?"

"Detective Jones."

Lee stuck out his hand and shook Ed's enthusiastically, then was on the move again. "I'm afraid we've never met. Always good to meet a member of Chicago's law enforcement."

Ed's smile never left his face. Sam thought Ed could give Lee a run for his money in maintaining a friendly appearance. Ed released Lee's hand but didn't relent. "Yeah, that business at City Hall. Pretty crazy, huh?"

"City Hall's a pretty crazy place sometimes."

"Truth, my man, truth. But yeah, that rat that got loose. Bet that's never happened before."

"I wouldn't know too much about that."

"Well, what would you know?" Ed asked. Ed and Sam lengthened their strides and got ahead of him just for a brief second, then slowed down, pinning Lee between them.

Disbelief flickered across Lee's face for just a split second, echoing his thoughts, but he got control and smiled again. "Like I said, I don't know much. I got a call, saying a rodent was loose in the building. I deferred it to my supervisors and I have full confidence that they handled the situation as needed. Now, if you gentlemen don't mind"—he checked his watch—"I'm afraid I'm late for a meeting."

Ed and Sam blocked the door. Ed scraped his thumbnail through the stubble on his chin and said, "One quick question. See, we got a call earlier, saying that one of the guys, one of your employees, one of your employees who dealt with that rat yesterday, well, we got a call saying that he's been admitted to this hospital this evening. Problem is, we can't seem to find him."

Lee said, "I'm sorry, I don't know how I can help you. I don't know anything about it." He nodded back toward the nurses' station. "You really should ask the hospital."

Sam gave a smile of his own. It was more like the expression on a corpse of a primitive man who had been caught in an iceberg for a few thousand years. "Can I ask, what exactly is your business here tonight?"

Lee blinked. "I don't see how that is any of your concern."

"We're detectives." Behind them, Sam heard the elevator doors open. "Everything related to our case is our concern, Mr. Shea." Sam still didn't want to turn around, still wanted to keep Lee pinned. He heard at least three, four men behind him.

Ed's right hand fell. It was now a full half second closer to his revolver.

Lee noticed this; his expression went blank, unreadable.

"Gentlemen," a harsh, brittle voice called out behind them. "Federal law maintains than anyone within a restricted area will surrender identification immediately."

"You haven't answered my question," Ed said to Lee and didn't move.

Lee shrugged. "I'm sorry. I'm afraid I don't even know which employee responded to that call. Now, if you will excuse me, I am sure these gentlemen would like a word with you. Maybe, if you play nice, they'll extend their professional courtesy and assist you with your case. Good night." He gave a slight bow and turned away.

Sam glanced over his shoulder and saw four soldiers waiting.

Qween heard the cruiser well before the spotlight danced across her part of the shore. She had plenty of time to simply slide a little lower, hidden in a little alcove formed by a tumble of concrete slabs that had been tossed along the edge of Lake Michigan to stop the waves from tearing out any parts of the park along Lake Shore Drive.

She listened to the cops drive past, along the bike path, and enjoyed her own private view of Lake Michigan at night. The moon was behind her, off to the right, so she could see stars, something she couldn't see from any of her hideouts downtown. Once in a while a feeling took hold, and she got to missing taking a long look at the night sky, so when she found a bottle, she would stash the cart, and spend the night two miles north, hiding out by the golf course.

The wind had died, and the air was growing hotter and stickier. She stretched out on the slab and listened to the water as it leisurely lapped at all the concrete and broken glass, hoping for a hint of wind. She closed her eyes for a moment.

A sound grew out across the lake, a droning storm of violence. Qween wanted to ignore it, wanted to pretend that it was part of her dreams. Eventually, though, she sat up and squinted at the horizon.

The turmoil took shape. Six or seven helicopters raced across the water, dropping in from the northeast. She counted at least three big fat ones, and four or five thin surrounding choppers. They roared overhead, low enough that she could see the outlines of guns or missiles or whatever the hell they were, and screamed across the golf course, passing over a nearly empty Lake Shore Drive, and climbed over the apartment buildings.

Fourteen seconds later, the helicopters crossed the Chicago River.

Qween settled back in and stared for a while at the seemingly endless stretch of water. She finished her bottle and struggled to her feet. She replaced the cap and stowed the empty bottle safely under her poncho. A lot of people would have been tempted to just toss the bottle in the lake, and while she had to admit the idea held a certain appeal, she knew better. She might be homeless, but that was no excuse to disrespect the environment.

She crawled over the concrete slabs until she reached the grass of the golf course. She paused a moment, catching her breath. The lights of downtown looked the same as always, but she knew better. Something in her city was cracking; some sort of cancer was seething under the surface, something that threatened her home.

She rolled the kinks out of her shoulders, scratched an itch under the Viking helmet, and headed south, moving parallel to the bike path, following the helicopters.

# CHAPTER 33

**11:56 PM**
**August 12**

Deep in the tunnel, Lee leaned against the hood of his Mercedes and hit the button to make his watch glow. Fuck. Kimmy was going to give him hell later, guaranfuckingteed. He was supposed to take her out to some restaurant with an unintelligible name that all the papers had been raving about. Didn't look like that was going to happen anytime soon this evening. And he couldn't call her, because there was no reception in the tunnel.

She was such exquisite eye candy that he'd taken to pulling her in close when the cameras were around, even the stupid kid, but he still didn't know if he was going to keep her around for the long term or not. She had a body that wouldn't quit, and had even started wearing the handcuffs that he liked in bed, but goddamn, she could be one hell of a cunt sometimes.

As soon as he left the hospital, he'd called his uncle. Phil audibly winced when Lee told him the detective's names.

"Look, those guys are fuckers," Phil had said. "Two pissed-off drunks. They've been with the department enough years that they've got some clout. You go up against them, it's expensive. You'll win, sure. But it costs. You want my opinion? It's not worth it. These guys, they've been known to hold grudges for years. I'm telling you, treat 'em like a hooker with herpes. Steer well clear."

"Understood."

"So. No loose ends then? Nothing that can connect you with this trouble?"

"Hell, no."

"Are you positive? Think carefully before you answer."

"I don't see how."

"So there are loose ends."

"No. Dammit, no."

"You sure?"

"Shit." Lee rubbed his face. "Fine. I'll take care of it."

"You better." Phil hung up.

Lee called a guy he knew out in Elgin, named Robert Earl Bailey, a guy with certain skills. Robert Earl didn't have much of a chin, just a gentle bump from his mouth on down to his Adam's apple. His eyes didn't play well together, they kept threatening to find separate things interesting. Despite looking like he was a step away from assisted living, he'd worked at a Wal-Mart, a Best Buy, a fireworks factory, a gun store, a gun range, and a law enforcement and surveillance supply warehouse. He was a licensed transporter of dangerous materials, and had driven for Lee several times before.

He also knew more about the cleansing effects of fire than anyone else Lee knew. Lee had used these skills to collect insurance on a house he had been renting out in the suburbs. Robert Earl, who preferred people use his full first and middle names, had started replacing the floor and left a mixture of solvents and oily rags in the corner overnight and left the concoction to ferment and do all the work. The house had been empty, and no one had noticed until it was too late. The fire had gutted the house before the fire department had even been called.

However, these heavy rock walls were going to require

a bit more than tamping the lid down on a paint can and walking away.

The bodyguard had left the headlights on, illuminating Robert Earl Bailey. He was about twenty yards down the tunnel, assembling all his shit where the tunnel opened up into the vast space filled with garbage and hazardous waste. He had been kneeling in the same spot for damn near half an hour, preparing the explosives. Robert Earl might be an expert in all kinds of useful shit, but he was fucking slow.

Back at his house earlier, Robert Earl had brought his supplies out to the car from his basement, and the bodyguard had balked at putting all that shit in the trunk.

"What happens, we hit a pothole?" the bodyguard, Bryan, had demanded. Bryan didn't like Robert Earl, probably because the bodyguard was black, and Robert Earl had a giant Confederate flag hanging in his living room.

Robert Earl had snorted. "It's harmless. Watch." He'd dropped the heavy duffel bag on his driveway. Lee and Bryan had flinched. Robert Earl had giggled like a toddler who had just inhaled half a gallon of birthday ice cream. "See? Harmless. Until you send an electric current through it. Then it goes bang."

Now, an hour later, down in the tunnel, Bryan kept pacing, saying, "We shouldn't be here tonight. It's not smart, you being this close."

Lee waved that away. "Sometimes, you gotta make sure something is done right. That means being hands-on."

Bryan exhaled in a hiss. "Boss, I've been with you on some crazy shit, and most of it turned out okay. Some things, though, you and I both know, they sometimes turned out not to be good ideas. Hindsight being twenty-twenty and all that, and I gotta say, this does not look like a good idea. Just walk away. Nothing down here tied to us."

"They start poking around down here it won't take a

fucking genius to start looking around at waste disposal companies. And believe me, they'd start at the top. With me. This way"—meaning sealing off the tunnel—"they got nothing."

"You telling me you can blow up a tunnel this size under the city of Chicago and nobody's gonna notice?"

"We're not gonna blow it up. Robert Earl's just gonna make the roof cave in. Just seal it off. He says all they'll see is a blip, if they notice it at all. Just a burp."

Robert Earl came jogging back to the car, fiddling with the remote detonator. He put it on the hood between them and said, "Don't touch this," giving Bryan a meaningful look. He retrieved a box of drill bits and scuffled back where he had laid out the assembled explosives.

He hit the trigger on the DeWalt twice, tightening the drill's grip on the bit. The high whine filled the tunnel and echoed back into the darkness beyond the reach of the headlights. He rolled a pair of orange foam ear plugs between his thumb and forefinger and screwed them into his ears.

Lee and Bryan glanced at each other, then stuck their fingers in their ears.

Robert Earl braced himself against the wall and wedged the bit into a seam he'd chipped out earlier. He flexed his grip on the DeWalt, squeezed the trigger, and leaned into it, putting some weight behind the spinning bit.

This time, the drill's engine was engulfed in the sound of the grinding howl of the bit chewing into the rock wall.

Shards of something reflective flickered in the darkness beyond Robert Earl. Lee pushed off the car and took several steps forward. He turned back to Bryan and yelled over the sound of the drill, "Did you see that?"

Bryan squinted, put his hand over his eyes. "What?"

"I don't know. . . ." Lee moved back and stood in front of the right headlight. His voice trailed off. Then, in the darkness of his shadow, he saw them. Hundreds of red eyes, glinting at Robert Earl. He pointed.

"Holy fuck." Bryan jumped off the hood and went for his

gun. "Hey!" he yelled at Robert Earl, but the sound was swallowed by the sound of disintegrating rock. Bryan squeezed off two shots at the rats.

Robert Earl released the trigger, peering through the cloud of dust at the drill. He'd heard something, but couldn't tell if it had come from the drill or something else.

Bryan walked past him and fired three more times.

That got Robert Earl's attention. His head flicked around, but his hips and feet didn't move, anchored into the wall with the drill.

Back at the car, Lee snatched the remote detonator off the hood.

Bryan emptied the clip. He dropped it, slipping it into his jacket pocket, loading a fresh one in less than two seconds. He squeezed another burst into the darkness.

"Let's go," Lee shouted.

Bryan either ignored Lee or couldn't hear him and fired once more. He paused for a moment, ultimately realizing his bullets were futile. There was a moment of stillness. Bryan flinched at something. He hopped backwards, twisting in midair, and started running full out for the car.

Robert Earl watched him run past, hands still on the drill.

The rats swarmed out of the gloom and launched themselves at Robert Earl, slashing with inch-long teeth and ragged claws. The combined weight of the attack knocked him off his feet. His screams echoed through the tunnel. He managed to struggle to his feet once, standing against the onslaught. He ripped a rat away from his face. Most of his nose was still between a rat's front teeth. Other rats dangled from his arm. He stumbled forward a couple of steps, swayed. Rats writhed around his legs. One of them chewed through his Achilles tendon. He took one more step and the ankle gave way.

He fell into the swarm and disappeared.

Thousands of rats exploded out of the cloud of dust, a tsunami of rats shooting up the tunnel.

Lee saw very quickly that most of the rats were still chasing Bryan. He jumped behind the wheel and slammed the door. Bryan was halfway to the car.

More rats poured from the shadows, a goddamn tidal wave.

Lee said, "Fucking Christ," and started the car. He jerked it into reverse and hit the gas.

Bryan faltered, and risked a look behind him. "Oh fuck, oh fuck!" he yelled and ran even faster.

Lee guided the car by keeping an eye on the side mirrors. He flicked the detonator's protective cap open. When he judged the distance from the explosion to be at least fifty yards, he hit the brakes. The rats kept coming. Lee armed the detonator. Bryan ran and yelled, "Wait, wait, wait!"

Lee waited until Bryan was nearly to the car and clicked the button. Thunder erupted in the dust. The blast cracked the windshield and knocked the bodyguard on his face. Billowing clouds obscured the view and Lee couldn't tell what had happened to the structure of the tunnel. Pieces of rats splattered across the hood.

Bryan got up and held his head, making an irritated noise in his throat. He coughed and spit a wad of bloody phlegm at the ground. He pulled open the back door and fell into the backseat. The front half of a rat was stuck to his chest. He grabbed hold of one ear and peeled it off. Shredded internal organs came loose and plopped into his lap. He flung it out into the tunnel and slammed the door.

Lee watched the swirling nightmare of dust and smoke through the windshield for a moment, turned around to face the back window, and hit the gas. The Mercedes scraped the side of the tunnel once or twice, but Lee didn't slow down.

# PHASE 4

PHASE 4

# CHAPTER 34

**7:49 AM**
**August 13**

Ed's phone chirped, and he jerked awake. For a moment, he couldn't figure out where he was. All he knew was that his back hurt. He blinked sleep from his eyes, and found himself in the front seat of their Crown Vic. A black metal fence loomed in front of the hood.

Sam was behind the wheel, slumped against the driver's door, sunken eyes forever staring blearily at the world in that perpetual early-morning haze. "Morning."

Ed rubbed his burning eyes and twisted around. They were parked in the small lot of a 7-Eleven. His hangover was awful. He tried to remember the night and had the oddest feeling he'd just stepped sideways at the right moment, dodging some speeding eighteen-wheeler.

Ed took a deep breath, let it out slowly. Bits and pieces were coming back to him, especially the icy cloud of dread that settled around his chest, as if a corpse's hand had fallen on the back of his neck and squeezed.

He hadn't felt anything like it in a long time.

1968. He'd been sixteen, edging in close to the back of the crowd amassed at the corner of Balbo and Michigan, anxious to see the unrest, curious to see the anger at the government for himself. The closest he'd gotten was State Street, and when the cops arrived on Michigan and uncertainty seeped through the crowd, he'd bolted. The politics of the time weren't that important to him; the protests took a backseat to trying to get laid.

Later, having no luck with the ladies, he'd taken another hike up into the South Loop.

The streets were so empty it felt like a dream. He could smell the bitterness of something, maybe tear gas, in the air. He and his buddies heard the diesel roar of a bus, and hid behind cars along the curb, laying down in the gutters as it passed. The bus ran without lights, not even headlights. The streetlights gleamed dully off the scratched windows; the inside of the bus was darker than the sewers. It rolled through a red light, and in the wash of the stoplight, Ed could see the silhouettes of twenty or thirty riot cops.

Ed felt his insides clench, and for the first time in his life he'd faced the very real possibility of getting stomped and beaten to death by a squad of licensed white men. The bus kept rolling down Wabash and turned left, toward the lake. As soon as it was out of sight, Ed and the rest of his boys had sprinted west down Roosevelt.

The soldiers last night had given Ed the same feeling.

Last night scared him.

The soldiers last night hadn't done anything threatening, exactly. But they hadn't exactly been your typical weekend warriors either. They'd been older, for one thing. They wore a hell of a lot of extra gear for guys who supposedly did this soldiering thing once a month. They seemed awfully prepared for a bunch of gas-station attendants and insurance salesmen.

And why the hell were they at the hospital?

Ed dug his phone out of his sport coat. Checked the number. Carolina. He exhaled slow, knowing this wasn't going to be good. "Hey, baby."

* * *

Tommy clawed his way into the light. He tried to grab a breath, but something was in the way. He coughed and gagged. Something was blocking his airways; something had been shoved up his nose and down his throat. He went to grab for whatever it was, to rip it away, but he couldn't move his hands. It felt like he was drowning. Agony ricocheted through his body, and his lungs screamed silently for air.

"Calm down and open your mouth," a voice commanded.

Tommy's mouth opened and snapped shut, gasping for air. Whatever was in his nose slid away, leaving a burning path down the back of his throat. Air, sweet air, rushed in, filling his lungs and his blood bubbled with oxygen.

His panic slowly subsided, and the overwhelming light in his eyes swam into focus as a row of buzzing fluorescent bulbs. He blinked, and he jerked his head around, trying to see more, trying to figure out where he was, trying to figure out what had happened. He remembered little beyond riding the elevator with Lee . . . and beyond that, nothing, just a dream of being underwater.

He saw that he was in some kind of hospital room, but he couldn't move from his position, lying flat on his back on some sort of unyielding bed. He felt straps binding him tightly across his chest, his waist, and his knees. His wrists were also secured. He whipped his head to the side. Some kind of thick plastic covered the walls and maybe the floor, but he couldn't see from his bed.

"I told you to calm down," the voice said again.

Tommy whipped his head to the other side.

A gaunt face, covered in a blue surgical mask and small round glasses, loomed over him. "My name is Dr. Reischtal."

A visibly nervous nurse stood next to him, looking as though she wanted to bolt for the door. She wore a surgical mask as well and rubber gloves over her uniform. Tommy couldn't tell if she was more afraid of him or the doctor.

Dr. Reischtal unhooked one half of his surgical mask and let it hang from one ear. He said, "We have removed your feeding tube and oxygen. You are perfectly fine and able to speak. So just relax."

Dr. Reischtal's tone was anything but relaxing. Still, Tommy tried. He forced himself to slow his breathing, to stop fighting the straps. It took a while.

Dr. Reischtal was impatient. "Do you need a sedative?"

"No. No thanks. Untie me, and I might feel better."

Dr. Reischtal actually smiled, as if he'd just found small joy in watching an enemy stumble and fall and impale himself on a wrought iron fence. "I have a few small, but important, questions for you, Mr. Krazinsky."

"Okay. Sure."

"To begin with, Mr. Krazinsky, you need to understand that you are the possible vector for an infectious disease the likes of which humankind has never seen."

"Don't you 'hey, baby' me," Carolina's voice was loud enough for Sam to hear, loud and clear. "All night, and not a word? I thought we were past all this bullshit."

Sam gave Ed a nod and stiffly climbed out into the early morning light, giving his partner some space. The sun was hitting the tops of the buildings, lightening the shadows, bringing out the details of the gray and vacant streets. He wondered if his sport coat and shirt smelled and couldn't remember when he'd last changed his clothes.

Inside the 7-Eleven, Sam nodded at the clerk as he went into the restroom. He locked the door behind him and pulled off his vest. Using the underside of his fist to hit the hot water handle, he held a few towels under the ten-second dribble. He wiped off his face and the back of his neck and tried not look at himself in the mirror.

He thought about the soldiers from last night to distract himself.

Goddamn. Once he'd seen the guns, he'd known damn well they weren't National Guard. Shit, they weren't even regular Army. Or Marines, for that matter. They wore National Guard uniforms, but several key items were missing. All rank insignia had been stripped. And no name tags. Instead, they had a series of numbers on their backs, up high, on top of their shoulders, so someone could keep track of them from a helicopter. Or a satellite.

It looked like the uniforms were supposed to simply maintain the illusion of U.S. soldiers, at least from a distance.

The National Guard didn't carry weapons like this. Sam read all the gun magazines that were left around the police station. Some of the assault rifles the soldiers carried he'd recognized. Others had been modified beyond measure and he could only guess at the caliber, let alone the makes and models of the guns themselves.

These guys were well-financed, well-organized, and professional to the bone. Whoever was now in charge of the hospital had some serious muscle behind them.

And when the closest soldier had said, "Sir, my superiors would like to apologize for their behavior last night," the hairs on the back of Sam's neck prickled. Something was seriously wrong. "If you would follow me, I can escort you to my boss, who would like to apologize in person." The soldier stepped aside, clearing a path to the restricted elevator.

Before he realized what he was doing, Sam had a hand on Ed's arm, stopping his partner. He said, "Uh, you know what, guys? It's getting awfully late." He made up some bullshit about checking in with the watch commander and how this wasn't their only case. The whole time, Sam had the gut-churning feeling that if they got into the elevator, it was inevitable that these soldiers would take them to a basement somewhere under the emergency room and shoot them in the head. Whoever was in charge of the hospital could explain the deaths any way they wanted.

Ed had immediately sensed his partner's hesitation and didn't try to argue. They strolled out the front door and climbed into their Crown Vic, feeling the soldiers' eyes on their backs the entire time. They ended up just a few blocks north, at Monk's, and at midnight, when the bar closed, they found a 7-Eleven and spent the night drinking vodka and orange juice, trying to figure out their next move.

Sam took a leak and washed his hands and face again. He pulled out his phone and dialed the nursing home in Skokie. Despite the time, almost five o'clock, and her age, almost ninety-two, he knew she wouldn't be sleeping. She'd be sitting up in bed, watching the Weather Channel. Her cell phone would be on the nightstand alongside the remote control for her adjustable hospital bed. Sometimes, she wouldn't have the strength or coordination to open the phone, so she would gently tap the edge of the phone on the corner of her night table, like she was cracking an egg where she wanted the fluid shell of the yolk preserved.

"Hello?"

"How are you feeling, Mom?"

"Oh, you know, I've been better. Still, I can't complain. And you? How's life with the Chicago Police Department?" She would then go on complaining for a full five minutes, sometimes making jokes about how much it hurt getting off her ass and getting to the bathroom. At least she had stopped asking when he would get married again.

At some point, Sam would invariably say, "I'm doing well, Mom."

This morning, his call was interrupted by a call from Ed.

Ed said, "Turn on your radio."

Chicago detectives, like all Chicago police officers, were required to carry department-issued radios at all times. Most detectives clipped them into their bulletproof vests, another pain-in-the-ass direct order, but left the radios off. They knew the boss would use the phone. Almost all the time.

"Listen, sorry, Mom, I just got a call from headquarters. I have to hang up now. I will call you later, okay?"

"Well, if you have to leave your mom worried sick and everything just because of work, I understand," she said, both of them knowing damn well she didn't.

"I'm glad, Mom. Bye," Sam said, switching on his radio.

"—and therefore, district commanders will be in contact with their individual teams. All department personnel are required to report for duty, regardless of rank. This message will repeat every five minutes." A click. "All department personnel are on high alert for persons exhibiting unusual behavior."

*What the fuck constitutes unusual behavior?* Sam wondered.

"Specifically, be on the lookout for signs of an addict undergoing severe withdrawal symptoms. Pale skin. Uncontrollable shivering. Sweating. Bloodshot eyes."

Sam unwrapped a stick of nicotine gum. Were they fucking serious? By now, he was at the car.

"You hearing this *Dragnet* shit?" Ed asked, holding up his radio.

The radio continued. "First responders are required to wear appropriate protection when in contact with anyone displaying these symptoms. Members of law enforcement are directed to transport any individuals exhibiting these symptoms to Cook County General Hospital, where a team of emergency personnel has been established to counter the situation."

Sam and Ed looked at each other.

Ed's cell phone rang again. "Fuck. It's Arturo."

"Might as well answer it. Get it over with."

# CHAPTER 35

*7:56 AM*
*August 13*

"Have you heard of the rabies virus?" Dr. Reischtal asked.

"Of course," Tommy said.

"This new virus . . ." Dr. Reischtal trailed off, looking beyond Tommy. "It's not exactly rabies though, is it?" It was clear Dr. Reischtal was asking a rhetorical question. "Similarities, oh, certainly. But something else, indeed." He gathered his thoughts and pinned Tommy again with his gaze. "We believe you are hiding the virus."

"I'm sorry, what?"

"That is, I believe the virus is hiding from you."

"What?"

"You and your partner deliberately placed yourselves in a hot zone when you engaged in skin-on-skin contact with an infected rodent. You ruptured this animal's body with . . . an aluminum baseball bat, I believe, releasing possible airborne toxins. Blood-borne pathogens as well, with the remains left on the wall. You—knowingly or unknowingly, it makes no difference—infected an entire building, no less than the government building of City Hall of Chicago and Cook County,

Illinois. Whether or not you meant well or were being a bad boy makes no difference."

He gave that rictus grin again. "And this is why I retreated. I could not risk having my team exposed to a new disease. We were not properly prepared. Now, we are."

"That's good, right?"

"Precisely. This is why it is important that you answer the following questions. It is my job to track this . . . virus. It is my sworn duty. My sacred duty."

Tommy watched Dr. Reischtal warily.

"This city"—Dr. Reischtal sat on a wheeled lab stool and rolled closer—"this city is facing an invasion, do you understand this? The danger is there, waiting . . . waiting for us, to relent, to slip, to ignore it and turn our backs. If we fail to recognize the true signs, the pure signals, we are doomed. Organisms that exist, thousands of them, millions, within the dregs of your glass of water. A billion in the crumb of your donut. That breath you take between the kitchen counter and your refrigerator. The blood between you and a . . . partner." He fixed Tommy with his tiny glasses. "Was your partner bit?"

"Bit? By what?"

"Do not play games with me, Mr. Krazinsky. We are out of time and it is imperative that we trace the path of infection. Do you understand?"

"I guess so, sure."

"Was your partner bit?"

"No."

"Were you bit?"

Tommy forced himself not to look down at the scratches on his hands. "No."

"I am not a fool, Mr. Krazinsky. You cannot deny the evidence."

"Okay, fine. I was bit. Not by that rat."

"Where then?"

Tommy didn't answer. He didn't want to mention the house party. He didn't want to get anyone in trouble.

"Where did you and your partner go after leaving City Hall?"

"Nowhere. I mean, we did our job. Drove around, checked traps."

"I see." Dr. Reischtal pulled off his glasses and leaned in close. His eyes, without the glasses, appeared startlingly large and unblinking. "I will ask only one more time. Before you answer, consider this room carefully. It may be where you draw your final breath."

He replaced his glasses, pulling the curved wires over his ears. "Your partner is infected with a virus that, until now, was unknown. We have since determined this virus possesses the capability to devastate our species. I implore you to consider the implications. Now, for the last time, where did you go last night?"

Tommy was a guy who spent his life following the rules. Listening to authority. Deep down, he truly believed that fate worked out in the end, that life really would reward his patience and understanding, his genuine kind-hearted virtues, and that nice guys didn't necessarily finish last. He wasn't naive enough to believe they might actually come out on top all the time, but he thought once in a while, God might recognize someone who lived an honorable life.

Despite this, one did not grow up in Bridgeport, in the shadow of downtown Chicago, and not learn the hard way about a few of life's truths. Those in authority did not always have your best interests at heart. And some people simply cannot be trusted.

Tommy didn't trust Dr. Reischtal.

He shrugged. "Like I said, we did our jobs."

"You, sir, are a liar." Dr. Reischtal ground his teeth together. "Did you seriously think that we would not watch you? We know you went to a club with a clientele composed exclusively of city employees. Then you attended a private event in the southern suburbs. I want to know exactly what happened last night. I want to know who came into close contact with both you and your partner. I want names and I want them now."

"You know so much, you tell me." Tommy hoped that sounded a lot more badass than he felt.

Dr. Reischtal shook his head. "Very well. As I have stated, I believe you are hiding the virus. Perhaps there is more than one patient zero. Perhaps this virus is working with an unexpected dispersal rate." He got up. Knocked on the door. "Unfortunately, the only way I can be sure is to obtain a sample of brain tissue. Fortunately, modern science renders this procedure non-life-threatening. This is good news for you, yes?"

"Brain tissue?"

"Only a little bit," Dr. Reischtal came back and leaned on the table next to the bed. "Relax. Only a tiny sample is required. We can obtain this without anesthetic, if you prefer. Only a needle is necessary."

The door opened and three men walked in. One carried a tray, setting it up next to the table. The others interlocked their fingers over Tommy's face, locking their elbows, and held his head perfectly still.

Dr. Reischtal pulled the blue cloth off the sterilized surgical tray, revealing a syringe the size of a robust cigar and a tiny drill. "Of course, we need to get through your skull first." The needle on the syringe could suck up homemade spaghetti sauce. The drill made a whine like a dentist's tool. He said, "See? Only a small hole. I find that if possible, it is far more useful to keep a subject alive, so we can talk. Perhaps after, you will be more inclined to tell me the truth."

Sam could hear Arturo's voice just as clear as Carolina's. "Are you fucking serious? What is fucking wrong with you?"

Ed didn't bother to answer. Arturo kept shouting. After a minute, Ed put the phone on the seat and started the car. He pulled into the early-morning traffic and they listened to Arturo the entire way home. He finally handed the phone over to Sam as he unlocked the front door to his building.

Sam said, "Listen, Commander, I know it looks bad—"

"Is this fucking Johnson? Is fucking Johnson trying to speak to me? I was in the middle of a conversation with Detective Jones. What the fuck are you doing on the phone?"

"We got some serious problems, Comm—"

"You're goddamn right we got some serious fucking problems, Detective. How fucking astute."

"When I say we, Commander . . . ah fuck. You know what I mean. This city. Us."

"This city, Detective, has withstood almost a hundred and eighty years of everything God wants to hurl at it. How dare you align yourself with this city. And I know you wouldn't be stupid enough to try and involve your fellow brothers and sisters on the force."

Sam hadn't slept in thirty hours and he was stumbling through a fuzzy patch. He needed a moment. He needed a shower. He needed to sit quietly for about three hours and get up and make a pot of coffee. "Okay. Fine, absolutely," and hit the END CALL button. He realized he was still standing on the sidewalk, long after Ed had gone inside. He tucked Ed's phone into the inside pocket of his sport coat and stepped inside, firmly closing the door behind him.


The light above flickered and eventually broke apart in the reflections of a fluid sun on water. Tommy floated to the surface. They'd brought him out of his anesthesia and he had one hell of a headache, but he didn't feel much of anything else. This was mostly because some tech had jammed a suppository in his ass, flooding his system with oxymorphone. He blinked as Dr. Reischtal loomed over him.

"We have samples of your brain now. We will learn the truth very, very soon."

Tommy tried to move his mouth, hiss, anything. A low croak escaped his lips.

"You're welcome," Dr. Reischtal said and left.

# CHAPTER 36

Carolina poured coffee, then served them eggs, bacon, and toast. She said, "So. Sam. You got a girl yet?"

"No."

"That's your fault and you know it. Guy like you, you choose to, you can get a girl."

"Sure."

"Ed here, he's got himself a girl. Too dumb to know how good he's got it." She slammed eggs on Ed's plate. "But I bet you'd be a little more thoughtful, wouldn't you, Sam?"

"Sure," Sam agreed. He wasn't an idiot.

Carolina turned to Ed. "Hmm-mmm. See that. Man smart enough to go out and find himself a woman, he oughta treat her with respect. Don't you think?"

Ed nodded. He was no idiot either. "Sure."

The TV on the kitchen counter caught Sam's eye. Cecilia Palmers stood in front of County General with her concerned expression, the one she usually saved for major car accidents. The news crawl at the bottom read, BREAKING NEWS—POSSIBLE VIRUS OUTBREAK IN CHICAGO. SPREAD BY

RATS, BUT IS NOT FATAL IN HUMANS. THOSE WITH COMPROMISED IMMUNE SYSTEMS SHOULD SEEK TREATMENT IMMEDIATELY. A PRESS CONFERENCE HAS BEEN SCHEDULED FOR TEN A.M.

Sam said, "Turn it up."

Carolina caught the edge in his voice and didn't argue.

"—want to stress that this is not contagious, nor overly dangerous to most adults. However, young children and the elderly can be susceptible. Authorities are simply warning the public to remain vigilant and report any rat sightings to the police."

The male anchor broke in, "And Cecilia, is it true that they have taken to calling this the 'rat flu'?"

Cecilia stuttered a moment, her eyes flicking to someone off camera. "Uh, this has not been confirmed at this time. . . ." She trailed off helplessly, waiting painfully for someone to say something to fill the void.

The female anchor recognized her panic and said, "We would like to repeat that this is nothing Chicago's citizens should pan—for people to worry . . . unnecessarily about. This is simply a general warning, to keep everyone fully aware of the situation."

The male anchor wouldn't let up, though. "Is it true, as sources here at the station have said, that this is related to the escaped rat at City Hall two days ago?"

Again, Cecilia didn't know how she should answer. "We cannot confirm anything at this time. . . ." Her eyes checked with her off-screen contact again. "But that event, at this time, would appear to be an isolated, unrelated incident. Again, I have been told that the authorities are emphasizing that this is a general precaution and should not interfere with anyone's plans or daily routine."

Carolina asked, "Is this bullshit? Or should I be worried?"

For several seconds, Ed and Sam didn't answer. Finally, Ed said, "I don't know, baby. I just don't know. But I want you and Charlie to pack and leave as soon as possible. Get out of the city. Go visit your mother. I don't care. Just get out."


Work hadn't been quite the same for the two paramedics, Scott and Vince, since they picked up the Streets and Sans guy. Ever since they'd gotten the call to bring the patient to Cook County General, not Northwestern, they seemed to get all the sketchy calls. They weren't the only ones, of course, but pretty soon it seemed like the only calls they got were the weird ones.

First off, they always seemed to be the only guys who took care of the meatloaf calls. These were the traffic accidents, where there wasn't enough left of the poor sonofabitch to fill the body bag. It's tough to determine a pulse when you can't even identify body parts from the pile of slick meat scattered across the asphalt. Sure, they'd scraped their fair share of corpses off the streets over the years, but during these past weeks, something was off. It was like they were the only paramedics on duty when it came time to shovel the remnants of some poor bastard into the thick black bags. And the statistics were skewed. A hell of a lot of people in Chicago suddenly seemed to be driving the wrong way down the Kennedy or Ike, intentionally slamming into concrete dividers or semi trailers at seventy miles an hour.

Usually, this time of the year, the total deaths were somewhere between five hundred and six hundred. They had seen the death toll mount over the past few days to around fourteen hundred.

And it wasn't like Scott and Vince didn't notice that everybody else kept their distance when it came time for the wet work. The paramedics upgraded to thicker, heavy-duty rubber gloves and started wearing cotton surgical masks.

Then there were the calls that took them to single-family

homes, sometimes apartments, and they had a ride-along. The ride-along was usually some silent military guy, pretending to blend in by wearing surgical scrubs. The guns the guys carried tended to give it away. It was a different feeling, riding with a guy who never talked and carried a goddamn machine gun.

These military guys always rode with them when some psycho had butchered their family or roommates and had invariably barricaded himself in a bathroom or closet. The psycho was either shot or held down long enough to snap cuffs on his wrists and ankles, then hustled out to Scott and Vince's ambulance.

The next stop was always the CCG. Never any other hospital. They didn't know why. But they knew that dead-eyed bastard in the Hawaiian shirt probably had something to do with it. They would unload the patient, and drive off to the next tragedy, and once in a while, they would hear about the suspicious fires that had somehow erupted in the neighborhoods and suburbs they had just visited.

The days became a blur. Whenever they dealt with one of these calls, they had to wear a hazmat suit. Pretty soon, every call required these special requirements. Their hazmat suits were coated in some noxious liquid that burned if it touched their skin. Then a rinse. They peeled out of the suit helmet first, the first step in a long, complicated process. It was sometimes better and easier to simply sleep in the suits. Scott and Vince stewed in their own filth, sleeping at the hospital on the visitor benches. The body bags were sealed and placed in dry ice, then shipped to God knows where. They watched more and more soldiers come and go.

Until that night.

That dead-eyed bastard in the Hawaiian shirt had been waiting in the break room, wrinkling his nose at the awful coffee. He noticed Scott and Vince. "Hey, you guys want some real coffee? I know they've got some decent sandwiches upstairs. No reason for you two to try and survive on this shit."

It sounded awfully tempting for Scott and Vince. Something inside told Scott that it wasn't a good idea, something about it felt wrong somehow, but he was so damn tired and hungry. They followed the man in the Hawaiian shirt to the elevator and rode it up to the sixth floor.

The man in the Hawaiian shirt didn't get off the elevator. He said, "There's plenty of food and coffee down there, down at the end of the hall."

Scott and Vince looked down the empty hall. It didn't look inviting.

"It's down there. Trust me," the man in the Hawaiian shirt said. He hit a button and the doors closed.

Vince shrugged. Scott started down the long hallway, wondering if he had time to get out of the damn suit. As he passed each room, he noticed every single door was open. From what he could see, the rooms were empty, but he couldn't help but feel as if there were people on this floor, people hiding out, people waiting for the right moment to appear.

A low, keening moan. Down on the right.

Some kind of banging, way down at the far end of the left side.

Nothing else. Just those horribly empty hospital rooms.

Scott said, "Fuck this."

Vince turned to the elevator, wanting to hit DOWN. He found the control panel open, hanging broken and limp. Inside, every wire had been cut. He slapped the panel aside in frustration.

It banged into the wall and the sound echoed along the corridor.

Scott found a chair on its side, used it to fling at the video camera, a clear fuck-you to whoever left them on this floor.

The chair hit the ceiling, missing the camera, and crashed back to the floor.

A few howls and screams echoed in answer.

Scott turned back to Vince, started to ask, "Where's the goddamn stairs?" when the first one came out of one of the rooms.

By the time they saw the running woman, it was too late. She had cracked under the strain to maintain the quiet, and came at the noise, bludgeoning Vince, the closest, with a wooden chair leg.

The rest came screaming out of the rooms. They swarmed the paramedics, striking, slashing, biting, sometimes each other, in a frantic effort to silence their world.

# CHAPTER 37

*10:23 AM*
*August 13*

Ed drove. South on Canal. Left onto West Monroe, heading east, to the lake. The morning sun hung in the sky in the upper right corner of the windshield. After showers, breakfast, two pots of coffee, and surviving his girlfriend's wrath, Ed explained that they were not to go within ten blocks of the hospital. Seemed that the word from above had come down on Arturo, with the weight of none other than the federal government, and this time, there was no way he would stick up for the two detectives.

"I guess we better find Qween," Sam said.

"How?" Ed asked.

"We go looking for folks that look like they live under a rock. See if they know her."

"That's a hell of a plan."

"It's been a hell of a couple of days," Sam said, readjusting his bulletproof vest, tightening the Velcro straps.

"Which way?" Ed looked north and south along State, then west along Madison.

"Let's hit the river. Should be plenty of folks along there that know her."

They parked on the sidewalk along Upper Wacker. Nobody would mess with the Crown Vic.

At the stairs down to the River Walk, Sam sank onto the top step to catch his breath. He pulled out his flask and Ed sat down heavily next to him. They passed the flask back and forth for a while, not saying anything. When it was empty, they got up and descended the rest of the stairs. They headed east along the river, moving almost as slowly as the water as it sluggishly flowed away from the lake.

Most of the usual haunts, the man-made caves and hollows, were vacant. They could see the remnants of the inhabitants, such as empty bottles, food wrappers, old blankets, stacks of old newspapers. But everything was empty until they passed under the Wabash Bridge.

Sam saw the man's shoes first. He whistled at Ed, who was down near the water, peering over the edge. The shoes, a warped and cracked pair of black wingtips, ended in surprisingly clean white socks. Black wool suit pants disappeared in the darkness of the narrow culvert. Sam tapped the shoes. "Excuse me, sir."

"Fuck you." A rasping voice from inside the shadows. "Ain't hurting nobody. Leave me alone."

"Sorry to disturb you, sir, but I need to ask you a question."

"Got nothin' to say."

Ed was short on patience. "Listen, pal, I know there's all kinds of bad shit going on around here, but we need some help and we don't have much time. You want to stick your head out of your hole and help us, or am I gonna have to drag you out on your ass and throw you in the goddamn river?"

The wingtips didn't move, but the voice said, "Whatchu want?"

"We're looking for Qween," Sam said. "And before you jump to conclusions, she's helping us. She's not in trouble. Tell you what, I got ten bucks here if you help us out."

"What I gotta do?"

"Nothing. Just tell her, if you see her, that we need to talk. That's all."

The wingtips were still for a moment, then withdrew into the shadow as the man shifted position in the narrow space. Pretty soon, he stuck his head out. He was old, and it was impossible to tell his race. His oddly expressive features, like a clown in a silent movie, looked exotic one moment, and the next, like the perfectly ordinary lined and pitted face of a homeless man. The grime on his face didn't help.

It was clear he had been homeless for a long, long time. He didn't strike the detectives as the kind of bum who would sit with his back against a building, shaking a cardboard coffee cup for spare change. He would never beg out in public. Too proud. An unlit, half-smoked cigarette was clamped between the first two knuckles of his fore and middle fingers.

"The fuck you want with Qween?"

Sam said, "We need to talk to her. That's all."

"Qween ain't gonna want to talk to no cops."

"You tell her that Detectives Jones and Johnson are looking for her. We'll try and stick near the river, by Adams Street, Union Station." Sam pulled out a bill. Snapped it in front of the guy to get his attention. "You tell her if you see her, got it?"

"I ain't stupid, white boy."

"Never said you were. Making sure you're honest."

The old guy cracked up at that. "Shit. Nobody alive is honest."

Ed asked, "You heard about the rats?"

"Ever'body heard 'bout the rats."

Ed leaned closer. "What's wrong with 'em?"

"Damned if I know. Why'nchu watch the news? They got all the answers."

Ed caught sight of somebody on the Dearborn Bridge aiming a long lens in their direction. "Time to go. Some asshole's taking pictures."

"You just remember," Sam told the old man, "you see

Qween, then you tell her we need to talk. We'll hang near Union Station as much as we can."

"Fine, fine. I'm finna go up thataway m'self sometime." He held his hand out.

Sam slapped a folded twenty into the old man's palm.

Dr. Reischtal stepped into Tommy's room and stood over the patient for a while, silent. He kneeled at the side of the bed. Put his elbows on the mattress. The gloved hands came together and interlaced over Tommy's waist.

"Oh, Lord. Hear me. Hear me, oh Lord." Dr. Reischtal didn't say anything else for a while.

Eventually, Tommy wondered if Dr. Reischtal was waiting for an answer.

"Oh, Lord. You are the one, true god. Let me smite him, oh Lord. Let me smite him."

It got so quiet Tommy could hear the fluorescent lights' faint buzz behind the plastic. He decided that if Dr. Reischtal so much as picked up a syringe, Tommy was going to yell as loudly as possible. Beyond that, he couldn't move.

The silence stretched out several minutes, until finally, Dr. Reischtal took a deep breath. His voice was low and ragged. "I understand now. If that is your will, then so be it. He will lead us to the vector. Thy will be done. Until further reconsideration is necessary. Amen." He stood, and watched Tommy.

Again, he refused to say anything. Tommy would be damned if he showed any weakness to this asshole. It became almost a game, to see who would break the quiet first.

Dr. Reischtal seemed not to notice. Thoughts bubbled up and he merely said, "It will be interesting to observe your condition in the coming hours."

Tommy ignored the ominous aspects of this remark, and tried to push his luck. "You think you could turn me loose? I gotta take a leak fucking awful."

At first, Dr. Reischtal refused to answer. He walked to

the door and knocked. It opened almost immediately. "Mr. Krazinsky is in need of a Foley catheter," Dr. Reischtal told the tech. "See that it is done and soon. I would hate to think that he is in any discomfort." He stopped and looked back at Tommy. "One more thing. Upon further review of his case, Mr. Krazinsky will not need any further sedatives. I want him . . . alert."

"God is not in the details," Mr. Ullman was fond of telling his subordinates. "I am. And if you want to remain employed with this hotel, you will do well to remember me." This was true. Employees had found themselves in the unemployment line with a suddenness that made their heads spin for something as seemingly simple as an unshaven chin, an unequal portions of risotto, or missing a single pubic hair on the black tiles under the toilet.

In the six months since the grand opening, it had become clear that the name of the building had irrevocably become The Fin, and although the owners had initially balked at the simplistic nickname, they had since come to recognize the value of such a branding. In the first few months, they had quietly co-opted the name, trademarked it, and now they embraced it.

The incident involving the homeless and the resulting bedbug infestation had nearly ended Mr. Ullman's own career. After an unpleasant discussion with the CEO and board of directors, he had been allowed to keep his position, but he been placed on probation. Grateful for his second chance, he redoubled his efforts in making the Serenity the cleanest hotel in Chicago, if not the nation. He was merciless. His eyes would zero in on details such as a scuff mark on the inside of an elevator, a stray thread on a pillowcase, or a smudged fingerprint on a vase of flowers in the lobby. Every single employee in the building knew his name and feared his wrath.

In addition to the unprecedented levels of sanitation, he also went to war on the insect population. An army of contractors went through the skyscraper, injecting a silicone sealant in every gap, every crack. Entire floors were repainted to hide these efforts. Each room was then sealed off in a rotating basis and blasted with highly pressurized steam. Professional-grade insecticide was now standard issue along with the rest of the cleaning products. The union didn't like it much, but after one short meeting with the general manager, the hotel now included new heavy-duty rubber gloves and a surgical mask for the staff.

With Mr. Ullman in charge, the bugs didn't stand a chance.

Back in the car, Ed turned left onto Wacker immediately after crossing the bridge. They cruised along the emergency side of the hospital, noting the shadows of soldiers within the doors. He circled the block, slowed down, timing it so he'd hit a yellow stoplight, then red. That way, they could take a full thirty seconds to watch the hospital.

But they saw nothing.

They kept circling, weaving around a five-to-seven-block radius several times before they saw any movement. A bus had pulled up in the empty emergency lane, discharging a group of tired, confused-looking people, all struggling to haul medical equipment and small luggage bags inside.

"If I didn't know better, I'd say that a bunch of doctors or scientists or folks like that just got off that bus," Ed said.

"Good thing you know better," Sam said.

Ed drove down Monroe a few blocks, then circled around to Adams, and parked in the shadow of the Willis Tower. "I'm getting sick of driving in circles."

Sam nodded, watching the late morning commuters shuffle to work.

"We're not gonna see anything from the outside. Not anything that they don't want anybody to see."

Sam nodded again. "You wanna go inside?"

"Not especially."

"Me neither. Not yet, anyway."

"Any ideas?"

Sam sat for a moment and didn't answer. He shrugged. "Make some calls. Check email. Listen to the radio. Go for a ride." They said together, *"What the hell, I ain't paying for gas."*

Ed plotted a course west out of downtown to Lake Shore Drive and turned south when he hit the lake. They passed the Field Museum and Soldier Field.

Sam yawned. It surprised him. He turned his radio off. "I think I'm gonna try to sleep," he said.

Ed nodded, turned down his own radio, and found a talk-radio AM station on the car's stereo, the frenzied hosts doing whatever they could to make everything sound like the world was about to crash into chaos and death. He turned the volume low, so it could serve as soothing white noise for Sam. Ed knew the truth.

Sam had never talked about his insomnia, but he'd never tried to hide it either. He adjusted his seat back, getting just enough of a incline to rest his skull against the doorframe, just out of sight of the side window. He held his notebook in his lap, and sunglasses so he could close his eyes and no one could tell he was asleep.

Ed drove while Sam slept. Since his partner was out, he tried to look at the world with both of their eyes. Problem was, Sam was more paranoid than a meth addict on a seven-day bender; but he still had this preternatural sense of who was dangerous and who wasn't.

Ed never could find that fine line; almost always he was either too disbelieving or too trusting. He drove slowly, letting the motions of the car help Sam get some sleep. They passed hulking shells of empty project homes. This was August, and nature ran rampant through unkempt concrete. Trees, bushes, grass all exploded with life, as if the warm, thick air acted as a kind of steroid.

He kept the AC on for Sam, but rolled down the driver's window. When he was thinking and driving through the city, he preferred to breathe the same air as everybody else on the streets. He wanted to hear everything, to feel the heat.

Nothing was happening, at least as far as this new threat was concerned, though. Oh, there was the usual shit, of course. Gangbangers swaggering down their blocks, itching for any excuse to prove their manhood. Certifiably brain-dead patients behind the wheels of vehicles. Public intoxication. Crack passing hands in the open sunlight. Zombies, almost always women, stumbling along, clear victims of domestic abuse, all bruised up. Some with blood still in their hair. If Ed felt like it, he could park the damn car on one corner and arrest five people inside of fifteen minutes.

But there was nothing concrete he could put his finger on, nothing that he could stop and wake Sam for, nothing that he could point to with clear conviction and say yes, there, right there is irrefutable evidence of the problem. So he kept driving. Up and down avenues along the South Side. Through areas that resembled nothing more than bombed-out wasteland where people eked out a living, once step ahead of homelessness and starvation.

The unwelcome cousins of paranoia and frustration started creeping into his thoughts and he decided that a possible solution was simply to become more paranoid, like Sam. So he found a quiet street lined with limp, lifeless trees and ravaged three-flats, pulled over, and fished in his sport coat for a blunt. He fired it up, took three deep hits. He stubbed the end out and stashed the blunt back in an inside pocket.

He drove to the end of the block, exhaling through his nose. Already, the air felt denser, the sounds were crisper, and the situation seemed more definable in his head. He turned off the radio, driving aimlessly, and tried to lay it out.

The CDC was in town, scared to death. They knew something was wrong with the rats, and apart from some bullshit "rat flu" story they'd released just to cover their ass, they weren't talking. Nobody else knew anything. Ed and Sam only had one person telling them anything, and that was a deranged homeless woman who liked to turn live rats loose in government buildings and drink everybody else under the table. And Ed had to face facts: nobody was going to listen to her.

But Ed had been there; he'd been under the city, He'd seen those rats in the subway tunnels, heard them hissing and scrambling over themselves as they tried to attack any humans who got too close. The three of them couldn't be the only ones to have witnessed anything.

And then there were the deaths. So many this year. All those in the subway, started by that college student falling on the third rail in an empty subway station. The suicides. The blitzkrieg of traffic deaths. Unusual heat. A man going berserk for no apparent reason, attacking people on a downtown street with a pair of scissors. Rumors of disappearances. Rumors of more deaths.

None of it made much sense.

He kept driving.

# CHAPTER 38

*3:32 PM*
*August 13*

Even with the somewhat extreme new measures, Roger Bickle and Daisy made weekly rounds throughout the Fin. In six months, they had not found a single bedbug. Roger still wore his uniform, and he only let Daisy loose to sniff at the bottom of the doors in the middle of the day, after the guests had either checked out or left for the day, and before any new guests checked in. If anybody asked, Roger was supposed to answer in a cheerful, yet vague manner. Yes, he could admit that he was from a pest control company. He was merely engaged in a routine patrol. Since he had been working here, he had never found any pests.

He was never, under any circumstances, supposed to mention bedbugs.

Daisy ran from door to door, keeping her nose in the corner where the wall and floor met. She would slow down at each door, taking great snuffles at the slight gap at the bottom. Sometimes up along the door frame, then pushing off, loping to the next one. After about five or six doors, Roger would call her back and she would cross to the other side of the hallway and check the doors along that side as he walked to the next group of doors. This way, they could cover each floor of the hotel in about two to three minutes.

Fifteen minutes in, Daisy was working along the fourteenth floor when she stopped. Drove her nose into the carpet in front of Room 1426. Took three snorting deep draughts of air. She sat, wagging her tail.

Roger stepped up and knocked. He waited, patient. After a full minute, he knocked again. After another minute, he knocked a third time and called the front desk. He gave them his name and consultant number, and asked if the guest in room 1426 had checked out yet.

"Just a moment, sir."

From inside the room, he heard a moan.

"No, I'm sorry, sir. That room is still occupied."

A sharp cry from inside.

Roger said, "Then I'm afraid I am going to have to speak with your general manager immediately."

Something shattered against the inside of the door. It sounded like one of the room's glasses.

Roger said to the clerk on the phone, "I think the guest in Room 1426 might be having a problem."

Two more tinkling crashes against the door. There went the rest of the glasses.

Daisy barked.

"Shhhh," Roger hissed.

"I'm connecting you now, sir. I will try and contact the guest." A click, and Roger heard ringing inside the phone, then inside the room.

Mr. Ullman picked up on the second ring. "What?"

A wavering scream erupted from inside, echoing the electronic ringing of the room's telephone. A deep, thudding crash. The screaming did not stop.

Daisy gave another worried bark.

"Where are you?" Mr. Ullman asked.

"Fourteenth floor," Roger said, horrified at the violent

sounds from within. "Tell them to stop trying to call this room. I don't think the ringing is helping."

Mr. Ullman gave a curt order; the telephone in the room went silent. The heavy banging did not stop. In fact, it grew in volume. Underneath it, Roger could hear sobbing.

Roger said, "Listen, somebody better get up here like right now. Something is terribly wrong in there." He realized he was talking to a dead phone. The connection had been broken. Roger dialed the front desk again. "Have you called the police yet?"

"I'm sorry, who is this?"

Roger repeated his information and said, "Listen to me, dammit. Someone is in trouble in there. If you won't call nine-one-one, then I will!"

"The proper authorities will be notified once we have ascertained the problem," Mr. Ullman said as he rounded the corner down by the elevators, moving swiftly and silently on the thick carpet. "Many of our guests do not wish to involve any authorities unless it is absolutely necessary. It is our re-sponsibility to respect their wishes."

From inside the room, they both heard a final, crunching crash, then nothing.

As Mr. Ullman got closer, he produced an electronic key card. "Please step back and for God's sake, get that dog out of here."

He inserted the key card into the slot above the door handle. There was a click, and the light flashed green briefly. Mr. Ullman swung the door open, sweeping the broken glass aside. From the doorway, they could only see down the short hallway, past the bathroom, and the edge of the bed. A breeze stirred the rumpled sheet that hung off the bed.

There was no sign of the room's occupant.

Mr. Ullman called into the room. "Hello? Hello? This is Mr. Ullman, general manager of the hotel. I hate to trouble you, but we have had a number of calls regarding the volume of activity in this room. I'm afraid I need to speak with you. Hello?"

Still nothing. Just the corner of the sheet fluttering.

Roger could feel warmth. He held out his hand. Warm air was definitely flowing from inside the room. Had the guest turned on the heat?

Mr. Ullman took one step inside, knocking one more time. "Hello? Hello?"

Before Mr. Ullman stepped fully into the room, Roger realized why the room felt warm and why a breeze was moving the sheet when skyscraper windows do not open.

The room was demolished, as if the occupant had been given a shot glass of cocaine and a sledgehammer. The bed frame had been ripped away from the wall. The plasma television had been driven through the glass coffee table. Something had ripped great tufts of stuffing out of the chairs. And the desk chair had been used to shatter the floor-to-ceiling window.

A hot wind surged through the room, pushing aside the ripped curtains and making the sheet billow out a moment, before settling back against the corner of the bed. Roger stepped toward the window, saw blood on the edges of the glass. He got close enough to the edge to see the deep shadows on the building across the street when vertigo dropped into his gut like a bomb and he clapped a hand over his mouth, afraid he might vomit.

He screwed his eyes shut and tried to breathe through his nose. He kept imagining the fall, throwing yourself out over the abyss, feeling nothing but the humid summer air as the windows streaked past, faster and faster, the sidewalk rushing up in a brutal embrace. With his eyes closed, it was almost worse; he imagined he could feel the building swaying gently in the wind.

He popped his eyes back open and stumbled back to the couch, where he collapsed. He put his head between his knees and focused on his breathing. Daisy came up and licked his face. He scratched behind her ears and that calmed him.

"Don't touch anything," Mr. Ullman said, his voice strangely calm, almost placid. He was over his shock now, and a coolly efficient crisis mode had taken over. "The police will want a word. We will conduct the interviews in my office, not in here." He called the front desk. "The police will be arriving shortly. Please send them up to room 1426. Thank you."

Daisy sniffed around the bed and promptly sat down.

"Get that dog out of here. Now." Mr. Ullman was on the phone with the CEO's secretary. "Tell him that we have an emergency situation, and he needs to call me back immediately. I will be contacting Benny Weisman myself."

The sound of sirens from the street reached them.

Roger went to snap Daisy's leash onto her collar and froze.

A single, tiny bedbug trundled out from under the sheet and headed for the bottom of the mattress.

"Good girl, good girl." He patted Daisy's head and gave her a treat.

Mr. Ullman hadn't noticed, phone still glued to his ear. "Benny? Benny! Drop everything and get here now. I need you ten minutes ago. What? No, no. Drop it. I don't care. This is an emergency, I—" He broke off, those detail-oriented eyes zeroing in on the bug as it wound its way down the side of the mattress and disappeared underneath. "What? Benny, listen to me. Get here now." Mr. Ullman hit END CALL.

Roger lifted the mattress and followed the bug with the beam of his flashlight.

The Mr. Ullman ran a shaking hand through his thinning hair. "Please tell me that is not what I think it is. Please."

Roger shook his head. "I hate to make your day worse, but somehow, they got back inside."

"I don't understand. We spent thousands. . . . How is this possible?"

Roger knelt and flashed the beam at the carpet, then the

molding, following it to the corner. He fished out his pocketknife and picked at the painted silicone strip. He pinched the end between his thumb and forefinger and pulled, ripping it away from the trim along the floor for about a foot or so.

Bedbugs spilled out like clotted, reddish-black oil. Hundreds of them.

"Oh dear me," Mr. Ullman muttered.

Roger snapped his pocketknife shut and pulled a canister of bug spray from his bag. He hit the bugs with a short burst. The effect was almost instantaneous. The bugs shuddered to a stop, then slowly curled their legs around themselves and stopped moving forever. More bugs seeped from the crack, so Roger gave them another blast. If there were any more inside the wall, they got the message.

Mr. Ullman's wingtip nudged the silicone strip back into place. He scattered the bugs under the bed, so they almost looked like flecks of pepper from a distance. He stared down at Roger. "This stays between us, do you understand?"

Roger shrugged, and got to his feet. "This is very unusual behavior for bedbugs, I have to say. But if this is what you want, then I—"

"This is absolutely what I want. This cannot get out. You do whatever you have to do, and I will deal with the police. Find out where these godforsaken bugs are coming from and kill them. Kill them all."

"When he was first brought in, we thought he might be a suitable candidate for . . . testing." It was clear to Dr. Reischtal that the tech was having trouble facing certain realities about the homeless and indigent people the soldiers had been rounding up to use as guinea pigs. The tech pulled off his glasses and cleaned them with his tie. His hands shook. "The . . . subject collapsed during intake."

"Before the dosage was administered?" Dr. Reischtal asked.

"Yes, sir," the tech said, hurrying to keep up as they barreled through the busy corridor. "The decision was made to quarantine the subject until tests results could confirm infection."

"And what have these results revealed?"

The tech nodded, flustered. "That yes, he is indeed infected with the virus."

"I still fail to see why I was summoned. The man is homeless. It is reasonable to assume that he was bitten by a rat."

"Uh, that's the thing, sir. We have been unable to locate any rat bites, any significant scratches of any kind."

Dr. Reischtal stopped suddenly and the tech nearly collided with him. The doctor whirled, eyes laser sharp behind the tiny lenses. "If I understand this correctly, you are telling me that we now have an infected patient that does not bear any evidence of virus transmitted by a rodent?"

"Yes, sir. Uh." The tech studied his shoes, unsure of how to phrase the next piece of information. "The attending found . . . something else." He felt the cold glare from Dr. Reischtal and refused to look up. "It might be best, sir, if you were to see for yourself."

Dr. Reischtal gritted his teeth, biting back a savage response. With this unprecedented level of incompetence, it was little wonder the virus was still spreading out in the streets. "Very well," he managed. "Where is the subject?"

The tech led him farther down the corridor. Dr. Reischtal followed without another question. The tech pointed to a door that, despite the urgency in the hustle of the passing techs, nurses, doctors, and soldiers, everyone still managed to avoid any close contact with, instead choosing to walk along the far side of the corridor. This created a bottleneck, which further enraged Dr. Reischtal. Even the tech wouldn't get any closer than fifteen feet.

Dr. Reischtal stopped outside the closed door and willed himself to ignore the ineptitude and downright superstitious nature of the personnel, letting them squeeze along the wall behind him. Without any further ceremony, he opened the door and stepped inside.

An old, naked, black man was strapped to the bed. A bundle of ragged clothes had been piled over a sharp pair of wingtips in the corner. Dr. Reischtal took in the long, stiff hair, the dirt under the fingernails, the grime of the streets that had settled in the lines that shaped the man's oddly beautiful face. Clearly, he was homeless scum and nothing more. Dr. Reischtal felt his anger building. This was a waste of time. Someone had lost their nerve, and had failed to locate a bite mark. Or, at the very least, a scratch. Whoever was responsible was about to find themselves permanent guests on the sixth floor. And he would start with the tech outside.

But then he saw the tiniest hint of movement in the man's long hair. A bug, so small it might have been a slow moving freckle, crawled from the top of the man's ear over to hide in his wiry eyebrows. Dr. Reischtal cocked his head.

Another bug crawled out of the man's surprisingly thick patch of pubic hair and disappeared over his hip. And still another wandered out from the man's armpit, appeared to test the air, and retreated back the way it had come.

The old man moaned once and shivered. He did not awaken. More bugs scurried across the dark, cracked skin.

Dr. Reischtal took a step backwards, eyes suddenly flicking around the room, the ceiling, the walls, the floor, tuned to any tiny movement. A storm of understanding gathered behind his eyes, threatening the feeble dam that he and the rest of the team had erected in their rush to understand and explain the virus. He left the old man alone in his room and shut the door securely behind him.

The tech was waiting with wide eyes. "You saw them?"

Dr. Reischtal did not respond at first. He was too busy re-organizing the information that he had believed, up until thirty seconds ago, to be reliable. The new pieces fell into place, revealing the inescapable path of the virus. Several parasites had been found on the animal smuggler's body, as well as the bats themselves. Except, of course, for the missing bat. He had read reports that detailed how bat bugs and bedbugs were nearly identical, and would invariably mate if one colony came into contact with another, since both used traumatized insemination. Only one in sixty would produce living offspring. However, the offspring of that mutation had been known to be eighty-six percent successful when producing offspring of their own.

He was no arbovirologist, but as far as he understood, the supposedly established fact within the scientific community that bedbugs could not transmit diseases was hypothetical, nothing more. In fact, bedbugs had been discovered to be infected with MRSA. It was entirely possible that the mutant offspring of bat bugs and bedbugs could carry a new virus.

If it was true, then he had been hunting the wrong species. In many ways, he wasn't surprised. This new revelation fit what he knew about the Ancient One. Why hide in rodents when he could disguise himself in something even smaller, something even more insidious? Dr. Reischtal thought about the Black Plague, and how all the holy men had blamed rats, when in reality it was the lowly flea that had spread the devastation.

He spoke without looking at the tech. "Please tell me a sample of . . . these organisms has been obtained."

"Yes, sir. Identified as *Cimex lectularius*, the common bedbug."

"And was the virus present?"

The tech was silent for a moment. Dr. Reischtal could tell that the tech knew damn well, just as he did, that bedbugs had never been found to transmit any significant virus, unlike say, mosquitoes with malaria or even the West Nile virus. The bedbug was a nuisance; that was all.

Until now.

The tech finally took a breath and nodded. "Yes, sir," he

said in a small voice. "It appears that these bedbugs are carrying and transmitting the virus."

Dr. Reischtal allowed nothing to show on his face. "Very well," he said. He pulled out his phone and called Sergeant Reaves. "I want a flame thrower team up on the fourth floor immediately. Everything within Room 417 is to be burned. I want this room erased, do you understand?"

Sergeant Reaves understood.

Dr. Reischtal said, "Every single last patient is now under quarantine. No one is to enter an infected room unless fully protected by a fully enclosed hazmat suit. Contact pest management. I want every common area in this entire building sterilized. Highest priority." He hung up and turned to the tech. "This information is to be kept confidential until if and when I decide to report this to the proper authorities. Right now, I want anyone who has touched him, anyone who sat next to him, anyone that was in the same room as this man, isolated. Starting with you."

# CHAPTER 39

**4:21 PM**
**August 13**

Mr. Ullman finally forced Roger to lock Daisy up in their animal hospitality suite. Apparently, a lot of celebrities like to be seen travelling with their pets, but have no interest in actually taking care of the damn things. The Fin was equipped to accommodate dogs, cats, birds, lizards, pretty much anything smaller than a horse. Roger left her in a crate in a quiet room on the third floor, buried back by the washing machines.

They went back up to the fifth floor to Mr. Ullman's office. He kept his keys in a small safe under his desk. He spoke quickly; he was due back upstairs to finish giving his statement. "If you think the storage facility has anything to do with this, then have at it, by all means. Investigate to your heart's content. Just promise me that you can kill these things once and for all."

"I'll do my best."

"I shall expect this key back by the end of the day. If I do not see some results by then, please inform your employer that I will be speaking to the competition first thing in the morning."

Mr. Ullman ushered Roger out of his office and locked the door behind them. Mr. Ullman headed for the elevators, while Roger went down the stairs, following a hand-drawn map. Mr. Ullman thought it would be for the best if Roger did not take the elevators; there was a chance he might run into a guest or police officer. So he took the service stairwell down until he hit the basement. He worked his way through the kitchens to another service door, which led to another stairwell, dropping another four floors.

He descended the stairs all the way to the bottom. He had to unlock the door, and found himself in a narrow utility hallway. The floor was metal grillwork, and Roger could see that the pavement was wet under the walkway. His footsteps made a hollow, banging noise as he strode down the hallway. He continually had to duck under exposed pipes in the ceiling. He whistled; they must have had a hell of a time moving all the furniture down here.

The door wasn't quite at the end where the hallway dead-ended in a spiderweb of pipes, but it was close. He fingered the key and checked the padlock. Still locked. A thin layer of dust covered the lock and the door handle. Mr. Ullman was right: no one had opened this door in months.

Roger twisted the key and the lock popped open with a click that sounded unnaturally loud in the confined hallway. He thought he heard a high, urgent squeaking on the other side of the metal door, shrugged it off. It was just water or something in all the pipes. He slipped the lock out of the hole, pocketed the keys, and grasped the cool door handle.

He felt very alone for a moment and felt acutely aware of Daisy's absence. It gave his chest a quick ache. He promised himself that as soon as he confirmed that the furniture was still secure and sealed, he would take Daisy out to their favorite burger joint, where they let her sit with him out on the back patio. He decided he might just throw caution to the wind and order at least two beers tonight. Heck, maybe three. After the day he'd had, he felt like he certainly deserved it.

He twisted the handle.

The door popped open, showering Roger with debris, the air suddenly full of cotton snow, scraps of fabric, and slivers of wood. It poured over and around him like a soft avalanche. An awful, foul odor followed, and in its own way, was almost more powerful than the shredded wreckage. He instinctively breathed through his open mouth; it was as if a tornado had ripped through a furniture store, grinding and chopping everything and throwing all of it against the door.

He took a step backward, out of the mess, and picked some wiry fluff out of his hair. Much of it was somehow wet, and clung to him. He realized that the moisture was actually rat urine. A dead rat slid out of the stuffing near his feet. He still hadn't figured out that he had just disrupted a gigantic rat nest until he found a baby rat clinging to his tie.

The thing was smaller than a spark plug and neon red. It looked like some kind of crazy Japanese soft candy. He brushed it away with a gag of disgust, then saw another one clinging to his arm. He could hear it squeal in terror. The cry echoed around him, and he realized that the wreckage was full of baby rats. The shrill squeaks filled the hallway. He swatted them away, stumbling back. He stepped on something that felt like a rotten plum, and when he pulled his foot away, he saw that he had just crushed one of the babies.

An adult rat, a giant covered in coarse black fur, squirmed out of the nest and hissed at him.

His nerve broke completely and with a hoarse shout, he turned and lurched back towards the stairs. His pounding footsteps sent vibrations deep into the foundation of the building, and that, combined with the screaming babies, attracted the rats. They erupted out of the open doorway in a cascade of densely muscled bodies, sharp claws, oversize teeth, and naked, segmented tails.

Roger heard something, and risked a look behind him.

The rats swarmed up the hallway with a speed that sent ice-cold panic shooting through his veins. He cried out and tried to run faster. His only chance was to make it through the doorway and somehow shut the door behind him. There. He could see the door now, and forced himself to not think about the horde that filled the hallway, a cyclone of teeth and claws and rage that roared and snapped at his heels.

He slammed into the door, hands slapping at the handle.

It was locked.

"Oh, Jesus," he whimpered, digging into his pocket for the keys. He refused to turn to see how close the rats were as his fingers closed over the keys. His hand shook as he jammed the key into the handle. The first key was the wrong one. He fumbled with the next key and they slipped out of his sweating fingers and fell through the metal grille.

He had almost a full second to stare at the keys, lying just inches out of reach on the wet concrete, and then the rats were on him. They hit his left leg first, then his right. He had a very clear sensation of the first few bites, those long teeth snapping together into his flesh, like a prehistoric stapler. Rats scrabbled up his body, biting, clawing, tearing, and agony blossomed in his mind. His knees collapsed, and he fell backwards, head propped awkwardly against the door.

The rats tore into him.

And ate him down to the bone.

# CHAPTER 40

**5:02 PM**
**August 13**

Dr. Reischtal locked the door to the women's restroom behind him and put the square package on one of the sinks. Bright florescent lights buzzed overhead, which didn't hurt, but Dr. Reischtal had chosen this particular restroom because of the full-length mirror next to the paper towel dispenser. He set a bottle of medical lotion and a Mini Maglite on the tray over the sinks. He tested the lock one more time, then began to strip.

He removed his clothes with a methodical resolve, folding them neatly and stacking the items carefully on the sink. First was the lab coat. Then the stiff white button-up shirt, then the white T-shirt. Next came his slacks. His socks. And finally his underwear.

He scrutinized his naked body for a few long seconds. He stepped closer to the mirror. He turned the flashlight on his skin and examined the reflection. He started with his skull, moving quickly through the short bristles of gray hair, checking behind his ears, then down to his neck, his chest. He spent a long time studying his armpits. He poked a finger in his belly button and ignored the bizarre signals from the cluster of nerves inside. That was normal. It was empty, and that was all that mattered.

He slowed down again when he got to his crotch, meticulously combing through his graying pubic hair. Nothing. He continued down his legs, and once he had peered between each toe, he turned and started over using a small mirror to inspect his back. When he got to his buttocks, he bent over and spread his cheeks apart, satisfying himself that no multi-legged horror had latched onto the sensitive skin around his anus.

When he was satisfied that no parasite was lurking on his skin, he opened the square package and unfolded the hazmat suit. After squirting a liberal amount of lotion into his palms, he slathered the lotion across his body, this time working from the ground up. When he was finished, the bottle was nearly empty. His skin shone under the fluorescent lights. He knew that he might be forced to wear the suit for a long duration, and the lotion would help.

He stepped into the hazmat suit and zipped it tight.

Sealed in now and secure, he felt his muscles relax slightly. It wasn't much, about the same as relaxing your fist just enough to let an excited dog pull its leash through your grip, but it was enough for Dr. Reischtal to take a slow breath and let it out of his nose.

He was safe from the bugs.

When Sam woke, Ed was driving through an industrial wasteland on the West Side. Sam stretched and checked his watch. He rubbed his eyes and scraped his tongue against his teeth. He found his flask, took a long sip, and passed it to Ed. "Miss anything exciting?"

"Oh, sure," Ed said. He took a long drink and handed it back.

Sam watched the abandoned factories slide past. "So what's our next move?"

"Shit. I been driving all damn day and still haven't gotten any closer to figuring any of this out."

"Well, hell. We're goddamn detectives. Let's detect."

"You're a fucking genius. Wish I'd thought of that."

Sam watched the cracked pavement, weeds, and sagging, abandoned buildings slide past the window for a while. "I'll tell you what's been troubling me. Where the hell are the two guys from Streets and San?"

"Cook County General."

"Right. But why hide 'em away? Why not let us talk to them?"

Ed was quiet for a moment. "It's the rats. They caught whatever the rats have?"

"But why cover it up? Why lie to us?"

"Something else is going on. Something they want to keep quiet. Whatever this rat flu bullshit really is, I'm betting it's a hell of a lot worse than they're telling us."

"Where are we?" Sam sat up, got his bearings. "Tell you what. Let's hit that bar where all the Streets and Sans boys hang out, see if we can't find anybody who works with 'em. Maybe they can give us something."

Ed nodded his head. "Okay. But it ain't gonna work." Despite having essentially the same employer, the City of Chicago, the public workers, the rat catchers, the electricians, the IDOT men, the garbage collectors, all of them didn't mix much with the first responders, the cops, the firemen, the paramedics. The pay scales weren't much different, but folks at the bar looked at it as a kind of class issue, and they were proud to consider themselves blue collar. Cops also saw themselves as being blue collar, but for whatever reason, the division remained.

"Maybe so." Sam shrugged. "Try and convince 'em that all we're doing is trying to find out what the hell happened to their buddies."

Ed gave a tired smile. "Sure. Easiest thing in the world, trying to convince a city worker in this town to trust a damn cop."

"Beats the alternative."

"And what's the alternative?"

"Shooting all the assholes in that hospital and making 'em tell us what the fuck is going on."

Tommy blinked his way out of a dreamless sleep to find Dr. Reischtal sitting in the folding chair next to the door, quietly watching him. Tommy let his bandaged head fall back against the thin mattress. He wanted to let himself cry. He'd been hoping for a dream of his daughter, just so he could see her face when he slept, but sleep had been thin and elusive.

"I trust you slept well," Dr. Reischtal said.

Tommy wondered if Dr. Reischtal was making a joke. Probably not. The man gave off the peculiar impression that he had somehow been born without a sense of humor.

Tommy didn't bother to answer. He didn't say much these days.

He sure as hell didn't sleep well. In fact, he wasn't sure if it could even be classified as sleep, if that's what you would call passing out from exhaustion for a few minutes at a time, on and off throughout the day. He was still strapped to the bed, for one thing. He had some kind of tube up his ass and a goddamn needle up his dick. The pain in his skull was constant, and with no medication, the dull ache clung to him like a stubborn shadow.

The hospital had been growing louder as well.

Especially at night. Tommy would lie in his bed, listening whether he wanted to or not, as more and more patients were brought to his floor. There was no shortage of screaming, as if demons chewed on their brains. And sometimes, when the doctors finished, giving up in disgust, the undisturbed silence was somehow worse.

Dr. Reischtal rose to his feet, crossed the small hospital room, and loomed over him. He now wore some kind of biohazard suit.

Dr. Reischtal's cold, clinical eyes studied Tommy. "I still

believe you know something. Something that you aren't telling me."

Tommy didn't bother to answer. He watched the almost imperceptible flickering of the fluorescent lights.

"There must be a reason." Dr. Reischtal continued, as if Tommy was some kind of exotic plant, incapable of communication. "Some reason why you haven't contracted the virus."

Tommy's head hurt. He said, "Must be God's will."

Dr. Reischtal drew back as if the virus itself had attacked his faceplate. "Do. Not. Mock. Me." He placed one gloved finger on Tommy's right temple, pushing against the bandage where he had drilled into the skull. The pressure increased.

Brilliant red and violet clouds unfurled in Tommy's vision. The pain made his toes curl, his fingernails dig into his palms.

"I will fill you full of drugs that will render you incapable of movement. Of speech." Dr. Reischtal did not pull his finger away. "I will paralyze you. I will rob you of everything except the ability to feel pain and leave you helpless on Lower Wacker for the rats to chew on at their convenience."

Someone knocked at the door. One of the techs stuck his head inside. "The connections have been tested and we are online, doctor."

Dr. Reischtal withdrew his finger.

Tommy tried not to gasp, and swallowed hard instead.

Dr. Reischtal nodded. "Very well. Notify Sergeant Reaves," he told the tech. "Mr. Krazinsky is awake."

The tech said, "Yes, doctor," and left.

Dr. Reischtal looked back down at Tommy. "While I still believe that you are hiding something, others are convinced that you may be of some assistance in our war. Therefore, if you cooperate, I am willing to grant you limited freedom. We will remove your restraints, for one thing. Perhaps even a telephone call to your daughter."

Dr. Reischtal saw the look in Tommy's eyes that Tommy

couldn't hide and gave a thin, emotionless smile. "I will expect your full cooperation, yes?"

Despite himself, Tommy nodded.

They lifted Tommy off the bed and settled him into a sturdy wheelchair. Tommy was hoping they would remove the damn catheters, but no luck. They used the leather straps on the wheelchair to bind his hands and feet and hung his bags from the IV stand connected to the chair.

All in all, it was a nice change of pace from the bed.

Two techs, both wearing full biohazard suits, performed the task. Sergeant Reaves supervised. He wore a bulletproof vest, a blue surgical mask, and a holster on his hip, but never took the handgun out. Instead, he hung back, said nothing, and kept his hands clasped loosely in front of him.

They wheeled him out, and Tommy was shocked at the amount of movement in the hospital. He'd been listening to the increased activity from his room, but it was quite a different feeling to actually see the change. Plastic still lined the walls, floor, and ceiling. Biohazard suits rushed around, carrying equipment or laptops, or pushing gurneys. Most of the rooms appeared to be occupied.

They pushed him into the elevator and hit the button for the second floor. Tommy shifted in the wheelchair, trying to get more comfortable, and felt Sergeant Reaves stiffen beside him. One hand went to the holster. Tommy tried not to smile. It felt good to make the pricks nervous. He wondered if he might be able to use this to his advantage. The techs affixed a surgical mask over his nose and mouth.

The doors to the second floor opened, and he was pushed out into much brighter light. No more rooms for patients— this was the lab floor. Tommy could only guess at what all the shit was used for. Only a few of the hospital personnel on this floor wore complete biohazard suits. Most only wore scrubs, rubber gloves, and surgical masks.

They wheeled him down the wide hallway. The rooms were mostly open on either side, filled with a dizzying array of medical equipment. They passed a table piled high with what looked like clear garbage bags. As he rolled past, Tommy realized that the bags each contained a dead dog. At the far end, he thought he recognized one, and he said, "Wait, stop!"

The tech, startled by the first words he had heard Tommy say all day, actually stopped.

Tommy stared through thick plastic at Don's dog, Rambo. It looked like Rambo's throat had been cut. The top of its skull had been removed, and most of his brain was missing.

Sergeant Reaves gave the tech a hard stare and they were off and rolling again, moving faster this time. They pushed Tommy into a conference room at the end of the hall. The room was empty, save for a large square table and a row of televisions, each tuned to a blue screen. A small video camera on a tripod had been set up in front of the TV. Cables snaked away to a computer in the corner. They left Tommy in front of the camera. Tommy heard the techs leave the room.

Sergeant Reaves, standing as always right behind the wheelchair, said, "Mr. Krazinsky is ready."

A red light appeared on the camera.

One by one, the televisions blinked into shots of various people in lab coats, surgical scrubs, even a few in biohazard suits. Some of the people appeared to be set up in labs, and Tommy wondered if they were in some other room in the hospital, instead of an office, like the rest. A TV near the top displayed an image of a young man with dark, sunken eyes. A yellowing bandage was wrapped tightly around his head, just above his eyebrows.

With a start, Tommy realized he was looking at himself.

A woman, with glasses and hair pulled back into a haphazard ponytail, sitting behind a dark mahogany desk, spoke first.

"Good morning, Mr. Krazinsky. My name is Dr. Halsey.

First off, let me apologize on behalf of some of my colleagues. You must understand the hazards in the hospital there; the risk of infection on a large scale has everyone on edge. Those in charge of this operation feel force is necessary for the safety of the nation. Some of us do not. However, time is short. We need to speak to you regarding the incident at City Hall two days ago. The official report has yet to be released, and reports from the scene are thin to say the least. We need to ask you about the rat."

Tommy found the camera and stared into the lens. "I'm not talking to anybody until I hear my daughter's voice."

Dr. Halsey looked flustered. "Mr. Krazinsky, I can appreciate your situation—"

"I don't think you appreciate shit, lady."

Dr. Reischtal spoke up. "Perhaps I can solve this problem." He was on a TV on the bottom, his biohazard helmet on the desk in front of him. He held up a cell phone, dialed, and hit another button. The digital ringing from the phone popped out of the speakers.

"Ahh, hello?" It was his daughter's voice.

Tommy took a long shuddering breath through his nose, struggling not to let any tears out.

"Hello. Is this Grace?" Dr. Reischtal asked.

"Umm, yes? Uh-huh."

"Grace, this Dr. Reischtal. I am your father's doctor. You father is very sick, did you know that?"

"Ummm? Is my daddy at the hostable?"

Tommy knew that Grace didn't understand. God only knew what Kimmy had told her. He suspected that Kimmy was in the same room as Grace, probably being coached through her own cell phone by somebody from the CDC team here at the hospital.

"Grace, I want you to hang on to that phone because I am hoping your father will be well enough to call you in a little bit. Do you understand that? I am sure that he will want to speak with you."

"Can I talk to Daddy?"

"I certainly hope so."

The confusion in his daughter's voice hit him cold in the gut and he could only imagine the flurry of half-formed questions in her eyes as she said, "Ahh, okay?"

Dr. Reischtal hung up. He stared out of the TV. "Now. You have heard your daughter's voice. Do not ask me again. I will give you a chance if you answer the questions honestly and without delay. This is my proposition. Does it suit you?"

Tommy nodded. He took a deep breath, then went through the entire thing once again, starting with pulling up to City Hall. He went into detail about the state of the rat, describing the near-starvation, the foam in the mouth, the way it had initially appeared dead, and the look in its eyes when it attacked. He talked about when they went to the bar after City Hall and how Don showed off the torn leather glove. He even talked about how they went down to Blue Island and how he was bitten by the raccoon. He answered every single question. He did not hesitate when they asked him to repeat details.

He was a model of cooperation.

A large man with scraggly hair and an unkempt beard squinted out of the TV. "Is there anything else about the rat, anything about how it moved, maybe the sounds it made, anything at all that you noticed? We're trying to figure this virus out, and we need—"

Dr. Reischtal broke in, his voice sharp and direct. "I will remind all of you that this operation is working with classified information. I am afraid Mr. Krazinsky is here in a debriefing capacity, not as a consultant. Please refrain from disclosing any sensitive information during this interview session."

The shaggy man threw up his hands in disgust.

Dr. Reischtal said, "Mr. Krazinsky, you may answer the question."

Tommy thought for a moment, then shook his head. "Look, me and Don, we never had much experience with live rats. We pretty much only put out poisoned bait, then collected the dead ones. All I can tell you is this one was seriously pissed off. I don't think I've ever seen any animal with that much . . . rage, aggression, whatever you want to call it. It looked like the only thing this rat wanted was to kill us."

Eventually, they reached a point where Tommy had no way of answering any more questions. He did not know where the homeless woman was who had found the rat. He did not know the age of the rat. He did not know why the Streets and Sans workers' quotas had been lowered or eliminated completely.

Dr. Reischtal said, "I believe the questions have run their course. Unless there is any other pressing business, this interview is over. Mr. Krazinsky needs his rest."

"Very well," Dr. Halsey said. "The interview regarding the rat situation may be over, but I believe there is still the matter of Mr. Krazinsky's civil rights to be discussed."

"Of course," Dr. Reischtal said. "But not at this juncture. Thank you."

Some of the doctors and scientists started to protest, but their voices were silenced as the televisions blinked over to a blue screen, one by one, until only two images remained. Dr. Reischtal and Tommy.

Dr. Reischtal said, "Very well. Sergeant Reaves?"

From somewhere behind him, Tommy heard Sergeant Reaves say, "Yes, doctor."

"Give this man the phone."

Sergeant Reaves placed a cheap cell phone in Tommy's right hand. He figured it to be some pre-paid, disposable phone. Something with no paperwork. He turned it over and opened it with his thumb. The phone was fully charged and waiting. He wondered if he could dial nine-one-one before Sergeant Reaves took it away.

Dr. Reischtal said, "I feel . . . compelled to inform you that the outgoing call function has been disabled." He checked his watch. "In less than thirty seconds, you are to get a phone call from you daughter. Sergeant Reaves will observe. So please remember that your daughter's well-being is at stake here as well as your own." Dr. Reischtal's picture disappeared, leaving only a blue screen.

A moment later, the red light on the camera winked out.

The phone rang.

Tommy tried to stop his hand from trembling. He didn't recognize the number. He hit the CALL button. Since he couldn't lift it to his ear, he hit SPEAKER. He croaked out, "Hello?"

No answer. Some sound. Breathing maybe.

"Hello? Grace?"

A soft laugh. "Jesus, you're a fucking moron."

Tommy froze. He knew that voice.

It was Lee.

Tommy whipped his head around to glare at Sergeant Reaves. But the man simply stared straight ahead, face set in stone.

Lee's voice continued. "Nah, Grace isn't here right now, asshole. Want to leave a message?" Another laugh. "I don't know what kind of deal you had with that wack job at the hospital, but let me explain a few things. You work for me. I tell you to shit, and you ask how much. You are mine. You and that fucking idiot Wycza caused me so many goddamn headaches, you have no idea. Jesus Christ. I got half a mind to go beat it out of your daughter. Maybe make myself feel better."

"You touch her, and I will kill you."

Lee laughed again. "Oh, yeah? You gonna take me on? Ten minutes with me and my boys, you'll be wishing you was back in that fucking hospital. So think very carefully about that, tough guy."

Tommy resisted the overwhelming urge to hurl the phone at the televisions. He pictured Grace, sleeping somewhere in this sonofabitch's condo. "What do you want?"

"Shit. I want you right there. I want you with a hundred needles in your eyes. I want you in pain, day and night. I want you to regret the day you ever went to work for me. I want you to die a slow, painful death. How's that sound?"

Tommy didn't answer.

"I want . . . I want you to understand how bad you fucked up. I want you to know that when I'm done with this fine piece of ass, your ex-wife, I want you to know that I'm putting her on the street. See how badly she wants to make rent for her and that bitch daughter of yours. I want you to know that soon, very soon, I'm gonna sell this daughter of yours to a couple of very bad customers. People that truly enjoy young flesh, if you catch my meaning. I want you to say good-bye to everything you loved in your pathetic life."

Lee paused, enjoying himself. "I want you to know that you do not fuck with me. I want you to be an example. I want people in this town to whisper your name and know that if you fuck with me, I will destroy you. I will destroy your family. I will destroy your soul. You got that?"

"Yeah."

"Good." Lee hung up.

# CHAPTER 41

Ed parked in the middle of the countless Streets and Sans vehicles. "All right, let's give this a shot. Put on your friendly face." Sam did his best to pull his features into a soft smile. Ed sighed and shook his head. "Do me a favor. Don't fucking smile. You're gonna scare the hell out of people."

They got out and walked through the August heat that reverberated off the blacktop with a vengeance. By the time they stepped into the air-conditioning of the bar, they were soaked in sweat. They knew they would be under scrutiny the second they stepped inside, knew they would be made as cops instantly. There was nothing for it, nothing they could do. Just order a beer and make a general announcement explaining their position.

The bar was packed, but not one patron turned to look at them. Everyone was glued to the televisions. All seven were on news channels. Anchors stumbled as they read their lines. "—authorities can neither confirm nor deny any of these random killings are related." Sam wandered over and watched WGN above the bar.

WGN cut to a reporter down in a subway station. His expression was grave. "At this point, Jim, we just don't know."

"Well, we know that no official statements have been released at this time, but have you heard anything? What can you tell us about the authorities?" Jim, the anchorman, was getting impatient. "I mean, what are they doing to—wait a minute, Chester. I'm being told—what? Wait." Jim broke from his lines and looked away from the teleprompter directly under the camera. "I'm sorry, but this is too—too—this is the news, for god's sake. They can't tell us what to—"

The director cut back to Chester, who was busy adjusting his tie.

Ed was drawn to two different news reports across the room, his attention torn between CNN and Fox News. CNN had a correspondent outside of the White House saying that the president was aware of the elevated number of deaths in Chicago, and was monitoring the situation, but that was all for now.

Fox News speculated about possible rioting and looting in Chicago. They cut to a fat white guy, an American flag pinned to his lapel. "Mark my words, you will have people wanting to take advantage of the chaos caused by a particular nasty version of the common flu bug. But that's all. It's just your common cold. Bird flu. Swine flu. Big deal. Look folks, there is no cause for alarm. We humans are a resilient bunch." Everybody at Fox enjoyed a good chuckle.

WGN cut to the reporter down in the subway holding his mike and talking to the cameraman and sound guy for a moment. "Any interference this way? I like the lights over here. Put me in profile. Okay. I can do another take. No sweat. And in three-two-one." His pitch dropped while his cadence quickened. "I'm Chester Hackensack, deep in the Washington subway station. During any weekday rush hour, thousands of commuters use this particular station every five minutes at peak capacity. Tonight, it is practically empty. It is literally a ghost town." The camera panned over to show two or three people standing in the brightest light in the middle of the station. "The soldiers up top won't authorize any audio or video, so we're shooting down here. No one is here, and yet, no one is talking." As if he realized that made no sense at all, he took a breath, giving time for someone to jump in. No one did. Chester nodded. "At this time, these few commuters are waiting for a presumably vacant train. Back to you in the studio, Jim."

Chester waited another beat. "Wish I could tell you more. Back to you, Jim."

CNN and FOX News had cut from the experts and were now showing the same shaking, blurry footage. The shot was from overhead, definitely from a helicopter, of police chasing a frightened, scurrying figure into a playground. From the angle, it was impossible to tell if it was somewhere in the city itself or out in the suburbs. The figure, a woman, raised her arms, and kids started falling around her. There was no audio, but Ed didn't need it. He knew only too well that he was watching a woman with a gun. Parents scooped up children and fled. The woman crawled under the slide, out of view of the helicopter. Chicago cops moved in. They surrounded her, all firing.

The CNN anchor said in halting tones, "This video was taken approximately thirty minutes ago in Chicago's Near North neighborhood. Few details are known at this time. We can tell you that the attacker has been shot to death by the police. It is believed that at least four children are dead, with several more in critical condition in area hospitals. The names of the deceased have not been released, nor are authorities speculating about a motive."

Fox News kept showing the footage, over and over, zooming in when the woman started shooting, while experts debated what exactly had driven the shooter to the playground. They kept repeating the word "terrorist," sometimes with a question mark, sometimes not.

A record of fifteen homicides and counting. A husband bludgeoned his wife to death with her own clothes iron. A woman stabbed her youngest child to death with a seven-inch stainless steel knife designed to chop vegetables. A man drove his car into a line of people waiting for the bus at the corner of Michigan and Adams.

Sam caught Ed's eye, tilted his head at the door.

They got in their car and drove east, toward the lake, toward the Loop.


Tommy clutched the phone so hard he heard the plastic crack. He forced himself to unlock his fist. The cell phone fell from his rigid fingers to the thin, industrial carpet. Deep in his mind, he knew he should have tried to keep hold of it, tried to smuggle it back to his room. Maybe he could figure out a way to make it work, to call outside the hospital, or at least text something to alert the outside world.

A single television in the center of the wall went from a blue screen to an overhead shot of a patient strapped to a bed. It was a man, a large man, and as he writhed against the re-straints, his tremendous gut rolled back and forth. Tommy recognized Don almost immediately.

Don was in agony. There was no sound, but Tommy could see the open, screaming mouth. Fingers scrabbled at the mat-tress. The toes curled. Don's back arched in one unending spasm. Tommy kept waiting for him to stop, to fall back slack against the bed, to collapse with fatigue, but Don never showed any sign of release. It was as if he was connected to a live wire that was sending a relentless, unbroken high-voltage stream through his battered body, and the torturer had fallen asleep at the switch.

It was exhausting just watching him.

A second TV switched over to another overhead shot of a patient. Tommy didn't know this one. The man was ragged and thin and dirty. Maybe some homeless guy. It didn't matter. The unsettling body language mirrored Don's thrashing. This man's mouth opened and closed, broken teeth crunching together. A glimpse of gauze inside the mouth meant that the irregular teeth had snapped shut on the man's tongue.

A third television blinked; another patient, this one also in the grip of agony. A fourth TV, a fifth. Soon the whole wall was alive with pain. The soundless cries filled the quiet room and Tommy recoiled in silent horror.

Dr. Reischtal whispered in his ear, "Do you see?"

Tommy flinched. He hadn't heard Dr. Reischtal enter the conference room.

"Everyone else around here calls it a dreadful disease. A horrible tragedy. A supervirus. How absurd. They don't see this for what it really is. They don't see it as corruption of the spirit. But you, you see the truth. You can see that these hosts, they are not victims. They are not simply infected. They have been consumed by the darkness. They are all lost souls. You can see this. You know this to be true."

Tommy didn't say anything. With his luck, he'd try and say something that the lunatic would agree with, but would end up being the absolute worst thing to say. Tommy would end up cementing his compliance with the virus, driving Dr. Reischtal deeper into madness. Tommy knew that his very life teetered on the edge of this doctor's insanity, hanging precariously on a thread in the cobwebs of Dr. Reischtal's poisonous mind. So he kept his mouth shut.

"Why doesn't this"—Dr. Reischtal nodded at the wall of TVs—"live within you?"

Tommy didn't bother to say anything. He figured it was another rhetorical question.

Dr. Reischtal leaned in close, tiny glasses focusing his

eyes like black lasers. "Obviously, there is still much we do not know. Therefore, you will be placed in close proximity to your partner, and we will observe the results." Dr. Reischtal drew himself to his full height and gazed down at Tommy. "We will find out, once and for all, what you are hiding."

# CHAPTER 42

**6:11 PM**
**August 13**

A riot of swirling blue and red lights and irritated horns surrounded the Loop. Ed and Sam found that Upper Wacker was a parking lot, so they tried Congress and found it blocked as well. Ed finally turned on the radio. WBBM was talking about the murders, of course, but took a break every ten minutes to give updates about the weather and traffic. As it turned out, Chicago police had restricted all of the interior streets in the Loop down to one lane in cooperation with a special unit acting as liaisons with a branch of the CDC.

"Sounds like more horseshit to me," Sam said.

"This is why I don't turn on the radio," Ed said. He flashed his lights, hit the siren, and whipped a U, heading south. He tore down Halsted to Roosevelt, turned to the lake. Left on Lake Shore Drive, this time heading north. Ed left the windows down. Sam cranked the air-conditioning.

Ed kept the siren and lights going as he raced up LSD, drifting across lanes with an almost drunken confidence. He turned left on East Monroe, heading west, back into downtown. They turned right on Michigan, then tried to go left on East Madison. A mass of cars blocked the intersection, all vying to be the next in line. Sam took the bullhorn and yelled at the driver of a silver Lexus. "Stop that car fucking right there, douche bag."

The driver reluctantly stopped and refused to make eye contact as Ed got ahead of him. "That's right, asshole," Sam yelled into the bullhorn, aiming it at the Lexus. "Next time you see lights, you fucking remember to pull over."

Streets inside the Loop were squeezed down to one lane, blocked with red and white sawhorses. The few pedestrians moved with an urgent purpose along empty sidewalks. They certainly moved faster than the vehicles. Ed and Sam's car crept forward with the pace of some old lady with a walker out on a sunny day in no particular hurry.

Ed squeezed the steering wheel until Sam was afraid it might snap. Ed said, "This is gonna take all night. We're never gonna find her going this slow."

"Fuck it then," Sam said. He tapped his badge. "We got ourselves an all-access backstage pass. Park anywhere you feel like. Let's go for a walk."

Ed pulled into the right hand turn lane at the intersection of Madison and State and killed the engine. Ed and Sam got out and stretched. The cars behind them waiting to make a right immediately started honking, but Ed reached back in and hit the spinning lights. The rest of the drivers behind him didn't like it much, but at least they stopped hitting their horns. They angrily waited for their turn to pull back into traffic and finally turn right once they were past the detectives' car. Sam waved as they went past.

Lee emptied the rest of the bottle of red wine into his glass. He set the bottle down harder than he'd intended, making a loud thunking noise on his glass dining table. Kimmy glanced at the empty bottle, but said nothing, focusing on her own plate. Good. She'd been a bitch lately, and he was in no fucking mood to listen to her nag, tonight especially.

He hadn't hit her. Yet. Their relationship wasn't that far along. But if she kept pushing him, by God, she was going to find out in a fucking hurry that he expected his women to keep their mouths open in the bedroom and zipped shut everywhere else.

Grace pushed soggy spaghetti noodles around her plate and made a face. "I wanted chicken strips," she said for the third time that evening.

"I've already told you," Kimmy said, "no one is delivering tonight. You're lucky that I had enough to make spaghetti. Now be quiet and eat your dinner." She looked up at Lee. "I hope it turned out okay. My mom made it all the time for us growing up. It's not as good as hers, but I hope it's okay."

Lee gave a noncommittal grunt. The meal had been awful. Who the fuck serves peas with spaghetti? But there was no point in making things worse. He slid his plate away, making room for his elbows. He swirled the wine in his glass, just for something to do. It beat checking his phone yet again for a call from his uncle.

Grace said quietly, "I hope Daddy is okay."

That about tore it. Lee drained his glass, went to pour another, and realized the bottle was empty. He couldn't remember if he had another bottle in the wine cabinet in the pantry or not. Typical. The fucking city was falling apart around him and he was stuck with this stupid cunt and her kid without any alcohol.

"I told you to be quiet and eat your dinner," Kimmy said. She tried to break the tension with Lee. "I used the whole-wheat noodles from Whole Foods, you know, to try and keep it healthy for you."

"I was wondering why it tasted like shit," Lee said. He threw his linen napkin at the table, knocking over the empty glass, and stomped into the living room. This room was the whole reason he'd bought the condo. All he could think of when he first took in the view was how much he wanted to bring people up to his place and show it off.

Harbor Point was perched at the north end of Grant Park. Lee's condo was on the fifty-first floor and had a southwestern view. The floor-to-ceiling windows allowed him to watch the sun set over Chicago's skyline every night. Tonight, the sun was nearly down, leaving the buildings of the Loop in silhouette. The remaining sunlight behind them was still strong enough to wash away any lights in the individual windows, giving the impression that Chicago was constructed of monolithic monuments, standing silent guard along the lake.

He blinked, shifting his focus from the darkening city to his own reflection as it grew stronger and more defined in the fading light. He didn't like the furtive, hunted look in his eyes so he turned his attention to the sixty-inch plasma above the fireplace and watched the news for a while.

Things hadn't gotten any better. Every goddamn channel in the world was focused on Chicago. It made the city look bad.

Fucking rats.

At least the federal government was in control. It wasn't official yet, and it might never be official, but the CDC owned Chicago right now. So whatever went down, Lee wasn't responsible. He couldn't be held accountable. Shit happens. It wasn't his fault. There was no way it could come around to bite Lee on the ass. And if things went real south, the boys in power always pinned everything on some pissant, second cousin to somebody low, and crucified him in the media. They'd do anything they could to aim the public's hate at one guy while the rest scurried for cover.

Lee turned back to his reflection in the windows. He didn't think he'd ever been this close to the real power in the federal government. It was like nothing he'd ever seen. All these guys had to do was snap their fingers, and entire streets got shut down like it was nothing. His reflection didn't reassure him. It had the opposite effect. He looked weak. He looked finished.

As much as he didn't want to admit it, it suddenly occurred to him that to these feds, he might be a small fish. Small enough that he could be the scapegoat. For the first time, Lee faced the uncomfortable truth that they could blame everything on him.

He wished his uncle would call.

# CHAPTER 43

Sam drank in the relative peace and quiet of the city. The horns had tapered off, and all the flashing police lights gave the darkening city a festive feel, like it was some obscure holiday, the offspring of Halloween and the Fourth of July. And normally, at this relatively early time of night, eight o'clock, the pedestrian walkway, over twenty feet above the river, would be half-filled with smokers, getting those last puffs in before they got to their cars after a long ride home on the Metra. Tonight it was empty.

Sam popped a piece of nicotine gum into his mouth and relaxed on the bench, enjoying the view. Ed waited next to him, staring at the blacktop under his feet, ignoring the view. Ed was troubled, Sam could see tell, but he didn't know what to say.

They'd passed Cook County General on their walk. The place was now surrounded by sawhorses with blinking lights, all wrapped in razor wire and supported with sandbags. It looked more like a barrack in Afghanistan than a hospital in Chicago.

"Where's the goddamn media for *this* shit?" Ed had asked.

They watched as several ambulances pulled into the emergency drive. Sam whistled low, as soldiers, not paramedics, hopped out and escorted the gurneys into the emergency room. The ambulances took off, lights flashing, sirens going.

It was Sam who noticed the late-model sedan with the tinted windows parked at the intersection of Wacker and Monroe. He caught the silhouettes of hulking figures inside as the ambulance roared past. Ed wanted to go over, show them his badge, see what the hell they were doing. With everything going on, he was feeling powerless, and wanted to bust some skulls.

Sam cautioned against it. He got a bad vibe from the car. If they went over, shoving their badges around, they might make themselves more of a target. All they'd do is give those soldiers an excuse to fan out through the streets and hunt them down. And there was no way they would stand a chance against that kind of firepower.

Ed reluctantly agreed that Sam might have a point. So they kept walking. Two more blocks until they crossed Adams and found all the benches empty. They had been sitting there for over an hour before they heard the rattle of the shopping cart.

"You seen Old Henry?" Qween appeared in the dim glow of the streetlights.

"Earlier," Ed said. "We need to talk to you."

"Damn right you do," Qween said, leaning on the handles to her cart. "'Bout time you figured that out. Where'd you see Henry?"

"Down by the river."

"When was this?"

"This morning sometime. Why?"

"He gone. We ain't talked all day. Ain't like him."

"I don't know about that. But this," Sam said, pointing at the hospital. "This is a problem." He stood and paced. "The government has taken over in that place. We stick our heads inside, we ain't gonna make it five feet. You say the rats are sick. The news is now saying the rats are carrying some kinda disease. And meanwhile, people are going bug-fuck crazy." Sam spread his hands. "So. Let's start with the rats. What's wrong with 'em?"

Qween worked her mouth, chewing on something for a while. Sam and Ed weren't sure if it was gum or something left over from dinner. She finally said, "I don't know if it's the rats or not. But if you wanna know about the rats, then go talk to the people that see 'em, day after day."

"Streets and Sans, they're not exactly cooperating."

"No, not them. You need to talk to some folks that are out on the streets, day in, day out." She looked from Ed to Sam. They didn't get it. "Folks like me."

"Foul-mouthed and cranky?" Sam asked.

The Man himself stared into the camera. "Doctor . . . Reischtal, is it?"

Dr. Reischtal said, "Yes, sir." He sat alone in the conference room on the top floor. He had pulled back the hood of his hazmat suit and taken off the faceplate and twin filtration bulbs. It rested on the table within arm's reach.

The Man got tired of waiting for Dr. Reischtal to say something else. "Understand the situation is critical. I've seen the news footage. Looks like things are going to hell in a handbasket." He was the placid eye in a hurricane of activity. Aides rushed around him, and high-ranking officials like the secretary of defense flanked him. Everybody else had a cell phone glued to his or her ear, but the Man ignored all of this, and barely moved as he watched Dr. Reischtal's video image.

Dr. Reischtal nodded. "The infection is reaching pandemic levels, yes. We are collecting and isolating individuals exhibiting any of the symptomology, as well as anyone else that may have been exposed. They are currently being treated at this hospital. However, we are running out of room." He clasped his long skeletal fingers and stared back at the Man. "If we do not destroy the root cause, the origin of the virus, we have no chance of containing it."

"Worst case?"

"Entire world. Within four or five months."

"Best case?"

"Isolate it and destroy it. Downtown is already lost, I firmly believe this."

"That's not what we're hearing from this end," the Man said.

"Your end is not here. I am here. I know what is coming. I know how the virus is spreading." Dr. Reischtal smiled. It did not contain warmth. "This is a species-ending virus, something that will latch on to anything you have in the way of a brain, and will live with the short-sighted goal to simply procreate and survive, even if it burns out an entire planet and ultimately kills itself." He struggled not to say the word "God" or especially "wrath."

The Man was silent for a moment. "Are you serious?" He turned to the secretary of the interior. "Is there any way what he's talking about is even close to the truth?" He looked back at Dr. Reischtal. "You people are supposed to be the best in the business. How did it get this far?"

"Until recently, we were unable to determine the exact transmission method. Now we know. Therefore, I need authorization to begin an evacuation of downtown Chicago in response to the virus outbreak. "

"Is that really necessary? I mean, extreme measures have already been taken, have they not? I understood that downtown was already restricted."

"I don't think you understand the ramifications of not taking decisive action immediately. The situation has escalated, and it makes no matter whether we want it to stop when convenient. We are about to engage in a war here, make no mistake, where we are fighting for our lives, our very souls."

Dr. Reischtal stood up and raised his voice. "It. Will.

Spread. Of that I have no doubt. Have your people described, in detail, exactly what happens when one is infected with this particular virus? Have they explained that after a brief coma, anywhere from twelve hours to one or two, the victim awakes to some of the most intense skin irritation I have ever witnessed? An irritation so severe it invariably leads the victim clawing his or her own skin off? I have personally witnessed a victim take a corkscrew to their thighs and chest in an attempt to satiate the irritation." He did not mention that the corkscrew was, in fact, a scalpel, and the blade had been provided to the patient for the sole purpose of observing the reaction. "And then"—he spread his fingers flat on the table—"the victim becomes hypersensitive to any kind of sound, and reacts violently. You do understand that these infected patients will not stop. They will attack and kill anyone in their paths, using anything at their disposal. Do you not see the possible consequences if this particular virus spreads beyond Chicago?"

"You said that you now know how the virus is transmitted. Can you . . . enlighten us?"

Dr. Reischtal paused a moment. When the arm of his hazmat suit rubbed against his torso, it squeaked like a children's bath toy. "Very well. But I believe this information should be kept from the public. It will only serve to hinder our primary focus, which is isolating the virus, studying it, and ultimately finding a vaccine." He took a deep breath. It was time to reveal the truth. "The virus is being transmitted by parasitic insects, commonly known as bedbugs."

The Man raised his eyebrows.

"Again, I must urge you to keep this information as quiet as possible. If you were to tell the general population what is really happening here, that death is crawling up through the cracks in the walls and hiding in their beds and couches, biting them when they sleep, feeding on them while they are hypnotized by their televisions, you would witness an unprecedented panic that will rip this country apart."

Dr. Reischtal wasn't the least surprised that the Old One had surfaced in a parasite, hiding in a bug that had once fed on the blood of mankind's ancestors as they slept in caves and trees. He faced the camera and tried not to let anything into his voice or escape through his face as he fought to control what he said out loud. It was so obvious. Why could they not see it? The Ancient One, the End Foretold, No Rebirth without Death. "You asked if an evacuation was really necessary to stop this, this abomination. It is. In fact, it is the only way to burn this virus out with all the fury of our Lord."

The Man shook his head. "I don't know if you can comprehend what factors are involved in such a decision. The consequences can be far-reaching and quite unpleasant to contemplate. I do not need to remind you that an election is imminent. This is unacceptable."

"And watching an entire city, then the entire country, fall victim to this virus, that would be acceptable?"

"Stop right there. I—"

"Listen to me!" Dr. Reischtal shouted, and if he felt any trepidation about interrupting the most powerful man in the free world, none of it showed on his face. He looked positively possessed. "This is what will be necessary."

Dr. Reischtal began to tell the president exactly what was necessary.

Qween insisted on bringing a bowling ball bag that she had pulled from under the cart. She left her cart on Monroe, taking only the wheels and the bag. God knew what was inside. Ed didn't think she could physically carry an actual bowling ball, but damned if he could figure it out; whatever it was, it was heavy.

She put her bag on the floor, stretched out in the backseat of the car, and made herself at home. She said, "Go south. Stop when you get to Roosevelt."

The bag made Ed nervous. He said, "If there's something

you ain't telling us, I will not appreciate it. I will take you in and make sure they put you in a hole for a long time. If this a wild goose chase, I will make it my purpose in life to make you unhappy."

"You need to relax, Ed Jones."

"What's in the bag, Qween?"

"Stop when you get to Roosevelt."

"Okay. Have it your way." Ed didn't say a word until they passed Eleventh Street. "Left or right."

"Right. We heading west."

Ed got into the right lane. They rode in silence for a while. Qween said slowly, "It used to be my mother's. We spent a lot of time at Providence Hospital when I was young. Had some problems. 'Course, we didn't start out there. Mama took me to the closest hospital first. Bunch of white doctors. Mama said that they took me in, but wouldn't tell her the name of the disease. A white doctor prescribed a bunch of pills. She never did like to admit it, but years later, Mama told me I came outta there worse off. Said she tried to take me back, but they wouldn't readmit me. I had been in there one night. That's all Mama would say.

"Had to hear the rest from my aunt, who went with us. She said we first tried to get in to see the doctor through the front entrance. The whites acted as though we oughta be embarrassed for making the white folks actually come out and say that the hospital was filled, and that we should try Provident, down on Fifty-first." She was quiet for a long time.

Sam and Ed didn't say anything. They knew that Provident Hospital had been established to care for black folks in the late 1800s, since none of the other hospitals would.

Qween said, "So we waited for the doctor to leave his hospital. Mama saw him on the sidewalk. Confronted him right there in front of all the other people, other doctors, nurses, everybody. She said, 'My girl hasn't been right since. Something is wrong, doctor.' Well, he just looked at her and said, 'I saved your daughter's life. Good day.' And that was that. I'll never forget Mama. He's walking away, and she screamed at him, 'You should have let her die.'

"I think she always felt bad for saying that. At least, saying it in front of me. So after we were done at Provident, we had to go back, over and over I remember, and so afterwards, she always took me bowling, down on Sixty-third Street. They had special hours for us black folks. We'd throw this nine-pound ball down the lane, praying it wouldn't end up in the gutter, you know. I remember it real clear. Like it was last week. Mama had this look on her face, flinging this big old heavy black ball at the white pins."

Qween gave a sly grin. "That's how I got the bag, Ed Jones." She gave him a few more directions, and they worked their way a few blocks south. Pretty soon they pulled past a big neon cross at the center of a long two-story building. HIS NAME BE PRAISED HOLY MISSION was spelled out below the cross in white neon letters. Ed pulled into the alley behind the mission.

"You better not be yanking our chain, Qween. This place— you know damn well what's really going on here. Last chance to tell us the truth."

"Yeah, yeah. You done warned me." She got a solid hold on the handle of her bag. "We here 'cause of the spacemen."

"The spacemen, Qween?" Ed asked and killed the engine.

"Spacemen. This place, they be selling people to the spacemen."

"Good enough for me," Sam said and got out.

He slammed his door to find three young black gentlemen in sharp suits and close-cropped hair. They all carried Bibles and gave him tight-lipped smiles. One of them said, "Evening, brother."

Sam grinned right back and flashed his star and his handgun. The three gentlemen faded back to the front of the building, joining a couple of others in shouting upbeat slogans at passing cars. Sam shook his head and spit his nicotine gum on the sidewalk.

Anybody who had spent any time at all on the streets knew this place was as crooked as the day was long. Like a lot of other nonprofit organizations, this place wore a mask. Out front, and on paper, this place looked like a god-fearing Christian charity, spreading the good word while they clothed and fed and sheltered the less fortunate. They paid the local cops and their alderman good money to make sure that mask stayed in place.

Under the mask, they used the homeless men as drug mules, carrying small shipments to the various gangs across the South and West sides. Nobody who knew said anything. You throw a wrench into the Machine, and no matter how strong the wrench, the Machine would chew it up and spit out shards of steel. If you were lucky, you lost an eye. If you weren't, your family would find what was left after you swallowed the business end of a twelve-gauge shotgun.

Ed helped Qween out of the backseat. She always walked a little bit like a movie cowboy, as if only her head and feet had received the original instructions, thanks to whatever childhood disease she had endured. When she carried the bag, the effect was more pronounced. She carried it close to her hip, back straight, bearing the weight with her entire body.

Ed opened the side door of the mission and waited for Qween and Sam to go inside.

Qween waited in the hallway for Sam, then followed him deeper though the next set of doors. Ed followed. Sam knew the assholes out front would be calling the office inside, and knew that he had only a minute. He moved fast, and Qween kept up. He had to give her credit; when she had to, the old girl moved fast and quiet. He avoided the chapel straight ahead and turned left in the next hallway, away from the music and candles. He guessed that the cafeteria tables and cots were to the right. He wanted the administration offices.

Sam didn't bother to knock. He twisted the door handle and slammed his shoulder into the door, hoping it was unlocked.

It was. He burst into the room, one hand holding up his star, one hand on his holster. "Evening, brothers."

He was in luck. This was the main office. Four men. Two were busy trying to sweep cash off a desk. One of them had a desk phone wedged between his ear and shoulder. Sam ignored them and concentrated on the two guys sitting on either side of the door. They were halfway up, reaching inside their suits.

Ed was immediately behind him, and he wasn't fucking around. He already had his .357 out. "You sit right the fuck down." The two big guys eyeballed each other and decided their cut wasn't worth taking on some pissed-off cop with a giant handgun. They sat.

While Sam angled toward the two guys trying to hide all the cash, Ed focused on the muscle. "That's right, fuckheads. Sit still. Don't give me an excuse, you got me?"

"Easy, easy," Sam told the accountants. "This isn't a raid. I couldn't give a rat's ass what y'all are up to in here. We're only here for some information. So take a deep breath. Leave that cash alone. It's not going anywhere."

Ed told the muscle, "I got an itch to put some holes in your heads, so do yourselves a favor and listen carefully. I don't give a fuck who is supposedly protecting you. He here now?" He showed them his handgun. "I am. Ain't no secret you packing. So here's what we're gonna do. You're gonna take those guns out, nice and slow, and put 'em on the floor. One at a time. You do it the right way and I don't paint the wall with your brains."

"Amen, brother," Sam said.

The two men didn't want to die. One at a time, they took out their handguns, holding them gingerly by the handles, and left them on the floor. Ed kicked them over to Sam. "Now then, since I don't feel like searching you, y'all are gonna lie down with your hands behind your head. We'll be out of your hair soon.

Sam said, "All we need is to talk to you about the spacemen." He was having a ball being the good cop for a change.

One of the muscleheads said in a muffled voice, "We didn't do nothing."

Ed said, "Shut the fuck up, 'less you got something constructive to say."

"All I'm sayin' is that we didn't do nothin'."

"Last warning," Ed said.

"Hey, man, what's your problem?" The musclehead was getting indignant. "You need to talk to your supervisor. This here, we're protected, you understand what I'm saying?"

Ed nodded. "I understand you didn't listen." He gave the guy a swift kick in the stomach. The air rushed out of the guy's lungs in a stunned hushing sound, and he made a strangled whining noise as struggled to take another breath. "Dumbass," Ed said. "Who's fucking next?"

Sam said, "Maybe violence isn't the answer here." He turned his attention back to the two men by the desks. "You seem like reasonable men. Care to enlighten my partner and me? Tell us about the spacemen and we're gone."

The two men wouldn't look up. They didn't say anything.

Sam said, "No? Okay then." He went around the desks, opened a few drawers at random until he found what he was looking for. A simple BIC lighter. He flicked it once, made sure it worked. He grabbed a stack of hundred-dollar bills off the desk, folded one over, and lit it on fire.

"You can't do that," one of the men said.

"I'm not doing anything," Sam said, holding on to the burning bill until the flames were licking his thumb and forefinger. He dropped it and ground the ashes into the expensive carpet. Sam lit two more bills. "File a complaint. Take me to court. Go ahead, prove this money ever existed." He lit the entire stack, burning at least four or five thousand dollars. "You can explain to your boss why you're a little short today." He grabbed another fistful of cash.

"Fine, fine, okay? Just stop," one of the accountants said,

patting the air in front of him like he was trying to get a bus to slow down. "It's got nothing to do with us."

Sam flicked his gaze to the groaning man on the floor. "That's what he said too."

"I just mean, all we do is call 'em if we got somebody in here that fits the description."

"And what would that description be?"

"Somebody looking like they going cold turkey. Shaking. Itching. Sleeping and won't wake up. Shit like that."

"Then what?"

"Sometimes they come here. The spacemen. Guys in rubber suits and masks. They take 'em away."

"Sometimes."

"Sometimes we take 'em ourselves. Sometimes they call us. When they want somebody."

"Somebody."

"Yeah, somebody. Those times, it don't matter. They just want somebody."

"Somebody that nobody'll miss," Ed chimed in.

The guy shrugged. "I guess so, yeah. We don't ask questions."

Before Ed could lose his temper again, Sam asked, "Where do you take 'em?" He was willing to bet all the money on the desk that the guy was going to say, "Cook County General."

But the guy said, "Loading dock on Lower Wacker. Between Monroe and Adams."

Sam popped more nicotine gum. Chewed slowly. It made sense. If they were dropping people off, whoever was in charge of the hospital wouldn't want anyone to see it. It seemed very likely that there was another way inside, not just the emergency entrance. Lower Wacker had loading docks that opened to Cook County General.

They heard a scream.

"Where's Qween?" Ed asked.

# CHAPTER 44

**8:46 PM**
**August 13**

Phil didn't call for a long time. Kimmy had put Grace to bed earlier, and had retreated to the bathroom to sulk in a bath she kept refilling with hot water, over and over, when it grew too cool.

Lee didn't give a damn. She could drown in there as far as he was concerned. He'd dug a bottle of cheap gin out of the back of his kitchen pantry somebody had left during his housewarming party and sat in front of the windows, staring at the Chicago skyline. The only light came from the television, but the sound was muted, so all Lee could hear was the hum of the air-conditioning and the occasional dull rush of hot water in the bathtub.

His uncle's voice was cold. "I told you this was going to come back and bite you in the ass."

Lee was drunk, but knew he'd better at least act like he was sorry. Arguing would just make things worse. And drunk or not, he needed his uncle's help. "My apologies," he mumbled.

His uncle sighed. "I've been up for the past three fucking days, trying to fix your mistakes. I'm tired and I'm pissed.

You're lucky you're my nephew, or I'd have some fellas I know come over and teach you a fucking lesson. Give you a chance to try wiping your ass with a fucking hook."

Lee stayed quiet, giving his Phil a chance to vent.

"As it is, there's no goddamn point. The big boys are scared. They're looking for a scapegoat. They're kicking around a few names, but I gotta tell you, yours is at the top of the list."

Lee shot to his feet. "So why'd you call then? Just to rip me a new asshole? Huh? What, make yourself feel better?"

"I called because I feel responsible, and to let you know that by this time tomorrow night, it'll be all over. All your friends are distancing themselves from you. Me included. Got no choice. You're goddamn toxic and nobody, but nobody, is going to want to be associated with you. I called to give you the name of a good lawyer. Forget about using the usual firm. No fucking way they're going near this shit."

"You can take your lawyer and shove him up your ass. I'm gonna ride this out and fucking bury you." Lee hung up. For several long seconds, he glared at his reflection in the windows. The rage built, vibrating up through his feet, his legs, his guts. He ground his teeth together. Luckily, the bathroom was silent. So instead of kicking the door down and dragging Kimmy out by her hair, he whipped his phone at the TV. It bounced off with a small popping noise, leaving a spiderweb of cracks the size of a coaster.

When Ed and Sam had gone into the office, Qween slipped back past the church and into the dormitory, her sneakers silent on the plush carpeting. The mission was a fixture in the neighborhood; it had been around for years. Everybody knew about the homeless men carrying drug money. Few, though, knew about the homeless women and sometimes young men who were enticed with promises of a hot meal, a warm place to sleep, and of course, eternal salvation and taken downstairs, given their own rooms, and told to wait patiently for a select group of clientele, who, as it turned out, liked to inflict a little damage with their love.

She found the door she wanted in the back of the mission and quietly unzipped her bag. She gently squeezed the door handle and twisted. The door opened on a small office.

An older man was asleep at the desk. He was wearing a suit, but it was about ten years out of fashion, faded and tight on his soft, bulging frame. She set the bag on the floor and shut the door, not bothering to be quiet anymore.

The man opened his eyes and blinked as she shot the dead bolt home.

Qween said, "Told you I'd be back."

The man nodded. "I remember you. I remember Jesus wouldn't forgive your sins, no matter how hard we tried to save you."

"You gonna wish Jesus was here to save you, mother-fucker."

He stood. Came around the desk. "I told you that if you set foot in this building again with that foul mouth I would—"

He'd gotten as far as the front of the desk when Qween pulled the bowling ball from her bag and dropped it on his foot. It landed with a jarring crunch and rolled away. He gasped, and bent over to clutch at his ankle, as if the foot hurt too much to touch. He stammered, "I'ma make sure—"

Qween wasn't paying attention. She retrieved her ball and lobbed it at him with an underhanded toss, using both hands. It soared up about six feet. She stopped to catch her breath, and eyed the room. It hadn't changed much in eight years.

The ball landed with a whispered crunch on the base of his spine and the man flopped forward. This time, he couldn't suppress a short scream. One hand shot to the small of his back and the other splayed out for support or mercy, Qween wasn't sure which. She didn't care either way.

Eight years. Long time to carry that much weight. She was

more than ready to unload it on the bastard who had raped her. She noted the same dark cheap wood imitation walls. The same puke-green carpet. The same set of Bibles. The same set of encyclopedias from 1974. Eight years ago the bastard had put a knife on the desk and said that if she gave him any problems, he would take this blade and shove it up her asshole. Then he would watch her try to get help as she slowly bled to death.

He'd smiled. Said either his dick or his knife was going in her ass and it was all up to her.

She picked up the bowling ball yet again and dropped it on his hand. Another scream. This one was long and heartfelt. She dropped the ball again on his broken foot, grinding fractured bones together.

There was a knock on the door. "Qween?" Sam's voice. "You good?" He tried the handle, but the dead bolt held the door.

The man rolled over, trying to find his breath to shout for help. Qween dropped the ball on the guy's crotch. Sour vomit spilled from between his teeth.

Qween called back to the door. "Not yet. But I'm getting there." She picked up the ball again. It was growing heavier.

"You got thirty seconds to finish your business," Sam said. "We're leaving."

Qween struggled to lift the ball higher. The guy was moaning at the floor, good hand held up as if to deflect the bowling ball, wherever it might land. Qween's breath whistled between the wide gaps in her teeth as she planted her feet, squared her hips, and slowly, slowly hefted the ball above her head.

"Oh God, oh God, don't, I have—"

She raised the bowling ball almost a full foot over her head and dropped it on his face.

# CHAPTER 45

They left Tommy alone in front of the TVs for a while to think about what was coming. For a while, he'd fought to maintain perspective, trying to convince himself that people weren't kept in hospitals against their will, that as soon as these doctors realized that he wasn't sick, they would discharge him. He would be allowed to leave. He would see Grace again. Soon.

That had been the old Tommy. The Tommy who had faith. In God. In America. In the government. In people.

The hospital had burned most of this faith right out of him.

Now he fought against the despair that threatened to sweep him away, that sapped his strength, stole his will to live. The throbbing in his head never left. When he did speak, his voice was wavering and weak. He lived on nothing but protein shakes he drank through a straw. His muscles felt slack and useless; he guessed he might have lost at least ten pounds. Maybe fifteen. If things didn't change, he was going to die, virus or not.

Tommy forced himself to slow down and concentrate. He let his eyes glaze over, so the disturbing images on the TVs sank into a blurry haze, and he focused on the face of his daughter in his mind. He could see her smiling. Hear her laugh when they threw the rubber chickens at the Son of Svengoolie. Feel her arms around his neck.

Same as before, two technicians and Sergeant Reaves came in to take him back upstairs. Tommy couldn't tell if it was the same two techs or not, but these looked like they'd been on duty twenty-four hours at least. Their eyes were sunken and dull. They moved like robots in need of oil. No weapons.

He wondered how much the life of a tech was worth to Dr. Reischtal. At first, Tommy would have assumed he could take a hostage to escape. He'd been planning on twisting his head when one of them grabbed the handles of the wheelchair and biting down on the tech's hand, threatening to rip the biohazard suit wide open if they didn't wheel him right out the front door.

Sergeant Reaves, as always, was the problem. He hung back, hands clasped loosely in front of him, eyes missing nothing. Tommy had no doubt he could have his handgun out and squeezing the trigger in less time than it took for Tommy to sneeze. Hell, he'd empty the clip into both Tommy and the tech before anybody could say, "God bless you." And while Tommy was the most desperate he'd ever been in his life, he wasn't suicidal.

They wheeled him out of the conference room. Tommy sank back in his straps on the wheelchair as they rolled him back to the elevator.

Back in the car, Ed asked Qween, "Did you take us back there for the reasons we talked about or for some kinda half-assed payback?"

"Didn't sound half-assed to me," Sam said.

Qween watched the lights slide past the windows. "Little of both, Ed Jones." She didn't say anything else, and seemed oddly contemplative. Whatever had happened back at the mission had calmed her. She sounded at peace with herself and the universe.

Ed didn't like it. "We asked you for help, not for an excuse to seek revenge. We got bigger problems here than you."

Sam nodded. "I know. But listen, we got what we needed. If that was the price, than so be it."

"I just don't like to be used," Ed grumbled. "If it was necessary, I would've been happy to go back there when all this other shit was finished."

"No point in worrying about it now," Sam said. "Like you said, we got other problems. Let's go take a closer look at that address."

Qween laid back on the seat and unfurled her cloak. With the windows rolled up to hold the air-conditioning in against the summer heat, it soon became clear that it had been a while since she had bathed. She pulled up her knees and crossed one leg over the other, her left foot braced against the back passenger window. She let out an "Oh, yeah . . ." that Koko Taylor would be proud of.

"Jesus fucking Christ," Ed said, trying to breathe through his mouth. Sam rolled down his window and stuck his head out, taking deep breaths of the sweltering heat.

Qween laughed. "You two need to get over your own damn selves."

There was no chance to try anything.

They wheeled Tommy out of the elevator and into Don's room without any preamble, just banged him into a door and there was Don. He had been lying so still before they came in that Tommy had thought he might be dead, but the sudden movement startled the large man, and he flinched against his restraints. His eyes, blood red and swollen, slid wildly around his sunken sockets, lighting briefly on Tommy.

There was no sign of recognition.

The techs left before Tommy's wheelchair had stopped moving. Nobody wanted to be in there any longer than necessary. The shock of seeing Don, up close and personal, made Tommy forget about his escape plans for the moment. He stared at his partner.

The skin around Don's stomach had pulled back, revealing a distended organ, while the flesh around his face had simply wilted and hung off his skull like fake eyelashes on a decomposing corpse. Dark saliva collected at the corners of his mouth. He struggled against the straps, but the movements were feeble. Large black bruises had formed along limbs, concentrating in his joints, as if slow-motion car crashes were happening under the skin.

Watching Don on the closed-circuit TV had been bad. This was worse.

Tommy could now actually hear the sounds coming from Don's throat. It wasn't screams exactly, it was more like someone trying to force air through a saxophone that had been buried in the bottom of a swamp for a long time.

The other thing was the smell. Tommy's neighbors composted their own fertilizer when he was a kid. They would dump everything into the box out back of their house. Coffee grounds, leftover eggs, bones, rotten fruit, everything. Every once in a while, the husband would go out and churn the decomposing mess with a pitchfork, bringing the dark matter on the bottom up to the top. Once, Tommy had tried to help. Until the smell attacked him and made him vomit. The neighbor had laughed and scraped the bile and half-digested scrambled eggs and toast into the compost pile with a shovel.

The putrid smell in Don's room reminded him of that decaying organic matter. Tommy breathed through his mouth, trying to be a silent as possible. He wanted Don to forget he was in the room. He wanted Don to rest. He wanted Don to find peace.

But Don wouldn't stop screaming. He was like some malfunctioning machine.

The hoarse cries grated against Tommy's eardrums. After half an hour, he could almost understand why some asshole parents hurt children who wouldn't stop crying. He just wanted it to stop. Finally, after another twenty minutes or so, Don's whispering squeals began to taper off. An hour later, Don was still and quiet once again.

Tommy didn't move. He barely breathed. He was afraid that any movement, any sound at all would trigger Don's panic once again.

After another hour, his own eyelids grew heavy. He fought sleep, because he was afraid of making some kind of unconscious noise, like snoring, or jerking against his own wheelchair straps, reawakening Don.

He was also acutely aware of the two cameras in the room. One was attached to the ceiling, aimed down at the bed. This was the feed that Tommy had been watching down in the conference room. The other camera had been set up on a tripod on the far side of the room, getting a closer view of Don's body. Tommy knew that he was in the shot as well.

Both cameras' red lights were on.

That helped to keep him awake. For a while.

# CHAPTER 46

**9:36 PM**
**August 13**

Lower Wacker was an industrial tunnel that ran along the Chicago River, originally designed for through traffic and deliveries to the buildings above. Ed coasted past the loading dock and they all took a good look. There was nothing special about the dock; it looked like a hundred others that were spaced out along the street.

Ed checked the mirrors. The street was practically deserted. Only a few parked cars dotted the sides. He cruised down another hundred yards, whipped a U-turn at the next intersection, and parked so they could watch the loading dock. A cab passed them, going fast and gaining speed, as if it was nervous about being underground.

"Now what?" Qween asked. She seemed happy to leave the decision making up to the detectives now that they had finished with the homeless shelter.

"Let's sit tight for a while," Ed said. "See if we can't spot anybody going in or out."

Qween grunted. "Shit. You two ain't gonna bust any heads open, I'm goin' to sleep."

Sam popped more nicotine gum and got comfortable. Most of the time, he had about as much patience as a pregnant woman waiting to use the restroom. With stakeouts though, he adjusted, somehow slowing his internal clock, altering his rhythms to endure long periods of sitting still, often watching a home or building where nothing would move for hours. Ed thought it might have something to do with Sam's insomnia. The detectives' combined ability for patience when necessary was part of the reason they worked well as partners.

An hour passed. Two.

This time, Ed was the one getting impatient. "I'm thinking we might be wasting our time out here. Maybe we should take a closer look. See if that door's really locked."

"And if it isn't?"

"Might be a quiet way of getting inside. See if we can't take a look-see."

"And Sleeping Beauty?"

Ed glanced at Qween, snoring in the backseat. "Let her rest."

Sam opened his door, but Ed said in a sharp voice, "Hold up."

A rumbling reached them. Sam eased back into the car, pulling his door closed in a smooth, unhurried motion. Headlights filled the car. Ed and Sam sank down in their seats. The roar of diesel engines grew louder, shaking Lower Wacker.

A convoy of M939 military trucks thundered past the Crown Vic. They were all painted in gray and black camouflage instead of the usual green and brown. The first truck pulled left, bouncing up over the center divider between the heavy concrete columns, then backed up to the loading dock.

Someone had been waiting for the trucks. The heavy loading dock door rolled up as soon as the brake lights flashed, and four soldiers stepped out and opened the flaps at the back of the truck. Dozens more soldiers hopped out and disappeared inside the dock. As soon as the last soldier left, the first truck pulled away and waited fifty yards up the street. The second truck repeated the process. As did the third and the fourth.

There was no confusion, no hesitation. The entire operation was finished in less than three minutes. Ed counted a dozen trucks. He guess there must have been at least twenty to twenty-five soldiers in each truck. The last truck pulled away and the first four soldiers slammed the loading dock door. When they were once again in a line, the trucks smoothly accelerated toward Congress, leaving nothing but a cloud of diesel exhaust in their wake.

Lower Wacker was silent and still.

"I got two-eighty. Three hundred, tops," Sam said.

"Same here," Ed said.

Qween rested her chin on the back of Ed's seat. "So much for your big plan to sneak inside."


The grumbling, rhythmic thud of boots in the hall jerked Tommy out of his sleep. For a moment, he wasn't sure where he was. He remembered a faint sense of being in his parents' kitchen, the vague memory of sitting in the old vinyl chairs and a whisper of the smell of bacon. It was nothing of particular importance, not really, but for some reason, it all seemed very special. Even as he clung to the image, the smell, the comforting sense of safety, the memory or dream slipped through his grasping fingers, like wisps of fog in the sunlight.

The figure on the bed came into focus and everything came rushing back. The hospital, the rats, Dr. Reischtal, Grace in danger, all of it. Tommy froze, afraid he had awakened Don, and he couldn't stand to watch his partner writhe and scream anymore.

Don was already awake. His mouth was open, but Tommy couldn't hear anything.

Don's mouth was full of black, clotted blood. He vomited, spraying bloody chunks across his right arm and the side of the mattress. His nose bled in a steady stream. It leaked from his eyes.

The blackened tongue tried to push the viscous fluid out of his mouth so he could breathe. He sucked in a gurgling breath, enough to galvanize the oxygen-deprived muscles, and he spewed out more of the thick, rotten glop with a wet, gagging sound.

Globules hit the carpet and quivered like half-digested Jell-O.

Tommy twisted his ankles against the straps and strained to reach the floor. His bare toes managed to graze the plastic. The slick sheet slid against the tile floor underneath, stopping any movement of the wheelchair. He shoved his hips forward, putting more weight on the restraints. This time he gained enough traction to push the wheels backwards an inch.

On the bed, Don continued to shiver and flail. The sad, liquid sound of the expulsion of gas came from underneath him. The unbearable stench of shit and blood and rotten flesh filled the room. An impossible amount of blood kept erupting from his mouth, steadily pumping it out of his body and onto the bed and floor.

Tommy threw his body into pushing himself backward, one squeaking inch at a time. He didn't think the virus could spread through the air; if that was the case, the whole bar full of Streets and Sans guys would have come down with it. No, the virus probably wasn't airborne, but he sure as hell didn't want any infected blood touching his skin.

He heard a soft *pop* and froze. It felt like one of the leather restraints had torn, just a bit, but he didn't want to give it away. The problem was, he wasn't sure which leg might have torn. He looked around, and found he was nearly back against the door. There wasn't much else he could do. If the virus was now airborne, then he was dead. If it wasn't, then hopefully he was far enough away from Don to avoid contamination.

He forced himself to concentrate on the wheelchair. He mimed rocking around, still thrashing against his restraints for a while, but he was actually trying to read anything he could off of the wheelchair. He discovered that it had a certification sticker on the arm, and this particular wheelchair's certification was over fifteen years old. If the leather had not been taken care of properly, it could be brittle by now. That might be what he'd heard. He thought about that faint tearing sound, lingering in the air for a quarter second. Maybe less. Wondered if THEY had heard it. Wondered if it truly had torn something major, something that he could tear completely away, or if it was nothing, just a cruel joke to get his hopes up.

Don flopped against the bed, still vomiting. He was blind now; two pools of blood filled his eye sockets. The thrashing slowed. His fingers fluttered. The legs stopped moving. The chest rose, sank, rose once more, then slowly sank. It did not rise again. Blood bubbled out of the mouth, pulled by gravity, instead of forced out by muscle contraction.

Don was dead.

# CHAPTER 47

Dr. Reischtal hated meetings. They gave everybody the illusion their opinions were important. That they had some kind of right to be included in making decisions. Especially the slob, Dr. Menard or something. Dr. Reischtal didn't care if he was one of the top vector-borne virus men in the country. He seemed to still think that he was part of a team.

And he wasn't the only one. Dr. Halsey had actually had the audacity to challenge his decision regarding Krazinsky, in front of the others, no less. Dr. Reischtal promised himself that she would pay for that deliberate breach of protocol. Once this current situation had been resolved, she would never again work on anything at the federal level.

The insubordination was spreading. Instead of following their orders, some of these doctors seemed to think it was their duty to "think outside the box." Dr. Reischtal would like to rip out the fingernails of whoever had come up with that asinine phrase, but he had to admit, even he found himself using it on occasion. Nevertheless, it was beyond him why these doctors and scientists couldn't simply do what they were told.

It was time to remind them who was in charge.

"I would like to begin by clearing away any misconceptions." Dr. Reischtal glared around the table. Everyone had stopped talking and stared at his biohazard suit when he strode into the room. No one was sure right off if they were supposed to be taking such extreme precautions outside the patients' rooms. They were dressed in scrubs, mostly because they hadn't had a chance to change.

Dr. Reischtal drew it out, knowing he had their full attention. "You were brought here because you are expert virologists. To decipher this organism, we need your full cooperation, and that means—"

Dr. Menard raised his hand. "Is this a test or something, doctor?" He gestured at the hazmat suit.

"I can assure you this is no test. For myself, the suit is a necessity. If you do not feel that is it necessary . . . that is your decision."

"What are you not telling us?"

"You are being told everything you need to know. Now, as I was saying—"

Dr. Menard held his hand up again, like a kid in fifth grade who has to go to the bathroom. "Need to know? What does that mean? You mean to say that you have information that you won't tell me?"

"Possibly. I am providing you with the information that you will find important. Is that clear?"

"Not really. What information?"

"I can assure you—"

"We're all dealing with a drastic virus here. Something that's dangerous as all hell. If you know anything else, you are obligated to let us all know. So, is there any news on Mr. Krazinsky?"

Dr. Reischtal fixed Dr. Menard with an ice-cold stare. For a moment, all anyone could hear was Dr. Reischtal's metallic, amplified breathing. "Tell me, Doctor . . . Menard, is it? Tell me, Dr. Menard, is it customary to interrupt your superiors out west, or wherever it is you are from?"

"I just want some straight answers. I—and I think I speak for many of us here in this room—we're sick and tired of all the limited information and clandestine bullshit around here."

"I concur," Dr. Halsey said. "What about the original patient, Mr. Wycza? What is his status? I am hearing reports that his door is locked." She clicked her pen as if it were a weapon.

Dr. Reischtal drummed his gloved fingers on the table. Rather than face a full-scale mutiny, he decided to pacify the usurpers. For now. For later, he had methods of dealing with troublemakers like Dr. Menard and Dr. Halsey. And if they would not listen to reason, there was always a solution to be found in Sergeant Reaves.

"Very well," Dr. Reischtal said. "Mr. Krazinsky is resting comfortably. As for Mr. Wycza, I regret to inform you that he passed away earlier this evening."

"Why were we not notified? Who is doing the autopsy?" Dr. Halsey demanded. "I would like to observe."

"There will be no immediate autopsy. The remains are far too infectious and the room is contaminated beyond measure. My team will be responsible for all postmortem investigations."

Dr. Halsey muttered under her breath, "This is absurd."

"If there are no more interruptions," Dr. Reischtal continued, "we now have a timeline for the virus. Mr. Wycza was the first living host that we were able to examine. We also have a fairly accurate timeline. Once infected, estimates place the host's life expectancy at approximately ninety to one hundred hours."

"Four days. Jesus," Dr. Menard said. "Is Mr. Krazinsky displaying any symptoms yet?"

"Mr. Krazinsky's symptomology does not follow the usual pattern, no."

"Then why the hell do you still have him on a floor with a known contamination?"

"I believe he is a carrier."

"This virus has shown zero inclination to simply ride along in a host. It is destroying every single infected patient in this hospital as we speak. And yet, you insist on keeping an otherwise healthy, non-infected patient within close contact with other patients."

Dr. Reischtal placed his hands flat on the table. "Do you not understand that this individual had more contact with the infected rat than Mr. Wycza? By all logic, the virus should have spread through his system like wildfire. Why is it that the disease ravages anyone else that gets close, but Mr. Krazinsky has remained untouched? There are many, many unanswered questions about this man."

Dr. Menard frowned. "There are many, many unanswered questions about your methods, doctor."

Dr. Reischtal struggled not to draw his hands into fists. "I would suggest, Dr. Menard, that you choose your words carefully. It appears that you are obsessing over a single individual that may hold valuable clues to a virus with the power to wipe out the other three million human beings in this city, if not the entire country. We are on the precipice of an outbreak the likes of which this world has never seen. That, Dr. Menard, is my responsibility." He saw no reason to discuss how insects were transmitting the virus. It would only serve to muddy the waters and distract them from focusing on a way to defeat the virus. He would leave the decision on when to reveal the truth to the President, and deal with the fallout at that point. If these people were beyond saving when that happened, then so be it.

His gaze swept the room. Even through the plastic faceplate, his stare held an almost physical impact. "I would encourage my fellow doctors to, if you feel I am in any way failing in my capacity as special investigator to unknown viruses, please, by all means, speak up. Voice your dissent."

The table was silent. Dr. Menard tried to meet everyone's eyes, but no one would look up from their notes. Even

Dr. Halsey placed her hands in her lap, endlessly twisting her wedding ring.

"I believe you stand corrected, Dr. Menard," Dr. Reischtal.

Dr. Menard met Dr. Reischtal's glare. "Intimidation may achieve results, but it is temporary and has many unanticipated consequences. Remember that. In the long run, the truth will come out. It always does. This entire operation is a farce, for chrissakes."

Dr. Reischtal said, "I will not tolerate blasphemy. Watch your language."

"What?"

"As a man of science, you may find matters of faith contemptible. I, however, do not."

"Goddamnit!" Dr. Menard pounded on the table. "Explain yourself! You are putting every single one of us at risk, not to mention the rest of the population of the city. You need to be held accountable."

Dr. Reischtal spoke slowly, carefully enunciating each word. "This is your last warning, Dr. Menard. I will not tolerate any more dissension on this team. I sincerely hope you understand."

"Or what? Or what? Is that a threat? You'll sic your attack dog on me? Huh? Your shadow?"

Sergeant Reaves, leaning against the wall near the door, did not change his blank expression. His eyes, dull and lifeless, stared out at the room, focusing on nothing and everything at the same time.

Dr. Menard said, "We're not fooled. These soldiers, they're not part of the U.S. Armed Forces, so who are they? Who do they work for?"

Dr. Reischtal picked up the conference room phone and said, "Please escort Dr. Menard from the property."

Dr. Menard stood and it became clear that he was a fairly large man. "What if I decide not to leave? What are you going to do, shoot me?"

Sergeant Reaves remained motionless.

"Only if you make it necessary." Dr. Reischtal gave a thin smile.

The doors swung open. Two soldiers stood at attention. Behind them, the hallway was filled with more soldiers. Dozens and dozens of them. The entire line bristled with the black muzzles of assault rifles, as if the men were a single organism, a spiked, heavy metal caterpillar.

The two soldiers entered the room, split apart, and came to rest on either side of Dr. Menard. He refused to acknowledge them. Instead, he pulled out a pack of cigarettes, put one between his lips.

Dr. Reischtal said, "Dr. Menard, I certainly hope you understand there is absolutely no smoking in this facility."

Dr. Menard mumbled around the cigarette, "Blow me." The soldiers walked him out.

Dr. Reischtal spread his hands, swept his gaze across the room one more time. "I certainly hope everyone can appreciate how crucial our work is here. If the virus spreads any further, this situation could be nothing less then the end of times."

# CHAPTER 48

*10:29 PM*
*August 13*

Sam was just about to say, "Let's go get a drink," when the door rolled up on the loading dock once again, and a large man in a white lab coat stepped outside. The door rolled shut behind him. He looked up and down the street for a moment, lit the cigarette clamped between his teeth, and ambled south.

Ed and Sam exchanged glances. Ed nodded and twisted the key. He hit the gas and pulled up alongside the large, shaggy man. Sam had the door open and his pistol out before Ed had even stopped. "Chicago PD. Get in the car."

The man gaped at them, cigarette halfway to his mouth. "I'm sorry, what?"

Sam said, "Shut the fuck up and get in the car." He opened the back door.

The man looked up and down the deserted street as if seeking any witnesses, then climbed in the backseat with Qween. Sam kicked the door shut and jumped back into the front seat. Ed headed south in a short squeal of rubber.

Sam twisted in his seat to face the big man and found that Qween already had a straight razor buried in the guy's straggly beard, pressed firmly against his throat. The big man was holding his chin so high the top of his head brushed against the ceiling of the Crown Vic.

"You just sit still now, you hear?" Qween said.

Sam had no idea where the hell she'd been hiding a straight razor. "Easy, Qween. He's not going anywhere, are you, pal?"

The big man's stare went from Qween to Sam to Ed, then to the buildings whipping past. Ed hadn't slowed down yet; the car was approaching fifty miles an hour as it roared through the empty downtown streets.

"Suit yourself," Qween said and slipped the razor back into the folds of her cloak.

The big man swallowed. Sam could tell he wanted to touch his throat to see if it was bleeding or not, but fear kept his hands frozen in his lap.

Sam said, "What's your name?"

"David Menard."

"You a doctor?"

"Yes. Dr. David Menard."

"You work at that hospital."

"No. Yes, well, I mean, I don't know how to—"

Sam tapped him sharply on the forehead with the barrel of his pistol. "I want some straight fucking answers, you got me? You try to lie to me one more time and I'll let my girl here cut your balls off."

"I wasn't lying! Swear to Christ, I'm not lying."

"Let's hear it then."

Dr. Menard talked so fast that at first, it sounded like the babbling of one of the speed freaks they would occasionally confront in an interrogation. "I was working there, yes. Me and others. The CDC brought us in to work with their team. I study viruses, that's my real job. This, this was something— I got a call in the middle of the night, telling me to pack up. Hopped on a plane in Sacramento, and they flew me out here. Next thing I know, we're studying a new virus. From the little bit I've been allowed to see, parts of three floors, I do know this. There are a large number of seriously ill patients back there and God help us if there's any more."

"Why?"

"If this spreads, we're . . . over. I've never seen anything like this. Nobody has seen anything like this. This is . . . this virus, they don't even have a name for it yet."

"How do you catch it?"

"We don't know exactly. Based on the information we've been given, it appears that close proximity to a rat that is carrying the virus can be a source of the infection. It is certainly present in the rat saliva, much like rabies."

Ed and Sam glanced at Qween. She ignored them.

"But that doesn't explain all of the cases," Dr. Menard said. "Many of the initial patients were homeless individuals, and therefore, we had to assume that because of their lifestyle, contact with a rat was certainly possible, if not likely, since the infected rats have shown to be quite aggressive. But within the last twelve hours, the number of patients that presumably would have no reason to be near a rat skyrocketed."

Sam interrupted, "Just exactly how many patients are in there now?"

Dr. Menard shook his head. "I don't know. Fifty. A hundred. Two hundred? I'm sorry. Dr. Reischtal, he's in charge, and he kept all records classified."

"Why?" Ed asked.

"I have no idea. Look, I don't know what to say. We just started two days ago. Nobody has had any sleep." Dr. Menard rubbed his face. "All we know is that it appears to be fatal in every case of infection."

"What are the symptoms?" Ed asked.

"At first, apparently nothing. The patients sometimes fall into a deep sleep, when they awake, they often suffer extreme discomfort on the surface of the skin."

"What kind of discomfort?" Ed asked.

Dr. Menard gave a heavy sigh. "They itch," he said, meeting Ed's eyes in the rearview mirror. "It must be awful. We have been observing patient after patient claw at their skin until they bleed. Back in my grad school days, I worked with addicts going through withdrawal, serious stuff, and I never encountered anything like this. And then, at some point, they begin to act . . . irrationally."

"They get violent as fuck," Ed said.

Sam glanced at Qween again, hearing the screams from the homeless shelter.

Dr. Menard nodded slowly. "Yes. Postmortem examinations of some of the bodies, people that had been shot and killed by the police—after the attacks, you know—they have revealed some clues about the damage the virus causes, but not nearly enough. The problem is, we have gotten so few specimens with undamaged tissue, it's been impossible to tell what the effects of the virus actually are." He gave a hollow laugh. "One guy got hit by an SUV. All that was left fit into a box this big." He held his hands about two feet apart. "What little we do know is that it appears to attack the amygdala. You're familiar with the term, 'amygdala hijack'?" He caught the blank looks of the other three. "Okay. 'Road Rage.' I'm sure you have encountered this in your jobs. There's an over-whelming sense of fury, when someone just snaps."

"Sounds like a few domestic disputes I've seen."

"I would imagine so, yes. But this, this is something else. Increase that fury by tenfold. Maybe fifty, a hundred. This is all such guesswork at this point. We need literally years of research before we'll know anything for sure. Anyway, as far as we can tell, the virus seems to travel along the peripheral nervous system and it shoots straight into the limbic system of our brains, specifically the amygdala. They're two little buds, tucked away deep inside your head. If you were to drill straight through here and here"—Dr. Menard pointed at his right eye and right ear—"you'd find it at the intersection of those lines. The amygdala is one of the oldest parts of the brain. It controls emotions like fear and anger. You've heard of 'fight or flight,' right?"

Ed and Sam nod.

"The lizard part," Sam said.

"No. You're thinking of stuff like keeping your heart going, breathing, blood in your brain, that kind of thing. This is a step higher on the evolutionary ladder. The amygdala dumps tons of adrenaline and cortisone into your system, so you can run. Fight. Take action, whatever. The thing is, there's no direct connection between the prefrontal lobe"—Dr. Menard tapped his forehead—"and the amygdala. The body doesn't want to waste any time thinking about what it should do when it's in danger. It has to react. Immediately. And that's the problem here. The virus attacks the prefrontal lobe. We don't know why. Maybe it likes the taste. It multiplies astonishingly fast, wiping out your ability to think with any reasoning or logic. Meanwhile, while it is destroying the prefrontal lobe, it is attaching itself to the amygdala, causing the body to go into overdrive."

"So it's driving people crazy," Ed said.

Dr. Menard gave a slow shrug. "I guess you could say that, yes. It is literally driving them mad with fear. With the amygdala going berserk, and the prefrontal lobes being chewed up and spit out . . . the infected are unable to stop themselves. They're unable to think logically. And so they lash out. Violently. A lot of times, it's sound that triggers the rage. Like with rabies. In the later stages, the virus attacks the rest of the body, causing massive internal bleeding. You've heard of the Ebola virus? It literally liquefies your insides. Ebola and rabies are similar, in many respects."

"Where did it come from?" Sam asked. "Why did it show up in the rats?"

Dr. Menard shook his head and shrugged again. "It is believed that an infected bat escaped from an animal smuggler at O'Hare and somehow passed the virus along to the rats."

Sam and Ed exchanged a look.

"All we know is that it appears to move slower in rats. They can survive for a month or two, sometimes three. We don't know why it takes more time with them. Humans . . . it takes only three, four days."

Ed whipped through streets, unusually quiet in the night hours, heading north. Dr. Menard, still anxious and unable to stop talking, said, "I can't get the beginning from Poe's story out of my head."

Nobody said anything for a moment. "I don't know about you two," Sam said, nodding at Ed and Qween, "but I'm a proud product of the American public school system and I don't have a goddamn clue what you're talking about."

Dr. Menard said, "Poe. Edgar Allan. You know him. *The Tell-Tale Heart*. Surely you read it in high school."

Sam shrugged.

Dr. Menard cleared his throat. "'True!—nervous—very, very dreadfully nervous I had been and am; but why will you say that I am mad?'" He quoted haltingly from his memory. "'The disease had sharpened my senses—not destroyed—not dulled. Above all was the sense of hearing acute. I heard all things in the heaven and in the earth. I heard many things in hell. How, then, am I mad?'"

For a long time, nobody said anything else.

Eventually, Sam stared out the window, chewing on a new piece of gum, said, "I still say sooner or later it all comes down to the lizard part."

# CHAPTER 49

**10:33 PM**
**August 13**

Dr. Reischtal held his phone up, listening to it ring, as he double-checked his suit for any rips or tears. He had a roll of duct tape ready, in case.

A click. "Yeah?" The voice was dry as smoke.

Dr. Reischtal said, "Good evening, Mr. Evans. I have a job for you."

The voice at the other end was quiet for a moment.

Dr. Reischtal was patient. He understood his call was not good news. "I need you to gather a team of drivers and pick up a special cargo from our mutual friends out in Denver, and arrange transportation to Chicago."

"How large is the cargo?"

"You will need at least thirty rigs."

"Where the hell am I gonna get thirty drivers right now?"

Dr. Reischtal said, "That, Mr. Evans, is your problem. I will expect the entirety of this cargo on its way to Chicago within six hours."

\* \* \*

Tommy sat in his wheelchair, facing the corpse, and waited. Waited for someone to notice that Don was dead. Waited for someone to come get him. Waited to get sick. The fluorescents hummed and flickered almost imperceptibly, casting a twitching glare throughout the room. Air hissed from the filters. Blood dripped from Don's bed.

Tommy watched the puddle on the right side grow larger. He winced at the spatter when each drop hit the puddle. He couldn't stop imagining what happened when the drops hit the plastic, sending microscopic slivers of voracious organisms, tiny explosions of death, naked to the human eye, as it scattered the virus into the air of the room.

Maybe he was already infected. Maybe that was why the drops of blood splashing against the plastic sounded so loud in the stillness of the room.

The other side of Don's bed started to leak, creating a new puddle.

A speck of movement, down near Don's bare feet. Tommy squinted, but saw nothing else. Maybe it was simply the maddening stuttering of the fluorescent tubes, creating buzzing, shadowy static among the tufts of hair along the top of Don's feet.

Tommy wondered if the virus was already in his system, wondering if he was about to face the long sleep, followed by the horrible itching, until finally the rage rocketed through his system, and he had to endure the agony of spending his last days, screaming hoarsely, pathetic, weak, strapped to a goddamn hospital bed.

Something definitely moved on Don's skin. Tommy blinked, squinted again. There. It was a bug. Something reddish-brown, creeping along like a crab, although it wasn't any bigger than one of the spatters of blood on the floor. He wondered if Don had lice. The bug scurried across the mattress and disappeared behind the rails.

A thought struck him, and he forgot about the bug. This

thought was something that he deeply understood to be true, but had never dived deep to examine. Now, faced with the icy, stark recognition, Tommy knew he was going to die. This was something most people held off at a distance. It fades into the background. Nobody but the suicidal and teenage goths linger intentionally in that part of the mind.

There was no pushing it away. He was going to die. One way or another, sooner or later, he was going to die. It might be the virus now, it might be some organ or another falling apart when he was an old man, seventy or eighty. He would've preferred to live to old age, but he started to understand that either way, quick or painful, he wanted to die having lived his life as best he could, taking care of himself and his family.

He remembered the tune, and a couple of words, to an old Monty Python song that his old man used to listen to once in a while. He couldn't remember much of the words so much as the intent, to remind you that you live in a universe hell bent on reaching for infinity, and you were but a speck of nothing. . . . However, the simple fact of your birth amid such vastness told the math to go to hell.

He understood the universe was entirely indifferent to his existence. He could not look to anyone for help. His parents? God bless 'em, but they couldn't make it to Dominick's for the weekly groceries without getting lost. Kimmy had stopped caring where he was at least four years ago.

His partner was dead.

And his boss wanted him here.

There was no one else. No one but Grace.

Tommy slumped in the wheelchair, fighting to slow his galloping heart. The panic fed at his consciousness like a fast-moving fungus, crawling underneath his sanity, tugging gently, looking for weak spots.

He tested the straps again, listening for that elusive sound of leather or thread ripping. Nothing. The restraints might as well have been made of steel. He pulled harder, harder. There was no give, no tearing noise, no nothing. Had he imagined the sound earlier?

He struggled to slow his breathing. Tried to refocus. Tried to think of anything except the fact that he was strapped to a wheelchair and locked in a room with a corpse. He found himself staring at the figure on the bed.

There should have been some sort of peace, now that Don was dead. His partner wasn't screaming anymore. He wasn't thrashing around, he was simply motionless.

Tommy decided the silence was worse. The stillness was worse. He tried to remind himself of how tortured Don had sounded, but already the memory was beginning to fade, that sound of utter hopelessness was gone, and all that was left was complete fucking silence and so all Tommy could focus on was his own hope, his own faith, that somehow it would all somehow work out in the end, and that the universe or God or whatever would recognize that he had been a decent, caring human being.

There wasn't much left of that feeling.

God did not care.

The universe did not care.

There was nothing left inside.

It was either fight or die.

And fighting was futile.

# PHASE 5

# CHAPTER 50

OMG. Mr. Ullman could be such a *bitch*.

No, Janelle decided as she rubbed her temples, *bitch* wasn't strong enough. He was a cocksucker, that's what he was. The city was half deserted, and hardly anybody was left in the whole damn Fin, but he wanted her here right at the crack of dawn. Didn't he know that she had a life outside of this friggin' job?

Apparently not. He met her at the employee entrance, all looming angles and aggressive cologne. Yes. Yes, Mr. Ullman. Of course she would give today everything she had. Oh, yes, you cocksucker.

*It's your own fault*, a voice said inside her throbbing head. The voice belonged to her roommate, Brandi. Now Brandi, she was a bitch; that was for sure. Yes. Brandi was a bitch, and Mr. Ullman was a cocksucker. That declaration felt right, but it didn't ease Janelle's hangover.

She sat by herself behind the desk in the grand lobby for ten minutes, and quickly realized that if she didn't make it to the restroom, there was going to be a mess that she didn't want to explain. Instead of using the more convenient restroom on the first floor, she decided it was imperative that she reach the employees-only bathroom downstairs. She hated going number two at work, and would avoid it if at all possible, but this morning was an emergency. She knew that very few employees would be around at this time of the day, and she could probably slip in and get out before anybody came in and smelled what she'd left.

Janelle massaged her temple and squeezed the bridge of her nose with her left hand while her right clutched the stairway railing. She eased her way downstairs, down the concrete steps to the employees-only restroom. Why the hell had she decided to wear her highest heels this morning? Any other day, she could practically run a marathon in any of her shoes, but right now, the tequila and tacos from last night at Taco Loco were threatening to erupt, and Janelle, quite frankly, wasn't sure which orifice they might spew from. The way she felt, the contents of her entire intestinal tract might just squirt from her goddamn ears.

*You knew you had to be at work at six, so quit 'cher bitchin'*, Brandi's voice sang in her aching head. Brandi, that tanned bitch, didn't have to be at work today. Brandi worked at some chic travel agency, fawning over rich pricks and gushing about Caribbean vacations all damn day, but her boss had told her to stay home until this mess with the rat flu was straightened out. So she was home, curled up in her bed in their apartment in Lincoln Park.

And to top it off, Janelle's period had hit with a vengeance last night. She'd slapped the shit out of her alarm clock only to find her eight-hundred-thread-count sheets spotted with blood. She couldn't win. She'd dragged the sheets and comforter off the bed, praying she hadn't stained the mattress, and dumped the mess in a corner of her room. Somehow, she'd managed to find her way into the shower, where she'd watched the sad remnants of last night's chicken and lettuce collect on the silver holes of the drain after she vomited. Twice.

Still. She'd made it to work, even with only half the buses running. So fuck everybody. Who cared if she could barely walk. She'd punched in, dammit. And just like she had thought, there was nothing happening at work. Nobody was checking out, and there sure as hell wasn't anybody checking in. Not at six in the fucking morning anyway. And the thing of it was, nobody else was at work either. That was the worst part. She'd been the only one dumb enough, the only one desperate enough, to actually come in to work.

Last night, you would have thought that the whole rat-flu thing would have scared everybody off, but God, she'd never seen Rush Street so crowded. The bars, the clubs, everything was full. There was this vibe in the air. Janelle couldn't quite put her finger on it, but it was as if the thought of danger had amplified the desire to escape into music and alcohol and lust. Everybody was going crazy, even the bartenders. She hadn't bought one drink all night. She couldn't move two steps in any direction without bumping into cute guys. She still couldn't quite figure out how she and Brandi had ended up back at their place by themselves. Maybe it was for the best. She did have to work the next day after all.

Once downstairs, she was in luck. The women's restroom was empty. It wasn't nearly as extravagant as the guest restroom just off the lobby, but here, she knew she probably wasn't in any danger of being disturbed. She stumbled past the sink to the two stalls, locking the handicapped door behind her. She wriggled her pencil skirt down to her knees and sank gratefully onto the toilet.

She set her phone on the toilet roll dispenser and pulled out her tampon. Just as she had thought, it was soaked. The sight and smell of the blood threatened to make her gorge rise, and that was the last thing she needed, to puke all over her panties and skirt, which were sketchy enough anyway, while she sat on the friggin' toilet.

She gritted her teeth as her body evacuated what felt like white-hot lava into the bowl while she pinched the tampon string. She couldn't dispose of it because some idiot, most likely a cock-sucking *man* who had no idea what he was doing, had installed the receptacle out of reach of anybody sitting on the toilet. Beads of sweat popped out on her forehead and she tried to only breathe through her mouth.

The thought of the used tampon dangling from her hand made her stomach roll uneasily yet again, and in a moment of rage, she simply threw the damn tampon at the uncomfortable box on the wall. The tampon bounced off, leaving a streak of clotted red viscera, and dropped to the floor.

If she made it through the day without staining her clothes, she promised herself a long hot bath tonight, to hell with the period, and a glass of red wine. And if Brandi wanted in the bathroom, well then, too damn bad.

Janelle started to see how this was all Brandi's fault anyway. Sure, Brandi would blame her, but who had been dragging whom to the bar for all those flaming shots with those DePaul frat boys? The more she thought about it, the more she thought Brandi needed to be suffering right along with her.

She fumbled for her phone and knocked it off the toilet paper dispenser. It bounced on the tiled floor and came to rest out of sight, behind and under her. "Really? Really?" she said under her breath, eyes on the ceiling as her fingers swept across the tiles, searching.

Something heavy, with matted, wet fur brushed against the back of her hand.

Janelle shrieked and jerked her hand back.

The thing hissed at her and scrabbled across the floor, darting through her stall, before disappearing around the corner to the sink.

The awful sensation of being chained to the toilet seat as seemingly everything inside of her, including all of her internal organs, slid into the bowl finally passed, and she cautiously bent over, peering under the stall wall. The bathroom was empty.

She sat back, worried that the fear might make her vomit.

She tried to control her breathing. In through the nose, out through the mouth. Relax. It was just a rat.

She gave a hitching exhale, like she was sliding down an icy road and flinched every time she bounced over crack. Just a rat. It was gone, under the door. She wasn't happy to see a rat in the restroom on the best of days, but now, with all that flu stuff in the news, it made her want to cry.

She sniffed, looking at the ceiling again, determined not to smudge her mascara. She looked bad enough as it was. She bent down again, this time looking at the phone. It sat by itself. No more rats. Staring at the phone, she could think of one person that deserved to share her misery. It was the least she could do.

Brandi's groggy voice said, "Oh, you bitch."

"Oh, don't 'oh bitch' me, you bitch," Janelle said. "You won't believe me. I just saw a rat. I'm dying in here, and there's a damn rat running on the floor."

Underneath her, out of her sight, two bedbugs wriggled out from under the toilet, where the bowl was bolted onto the floor. It had been sloppily sealed with silicone and the bugs oozed from a small gap. More bugs followed.

Brandi yawned. "You called me 'cause of that, are you kidding me?"

"Don't you know anything? The rats, you know, the rat flu?"

Brandi grunted sleepily, said, "Yeah, that's awful."

A steady line of bugs emerged through the hole under the toilet. More crawled from the air vent in the ceiling.

Brandi yawned again.

"Oh, no. No. There's no way you get to go to sleep. Don't you hang up. I'll keep calling. There's nobody at work. So don't think I won't. I'll call and call and call, and you're gonna have to talk to me sooner or later so it might as well be now, bitch."

Bugs burst from the gap between the toilet tank and the wall and marched steadily down the wall.

A fresh spasm jolted Janelle's abdomen and she closed her

eyes, riding the latest wave out. Brandi heard the sounds and wrinkled her nose, "Are you fucking kidding me? Please don't, oh no. You're in the bathroom right now, aren't you? Oh. My. God. You are sooooo disgusting."

"Bitch, please. Don't. Just talk to me. I just wanna die."

"I know. I'm sorry. It's okay. That bathroom, what? It's in the basement, you told me. So it's probably just a rat that's trying to get to shelter or something. It doesn't care about you. It's gonna be okay. Really."

"But what about the disease?"

"It's only if they bite you or something. So just chill, you're okay, okay?"

The spasm passed, and Janelle wondered if she should dare to wipe herself and insert a new tampon. She had to get used to that thought for a while, and rested her head on her knees. Through half-closed eyes, she watched a little bug trundle confidently along between her shoes. She blinked, and watched the bug move with a purpose, straight to the used tampon.

The bloody cotton tube was crawling with insects.

She gasped and jerked her feet off the floor. "Oh my god. Oh my god."

"What? What's wrong?"

"You won't believe this. Oh my god."

"What?"

"This, this is how my morning is going. I'm not even going to try to tell you." Janelle gave an unhinged giggle. "You need to see this yourself so you can see. I'm going to send you a video."

"Oh, come on, I—"

Janelle hung up. Clicked on CAMERA, then switched over to VIDEO. Bracing her feet on the walls, she got a shot of the tampon, with what looked like fat red ants clambering all over it. She zoomed in. The lighting was awful, and the zoom didn't do much but blow up all the pixels, but it looked like the insects were relishing the fresh blood. She zoomed back out to give some perspective. Several lines of bugs marched on the used tampon, all from under her toilet.

She scratched absentmindedly at her waist with her left hand, still focused on the phone in her right. The sight of the bugs had not sickened her; they hadn't added to her nausea. Instead, she found the movement and documentation of the bugs fascinating. The opportunity to prove to her roommate that this morning was by far the worst morning in the history of the world was enough to satisfy her and settle her gag reflex.

Even when she looked away from the phone's display and saw that the bugs had moved up the toilet en masse and were now crawling across her thighs was not cause for immediate panic. She stood, forgetting the lines of bugs that crisscrossed the floor, and experimentally tried to brush the bugs off her torso. They weren't much bigger than bell pepper seeds, and clung to her skin with the same stubborn tenacity as those same seeds, resisting being washed away by the kitchen sink faucet or even the vegetable knife.

She finally realized that the bugs were now surging up her high heels and up her legs, settling on her bare skin and latching on somehow. Before, when she had first seen the bugs, there had been dozens. Now, there were hundreds, maybe even thousands, jockeying for position, fighting to find an empty patch of skin, so they could sink their strange, undulating teeth into her exposed flesh.

And only then did she start slapping at the bugs. She might have been slapping at the wind. The bugs continued to rise from the floor, unfolding up her legs like a horrible wave. She grabbed at her skirt and tried to pull it up in a vain attempt to stop the bugs from crawling into her pubic region.

The bugs though, smelled blood, and flowed up her legs and wriggled under her damp panties.

Janelle jerked the bolt open and stumbled out of the stall.

The bugs had reached her armpits. Her heels slipped. The phone dropped from her hands as she reached out for support. Dizzy from the loss of blood, she fell into the wall, and sank to the floor. There was time for a final exhale, and the bugs swarmed over her skull, crawling into her open mouth. Her nose. Her eyes.

# CHAPTER 51

They spent the night at the bar until the bartender kicked them out at four. Ed, Qween, and Dr. Menard crashed at Sam's apartment, while Sam sat in the kitchen, chewing nicotine gum and drinking ice water. When the sun filled the kitchen, he woke everyone up and they wordlessly piled back into the car.

Ed decided to go out for breakfast at The Golden Waffle. They filed inside, exhausted. The place was empty except for one cab driver who didn't want to go home to his wife. A sleepy waitress gestured at the empty dining room and told them to sit anywhere they felt like. The cook eyeballed them from inside the kitchen as if they'd interrupted something important.

The meal was a quiet affair. When they were finished, Sam took the check and told the waitress, "More coffee."

They sipped their coffee in silence. Qween finished her mug and snapped her fingers to get the waitress's attention. She pointed at the empty cup and waddled off to the bathroom.

When she was out of earshot, Sam spread his hands, palms

out, and looked Dr. Menard in the eye. "Sorry about the tap on the head there. I jumped to conclusions. I ah . . . sorry."

Dr. Menard touched the raw spot on his forehead and winced. He shrugged. "I'll live. Could have been worse, I guess."

"Things can always be worse," Ed said. "You'll have to accept our unofficial apologies for the time being. You want to file a complaint or anything like that, I suppose somebody might get back to you in a couple of months. Or years. There's not much rush to investigate things when cops overstep their bounds here, you understand."

Dr. Menard shook his head. "Understood."

The waitress refilled their mugs. More customers trickled inside. The place grew louder.

"So what now?" Dr. Menard asked.

"We find ourselves a bar, baby," Qween said, settling back into the booth.

"Damned if I've got a better idea," Sam said.

"I could go to the media," Dr. Menard said. "Let people know what's really going on down here. Get the public's attention. You guys know somebody at the newspapers or one of the TV stations, right?"

Sam snorted and shook his head. As a general rule, detectives did not hang out with anybody associated with the media.

"Maybe," Ed said. "I got maybe someone that would listen."

Sam was curious. "Who the hell do you talk to?"

Ed said, "None of your damn business."

Sam grinned. "Oh, now I know. It's that short one, that poor girl they send out to car crashes and bad weather."

"Yeah. So what." A pause. "Don't you dare tell Carolina."

"Never."

Ed wandered away to make the call. They heard him say, "Is this the famous hotshot girl reporter, Cecilia Palmers?" and laugh.

Qween said, "I already tried this, and nobody listened."

Sam said, "I know, Qween. I know. It was a good plan. Wish to hell somebody had listened. Maybe things would be different. All we can do now is let folks know the inside story. Put some pressure on these assholes."

Ed slid back into the booth. "It's all set. We're gonna meet Cecilia out in front of City Hall in an hour. Just so we're clear, me and Sam won't be anywhere near the cameras and you are not to mention our names under any circumstance, all right? All I want is for people to start wondering what's going on in that hospital. Let's put it out there, and let somebody else start poking around. We don't need that kind of exposure. Like it or not, you're gonna be the face of this thing. You ready, Doc?"

Dr. Menard rubbed his face. "I don't know. I guess so."

"That's the spirit." Ed grinned. "Fuck it. You're gonna be a hero. Go on *Oprah*."

"Maybe she'll give you a car," Sam said.

Ed rapped on the table. "That's it then. We're gonna get your story out in front of the public, and damned if we're aren't gonna bring justice to the mean streets of Chicago."

"Hell, that's our job description," Sam said.

Ed's phone rang. He checked the number. It was Arturo.

Across the restaurant, the cook yelled, "Holy shit, turn that TV up."

# CHAPTER 52

**9:09 AM**
*August 14*

Kimmy awoke to pounding. At first, she wasn't sure what was making the noise. She realized it must be Lee. He'd left his phone when he stormed out last night, and he must have left his keys as well. She just hoped he had burned off the anger.

She wanted to slip into some lingerie, coax him back into bed, see if she couldn't improve his mood, but she didn't want to risk enraging him further if she made him wait. She threw on a silk robe instead, deciding that she could always make him coffee and then change. She closed Grace's door as she passed, and hurried to the front door.

It was Phil. "I need to talk to Lee. Immediately."

"He's not here."

"Then where the fuck is he? He won't answer his phone."

Kimmy shrugged. "He took off last night. I think he broke his phone before he left, so he didn't take it."

"Jesus Christ." He eyed her suspiciously. "You sure he's not here? You're not covering for his dumb ass, are you?" He pushed past roughly past her and banged on the walls with his fist. "Lee! Lee! You better not be hiding, you stupid sonofabitch." He poked his head in the master bedroom, even checked the bathroom. On the way back, he opened Grace's door, stuck his head inside.

He circled the living room, squinting at the brilliant sunlight sizzling through the floor to ceiling windows. He whirled on Kimmy in the kitchen. "Goddamnit, I've been up all fucking night, trying to save his career."

Kimmy crossed her arms. She didn't like the way he looked at her. "I told you. I don't know where he is. He left without saying anything."

Phil ran a shaking hand through his wild hair. "Make me some coffee. I need to sit and think a minute." He dragged a chair back from the dining table and collapsed into it.

Grace appeared, rubbing her eyes. "Mommy, can I watch TV?"

Kimmy shook her head and muttered, "Goddamnit." She threw Phil a furious look, then turned to her daughter. "Go back to bed. No TV. Not now."

"But Mommy," Grace whined.

Kimmy smacked her on the butt. "I said get back into your bed. Now!"

Grace started to cry.

"Go! Now!"

Phil's phone rang. He checked the number. "Shit." It wasn't Lee. He flipped it open. "Yeah, what?" He was silent for a moment. "You're shitting me." He snapped the phone shut, stood up, and strode into the living room.

He stood for a second, scratching his head again. He finally located the remote and turned on the TV. "What happened to your TV?"

The picture worked, despite the spiderweb of cracks in the center. Phil flipped to one of the news networks. The president's face appeared. He had a grave look on his face, but Phil couldn't hear anything. He shouted, "Sound, goddamnit! Where's the sound?"

Grace muttered, "I wanna watch *Kipper*!"

Kimmy shot Phil a withering look as she walked over and hit the POWER button on the audio receiver. The president's smooth baritone voice came out of all eight speakers, sounding as if he was there in the room with them.

"—unprecedented scale. Drastic measures must be implemented to counteract this unparalleled threat to our American way of life. I have appointed a special task force to work in conjunction with the CDC response team already in place in downtown Chicago."

"Aw . . . fuck." Phil looked like someone had just cut a small hole in a blow-up doll and it was slowly but steadily losing air. He took a step backward and looked like he might just sink to the floor, everything inside of him gone.

The president continued. "Evacuation of the Loop is scheduled to begin in less than two hours. I want to emphasize that this is strictly a precautionary measure, one that will ensure that this virus does not spread beyond the confines of the Chicago Loop. Our thoughts and prayers are with everyone within this magnificent city. To repeat—"

The front door open and Lee stumbled in. His tie was gone, shirt untucked. He spotted Phil. "Fuck you want?" he said. His breath made Kimmy's eyes water.

In the hall, Grace burst into tears, squeezing her fists.

"Shut that fucking brat up," Lee said, rubbing his temples. He blinked at Phil, trying to refocus his bloodshot eyes. "I asked you a question."

Kimmy smacked Grace again and dragged her back to the bedroom.

Phil drew himself up, set his jaw, and found the strength in his legs. He waved a hand at the table. "Sit down before you fall down. Then get your girlfriend to make some coffee. We got a lot to talk about."

"Why? Thought you were finished with me."

"You're not dead yet, not as far as the public is concerned. Believe me, you ain't on the front page anymore. You been watching the news?" Phil gestured at the TV. "All hell is breaking loose. Maybe we can make it work for us."

Lee glared at the president, who was saying, "—information we have received, information that is currently being confirmed by no less than the U.S. Army's Infectious Disease Center. At the moment, however, it does appear that the virus, initially thought to be spread by rats, is actually being spread by the common bedbug. Again, I want to emphasize that everything able to be done is being done, and there is no need to panic."

"Fuck did he just say?" Lee demanded.

Phil ignored the question. "Remember that freak from the CDC? Dr. Reischtal? Turns out he wants a meet. Needs some help. From you."

"What? Okay? When?"

Phil checked his watch. "Just under an hour. You've got just enough time to shower and shave. This might be just the break we need, so look sharp." He indicated the TV. The president was still justifying drastic measures. Phil shook his head. "I wouldn't dillydally. No telling what the big boys have got cooked up."

# CHAPTER 53

*9:10 AM*
*August 14*

"Here's the deal," Ed said as he raced south down Clark, lights blazing, siren going, weaving around people and blindly sailing through intersections. "We're fucked."

While Sam, Qween, and Dr. Menard had wandered over to the counter to watch the president's news conference, Ed took the call from Arturo. Arturo laid everything out. Word was that the president was about to call a press conference and declare martial law in downtown Chicago. The feds were about to evacuate the Loop and Arturo needed Ed and Sam back on the job. Immediately. All past sins would be forgiven if they pitched in and helped Arturo out. Arturo had a lot of shit to coordinate and zero time. Ed didn't have much of a choice. He said yes, hustled everyone out to the car, and took off.

"We, the CPD," Ed said in a flat, official voice, hammering the Crown Vic's horn at a guy in a white van that wouldn't move over at a light, "are working in conjunction with special representatives of the forces of the federal government." They flew through the intersection at forty-five miles an hour, missing the van's bumper by less than four inches. "That's what they're forcing on Arturo. CPD and CFD are responsible for executing a mass evacuation of downtown, using some plan they drew up after oh-one. Platoons of soldiers are responsible for the bugs and rats. And don't ask me what the fuck that means, 'cause I don't have a clue."

"It's easy," Qween said. "Uncle Sam just declared war on that virus."

Sam said, "That's the dumbest idea I've ever heard. There's no fucking way they're gonna get all the fucking rats, let alone a billion bugs."

"Maybe so." Ed shrugged. "But apparently this Dr. Reischtal believes he can make a serious dent in the bug population, get this virus under control."

"How the hell are they gonna do that? They're gonna have to seal off every goddamn tunnel and sewer and drain. . . . What about the fucking river?" Sam was livid. "Nobody's figured out that rats can swim?"

"I guess they got themselves a plan."

"It's the stupidest fucking thing I've ever heard," Sam repeated. "This Dr. Reischtal, he needs his head examined."

"I told you," Dr. Menard said, trying to pull his seat belt tighter.

Ed said, "That's not the scary part. The scary part is, your Dr. Reischtal, he's in charge now. The president has just declared martial law in Chicago."

The color left Sam's face. He stared at Ed. "You're shitting me."

Ed shook his head, weaved around a long line of cars and went barreling down Clark in the oncoming lane. "They're not gonna call it that. They're gonna use something like a state of emergency or whatever, but it's the same damn thing. It'll never make the news, but Arturo said it's been made quite clear to all the concerned parties. The federal government is in charge, but they're handing the ball over to a special branch of the CDC. Dr. Reischtal is the last word. We're supposed to steer clear."

"Oh yeah?" Sam asked. "What are we supposed to do then? Aren't we helping out with the evacuation?"

Ed got back in on their side of the yellow lines and hit the horn again, trying to get a cab driver's attention. "Sort of. We got ourselves a special assignment to make sure that some VIPs get out without any trouble."

"Oh yeah?" Sam perked up. "Politicians? Celebrities? Athletes?"

Ed gave a grim smile. "We get to babysit all those bad boys and girls at the MCC, make sure they get out of the city okay."

Stunned silence from Sam. Qween chuckled. Dr. Menard was confused, but decided it was best to keep quiet. Finally, Sam managed to get out, "You said yes to that job? What's wrong with you?"

Ed shrugged. "We don't do it, a lot of people are going to get hurt."

Sam said, "And if we do it, there's a damn good chance we might get hurt."

Ed lifted his eyebrows. "Never knew you to be scared."

"Not scared, brother. Just . . . concerned. Driving busloads of hate ain't my idea of a good time."

"Me neither, but you got something better you'd like to do with your time?"

"Yeah. How about driving a bus full of swimsuit models out of the city?"

"Shit," Qween cut in. "You boys be driving me around. What else you want?"

Sam watched the warehouses and fast food joints give way to the bars and upscale shops and tourist honeypots of the Near North Side. They drew closer to the bridge. On the other side of West Kinzie, two police cruisers were cutting off both lanes, directing people to take alternate routes. Ed flashed his star at them and they moved aside.

As they hit the incline for the Clark Street Bridge, they saw that instead of another police car and sawhorse like they had seen last night, constricting the bridge down to one lane, there was now a Stryker and sandbags, blocking both lanes between the faded purple trusses.

The Stryker was a no-nonsense military vehicle, no less than eight wheels slapped under a wedge of gray, riveted steel, with a .50 caliber machine gun mounted on top like some cherry on a sadistic birthday cake.

"Fuck me sideways," Sam said. It was one thing to hear about some military force taking over the Loop and quite another to witness it firsthand. Ed pulled up to the gap between the walls of sandbags. A soldier stepped away from the Stryker, holding his assault rifle casually, though it was still pointed in their general direction.

Three more soldiers materialized, ready behind the sandbags. The first soldier said, "Please roll your window down, sir."

Ed rolled the window down and held up his star. "We've got urgent business downtown. You make us late, you can talk to my commanding officer, Commander Arturo Mendoza. You go ahead and take the time to ask him, you feel it's necessary. Don't blame me when he rips you a new one, dickhead."

The soldier eyeballed Qween and Dr. Menard. "You all cops?"

"My partner just explained that we have urgent business downtown. You born this stupid, or did you have to work at it?" Sam said.

A belligerent cabbie pulled up behind the Crown Vic and hit his horn. He rolled down his window and started yelling. "Hey! Hey! You have no right, no right, to block traffic. I am a man making a living here. Hey! I am talking to you. I pay taxes. I am a legal immigrant. Legal! You cannot cut off the streets! Hey! You listening to me?"

"What Detective Johnson means to say is that these people would not be with us at this particular moment unless their services were required," Ed said. "Seems to me you got your hands full with more important problems."

The soldier finally stepped back. "Drive safe," he said, and waved them through.

The cab tried to follow close behind, but the soldiers formed a line across the bridge. Another soldier was now behind the .50 caliber. He racked the bolt back and settled the crosshairs on the cab's windshield. That got the driver's attention.

As they crossed over the bridge, a deep thrumming sound reached them. Ed hit the brakes. They twisted in their seats to watch as the bridge, split in the middle, began to rise. It took less than two minutes. The Clark Street Bridge was up. A quick glance up and down Upper Wacker revealed that every bridge in sight had been raised.

As they headed south down Clark, Ed noticed lines of CTA buses, dozens of them, maybe even hundreds, lining the streets that ran east and west. More Strykers and low walls of sandbags had been set up during the night at nearly every intersection.

"Better call Cecilia. Neither one of you is making that interview," Sam said, nodding at the clusters of soldiers at the corner of each block. "It's already a done deal. This city has given up."

"The real question is, for the moment at least," Dr. Menard spoke quietly from the backseat, "is what are we going to do? You two have a job. Personally, I'd like to get closer to the hospital. See if I can't grab anything that looks like it might indict Dr. Reischtal. Records. Videos. Something."

"Doc, you want to go after him, fine," Ed said. "I don't know how you can, but understand this—we can't help you."

"I know. It's okay."

Qween said, "You're kinda cute, sugar." She gave Dr. Menard a wink. "I'll show you a few shortcuts."

# CHAPTER 54

**10:24 AM**
**August 14**

Mr. Ullman was almost glad that the president had declared a state of emergency and ordered the evacuation of the Loop. It saved the general manager the embarrassment of explaining to the guests that they were being kicked out of the hotel so the management could exterminate a colony of bedbugs. This way, he could simply spread his hands in mock impotence and point to the official orders coming from both Washington and Chicago's City Hall. It was all the government's fault.

Not the hotel's.

Not the bedbugs'.

In fact, he didn't have to mention bedbugs at all. Most of the guests were more than happy to check out, and couldn't get on the hotel's shuttle buses fast enough. A few, though, were refusing to leave immediately. They were either waiting for their own limos or thought the whole thing was a hoax or wanted to simply sleep through their hangovers. Some of the guests didn't answer their room phones.

Mr. Ullman guessed he had at least an hour or two before

the soldiers entered the hotel and forcibly ejected the stragglers, something the TV newscasters breathlessly told their viewers would happen with each and every building in the Loop.

Since there were still guests inside the hotel, he gave strict orders for what was left of the staff to remain. They weren't happy, but it wasn't his job to make sure his employees enjoyed their jobs. It was his job to make sure the hotel was in the best possible hands, and therefore, he wanted everyone on hand in case the guests needed anything. He suspected that many of them had already left before being given the official green light.

He decided that he would give them the benefit of the doubt, and when all of this nonsense was over, he would welcome them back to start with a clean slate. The only problem, a minor irritation really, was that the ineffectual little man from the pest exterminator company, Roger Something or other, had never checked back in with him. He had probably run off with all the rest.

Mr. Ullman rode up to the top floor alone in the elevator. He was determined to verify that every single door to every single room in the hotel was not only shut, but locked as well. He did not trust the officials, some of whom were trying to quell panic by reassuring the city that this evacuation was only for twenty-four hours. The possibility of looters was very real and he couldn't stand the thought of someone soiling the image of this pristine hotel. So he started at the very top and worked his way down.

On the fourteenth floor he came to room number 1426. The door was still open, forgotten in the chaos. The detectives poking around had suddenly been called away, and even the uniformed officers had vanished, pulled by more pressing matters.

Mr. Ullman couldn't help himself; he had to step inside and look around. The room was still a mess. The shattered window had yet to be repaired. White fingerprint dust filled the air and formed a fog that clung to the floor and roiled in the ebb and flow of the hot wind.

He made a note to get on the phone immediately and get this window replaced. He could only imagine the shots from the helicopters, zooming in on the lone shattered window in a high cliff of glass, occasionally catching a glimpse inside the sad, empty room. Those soulless producers would die for a shot like that.

The last thing he wanted was that kind of image to linger in everyone's minds.

He stepped around the bed, calculating the damage. The room was in such a state of destruction that the amount needed to repair everything staggered even him. His initial reaction had been to start the process of billing the estate for the damages, but he'd reconsidered after someone had mentioned the negative publicity he would attract by charging the family of the suicide victim.

He edged around the couch, watching the space under the bed. He bent closer. He couldn't see any bugs, but Roger had assured him that that didn't mean anything necessarily. The image of their fecal matter filled his thoughts, no matter how much he wanted to pretend the clotted droppings didn't exist.

His gaze landed on the corner, behind the nightstand. He pulled it away, shining his flashlight at the partially peeled silicone, the painted trim that had been pried away from the wallpaper. Nothing moved in the light. The dead bugs from Roger's insecticide were still there, as if someone had scattered wet coffee grounds. Once again, he couldn't help himself; he had to expose the worst wounds of the hotel, and tapped the silicone with the toe of his wingtips. Living bugs erupted around the floor trim in the hundreds. Thousands. It was as if the building itself had vomited the tiny parasites into the room.

The bugs spilled over themselves in an almost liquid

movement as they oozed from the cracks. The carpet grew alive under his shoes. They swarmed up the legs of the nightstand. His leg brushed the mattress and he flinched as bugs gushed from the seams.

Mr. Ullman didn't waste any time getting back to the doorway. He slammed the door shut and locked it. He hustled down to the elevator and hit the button and fought the urge to hit the button again. That little shit Roger was going to hear about this.

Mr. Ullman checked back down the hall. The shadows around the door seemed to grow. He blinked, ran one hand through his thinning hair. The only thing he could hear was the thrumming of the cables and the rest of the elevator, but his eyes caught movement, down at the door to room 1426.

Shadows dripped from under the door. They grew along the corner of the hall. Flowed down the carpet at Mr. Ullman. He punched the down button, over and over.

The darkness grew, still utterly silent. Millions of the bugs flooded the hallway, washing across the carpet in waves of foul-smelling tiny bodies. He heard the elevator come to a slow stop on his floor.

The elevator doors split in half and he fell inside. He leapt for the CLOSE DOOR button, and jumped up and down to activate the capacity indicator, anything to close the doors. Bugs spilled inside.

The doors slid shut.

Mr. Ullman stomped on the bugs, grinding them into the thin carpet. He hit the basement button. He planned to deactivate all of the air systems throughout the hotel, all of the air intake and circulation, anything he could think of. He hoped that it would at least stop the bugs from spreading to different floors. The only way to accomplish this task was to gain access to a secure terminal in the basement, behind ten inches of steel. There were only three keys. Mr. Ullman had one. The facilities manager had a copy. One of the elected officials of the board had the other.

He stepped back to assess the bug situation in the elevator. He couldn't tell how many he'd killed; if you scraped it all together it might be enough to butter a slice of toast. More were still crawling around the doors, about three inches off the floor. Mr. Ullman stepped in close, bent his toes on the door just above the bugs, and slid his shoe down, crushing the bugs with the ball of his foot.

The floor numbers flashed. His ears popped.

Once he shut the air circulation down, his next move would be to visit each of the remaining guests' rooms. They could either leave under their own volition, or be removed by the soldiers who were even now marching through the city. After his encounter with the bugs, he did not care.

Once the guests were no longer on the premises, he would inform the staff and they would file out in an orderly fashion. Of course, being the general manager, he would be the last out of the building, handing the operations key over to the emergency personnel.

The elevator slowed, stopped.

The doors opened and Mr. Ullman stepped into the basement, full of visions of handing the damn key over to somebody else. He was four or five steps down the corridor before he realized he was walking through an inch or two of the bugs. They were up his pants before he had a chance to even register the sounds of all of them under his shoes. He tried slapping at them with his clipboard, but he might as well have been trying to stop the rain with fresh laundry in a Midwestern thunderstorm.

He went to his knees.

The virus was already slipping into his brain, slinking into the cells, corrupting everything exponentially. He didn't know that he was already infected, and still fought as he fell forward. Waves flowed to him, as if the tide of bugs had been lovingly called to the moon. They covered him, crawling over his face, into his hair, down his suit, fastening those horribly efficient tubes to every inch of his skin. He held on to the key until it was nudged aside by bugs looking for a place to feed.

# CHAPTER 55

*10:27 AM*
*August 14*

Ed tried to turn right on Randolph and head west between City Hall and the Thompson Center, but found himself face to face with the imposing grille on the front of a CTA bus. All three lanes of the street were blocked by buses, all them going the wrong way, streaming toward Grant Park and the lake. The sidewalks were full of civilians, lining up to climb aboard. Soldiers stood back near the buildings, watching everything.

Ed spun the steering wheel back to the left, drove through the intersection, and pulled over. He killed the spinning lights and said, "This is as close as I'm gonna get to that hospital. It wouldn't do you two any good to be seen driving up with us. Be a good idea to get in quiet."

"No shit?" Qween said. "They must pay you extra to figure shit like that out."

Dr. Menard opened the door and climbed out. Qween followed, making popping noises with her tongue. She slammed the door.

Sam lowered his window. "You're a cranky little minx, you are, so go easy on any sonofabitch you come across."

Ed looked them over one last time, this old woman who had been living in the streets, the haggard doctor with the broken glasses, gave them a solemn nod, and pulled smoothly away. He wound down Clark, threading his way through the sandbags, Strykers, and trucks full of soldiers, and hit the siren again.

Qween pulled Dr. Menard close and spoke very quietly. "Look around. They're gonna haul everybody's ass they can find out of here. Right now, try and look like we're jus' waiting for the bus, like ever'body else." She took a moment, turning slowly, taking everything in, as people ignored them and flowed around them like water around the remnants of an ocean pier.

She sensed the panic seething just under the surface. Their eyes spoke volumes. Too wide and uncomprehending for people that had lived and worked in the Loop for years. These people looked like Midwestern tourists who had found they had been mistakenly dropped off in downtown Baghdad.

It wasn't just the expressions. One woman had bottles of water stuffed in a bulging purse, a man carried three briefcases, and another man awkwardly carried the large hard drive of a desktop computer. Nobody was flat-out running, but they looked like they wanted to. Instead, they formed shuffling lines until the next empty bus rolled into place.

Qween figured the soldiers and the guns helped some in keeping thing orderly.

Whistles broke the grinding monotony of diesel engines and buses halted at the Clark crosswalk. Soldiers cleared the intersection as a covered truck rumbled up to the intersection.

"Gonna be movin' quick. Get ready," Qween said to

Dr. Menard without looking at him. "You stick to me like syrup on flapjacks."

A squadron of soldiers in hazmat suits jumped out of the truck and a collective gasp rippled through the crowd. The orange figures carried a variety of weapons, from the standard assault rifles to mundane pesticide canisters to what looked like flamethrowers with heavy tanks on the soldiers' backs.

As the squad headed for the front doors of the Thompson Center, and everyone was watching the soldiers, Qween tapped Dr. Menard's hand and said, "Now." Then she was off, not running exactly, but moving quickly. She led him into the street, scuttling through a break in the buses, and instead of crossing to the other side, she turned up Randolph and they moved west, using the buses to hide them from the soldiers on both sides of the street. They travelled two blocks this way, fighting against the inexorable current until they reached Welles without being stopped.

Once under the El tracks, Qween led Dr. Menard back to the sidewalk, where they slipped through the crowd and into a massive parking garage. They went up six flights of stairs, taking it slow, and came out onto an empty roof, into the muted, hazy sunlight.

Qween didn't stop until she leaned on the edge and could look over. Dr. Menard sagged gratefully into the low wall and caught his breath. The east–west streets were jammed with buses, all headed toward the lake. The north/south streets were full of soldiers, funneling civilians out of buildings to the buses.

A short, guttural cry caught everybody's attention. A bike messenger, wielding his U-lock and a switchblade, stumbled out from between the parked cars. Soldiers kept their distance, but they eventually formed a ragged half-circle around him. One of them, apparently some sort of officer, edged forward and shouted, "Cease and desist!" The kid moaned

at the harsh sound and leapt forward with the knife and the
lock, and the officer squeezed off a quick three-shot burst.
The kid flopped backwards, landing hard on his butt, missing
his nose and the back of his head.

The civilians on the sidewalk flinched away. One of the
soldiers stepped out with a bullhorn and his inflated voice
boomed out into the street. "Everything is under control. The
federal government is in charge of the situation. Everything
is under control." Without the constant rumble of the El
trains, his amplified voice exploded in the space under the
tracks and sent the fragmented echoes bouncing down the bus-
filled streets. The rest of the soldiers marched up the street,
shooting out the tires of the parked cars. Other soldiers
sprayed the white chemical foam over the body, then slipped
a heavy black bag around the bike messenger and hauled
him away.

The mournful cry of the tornado sirens pierced the unnatural stillness and Qween felt a chill, despite the stifling heat
and humidity. She had grown accustomed to hearing them for
a few moments every first Tuesday morning of every month
when they tested the sirens. Now, in the middle of a blistering
August, the sound was eerily out of place, as if a child
laughed in a morgue.

News and military helicopters filled the sky above the
Loop, endlessly circling, like lazy dragonflies.

Qween spit over the edge and watched the soldiers. They
were concentrating on setting up roadblocks and arranging
sandbags, but soon they would be watching for any civilians
left behind by the buses. There was nowhere to hide. Nowhere
to blend in. She took Dr. Menard's arm. "'Bout half an hour,
we gonna stick out like a busted big toe."

She sank heavily to the concrete, back to the wall. Since
the soldiers had shown they had no problems shooting
people, she didn't want to be seen. Here was a place to rest
out of sight. She didn't know if any the helicopters were re-
laying information down to the soldiers, and wouldn't be

surprised if they were, but they should be fine for a few minutes at least.

She got winded easily these days, but her body was conditioned to moving at a steady clip. Qween moved fast because she had a lot of practice. She had been through most every building in the Loop and had discovered that even when she was crazy-ass drunk, nobody usually hassled her if she kept moving. She couldn't just crawl through a place as if she was looking for a warm place to crash, because then they'd be on her ass immediately. If she kept moving though, at that steady chugging pace, as if she was in a hurry to get to somewhere important far from here and this was the fastest her body could move, which wasn't far from the truth, nobody would fuck with her. She figured it was because if she kept moving, she automatically became someone else's problem. She wasn't accosting anybody. She wasn't scaring anyone. She wasn't costing the city money. She wasn't damaging anything.

She was, however, taking it all in, remembering everything. She knew, for example, over at the elevator in the corner of the parking garage, that if you pried off the locked cover between the floor buttons and the emergency button, you could press a button that would take you to the sublevels, where the garage sold private parking spots for a steep monthly fee.

Down there, once you got past the storage area where they kept the snow blowers and salt, you could open a door to an access tunnel that led under the street, connecting to a maze of fire tunnels, forgotten corridors, and dusty storm shelters.

Qween explained her plan. "We can go blocks without them soldiers seein' us."

"It's not the soldiers I'm worried about down here," Dr. Menard said. "It's the bugs."

Qween shrugged. "Maybe. I'll take my chances stomping on dem bugs any day over tryin' to stomp on a bullet."

# CHAPTER 56

The convoy of trucks streamed east, strung out along I-80. Evans drove the third truck, and kept the drivers coordinated through a disposable cell phone. Every driver carried one. He kept them spaced roughly a quarter mile apart, allowing cars and even other trucks to slip into the convoy, all in the interest of maintaining the lowest possible profile. The trailers and tanks all sported different corporate logos.

Evans didn't want to think about what they were actually hauling, about the hell that would be unleashed if one of his drivers happened to accidently collide with a sleepy tourist behind the wheel of a minivan.

Evans called Dr. Reischtal. "On schedule," he said. "Should be arriving in the area by early evening."

"See that you do," Dr. Reischtal said, and hung up.

Uncle Phil pounded on the bathroom door. "I'd appreciate it if you could get out here right fucking now."

Lee raised his head out of the icy spray and yelled, "Heard

you the first time. Go wait downstairs." He added under his breath, "Ugly ass troll."

Phil thought Lee had said something else, but decided to ignore it. He continued to yell. "You're late, and if you fuck this meeting up, swear to Christ, they'll find a way to pin this shitstorm on you. It's your ass."

Lee reluctantly turned the water off. He loved his showers cold, with the handle twisted all the way to the right, craving how the freezing needles lowered his body temperature to a tingling numbness. There wasn't much worse than feeling his pores start to ooze sweat at the thought of stepping out into the goddamn humidity.

He dried off and went into the bedroom, threw on a suit. His new phone rang. Lee opened it, said, "What?"

Phil said, "Tell me you're on the way down."

Lee snapped the phone shut. Phil had left it for him. It was a cheap piece of shit, unable to connect to the Internet or any other bells and whistles, but his old one wasn't working right ever since he threw it at the TV. He didn't even want to think about the fucking plasma, let alone look at it. It didn't matter. All of this shit was temporary.

He walked into the living room, struggling with his tie. Kimmy and Grace were on the couch, faces plastered to the windows, watching the endless procession of dozens and dozens of CTA buses, all streaming through Grant Park before heading south on Lake Shore Drive. Good. *Let 'em stare at the spectacle*, he thought. It would keep them out of his hair for a while.

"Gotta go, babe. They need me."

Kimmy turned, confusion and worry crinkling her forehead. "Okay, but aren't we supposed to evacuate too? That's what the news said."

"You gonna listen to the news or you gonna listen to me? Who the hell you think has the inside scoop? Huh? No, you two stay here. You're absolutely, one hundred percent safe.

Believe me, it's already over. I'll be back quick as I can, soon as I get this business done. Then later on tonight, we'll all go back down to the press conference. So lay out your best outfit and be ready for a night on the town."

"It's all going to be okay? The city, all the sick people, I mean? They're gonna get all those bugs, right?"

"Of course." He gave her his best smile. "They're just being careful. And as it happens, it's gonna be the best thing that ever happened for us. I'll make a big deal out of how I'm volunteering to stay behind to protect my city. Phil says the media is gonna eat it up. Says it could be the defining moment of my career. You'll be at my side later when I give that press conference telling people that the city has been saved. You watch. I'm gonna be a hero. Trust me."

"Okay, baby. Can we bring Grace?"

"Yeah, I wanna come," Grace said, finally tearing her eyes away from all the buses when she heard her name.

Lee kept his grin alive. "We'll have to see, kiddo." He grabbed his briefcase. It was empty except for a *Maxim* magazine, but Phil told him he looked more professional carrying it around. He checked his watch. "I'm sorry, but I gotta run. Phil and Bryan are downstairs."

Kimmy came off the couch and stood in the sunlight, hands clasped at her chest. "Love you."

It was impossible to ignore the pleading, questioning tone in her voice. Lee struggled to keep his smile wide. "Yeah, see you later," he said and left.

As he walked down the hall to the elevator, he reconsidered his initial anger and outright revulsion at being around the brat at home, let alone in public. The more he thought about it, the more he came to understand that she might not be such a bad prop for the press conference. Might be the best visual confirmation that the city was safe, hoisting a four-year-old girl to his shoulders. Yeah. That would make a hell of a shot.

He made a final adjustment to his tie in the reflective

metal of the elevator. Funny how things turned out. Less than twelve hours ago he had been on his way to becoming one of the most reviled politicians in the city's history. And for Chicago, that was really saying something. The way Phil barked, he'd be lucky if he avoided jail time. But that was then, as they said, and now things had definitely swung back in his favor. He wondered what the hell that freak Dr. Reischtal wanted. He strode out into the lobby and saluted the doorman.

The doorman, some simpering idiot who couldn't find a real job, held up his hand. "So sorry, Mr. Shea, but I'm trying to get a tally of who is left in the building. Most of the residents have already left, of course, but I've been told that I need to give the soldiers a count of who is left on the premises."

"You can scratch my place off your list, then," Lee said. "It's empty."

"Oh, so Kimmy and Grace are gone, then? I must have missed them."

Lee was irritated that this piss-boy knew Kimmy's name. "I sent 'em to her mother's last night. Like I said, it's all clear up there." Lee didn't wait for a response, and strolled through the spinning doors, down the steps to where Bryan and Phil waited in the car.

# CHAPTER 57

*10:44 AM*
*August 14*

Farther down Clark, where it passed under the El tracks that covered Van Buren, a slim slab of beige granite sat all by itself in the midst of a perfectly average city plaza, filled with plenty of benches, a few ornamental trees, some shrubs and flowers in long cement planters. Lots of people who worked in the Loop liked to sit in the sun and eat their lunch before returning to the skyscrapers. If you weren't paying attention, you'd never know it was a maximum-security federal prison.

The windows gave it away. They were narrow slits and resembled ports for medieval archers to fire arrows, too small for anyone to squeeze through. A small, nondescript sign identified the building as the Metropolitan Correction Center.

Ed and Sam rolled into the secure parking lot next door. The guard at the entrance wasted time by having them wait in their car while he called his superior officer upstairs. He got the all-clear, but still demanded to know what he should do if he saw a rat—"or one of them bedbugs."

Sam said, "You got a sidearm. Use it."

Ed parked in a handicapped spot on the second level next to the walkway into the prison reserved for cops and prison personnel. The convicts were brought in through a different entrance, up on the sixth level, at the top of the parking structure.

The warden himself was waiting. "This, this is most unusual, officers." The warden was in his sixties, with a head full of brilliant white hair and soft hands. He wanted to stop and talk in the corridor, but Sam and Ed blew past him, heading for the elevators. He hurried to catch up.

Ed said, "Call the Cook County sheriff and demand at least ten prisoner transfer buses, more if you can get 'em."

"I talked to an Arturo Mendoza. He never did give me an adequate explanation."

"Call the sheriff. Get as many buses as you can. Then turn on the goddamn TV."

"I have received a call from the sheriff's department. They have promised us their full cooperation."

"What does that mean? How many buses, have they promised, specifically?"

"Three."

"We need more."

"It is my understanding that we are simply transporting the inmates to the holding cells at the Cook County facilities at Twenty-sixth and California. It may require two trips, three at the most. Three buses will be adequate."

Ed stopped and put a hand on the warden's shoulder. Ed said gently, "I'm not telling you how to do your job, but we're gonna need more buses." Sam recognized the good-cop, wise-older-brother tone. "Sure, we could pack everybody in here on a couple of buses, haul 'em down there and dump 'em, but there's a lot of variables in this situation. We haven't been able to talk to anybody down there yet, and so we're not taking anything for granted. What happens if we get down there and find out that there's no room? What then? You gonna leave eighty inmates locked on one bus with nowhere to go?"

The warden licked his lips and finally nodded. "I'll call them back, see what I can arrange."

He showed them into a briefing room, filled with guards. Most of the guards were watching the press conferences on TV. The cameras had just cut from the president outside the White House to the mayor at City Hall, who began to outline the details of the evacuation. The warden introduced Ed and Sam and explained to his men, "As many of you are aware, recent developments in the Loop have necessitated the evacuation of Chicago's entire downtown area. CPD has seen fit to send us Detectives Jones and Johnson to oversee the transfer of every prisoner inside the MCC."

The warden let that sink in. He turned to Ed and Sam. "Well, then. How can we help?"

Ed said, "First off, how many inmates are we talking about?"

"I believe the current population is five hundred and twenty-seven, both male and female. We'll confirm that number, of course."

"Where are they?"

The warden pulled down a large cross-sectional diagram of the prison and settled into the role of tour guide. "The MCC is a transition facility; that is, this is a way station for inmates who have been found guilty and are awaiting the details of their sentencing. Almost all of the inmates are waiting for further court hearings or to be transferred to a more permanent home. The average length of incarceration, at least within the MCC, is less than six months. We also feature a state-of-the-art hospital, and anywhere from five to ten percent of our population have been transferred from other prisons within Illinois to receive treatment."

He pointed to the diagram. The building had a triangle footprint, giving the guards clear sight lines for each narrow floor. "No prisoners are ever housed beneath the tenth floor. That gives us seventeen floors to utilize, and we have found it works to both our advantage and the inmates' safety to spread them out, housing as few inmates as possible per floor. We pride ourselves on keeping our guests calm and comfortable."

"Good. That's our key," Ed said and caught Sam's eye.

The transitory nature of the prison made their jobs easier. The detectives realized that because inmates did not stay at the prison for any significant length of time, the institutionalized tribes that flourished wherever prisoners would spend decades behind bars, in crews bound by race or gang or belief, had failed to find a foothold. In a typical maximum-security prison, many of the inmates were facing life sentences, and had the time to establish structured organizations, forming hierarchies, protecting their tribe, as well as coordinating clever, vicious attacks against other gangs or the guards.

"Best way to avoid problems," Ed said. "Keep everybody comfortable, but off-balance. I don't want them to know what is going to happening next."

Sam said, "We don't want to give them a chance to get friendly with each other. If these boys ever got organized, they could overpower a bus without much trouble, and then we've got a mobile hostage situation on our hands."

Ed addressed the entire room. "Understand this. Safety and security are our only responsibilities. There are only two things you are to communicate to the inmates. One, a state of emergency exists, and two, they are being transferred to a different location for their own safety. That is it. Don't tell them anything else."

"Except," Sam said.

Ed said, "Except that a policy of zero tolerance has been implemented. If anyone steps out of line, guards will be shooting to kill."

Ed and Sam watched as the guards had to fight their delight and hide their satisfied, victorious grins at finally being able to bolster their careers with a stamp of authority. Ed glanced at Sam. Sam closed his eyes and gave an imperceptible nod. The guards had been exposed to the institutionalized violence for too long, with no outlet, no way of turning the fear loose in a meaningful manner, no way of exorcising the demons that grew and multiplied in the dark in a place like this. In fact, letting off this kind of steam was frowned upon, and sometimes, it was flat-out illegal. Shooting ranges could only provide so much relief. It was like drinking near beer for an alcoholic.

Eventually, something had to give.

The guards were going to be a problem.

Sam could smell violence in the air, like a lightning storm on the horizon.

# CHAPTER 58

"That's not the suit you're wearing tonight, I hope." Phil's first words.

"No. It's the suit I'm wearing right now," Lee said. "The good ones are at the office." Phil's condescending attitude was getting tougher to swallow. "Never thought you'd be worrying about men's fashion."

"This might be the most important press conference of our lives. I'm worrying about everything."

Bryan accelerated and shot down the side street to Upper Wacker. Phil explained, "All the interior roads are blocked. Right now, the only streets open to get into the Loop are Clark and Congress."

"Shit. These people are serious."

"You have no fucking idea."

Bryan turned left on Clark, where they were met by staggered walls of sandbags and four soldiers, all carrying assault rifles and wearing surgical masks. They inspected Phil's ID and checked their list. They came back and looked at Lee's ID as well as Bryan's. It must have checked out, because the soldiers waved them through.

"So listen, please, no jokes, okay? Don't try to be funny," Phil said.

"Why not? Nothing wrong with my sense of humor." Lee tried to dismiss the whole thing.

Phil shook his head. "Absolutely not. Even those dago pricks only laugh to be polite, and they laugh at everything. You? You're about as funny as a case of the clap."

Bryan weaved through the sandbags and followed Clark down to City Hall. Lee glanced at the open plaza to the left, by the Daley Center, and was astonished to see that the giant Picasso sculpture was gone. He finally spotted it, lying on its side in the intersection of Dearborn and Washington, acting as a kind of barricade.

Phil caught his stunned expression and said, "They took it down because they wanted room to land the helicopters."

Lee actually liked the sculpture, the way it had some sort of invisible tether to the heavens, as if it was some sort of pet from someone above. Lee thought it was a bad omen, this desecration of a Chicago landmark. But Phil was pissing him off, so Lee didn't say anything. Bryan dropped them off in front of City Hall on the Cook County side. More soldiers checked their IDs once again.

Inside, they were directed upstairs to a large briefing room. The room had been built like an amphitheater, with descending rows of seats and tables curving around a central stage. A soldier directed Lee and Phil to one of the smooth tables with low lamps near the back. Some high-ranking official was down in the center, using a laser pointer to highlight areas of maps of the Loop and the subway system projected on the screens behind him.

The official, some major or general or something—Lee wasn't too clear on these things—was laying out plans in a dry, almost disinterested tone. He was tall, with dark, vigorous eyebrows that didn't match the gray, lifeless hair that had been cut close to his scalp. "Phase two is nearly complete, a total relocation of civilians to a neutral zone where they can be properly examined before being released into the public at large. Phase three preliminaries are complete and are ready to implement immediately. As we proceed with these two phases, phase four and five are being prepped." He gestured at the map. "Every bridge, with the sole exception of the Congress Street Bridge, has been raised. The river has been irradiated with a compound that will . . . inhibit life."

The officer traced the boundaries of the quarantine zone with his laser pointer. "The subway tunnels have been neutralized." Lee figured this was code for blowing the shit out of the things. He sniggered.

Phil refused to look at him.

Lee got the hint. *Play along. Don't make waves. And above all, don't draw any attention to yourself.* Fine. Lee decided to play along. For now.

"To repeat, every bridge has been raised, except for Congress, and that will be raised within the hour. The river has been treated. No rat will survive the swim. And here"—the red dot swept along Roosevelt Avenue—"a continuous firebreak has been established, stretching from the Chicago River to Lake Shore Drive. We have squads spread out along Roosevelt Avenue, equipped with both .50 caliber firepower and flamethrowers." He checked his watch. "In less than thirty minutes, the only access to downtown Chicago, in or out, will be restricted to this one lane of Lake Shore Drive." The red dot seared into a spot just to the left of the Field Museum.

Some other senior official asked, "What about the lakefront?"

The major or general or whatever smiled. "The CDC has informed us that a cutting-edge medical and military vessel will be in place in the next several hours. Until then, the Coast Guard has agreed to help patrol the waters." He surveyed his audience. "Trust me, gentlemen. Nothing, absolutely nothing, can escape the quarantine zone. This city will be locked down tighter than Fort Knox."

He turned back to the map. "We are directing most of our

forces down into the Blue Line subway stations, specifically Jackson Street Station. Platoons are gaining access to the underground through the post office and the Monadnock building. They will be spreading throughout the tunnels, forming an offensive that will be dispersing both fire and a lethal pesticide. This will provide an effective foundation, killing any infected rats, as well as any and all bugs with vapor chemicals that will reach into any crevice, any crack, any place where the bugs hide, and kill them."

He added as an afterthought, "And if it is deemed necessary, the solution within the Chicago River can be set on fire."

The speech had risen to a crescendo, and if this had been a political platform, that would be the cue to leap to your feet and start clapping like crazy. But since this was the military, the speaker took comfort in the total silence. He waited just as long as it would have taken for the applause to die down, and said, "Squads are currently conducting building-to-building searches, but this process takes time and manpower. Both of which we are in sore need of, I don't need to remind you."

Then he got into some math and started using words like, "kill ratio" and "projected casualties" and "dispersal rate" and Lee, too familiar with boring fucking governmental meetings, tuned him out immediately. Since his eyes had adjusted to the gloom, he took stock of the room.

Every emergency department in the city was there, along with soldiers. Damn near everybody was taking copious notes. The general, or whatever the hell he was up front, finally finished coordinating the underground sweeps with, "Remember, flush 'em out, get 'em up to the surface, where the burn crews will flash-fire 'em. Any questions?"

Phil gave Lee a sour look, as if telling him to keep quiet.

"Right, then," the general or whatever said. "You all have your assignments. I suggest you don't waste any time moving into position. This operation will start precisely at fifteen hundred hours. No exceptions, gentlemen."

The soldiers at all of the low tables gathered their notes and guns and filed out, leaving Lee and Phil alone with the projected maps of the Loop. Even the general left. Lee's patience lasted almost fifteen seconds. "Okay. Now what? Where the fuck is this guy?"

A cold, deliberate voice came from behind them, deep in the shadows of one of the alcoves that dotted the wall. "I wanted to say . . . thank you, for your cooperation in detaining two of your employees."

Lee whipped his head around to find Dr. Reischtal. The doctor's tiny glasses caught the reflection of the maps down in front and gave him the appearance of eyes that flashed with white fire. He was wearing an orange hazmat suit, and even though he didn't have the face mask covering his head, the outfit still made Lee nervous.

"Sure. Anytime," Lee said. "How, uh, can we help you?"

"I understand you are the man to speak with, if you have . . . special needs. Mr. Shea here"—Dr. Reischtal indicated Phil—"has kindly offered to further our business arrangement, by admitting that you, his nephew no less, are in a rarefied position to help government employees such as myself find quiet places to store some of the unpleasant consequences of my job description."

"Maybe," Lee said.

"Then perhaps you might be of some assistance. For the right price, of course. I have already negotiated a most generous donation to your reelection fund with your uncle, so if you are unhappy with your share, you can take it up with him."

Phil started nodding his head when Dr. Reischtal mentioned the fund, making a circle with his thumb and forefinger in the universal sign of "okay." He shook his head when Dr. Reischtal said the word "unhappy."

Lee nodded.

Dr. Reischtal stood quite still. "I have heard of a quiet, private disposal site under the downtown area."

"Maybe."

"I have heard that this space is accessible by eighteen-wheeled semi trailer trucks. It is my understanding that you know of a route that could provide access."

"I know of all kinds of dump sites. What I need to know is what you're dumping."

"I shall require access to this site."

"You haven't answered the question."

"Perhaps your uncle can satisfy your curiosity."

Lee didn't look at Phil. "That's not his job. You want to go under downtown, that's my job." Lee finally figured it out. "Okay. Okay. Maybe you could give me a better idea of what we're dealing with here."

"I don't see how that should concern you."

"If I'm deciding where to put something, I need to know some details. Like, how many?"

"How many . . . what?"

"How many trucks? How many loads? Three? Four? Five? Are you going to need special equipment to deliver the troublesome cargo? Or is it something that a couple of guys can manage? I need to know how much, you understand. Things like, is the product biodegradable? Would it benefit from close proximity to say, corrosive chemicals, which failed to find their way out of the city?"

"Perhaps as little as five. Perhaps as many as twenty-five."

"Twenty-five what?"

"Twenty-five tanker trucks."

Lee was impressed. "Whoa. Twenty-five loads. Shit. Okay. How long are you going to spread it out? You know, most of these guys, they drop off a load in February, maybe another in March. How do you want to space things out?"

"This will be a one time trip. Twenty-five trucks. Together."

Dr. Reischtal turned to the door. "Spaced around and under downtown Chicago."

Lee thought of the long tunnel and the explosion. "When?"

"Perhaps days. Perhaps hours."

Phil waved Lee over. He grasped Lee's shoulder and bent him close. "Listen to me very carefully. You want to take what he's offering. Please."

Lee said, "If this asshole wants to come on my home turf here—"

"Shut up for five seconds and listen. If you want to have any kind of career at this at all, for the love of Christ shut the fuck up and listen."

Lee swallowed his next sentence.

Phil tapped his chest. "It's an easy choice. You handle this right, and by God, in ten years, you're gonna be fucking president."


The sheriff's department would only provide three buses. No more.

"Fuck me," Sam said and spit his gum into the gutter. He'd gone out to check everything out, just to make sure that they wouldn't be putting federal prisoners on any kind of transport that might prove to be unstable and problematic. He stood at the curb as the three buses drove the wrong way down Clark and lined up along the curb. "Where's the rest?" he asked the first driver.

The driver shrugged. "All I know is they sent me here. You got a problem, call the sheriff. I drive the bus. That's all."

The two other drivers all said the same thing. Sam pulled out his cell and called Ed. "Hate to say it, but this is gonna be all we got."

Ed, watching the buses on closed circuit video monitors inside the main office, said, "Looks like we got the short end of the stick. Hold tight for a minute. I'll call Arturo, see if I can't get some answers."

Sam didn't bother to answer. He relayed the message to the drivers, who all sat snug ensconced inside a bulletproof plastic cocoon. This way, if the prisoners ever managed to gain the upper hand over the guards, they couldn't reach the bus drivers. When Sam delivered the news, each of the three drivers shrugged and shook out a folded newspaper over the giant steering wheel, settling down for a long wait. These guys didn't give two shits about the situation. The union only said they had to drive the bus, and nothing else.

Sam's phone rang. It was Ed. Sam answered with, "Any luck?"

"Arturo isn't answering his phone. So I called the sheriff's office. Turns out the boys from the CDC have commandeered a number of prisoner buses. Won't say why. Just that the buses aren't available. When I pressed the issue, they told me, strictly off the record of course, that the CDC and FEMA and god knows who else had already commandeered the rest of the prisoner transfer buses in Cook County. Sounded to me like they're anticipating some trouble in the evacuation. Either way, we got three buses, so we're gonna have to do this in shifts."

"Figures. Same old story. No help from anybody."

"You got it, brother. Sit tight out there, and I'll figure out who gets to ride the first merry-go-round."

Sam didn't bother to relay the message to the bus drivers. He didn't want to interrupt their reading. He wandered over to one of the empty benches, sat down, closed his eyes, and turned his face to the hazy sun for a few minutes. He wished he'd brought his flask along, but he'd left it in the car.

He wondered if he could sleep if he stretched out on the warm bench. If he could just close his eyes for a while, he could pretend that the soldiers behind him, busy setting up more roadblocks along Van Buren, were actually El trains clattering along the tracks. He knew deep down that it wouldn't work. The sound of the El trains screeching around corners and rumbling into stations was unique, and in that absence, he could never shake the feeling that armed soldiers now patrolled his city.

And so he would never be able to fall asleep.

Not until this was finished, one way or another.

# CHAPTER 59

*12:39 PM*
*August 14*

Qween and Dr. Menard picked their way through a sub-basement full of old conference chairs, outdated copy machines, and plenty of cobwebs. On the far wall, Qween found a large panel with three long lines scratched in the metal. At first glance, it looked as if it was just regular wear and tear, but if you cocked your head just right, the three scratches eventually arranged themselves into a ragged capital H. Qween pulled it away from the wall, revealing a large vertical air duct. "Old Henry told me about this place. He holes up back here when it gets too cold."

Dr. Menard peered down into the absolute darkness and sighed. "I don't know if I'll fit."

Qween snorted. "If I can fit, you can fit. I'll go first, ya big baby." It was old enough and big enough that she fit without straining too much, using her butt and knees to slow her descent. She looked up at Dr. Menard's silhouette, framed within a square of dusty light. "Almost there, Doc. Your hospital is on the other side of this wall. You want in quiet, this is how we get there."

Dr. Menard didn't say anything, but he climbed inside,

blocking the light. She heard him coming down in a shuffling slide. Ten feet down, Qween hit the bottom of the shaft. It stretched away on both sides. She called up, "Head to your left when you get down here."

She crawled along until a hazy blob of faint light appeared. The light sharpened into a square of horizontal strips as Qween got closer. She pressed her face against the grill, looking at another large, forgotten, filthy storage room, full of discarded furniture, outdated technology, and boxes full of mold.

Something was different about this one, though. It almost looked as if a flood had been flash frozen as it tore through the room, the murky water solidified midsurge. The edges clung to the corners and under conference room tables, and the shadows collected and pooled in the dim light.

She dug around in her cloak and found a tiny flashlight. She clicked it on.

Dr. Menard's voice was half-surprised, half irritated. "You've had a flashlight this whole time and didn't use it?"

Qween said, "You're a smart man. Woulda thought you'd know these take batteries. They ain't free and they ain't cheap. Ain't gonna use 'em up when I don't need to." She aimed the light down at the material, but still couldn't figure out what it was. It almost looked like black sand had collected in drifts over the years. She got impatient and gave the grill a solid thump with the bottom of her fist, knocking it out of the way. It hit something hard directly under the airshaft, bounced off into the center of the room, landing in the drifts with a soft thump, sending a cloud of the stuff flying into the air. The debris settled fairly quickly, and Qween decided it wasn't dust. Too heavy.

She stuck her head out and saw they had gotten lucky; a table had been shoved against the wall directly under the airshaft. She rotated her body and stuck her feet out first, then lowered herself to the table. She kept her flashlight on the whole time, watching to make sure that whatever the material was, it wasn't moving.

One wild thought kept bouncing around her head, and although she dismissed it as being too ridiculous, it kept coming back. She was worried that they'd stumbled into a nest of those damn bugs, but there was no way that many bugs would clump together in one place like this. No way. So she flicked the light around the mounds of what looked like rich black soil. But she knew it wasn't dirt. The particles were a touch too large for one thing, and the other was that they were flat, and lacked the way soil crumbled when it fell apart. It wasn't clay, or mud.

Dr. Menard climbed out of the airshaft and sneezed.

Qween got down and leaned over the edge of the table. She held the flashlight close to a stagnant wave of the substance. It wasn't exactly black; that was just the lack of light in the sub-basement. Up close, the stuff was a dark reddish-brown, and in some spots, almost translucent. Whatever it was, it wasn't alive. She reached out to touch it; most of it crumbled to dust under her fingers. She cupped her hand, and brought a sample up so they could get a better look.

"Any ideas, Doc?"

"I don't . . ." Dr. Menard trailed off. He pinched some of the stuff between his thumb and forefinger, taking the flashlight from her hand and holding the lens an inch away. The substance reminded Qween of fish scales for some reason.

"Oh good Christ," Dr. Menard whispered. "It's all the shells, it's their exoskeletons. These bedbugs, they molt. Five times, if I can remember it correctly. And this . . ." The flashlight swept the room. The dark material was a least two feet deep, sometimes higher near the walls and some of the furniture. "This is what is left, when . . . when they . . ."

"When they shuck they skin," Qween finished for him.

Dr. Menard's eyes raced around the huge room. "This city has got a bigger problem than anyone realizes. There's nothing on record. . . . I don't think there's anything that indicates . . . There's gotta be . . . millions of exoskeletons here.

Billions." He swallowed. "If these things carry that virus, we are all in such big trouble."

"I don't have no fancy degree or anything, but I coulda told you that. So let's get moving." She slid off the table into the drifts of the shells of dead bugs. They came up to her knees. It felt like when she was a little girl, playing in an old silo full of wheat chaff. "We ain't going back the way we came, 'less you can climb up that air shaft."

Dr. Menard tucked the bottoms of his pants into his socks, then retied his shoes as tight as possible. "If we can't get back out this way, how were you planning on getting out?" He pushed off the table into the dry swamp, feet disappearing from view as they slid through all those tiny exoskeletons.

Qween gave a dry, rasping laugh. "Shit. Never promised you a way to get out. Just a way to get inside. Once we're in there, it's your call. Figured you'd have an idea." She waded through the drifts, heading for the door.

"I'm not coming back this way, I can tell you that much," Dr. Menard said.

"What you worried about? Ain't nothing here but a bunch of old shells. Shit, you oughta see what's left after a crawfish boil on Maxwell Street. Now there, there's a mess. This? This ain't gonna slow us down. This is just a billion crunchy ghosts is all."

# CHAPTER 60

*12:39 PM*
*August 14*

Tommy still sat with Don's corpse. There were no windows, no clock. He had no idea how long he'd been locked in the room. The IV bags hanging from the rod that rose above his right shoulder were empty. The slick plastic bag attached to his catheter that hung down by his left leg was full of urine. He did not know if he had been asleep or awake; the edges between consciousness and oblivion were getting blurry.

Sometimes he thought he saw bugs. On the bed. Lately, on the floor.

Tommy wondered if he was starting to hallucinate.

Driven down to nothing, he went back to testing the leather straps, flexing each arm and leg, giving each side a chance to rest while he yanked with the other side. It didn't work. No matter how hard he pulled, he couldn't recreate whatever combination of movements had led to that wonderfully elusive sound of popping thread. He worried that he was getting too weak. He had no idea the last time his body had gotten any kind of nourishment.

Now, instead of phantom flickers in his mind of Dr. Reischtal laughing at him from behind the monitors, of infected patients running howling through the halls, he could only see his daughter's face. This was worse than anything. Watching her expression fall from warmth and joy to soul-crushing terror and pain as men's hands groped and clutched and squeezed.

Tommy bucked and flailed at the wheelchair straps, howling and weeping, sobbing promises to Dr. Reischtal, to anyone watching, begging for release.

Something gave. More movement from one of the straps. He realized that it was the combination of jerking his left arm and right leg at the same time that gave him enough leverage. He tried it again. The tearing sound was perhaps the most blissful thing he'd heard in his life.

Soon, he had enough slack in the leather strap around his right ankle that he could pull his foot free. He used it to get a better grip on the plastic covering the floor, and pushed back around, away from the door, toward Don. The wall behind the bed and camera was filled with cabinets and Tommy was hoping for some kind of blade.

He stopped. Cold. At least five or six bugs were now clearly visible on the floor. He could only guess that they were leaving Don to come looking for the only warm body in the room. Using his toes, Tommy got the wheelchair rocking and angled it to the side, crushing a bug. Rolling back and forth, he used the wheels to smash every bug he could find, one by one.

He edged around the bed and tried not to think about the cold, clotted blood under his bare foot and hoped that the virus couldn't survive for hours in a cool temperature. Once on the other side of the bed, the first thing he did was kick the camera over. It didn't shatter like he had hoped, but it still felt halfway satisfying. Of course, he couldn't do anything about the one in the ceiling.

Using his toes, he pulled the drawers open, swung the cabinet doors wide. Nothing useful. No scalpels. No bone saws.

Just soft supplies, like rubber gloves, sheets, replacement paper towels for above the small sink. A goddamn bedpan.

He looked back to the door. Maybe he could push himself back, see if he couldn't figure out how to unlock it. If he could get out of this room, he might be able to find something, anything that could help him get free of the wheelchair.

Tommy was halfway around the bed when there was a loud click, and Sgt. Reaves opened the door.


It wasn't until the third bus was almost full that Sam had to make an example out of somebody.

They'd brought out sixty-two prisoners, splitting them between the three buses. Over half of these were low-level security concerns, mostly old white guys with three DUIs and black kids who still didn't understand the difference between a federal charge of intent to sell versus the lesser Illinois charge of simple possession. These kids saw themselves as proud warriors, following in the footsteps of their fathers, uncles, and brothers. As if it was some kind of honorable career choice. However, they were still new enough that federal prison scared the living shit out of them. So they were fine, no trouble at all. Neither were the three or four junkies, so strung out that they thought they might be in hell.

The rest were career criminals, serial rapists, neighborhood narcotic kingpins, and guys who couldn't manage to walk past a car without trying to steal it. For the most part, they were docile, and didn't give anybody any trouble. The guards brought them down and out through the visiting area, further disrupting the prisoners' expectations. All prisoners were normally moved in and out of the Metropolitan Correctional Center through a special passageway along the fifth floor of the parking garage. Instead, Ed and Sam had them led out into the plaza, then around to Clark, where the buses were waiting.

Trouble came with Inmate No. 928743.

Inmate No. 928743 didn't want to get his wristband scanned. Every prisoner wore one. They were all brand new, made of the same plastic that was used in clothing store security tags. Shockproof. Waterproof. Came with a bar code that identified the prisoner. Ed had demanded that they scan the codes at every step, just to keep track, so a guard would scan the number of every prisoner as they got on the bus.

Ed monitored everything from inside, eyes flicking across a bank of monitors. He used his phone to talk to Sam. For everything else he gave orders to the warden, who passed it on to the appropriate personnel. He had just sent the first batch of truly dangerous repeat offenders out to the buses, mixed with an equal number of first timers.

The biggest threats to the MCC evacuation were the guys awaiting sentencing for heavy crimes like murder, aggravated assault, and rape. They'd already been found guilty, probably had burned through an appeal or two, and were just sitting around to find out how many years they were going to spend behind bars. They were the walking definition of nothing to lose.

Inmate No. 928743 clasped his cuffed hands at his waist when the guard held up the scanner and said, "No."

The guard stepped back across the sidewalk, putting some distance between himself and the prisoner, trained to withdraw from one-on-one challenges. The two guards on either side of the bus doors watched and waited for an order. Ed watched it on the video monitors. He called Sam.

Sam answered with, "Already on it." While Ed had been watching from deep inside the prison, Sam was outside, leaning against the wall, chewing a fresh stick of gum, and watching the prisoners step on the buses. He'd been expecting someone like this, an opportunist who could smell the insanity on the wind, taste the chaos impatiently waiting just under the crumbling surface of order, someone who would test the limits of authority.

Sam made eye contact with a guard who carried a twelve-gauge and made sure the guard was paying attention. Then he moved toward Inmate No. 928743. "Afternoon."

The prisoner cocked his head and regarded Sam coolly.

Sam smiled. "Listen, I don't care what your problem is. My advice, get over it. This is your first and only warning."

Inmate No. 928743 planted his feet shoulder-width apart, and smiled right back, equally scary and empty. Amateur tattoos, bluish gray in the hazy sunlight, crawled up his neck and all over his bald skull. "My civil rights are being violated."

"No, no, they're not," Sam said. "Not yet." With no wasted movement, he brought his lower leg up, square and true, smashing the tibia bone into Inmate's No. 928743's testicles. The seismic shock had barely begun rising from the prisoner's torso into his chest when Sam broke his nose with a fast little jab.

As a teenager, Sam had taken classes from an old ex-Israeli soldier who had showed the lanky boy a few vicious Krav Maga moves. The man's fighting philosophy was basically that if anyone was threating you, then you hurt them before they had a chance to hurt you, and hurt them bad enough that by the time they're even thinking about getting up off the floor, you're far, far way.

Blood exploded from Inmate No. 928743's nostrils the same time the devastating effect of his crushed testicles hit his brain. He went down like a rotten tree, every part of him collapsing into the concrete. Sam had to give the guy credit. Inmate No. 928743 still managed to crawl forward a few feet before he curled into a fetal position and vomited on himself. Urine stained the front of his pants.

Sam turned to the guard with the .12 gauge. The guard tossed the shotgun; Sam caught it, brought the stock around and cracked the prisoner's skull. Fresh blood erupted out of the man's shaved head, washed over the tattoos, and spilled down over his already bleeding nose and started a puddle on the sidewalk.

Sam had deliberately hit the guy in the head with the stock, instead of some softer, perhaps more painful location, because head wounds bled like a bitch. Both Ed and Sam wanted the rest of the inmates to see the blood. You could be borderline retarded, even damn near brain damaged, but everybody coming out of the prison would understand what blood on the ground meant.

The massive lobby of the Fin was cool despite the sunlight that flooded through the three stories of windows. The three soldiers pushed through the spinning glass doors and took a moment to enjoy the delicious chill as it settled into the sweat that coated the inside of their fatigues.

"That's what I'm talking about," one said.

"We got thirty seconds before McLeary is on our ass," another pointed out.

"Hello?" the third called out, moving toward the sleek front desk. "Hello?" he called again. "Anybody here?" He turned back to the first two. "Hey, you guys know if this building's been cleared yet?"

They shrugged. The third muttered, "Shit. Just what we need. Wasting time checking an empty building."

The second shook his head. "They shouldn't have. Supposed to be on our grid." He pulled out a radio and spoke into it. "Command? This is Charlie one-two-seven, that's Charlie one-two-seven. I need confirmation on a location. Over."

A burst of static from the radio. It swelled, then settled into a low hiss. "Command, you copy? I need verification that a building has been cleared. Over." Still no response. "Goddamnit. These pieces of shit."

"What do you want, man? They work in the desert," one of the soldiers said. "Too many fucking tall buildings here."

The third soldier stuck his head in the back office. "Hello? Hello? Anybody here? Anybody?"

Deep in the back office, Janelle was hiding under one of the desks, breathing fast, almost hyperventilating, sound asleep. She had curled up under of the far desks, wedging herself into the tightest corner possible, like a lost lamb under a dead tree, frozen in both snow and fear.

"Fuck it, dude," the other soldier said. "We don't get back out on the grid, McLeary's gonna shit a brick. 'Sides, isn't Winston and those boys supposed to double back through, confirm that everything's been cleared?"

"Supposed to. Let's head back outside, see if the radio works any better."

The first two soldiers groaned when they stepped back out into the sun. The third soldier hit the button on his radio again, suddenly shielded his eyes and pointed. The other two saw the rat at once, working its way along one of the graceful, curving flower beds, trying to remain hidden under the leaves. All three soldiers opened fire.

Chips of concrete, flower petals, dirt, fertilizer, and rat flesh exploded into a pink and brown cloud. When the dust settled, there wasn't enough left of the rat to fill a sandwich Baggie.

"I'd be lying if I said that wasn't fun," one of the soldiers said as they wandered over to the flowers to look for any more rats. The gunfire attracted the attention of one of the grid commanders. Once he understood that it was only one rat, he sent a decon crew over to spray the area down with the sterilization foam.

Behind them, the lobby remained empty and quiet.


Sergeant Reaves said nothing as he surveyed Don's hospital room. He wore a hazmat suit, minus the helmet. His expression never changed as he regarded bloody corpse, the tire tracks in the blood on the floor, the overturned camera, the open cabinets.

He paused and tilted his head when he saw the dead bugs. When his gaze settled on Tommy, Tommy tried not to look like a child who'd been caught trying to steal a cookie and had accidentally knocked the cookie jar to the floor where it shattered. Sergeant Reaves's gaze never wavered.

Tommy shrugged.

Sergeant Reaves blinked, took a deep breath, held it, and walked over to Tommy, rubber hazmat boots crunching on the dried blood. He leaned over Tommy, placed one gloved hand over his face. With his thumb and forefinger, he spread Tommy's right eyebrow and cheek, widening the eye to painful extremes. He repeated the movement with Tommy's left eye, peering intently at Tommy's eyeball. Satisfied, he released Tommy's head and spun the wheelchair around, so that Tommy faced the far side of the room.

Tommy had no idea how his eyes might give something away, and had a nightmarish flash that Sergeant Reaves was simply going to pull out his pistol and put a bullet in the back of his head. He tensed, waiting for that blast of oblivion, but Sergeant Reaves simply dragged the wheelchair backwards through the blood to the doorway and out into the hallway.

Sergeant Reaves exhaled outside the room. He wheeled Tommy down the hall to the elevator and they waited in silence for the doors to open.

Tommy wondered if he was being taken back to his original room. One entire wall had been covered with a heavy curtain, and Tommy was convinced it had concealed a window. If he could just get out of his wheelchair, he might have a chance at breaking through the window. And if he could break the window, he could climb out. He didn't care if there was a ledge or not, he'd take the risks of climbing out of a twelve- or thirteen-story room compared to facing Sergeant Reaves or Dr. Reischtal.

Tommy kept his right foot pulled in on the metal footrest, nice and snug, as if the leather strap was still wrapped around his ankle. He had no idea how he might break out of the wheelchair restraints, but he had one foot loose, and that was a start. He just needed some time alone in his room where he could break the window.

The elevator doors slid open. Sergeant Reaves wheeled Tommy inside and pushed the button for the lobby instead of going upstairs. Tommy wanted to keep quiet, wanted to be a hard-ass, didn't want to give Sergeant Reaves the satisfaction of hearing Tommy speak first, but as the descending floor numbers flashed, his will broke. "Where we going?"

For a long time, Tommy didn't think Sergeant Reaves would answer. Tommy knew he had fucked up, and swore at himself for being weak.

Sergeant Reaves finally said, "Dr. Reischtal has given instructions to transfer you to a more secure location. This building . . . is no longer safe."

Tommy didn't know what to say. He stayed quiet as they dropped. The doors opened on the first floor with a happy *ding*. They came out behind the front desk and beyond it, Tommy could see that the waiting room was empty. Sergeant Reaves pushed him out a back door into the thick summer air that hung over the river. The tables between the hospital and Chicago River were vacant. Even the benches stood alone.

Tommy watched a bus push over the Madison Bridge; then, as if this was the last CTA bus in the city, the bridge split in half and began rising. From the wheelchair, every bridge he could see had been opened, as if the stitches on a fresh wound had been popped, that black thread cut in a hurry with a bone saw, sparing the clean flesh from the infection.

An ambulance was waiting on the sidewalk. Two more soldiers, completely encased in hazmat suits, rolled Tommy up a ramp into an ambulance. They locked his wheels. He hoped they couldn't make out fine details with their plastic faceplates and wouldn't notice the broken strap around his right ankle. One sat in the back on the opposite bench and stared at Tommy.

Sergeant Reaves stood a ways from the ambulance, his

back to the river, and watched without expression as the other soldier slammed the back doors. He didn't move. Tommy hoped it was the last time he ever got close to the man.

The other soldier climbed into the front and started the engine. He turned the lights on and drove through the sand-bags until joining the parade of buses. Through the back windows, across the Chicago River, all along the river walk, Tommy could see trucks pulling massive tankers, arranging them into place next to the river, and more figures in hazmat suits uncoiling long hoses into the river. The ambulance turned onto Upper Wacker and the image was lost.

Tommy glanced at the soldier in the back with him. The man's eyes, encased behind protective plastic, were blank and dead. Tommy might as well have been looking into the eyes of some deep water shark, something that went blind in the light and hunted by some kind of primitive, almost supernatural sense.

The buses pulled to the side for the lights and siren, allowing the ambulance to streak through downtown. They flew down Madison, and turned right on Michigan. When they hit Monroe, they turned left, heading into Grant Park, toward the Lake. As they broke free of the shadows of all the buildings, Tommy again turned to the back windows, looking at the afternoon sun. It was the first time he'd seen true sunlight in two days. He closed his eyes, trying to imagine he could feel the rays on his face, and that somehow the warmth and security of the sun could pass through the thick glass of the back windows.

They followed Monroe all the way to Lake Shore Drive and turned south, where they joined a convoy of CTA buses, all merging into one lane, the only lane through the blockade on Roosevelt, next to the Field Museum. Tommy leaned forward and could see the line of buses snaking along Lake Shore Drive past the parks, past the baseball fields, past Buckingham Fountain, and once they were through the road-block, the buses turned east once more onto short McFetridge

Drive, and curled down into the Soldier Field underground parking lot.

While the buses descended beneath the stadium, the ambulance left the line and continued east, toward Adler Planetarium. They turned south and pushed through the clustered knots of trailers, trucks, and military vehicles strung out across Northerly Island Park. The narrow strip used to be a landing strip called Meigs Field, until Daley Junior had a bunch of bulldozers rip up the runway in the middle of the night back in 2003. Now it was a flat, grassy field, full of emergency equipment. Everything was pushed back as far as it could go, their backs against the water, as though they wanted to get as far as possible from the stadium.

The ambulance driver pulled around and backed into a narrow spot among a group of FEMA trailers. The soldier in the back didn't move and never took his eyes off Tommy. Out of the front windows, beyond summer docks and small boats, Tommy could see the line of buses disappearing under the northern end of Soldier Field. Out of the back windows, nothing but the endless blue expanse of Lake Michigan.

He heard voices outside, but couldn't make out any specific words. There was a muffled knock at the back doors, and the soldier in the back with Tommy got up and unlatched the doors, swung them wide open.

Dr. Reischtal stood there. The sun was not kind to his skin. "Good afternoon, Mr. Krazinsky. Sergeant Reaves has assured me that, for some unknown reason, you have not only survived the night with Mr. Wycza but as of yet, there is no sign of infection." His lips pulled back into a thin grimace that may have been a smile. "We shall soon discover why. A proper laboratory is en route. When it arrives, I will see for myself exactly what secrets live inside you."

The soldiers slammed the doors, leaving Tommy alone in the ambulance.

# CHAPTER 61

**2:47 PM**
**August 14**

The hospital lobby was empty. It made Qween nervous. The waiting room was silent. The nurses' station had been abandoned. The phones did not ring. The computers were dark.

But the old building didn't quite *feel* empty. This was why she was nervous. Something in the air, something just out of the range of her hearing, some kind of vibration through the molecules that her conscious brain couldn't pick up, something set off ominous warnings in her subconscious, the lizard part of her mind, as Sam would say. Somewhere, there was life inside the hospital.

Dr. Menard checked the computers at the nurses' station. He shook his head. "They aren't connected to the system that we used." He headed for the elevators. "We have to go up to the third floor. There's a central computer where I can access all the files." He didn't seem worried about the vibe of the place; he just looked relieved they hadn't encountered any soldiers.

"You sure this is worth it, Doc?" Qween followed, the

reluctant one now. "Smart money says there's a damn good reason ain't nobody here."

The elevator doors opened immediately, as if it had been waiting for them, and they stepped inside. "Five minutes, tops," Dr. Menard said. He fished a little plastic stick out of his pocket. "Just long enough to dump whatever I can find on this jump drive."

Qween looked at it skeptically. "You be quick, or I'll up and leave your ass here."

The third floor was just as empty as the first. Great plastic sheets had been stretched over every surface, and while they may have been tight at the beginning, now they hung in tatters, as if a violent wind had ripped through the third floor. Dr. Menard moved quickly to the bank of computers at the nurses' station in the center of the room. Cubicles with light blue curtains surrounded the area, beyond which, a long corridor stretched out. The end of the corridor was obscured with strips of shredded plastic hanging from the ceiling. It was impossible to tell if anyone was down there or not.

Dr. Menard tapped a few keys. While the system booted up, he dragged over a chair and then inserted his jump drive. "I'll be surprised if they didn't wipe these machines clean, but maybe we'll get lucky if they left in a hurry."

Qween said, "It's the leaving in a hurry that makes me worry. We got no business being in here." The plastic whispered under her feet, unnaturally loud in the empty area. She found herself wishing she had her cart up here; she missed the familiar bulk and weight. She had all kinds of weapons stashed inside, sure, but it had also been surprisingly versatile in a fight, all by itself. She had used it as battering ram, a shield, even an escape vehicle once, rolling away down the low hill on West Division over Goose Island.

As the computer screens flashed to life and Dr. Menard started muttering and clicking around, Qween eased down the corridor, avoiding the smears of clotted blood on the plastic. The ragged strips hanging from the ceiling caught the light from the buzzing fluorescents and shimmered with a faint green tint, like rotting strands of kelp. A medical cart lay on its side halfway down the long hallway. A couple of oxygen tanks had been forgotten at the far end. Piles of stained blue hospital gowns and scrubs had been scattered along the floor. Every single door was closed. The entire wing was so quiet she could hear the whisper of cool air hissing from the vents and the humming of some huge machinery several floors below.

Qween crossed over to the first door on the left and opened it. Inside, she found the bloody corpse of a woman strapped to a bed. It looked as if the woman had died in horrible agony, thrashing as she bled out of every orifice, spraying blood across the room in the final convulsions.

Qween backed out, wiping her hands on her cloak, and tried the door across the hall. Instead of just one corpse, she found a massive pile of body bags. All of the furniture and medical equipment had been removed, apparently to make room for the forty or fifty corpses. They had been thrown in haphazardly, as if whoever had been carrying them had been in a hurry. The bags weren't sealed with any kind of biohazard precautions; blood was seeping through the zippers.

She shivered and reached for the door handle. She was finished with looking around. Fuck that. It was time to leave. She shut the door with a solid click. The sudden, sharp sound made her flinch and an instant later, an agonized howl erupted from two or three rooms down the hall. Someone crashed into that door from the other side. The door rattled and the handle quivered. The screaming didn't stop. It got worse.

Qween moved quickly back up the hall. "Time to go, Doc."

"I know, I know," he called. He'd heard the shrieking. "Almost done."

Then, another scream. This one distant, from the fourth floor above. Someone else joined in. A chorus of cries echoed up and down the hall. Soon, the hospital was alive with screaming.

Dr. Menard rose out of his chair, watching the ceiling. It sounded like hundreds of people were howling in despair and agony. The wave of pain reverberated throughout the halls, the empty rooms, the elevator shaft, and then somehow, grew impossibly louder. The awful sounds shook the ceiling, the walls, the very foundations of the building. Even the plastic seemed to be vibrating.

Qween kept moving back to the elevators, her Chuck Taylors making crackling noises that were nearly buried under the avalanche of shrieking. She stopped, lifting her feet to check the soles of her shoes. Nothing was there.

Qween squinted at the plastic under her feet. She put one foot out, experimentally pressing down on the floor. The texture of the floor under the opaque plastic changed somehow, swirling around her footprint. She cocked her head, trying to make sense of it. It almost looked like the surface of the floor was moving like sand in an hourglass. She turned back, and now could see, quite clearly, the plastic was stuck to the floor in the shape of her footprints.

Dr. Menard said, "Thirty seconds. And we're out of here."

Qween took a few tentative steps toward a tear in the plastic, over by the wall. She reached out, pinched the very edge, and peeled it back several feet. It tore easily, like wet newspaper.

The floor was alive with bugs.

They had been flowing under the plastic the entire time, heading down the hall. The bugs that had been revealed in the new tear stopped in the sudden exposure to fresh air, and behind them, the current continued to flow, and so a mound of the bugs grew as they piled up. They spilled out over the plastic and started to crawl toward Qween over the top of the plastic.

"We're done here," Qween said, heading for the elevator. "Don't care if you're finished or not. I'm fucking leaving. Now."

Dr. Menard saw the bugs. He swallowed, tried to say

something, failed, and settled for yanking the jump drive out of the CPU. He quickly scurried to the bank of elevators, noting how the bugs were still moving under the plastic on the floor in a vast, seeping flood.

The elevator doors opened and they didn't waste time getting inside. The doors shut and the elevator dropped. "All those people—" Dr. Menard started to say.

"—are dead," Qween finished. "Ain't nothing you gonna do for 'em. They gone."

# CHAPTER 62

The buses were full. It was time to move out.

Ed walked down the sidewalk, heading for the last bus, going over the plan in his head. The job was difficult, but not impossible.

He knew all about the bridges and street closures; the only way out of the Loop was through the single lane down by the Field Museum. Sam would ride in the first bus with some of the worst offenders, while Ed would ride in the third, keeping an eye on things and coordinating the trip from the rear bus.

The plan was to turn right on Van Buren, roll out to Michigan, then down to Congress and onto Lake Shore Drive. In addition to the prisoners, each bus would carry three guards, all armed with .12 gauge pump Winchesters. Once they were in motion, the guards had been instructed, right in front of the convicts, to shoot to kill if anyone stepped out of line. The guards were more than happy to comply.

Once the three prisoner buses were through the blockade, a security detail was supposedly waiting to escort them down to Twenty-sixth and California. It wouldn't take much to ambush the convoy; anybody halfway organized could create problems, cracking open the buses like a can of cheap beer, leaving the inmates to go sprinting through the streets.

So Arturo had promised Ed and Sam four patrol cars, with two officers in each car, and a couple of wild-eyed cops on motorcycles who weren't part of the main force that surrounded the Loop. Everybody else was spread out across the rest of the city to maintain the illusion that the Chicago PD still had everything under control.

Once down at Cook County Jail, they would orchestrate the unloading of the prisoners, then head back with the empty buses for another load.

Ed boarded the third bus and scanned the faces, which ranged from wide-eyed and panicked to openly hostile. He called Sam. They were as ready as they would ever be. "Let's get going."

"Good. Sooner we start this shit, sooner we're done."

Ed hung up and nodded to the driver. The driver folded his newspaper and put the bus in gear. Ed turned to watch through the windshield. He could see Sam's lead bus roll up to the intersection of Clark and Van Buren and start to turn right. Ed felt a sense of calmness settle throughout his body; he almost felt as if he could breathe easily again. They had a long ways to go, but at least they were on the move.

Then the first bus stopped. One of the soldiers was waving his arms over his head, pointing north, to where the lines of CTA buses were trickling down Jackson. Sam hopped out of the bus and walked over to the soldier. Sam pointed east down Van Buren. The soldier shook his head. Sam pulled out his phone.

Ed answered the call. "Christ, what now?"

"Believe the old-timers called it a failure to communicate," Sam said. "Seems that nobody told these boys where we're headed, and it doesn't fit their plans." Ed could hear the soldier yell something at Sam. Sam yelled back, "And I don't give two shits about what you want, so go fuck yourself, pal."

Ed hung up and locked eyes with the driver. "You stay here, keep the engine running, and you don't move for anybody, until you hear from me. Got it?"

The driver shrugged, put the bus in park, and whipped open his newspaper yet again. Ed went down the steps and out into the heat and humidity. He was surprised he'd gotten used to the air-conditioning on the bus that fast. He quickly joined Sam at the front of the first bus.

Sam was still yelling at the soldier, "—tin star jackass wannabe hero. You ever pull that lump on your neck there out of your ass, you might try thinking for yourself for once."

"Okay, okay," Ed said. He shot Sam a look that said to keep his mouth shut.

Sam shrugged, put his hands on his hips, and turned his back on everything, watching the El tracks, missing the rumbling and sparks of the trains.

Ed approached the soldier. "What's the problem?"

The man wore a hazmat suit without the helmet. An assault rifle was strapped across his back. Extra clips sagged from webbing down the front of his chest. A throat mike wrapped around his neck. "You've been misinformed. I'm afraid there is no way these prisoners can be transported anywhere but Soldier Field for decontamination procedures, no exceptions, by order of the president of the United States."

Ed considered this, then spoke softly. "Do you have any idea who is on board these buses? Take a hard look at this building here. This is a maximum-security federal penitentiary, understand? We are currently transporting over sixty inmates down to the facilities at the Cook County Jail. To put them through some kind of decontamination process, along with regular citizens, this is out of the question. We don't have the man power. Are you following any of this? The president wasn't thinking about this when he signed that order."

"No exceptions," the soldier repeated.

Ed felt his blood pressure spike. He said, "I don't know who the fuck you work for. I don't care." He pulled out his star. "You see this? This gives me the right to do whatever the hell I deem necessary within the city of Chicago. And that, pal, is a fact."

The soldier permitted himself a crooked, faint smile. "Look around. We're in charge. And that, pal, is a fact."

Three Strykers came roaring down Clark, each of them taking a position across from each bus. The rear door of the closest one opened with a rough hiss, and two more soldiers got out. Neither one wore any kind of insignia on his hazmat suit, but it was clear from the behavior of the other soldiers that these two were superior officers.

One stomped over. He had close-cropped, iron-gray hair and goggle-like sunglasses that clung to his skull as if they'd been surgically attached. He asked the younger soldier, "What's the holdup?"

Ed said, "We seem to be getting off on the wrong foot here. These prisoners need to be taken down to the Cook County Jail."

The soldier with the sunglasses turned to Ed. "Who are you?"

"Detective Jones. Chicago PD."

"Well, I don't know what you've been told, but our orders are quite clear. Every single man, woman, and child inside the perimeter will be evacuated and complete the decontamination process. After that, there is a medical evaluation, and then, and only then, will they be released. No exceptions. If we do not follow proper protocol, we risk breaching our containment system, which could lead to an outbreak. Then it isn't simply Chicago that is in danger, it is the entire continent. We will not allow that to happen."

"So tell me, what measures have been put in place to minimize the possibility of a prison break? If you planned this out, you surely recognized the fact that over five hundred inmates from a maximum-security federal prison would have to be evacuated. How do you intend to deal with these violent, dangerous individuals who will happily seize this opportunity to kill anyone in their way and escape?"

"That is your responsibility."

Ed started to ask the hypothetical question of whether or not the man was fucking serious when his phone rang again. Shaking his head, he pulled it out to check the number. With any luck, it would be Arturo with a solution to this mess.

It was the warden. Ed answered it. "What?"

"We have a problem. . . . Something is happening. . . ."

Ed could hear chaos in the background. "Gonna have to be more specific."

"We've lost contact with several floors."

"Please clarify 'lost contact.'"

That got the military officer's attention.

The warden sounded frantic. "Guards were, uh, making a final sweep of the laundry facilities, I believe. There were guards lost . . ." More shouting in the background. Ed stuck his finger in his ear, straining to hear. ". . . floors thirteen through sixteen are not responding . . ." Gunfire, sudden and close.

Ed jerked the phone from his ear, turning to look up at the wedge-shaped building.

The officer stepped back, speaking low and fast into his throat mike. Hatches popped open on the three Strykers and soldiers appeared behind the .50 caliber machine guns like heavily armed jack-in-the-boxes. Another dozen soldiers ran along Van Buren and lined up on the sidewalk, their rifles unslung and ready.

The officer said, "I suggest you gentlemen step back and allow us to assess the situation."

Ed ignored him, concentrating on his phone. The warden had stopped talking altogether. For all Ed knew, the warden may have dropped the phone. One lone gunshot, more screaming. Then silence.

Another dozen soldiers lined up along the El tracks over Van Buren.

Sam tapped Ed's shoulder and pointed.

Ed turned and saw all the soldiers, the firepower. He lowered his phone.

The glass visitor doors opened and a man staggered out into the sunlight. He moved as if he couldn't see very well, taking conservative, hesitant steps, holding his hands up over his eyes, to protect them from the light. He wobbled, confused for a moment, then struck out, almost at random, in a direction that headed straight for the building's massive northern pillar.

Ed walked over, followed closely by Sam. A warning shout went up behind them. They glanced at each other, then at the figure that was stumbling along, trying to get as far as possible from the door. As they got closer, they could see that the man was wearing a guard's uniform, although that did not necessarily mean he was actually a prison guard.

They got within ten feet. The man stopped. He was white, mid-thirties, a little overweight, with red blotches across his skin. Ed couldn't get a fix on whether he was actually a guard, and eventually believed it because of how the clothes fit.

So far the man hadn't said anything.

"You okay?" Ed asked, watching the doorway. Sam had his Glock out.

A bug crawled out of the man's hairline and made its way down his puffy face to his nose, and disappeared under a nostril. He didn't appear to notice or mind. He scratched at his armpit, made eye contact for the briefest glimmer, and said, "It itches. Oh God, it itches."

"Why don't we get you some help?" Ed said.

Another bug crawled out of the guard's collar, over his jaw, braving the sun, and disappeared up the other nostril. A third came out of his hair and crawled across his open eye.

The eye imploded, and the back of his head crumpled into a pink mist.

The sound of the gunshot bounced around the plaza,

echoing between the El tracks and the building. Ed and Sam dropped to their knees, spinning, as Ed yanked his .357 out of his shoulder holster and Sam brought his pistol up with both hands. They faced over twenty soldiers, lined up along the sidewalk and the El tracks.

The body of the guard collapsed.

Ed yelled at the officer, "You said this was our responsibility."

"Until we visually confirm presence of either bugs or the virus. Then our authority supersedes everything."

Ed never got a chance to argue. Another man bounced out of the front door, but wasn't slow and hesitant like the first one, this guy was running for all he was worth. He wore a prisoner's jumpsuit and tried to slip around the corner to Clark. A three-round burst from one of the soldiers took him down in a tangled heap of orange cotton and splashes of blood.

Then a third. A fourth. More prisoners poured out of the visitor entrance, heading in all directions. It was almost like the bugs crawling out from the guard's collar, using their overwhelming numbers to escape. The prisoners, like the bugs, flinched at the sudden sun and heat but kept running.

Gunfire erupted around the small plaza in a sudden storm. The prisoners were literally blown apart, their heads folding messily into themselves, causing the sudden lurching expressions of astonishment, as their lungs popped and their legs split open horizontally across the kneecap. At twenty to thirty yards, it wasn't a challenge; it was more like shooting fish in a barrel.

The three machine gunners on the Strykers took that as a cue and unloaded on the buses. The ridiculously heavy bullets smashed through the windows, the side of the bus, through the seats, through the prisoners closest to the side, then more seats and the second set of prisoners across the aisle. Collisions with the seats and some of the major ligaments changed the original trajectory of the bullets, but they continued on, into the seats across the bus, smashing through more prisoners and seats, and out through the other side. They killed everyone on-board, including the drivers. The feather-like remnants of the newspapers floated serenely around the steering wheels and corpses.

When the third prisoner had bolted from the entrance, Ed and Sam dove to the side, rolling into shelter behind the north pillar. Gunfire came from Van Buren, then the deep, booming crackling from the Strykers' .50 caliber guns opened up from the west, on Clark. They crouched, heads down, elbows up, arms wrapped over their heads to protect themselves from the exploding glass wall that encased the first floor.

The gunfire trickled away as the flood of prisoners slowed and stopped. Several unnaturally quiet seconds ticked past. The soldiers started reloading. Then, new gunshots, somehow different. Ed risked a glance at the shattered remains of the first floor. More men were now fleeing the prison, both pris-oners and guards, but this second wave was armed. That was why the gunfire sounded different—it was coming from behind Ed and Sam.

The soldiers fell back into defensive positions and re-sumed shooting. The prisoners and guards dropped to the sidewalk and wriggled up behind the piles of corpses, using the bodies for cover. They stuck their shotguns and handguns over all the dead flesh and fired blindly.

Ed saw one soldier fall from the El tracks and land like a bag of loose laundry, sprawling over a low sandbag wall. But that was the only soldier he witnessed get hit. A few shot-guns, with shortened barrels for close-range defense, and a handful of Smith and Wessons were no match against thirty or forty state-of-the-art fully automatic assault rifles, and the slaughter continued.

However, the prison had the advantage of a seemingly endless supply of prisoners and even a couple of guards. Whenever one of them went down, someone behind them would pick up the fallen weapon and continue shooting. They kept coming, streaming out of the MCC.

At first, Ed couldn't figure out why the prisoners would face almost certain death, running face-first into a blizzard of bullets. Then he remembered the bug crawling across the first guard's face and realized the bugs must be infesting the prison, and they were driving the prisoners out of the prison, despite the gunfire.

He tapped Sam on the shoulder, and nodded toward the shattered buses. They needed to take advantage of the new distraction and at least get clear of the damn cross fire. They scuttled across the sidewalk on the Clark Street side, keeping the buses between them and those .50 caliber machine guns. They rolled through the shattered glass in the gutter and scooted under the middle bus. Gunshots continued to pop and crackle around them.

Ed fought to control his breathing, to slow his heart. His ears rang from all the shooting. His eyes watered from the stinging smoke and glass. The air smelled of harsh gunpowder and metallic taste of blood.

"When these boys finish cutting down the prisoners, they're gonna come looking for us, you know that, right?" Sam asked, half-whispering, half-yelling into Ed's ear to be heard.

Ed nodded. Still, he hesitated, watching the prisoners struggle forward, only to be blown apart. He hated to cut and run, leaving the inmates to their doom, but there was nothing the detectives could do. If the bugs had gotten into the prison, then the prisoners were as good as dead anyway.

"Any suggestions?"

Sam twisted around, getting a fix on the Strykers. "We try to just walk out of here, they're just gonna shoot us in the back and forget about it."

Ed nodded. He knew better than to think the soldiers were on their side.

Sam asked, "How bad you want to get out of here?"

Ed thought about Carolina and her son. "Bad enough to shoot my way out if that's what it takes."

Sam grinned. "Atta boy. You remember that." He crawled to the other side of the bus and surveyed the street. He called back to Ed, "Gimme thirty seconds, then come around to the other side of that tank down there or whatever the fuck they call it." He pointed at the Stryker farthest south on Clark.

Ed gave him the thumbs-up. Sam rolled out, got to his feet, and scrambled across to the far side of Clark. Ed took one last look back at the prison, noting how the shooting was slowing down. There weren't many prisoners left to fire back. He tried to ignore the shards of safety glass strewn across the asphalt as he used his elbows to pull himself along under the bus to the back.

He scurried across the gap to the third bus in the line and dove underneath it as well. He crawled the length of that bus, then figured at least thirty seconds had passed. He rose stiffly, knees cracking like frozen power lines in a high wind, and peered back at the plaza.

The soldiers were moving in now, finishing off the last of the prisoners. At least two or three guards had seen the writing on the wall, and while they couldn't go back upstairs, they weren't in any rush to stick their heads outside and get their brains blown out, so they'd holed up inside, behind the visitor desk. They'd pop up once in a while and fire a volley through the shattered glass, just to keep the soldiers keep their distance.

Ed knew the attempt was futile, and those guards were finished. It was just a matter of time. He tried not to think about the poor bastards stuck inside the lobby, still shooting it out with the soldiers, and hurried over to the last Stryker. Like he had promised Sam, his only responsibility now was to get out of the city alive. He ducked down under the nose to avoid being detected by the periscope and the driver's video image sensor.

The guy on top running the .50 caliber was too preoccupied with punching holes the size of softballs in the concrete above the guards inside to keep an eye on anything closer. Ed didn't think the soldier had enough of an angle to see where the guards were hiding, and seemed to be blasting away for the hell of it.

The unholy volume of the machine gun made it hard to think, so Ed just kept his head down and hustled around to the other side of the vehicle. The shock waves from each shell pummeled him with invisible fists and made him dizzy. He didn't even hear the shot from a handgun, only saw that suddenly the machine gunner stopped and slumped to the side. Blood poured out of his mouth and nose.

The rear door flopped open, and two soldiers jumped out, guns ready. They spotted Ed immediately. One of them screamed, "Freeze!"

The other one said, "Shoot him. Shoot the fucker."

Ed didn't even have time to raise his arms before Sam somehow materialized behind the soldiers. Two shots, so close together they sounded almost like one solid report. Blood spattered across Ed's sport coat. Both soldiers collapsed.

Sam slipped his pistol back into his holster and rolled the closest soldier over. "You take that one. Hurry." He felt around for the Velcro straps that protected the zipper. "We got a minute, maybe two tops, before they figure out they've lost these guys."

Ed finally figured out what Sam was doing. He got to work on the other soldier. As they struggled with the hazmat suits, Ed tried to process what had just happened. It left him feeling cold. Sam had just killed three men inside of ten, maybe fifteen, seconds. It scared Ed a little. "You sonofabitch. You use me as bait again, I'm liable to bust you in the chops."

Sam tried to wipe some of the blood off the hazmat suit. "Quit your bitchin'. I took care of it."

A minute and a half later, Ed and Sam helped each other zip up their suits and kicked their sport coats under the Stryker. They had left their own handguns back inside their shoulder holsters, and took the assault rifles from the dead soldiers. Sam pushed the bodies of the soldiers under the Stryker. Ed stuck his head inside the vehicle and found a couple of helmets, along with a backpack, on the front seat. He opened it and found it was full of foreign MREs, with no less than seven languages labeling the contents. Plastic water bottles. A map.

"Grab all the cool shit," Sam said. He squinted. Found his glasses. Used them to determine what he was seeing. He waved to one of the guards on the other side of the broken glass. The guard held a shotgun and two fingers up.

Sam got it. One gun. Two shells. He shrugged, and gestured at the Stryker, wordlessly telling the guard that if they could get outside, the Stryker was all theirs.

Ed found a pair of night vision goggles. More ammo. He dumped it into the backpack. Ed slipped it over his shoulder and handed a helmet to Sam. He said, "We supposed to just waltz right past 'em?"

"That's exactly what we're gonna do."

They pulled the helmets over their heads and left the Stryker, heading north. At Van Buren, they turned west, leaving the sporadic shooting behind. They passed through rows of sandbags, moving quickly. A group of soldiers came jogging along, heading for the firefight, and never looked twice at the two figures in military hazmat suits.

Ed and Sam faded into the shadows.

# CHAPTER 63

"You sure about this?" Qween asked.

Dr. Menard nodded. "It's the fastest way to get out of the city. Once I'm on the other side, I can get this"—he clutched the jump drive in his fist—"to somebody. Somebody not connected to the CDC. Somebody with some authority. Somebody with some power."

He pushed out of the front doors of Cook County General before he could change his mind. Qween followed him at a distance. It was clear to him that she didn't like the plan. He turned back to her as they headed for the street, knowing the answer, but asking anyway. "You want to come with me?"

Qween snorted. "Naw. I leave this town, it'll be on my own two legs. 'Sides, I gotta pick up my cart." She'd stashed her shopping cart the day before in an alley a block from the post office and was anxious to make sure it was still there.

Dr. Menard said, "There's nobody left on the streets, just the soldiers. They're gonna see you."

"Shit. They see me, then I deserve to get caught and hauled away. Don't worry, Doc. Gonna be night soon."

Dr. Menard stuck out his hand. "Thank you."

Qween shook it. "You just make sure you let folks know." She jerked her head back at the hospital.

Dr. Menard started off north along Upper Wacker. He didn't want to look back, didn't want to watch and see which direction Qween was headed. If things went wrong, and they wanted information, he didn't want to know where Qween had disappeared.

It wasn't long before a couple of soldiers noticed the lanky doctor shambling along. They shouted at him and he waved back, content to play the clueless scientist. They jogged over and demanded to know where he had been.

Dr. Menard acted confused. "I've been . . . working. What's happening? Where is everybody?"

"Where, exactly, have you been working?" one of the soldiers asked.

Dr. Menard turned back the way he had come, and pointed. "The hospital." He was glad that Qween was gone. There was nothing but an empty street behind him.

Both soldiers took a step backward. "The hospital," the first soldier confirmed.

Dr. Menard nodded.

The other soldier pressed the button on his throat mike and said, "We have a survivor from the hospital. Repeat, we have a survivor from the hospital, waiting for pickup, Wacker and Washington." He listened a moment. "Copy that." He released the mike and looked up at Dr. Menard. His smile was as hollow as an alderman's promise. "They're sending someone around now, sir."

"What is going on?" Dr. Menard tried again.

"Some problems in the city, sir. They're evacuating everyone."

Dr. Menard tried to go blank. "No kidding? I mean, I know things weren't good, but Jesus, I didn't think they'd evacuate the city."

"Please stand still, sir."

"Am I in trouble?"

"No, sir."

"Why are you looking at me like that? What's really going on here?"

"Just basic precautions, sir. Nothing to worry about."

Dr. Menard was getting nervous and finding it harder and harder to play dumb. "Look, I'm fine. Really. I'm not sick."

"I'm sure you're not, sir. We need to get you on a bus, sir."

Dr. Menard wanted to say, *Stop calling me sir, you little bastard.* Instead, he said, "Okay. Where am I going?"

"They're taking everyone to Soldier Field. For decontamination."

The second soldier shot the first a tight look, and the first soldier shut up. Something cold crawled up Dr. Menard's testicles. Soldier Field. For some reason, the idea of gathering all of the evacuees in one place scared the hell out of him. "Why?" he asked.

"That's our orders," the second soldier said. He didn't bother with the "sir."

"There it is," the first soldier said, sounding relieved. He pointed at an oncoming white bus in the wrong lane. With a sinking feeling, Dr. Menard realized it wasn't a CTA bus. It was a Cook County sheriff's prisoner transport bus. He swallowed. This was going from bad to worse. "Listen," he said. "I can walk. Really. It's no big deal."

"I'm sorry, sir. Orders." The two soldiers stepped apart, blocking both directions down the sidewalk. The bus got closer.

Dr. Menard stopped pretending. "You two have no idea what's really happening, do you? This virus, it isn't going to be stopped by an evacuation, do you understand? It is going to spread, unless we study it. We have to unlock it, don't you get it?"

The two soldiers stared at him but didn't say anything.

The bus pulled up behind him in a cloud of diesel exhaust. The driver, buried behind a layer of bulletproof plastic, opened the doors. Dr. Menard turned back and found the soldiers aiming their rifles at him. Mindful of the jump drive in his front pocket, he climbed aboard. The doors snapped shut behind him.

# CHAPTER 64

**5:22 PM**
**August 14**

Dr. Menard didn't think anything was wrong with the people on the bus at first. Sure, some of them appeared to be sleeping. Well, maybe most of them. And a guy in the back was weeping. Loudly. The rest of the passengers, the few that were awake, looked just like him, confused and scared and trying not to lose hope that the soldiers were there to help.

He moved through the bus, and the reality started to sink in.

The sleepers weren't just taking a power nap. They were out cold. These people had curled up into a fetal position across two seats, or had ended up on the floor. A few of them had been written on with permanent marker. Someone had scrawled, KICK ME across some businessman's face. Another guy, just a kid really, with long hair, dirty glasses, and a Death Cab for Cutie T-shirt, had HAVE FUN KILLIN PEOPLE, DUDE written in blocky letters from one cheek, across his nose, to the other cheek. Still another had a target circled on his forehead.

A tight, choking feeling enveloped Dr. Menard. He couldn't help but notice the heavy-gauge wire that covered the windows. He wanted to turn around and bang on the driver's plastic barrier and demand to be released. This bus was full of people infected with nearly every stage of the virus. But he knew that wouldn't work. It might get him shot.

No. The soldiers knew damn well this bus was full of the infected.

So Dr. Menard kept moving toward the back of the bus. Nearly all of the seats had been taken. He didn't know where to sit. At least none of the passengers had slipped into the final, violent phase. Yet. Almost at the very back, he spotted an Asian woman in surgical scrubs, staring morosely at her lap. Sensing a kindred spirit, he sat carefully next to her, trying not to let his elbow touch her arm.

The bus turned onto Upper Wacker and they drove past the hospital. He craned his head around, but he couldn't see any sign of Qween. He glanced at the woman next to him, but she still hadn't looked up. "Do you know what's happening?" he asked quietly.

She looked at him, eyes hollow and wet with tears. The prisoner bus passed an empty CTA bus, and the glass reflected a glare from the setting sun back into the interior of the passenger bus. Nearly everyone flinched at the sudden flash of light, including the woman wearing medical scrubs. She turned her head away from him, and he finally saw them.

Three bedbugs were feeding on the back of her ear.

Dr. Menard jerked away and stood up in the aisle. Down at the front, the driver's eyes met Dr. Menard's eyes in the mirror, then flicked back to the street. Dr. Menard did his best to stand while the bus turned left on Jackson and sped up. He brushed imaginary flecks off his clothes and couldn't stop. His hands shook.

He pressed his hand against the jump drive in his front pocket, just to reassure himself. It was still there; of course it was still there. He told himself that they would be unloaded at Soldier Field, and all he would have to do was make it through the decontamination process. It wouldn't be much fun, but he could handle it.

He knew he would have to say good-bye to his clothes. That would be first. He figured that he would either slip the jump drive in his mouth or, if push came to shove, so to speak, he could hide it in his ass. Then they'd be hit by some kind of powder? Hard to say. Showers were guaranteed, probably a number of them. God only knew the chemicals that would be sprayed on them. Heat definitely. Lots of heat, to kill any bugs. From there, he imagined they would turn people loose inside the stadium itself. He'd join everybody else, and they would wait.

Everything would be put on hold until the SWAT teams in the subways came up for air. Once the rats had been destroyed and the pesticides had been sprayed from one end of the city to the other, then the government would want to declare the evacuation had been a success. They'd have to let everybody go at that point. They couldn't rightly declare a victory without turning the survivors loose. It wouldn't suit their version of the truth. Hell, if the CDC or the president wanted, they could claim they'd saved everybody in Soldier Field.

*Be patient*, Dr. Menard told himself. There was a light at the end of the tunnel. He would live to see the end of this.

The bus turned onto Lake Shore Drive, and he marveled at the wall of tanks and trucks that had been arranged to form a barricade across both Lake Shore Drive and Roosevelt. Dr. Menard glanced through the back windows. There were no more buses behind them. In fact, as far as he could see, nothing else moved on the streets.

The prisoner bus barely slowed down as it slipped through the barricade. For Dr. Menard, this was not a good sign. It meant that they didn't want to stop and inspect the bus. It meant that they already knew who was on board, and wanted them through as fast as possible.

Soldier Field loomed ahead, the new gleaming steel and

glass addition dwarfing the original dignified columns and solemn structure. Dr. Menard was confident they would pull around to wherever they had set up the decontamination staging area, probably outside in a parking lot somewhere. The bus headed down into the underground parking lot.

*Of course*, Dr. Menard reassured himself. They must have a huge lot under the stadium, easily accessible by the buses, and easy to control. It made sense that they would set up the decontamination tents down here. But instead of going deeper into the parking lot, the bus rolled up a ramp, and before he fully understood what was happening, the bus emerged out from under the northern seats of the stadium, past the goal post, and across the end zone.

Some of passengers moaned at the sudden reappearance of light as the bus left the darkness of the underground parking lot. Dr. Menard ignored them and peered through the wires at the stadium as the bus rolled arrogantly over the grass, passing the ten-yard line. The twenty. The thirty. Until finally, it slowed and stopped around the forty-yard line, joining dozens of other buses, all lined up in neat rows on the field.

Dr. Menard stormed up the aisle to the driver's cubicle. He pounded on the plastic. "Where are the decon showers? What's the protocol here? You cannot just dump these people in here. We need to be screened, do you understand? You have infected onboard! Get us out of here." He pointed at the driver with one hand and clutched the jump drive with his other.

Something tickled the back of his neck and he slapped at it but he never took his stare off the driver.

The driver's expression was unreadable behind the hazmat faceplate. All Dr. Menard knew was that the driver was facing his direction. The gloved hand hit a button and the door behind Dr. Menard opened. Dr. Menard refused to turn around.

The driver opened his own door and stepped outside. And walked away.

Dr. Menard looked back at the passengers. Everyone was asleep now. He came to a decision and went purposefully down the stairs. He put his foot on the badly wounded turf and moved swiftly. As he rounded the front of the bus, the thing that surprised him was the quiet of such a huge structure. Apart from some asshole yelling garbled directions through a megaphone down around the southern food court, the silence that hung over everything was unnatural, this calmness.

He turned in a slow circle and realized the main reason that such a huge place was so quiet was because most of the people were sleeping. Down on the field, people had crawled under the buses to escape the light. All those people under the buses made him think that they'd created some kind of horrible nest or burrow.

He put one foot on the top of the front tire and pulled himself onto the bus's hood. From there he crawled up the windshield and stood on the roof, getting his first good look at the immense stadium. It looked empty. Then he saw the shapes wedged behind the seats, the rumpled seams of backbones and elbows and hair that skulked behind every row. Very few had fallen asleep sitting up. It looked like everyone had sought out the tightest, darkest, most secure spots as they drifted off, as if it was some kind of primeval ritual.

The few people he saw actually walking, or at least moving, all seemed unaware of each other. They stumbled through the rows of buses, looking for a quiet place to rest. For whatever reason, they seemed content to curl up next to someone else who was already sleeping. He couldn't quite tell, but from the buses nearby, it looked like the front doors were all wide open, and full of sleeping figures. The only vigorous movement Dr. Menard could see was inside the back of the CTA bus directly in front of him. It looked like a group of men were gang raping a young woman. He couldn't tell if she was sleeping or not. He hoped she was.

There was not one soldier, not one police officer, not one doctor, no one from the government on the field itself. After scanning the seats for a while, he finally saw a few soldiers patrolling the upper decks. There was movement behind the windows of the exclusive club levels, the expensive private rooms on the east side of the stadium. But that was all.

They had been abandoned.

He quickly slid down to the hood and climbed back to the grass. He got into the cab of the bus and closed the door firmly behind him. Of course the keys were gone. He slid his shaking fingers along the rubber molding that provided a tight seal against the elements. He kneeled on the driver's seat, following the seam where the stiff plastic shell had been bolted into the floor. It looked like it was tight enough to keep the bugs out, but he couldn't be sure. He explored under the dashboard and worried about the gaps between the dash and the steering column.

Hopefully the bugs wouldn't crawl up into the engine block. And if he was still in there when people started waking up and going berserk, it should hold. It had been designed to withstand potential prisoner hijackings after all. He allowed himself to sit back and look around the stadium once again.

He didn't understand how tens of thousands of people had been herded into Soldier Field. Why were they keeping everyone here? These people needed doctors. They needed to be decontaminated. They needed help.

The back of his collar rubbed at his neck at again and he pulled at it with irritation. His index finger brushed against something tiny, a speck of gravel or scab-like crust or something. Pinching it between his thumb and forefinger, he brought it around and held the squirming bedbug up to his face.

He watched the legs twist, felt the tiny shell undulate under his fingers, saw how the proboscis reached for his breath, and when it couldn't have that, it curled around to bite at the strip of soft flesh right up under the thumbnail.

He drove it into the center of the steering wheel. The horn echoed throughout the stadium.

# CHAPTER 65

As the sun sank behind the Loop skyline, Tommy waited in the darkness of the back of the ambulance.

Ideas, each worse than the last, swam through his head like dying fish trapped in a half-filled aquarium. Some, when he knew he was absolutely positive he was awake, seemed almost plausible. They had forgotten him when the virus had swept through the city, and they had abandoned everything. They were still watching him for any of the symptoms to appear. Or they were simply watching and waiting for his sanity to finally crack and for him to start screaming or drooling on himself.

Some of the worst ideas seemed to uncoil from the cold tendrils of his nightmares. Grace was strapped to an identical wheelchair, watching him on one of the monitors while Dr. Reischtal slid needles full of the virus into her veins. Or Tommy was trapped in a coma, only thinking he was awake, while the world withered away in dust and ashes outside.

But no matter the path of the theory, no matter what ghostly images swam into focus on the blank cellulose acetate of his mind, the utterly banal, inevitable fate waiting at the end of every train of thought was that the universe did not revolve around his problems. It was indifferent. It simply did not care.

The undeniable truth that lay in the darkest depths of his despair was the knowledge that he was going to die. Soon. And when he was gone, he understood now how little it would take, how a tiny ripple in the chaos of the world could hurt his little girl. There were so many ways to snap the life out of a four-year-old girl. Grace could die so easily.

Or maybe even something worse than death.

What would happen if Lee got his hands on her? Tommy kept seeing her in pain, hearing the anguish in her voice, watching those innocent, uncomprehending eyes as strangers touched her. . . .

A guttural cry escaped his clenched teeth.

Either he escaped or Grace died.

# PHASE 6

# CHAPTER 66

8:36 PM
August 14

Lee had promised her that they would be perfectly safe, but watching all the soldiers rush around all the sandbags and tanks, and listening to the distant shooting, Kimmy wasn't so sure. The men in the hazmat suits had made Grace cry, so Kimmy now had to keep the girl on her lap. Grace kept burying her head in her mother's shoulder, and Kimmy just knew that she was getting tears and snot all over her evening dress. But that wasn't the worst. The worst was the dust getting blown around from all the helicopters landing and taking off across the street, in Daley Plaza. The wind was wreaking havoc with her hair and the dirt was sticking to her makeup.

By the time the press conference started, she would be lucky to look like one of those insulting Bratz dolls that had been buried at the bottom of a trash heap for a few weeks. And with all these reporters standing around, with all their crews, not to mention the big trailers full of generators to run the lights, you'd think that somebody would have a makeup kit around. But no, all the reporters, even the women, seemed to be shedding the air of glamour and embracing the rough-and-tumble effect, as if to remind their viewers that being in the quarantine zone was serious business.

Kimmy wanted to shake them and say, *Puh-leeze. You're on TV, for god's sake. And those stupid clothes—you're not on safari here. Try not to look like you've been sleeping outside for the last two nights.* She shifted Grace to the other shoulder and was thankful that she could at least sit down. Around fifty folding chairs had been set up in orderly rows, facing the stage. Whoever had set them up had been either misled or optimistic; most of the chairs were empty.

The stage itself had been erected in the very middle of Clark Street, between City Hall and Daley Plaza. Two flags bookended the stage, the light blue horizontal bars and four red stars of the City of Chicago flag, and the stars and stripes of the U.S. flag. The solemn walnut podium stood empty in the center.

Kimmy tried to relax. She reminded herself that she was just being catty to the reporters because she was jealous that they finally got to look cool, like those foreign correspondents who were always broadcasting while bombs and bullets burst over their heads.

But not her. Oh, no. Lee had instructed her to look as flawless as possible. So she'd pulled out her best black strapless evening dress. Diamond studded choker. One-carat diamond earrings. Hair upswept, precariously held together with a few hidden hairpins, strong hairspray, and a lot of prayers. Even Grace was wearing her best Sunday dress and the stiff shoes that she hated, because they hurt her feet.

Lee had on one of his most expensive suits. His tie was the color of the red stripes in the American flag, with a matching silk handkerchief in the breast pocket. His hair was slicked back and gleamed in the media lights.

The fear was making her impatient. The press conference was supposed to have finished over an hour ago. She'd overheard some of the reporters talking, and they were apparently all waiting for one of the main guys from the CDC to show up. The CDC could give an assessment of the situation, and then Lee could step forward and take all the credit, offering up Kimmy and Grace as proof that the city was quite safe.

Apart from that, she didn't know anything else about the press conference. While she certainly didn't expect Lee to stand at her side the entire time, it would have been nice if he'd come over once in a while to check with her.

Instead, he was too busy huddling next to the stage with his slimy uncle. Phil seemed to be angrier than usual; Kimmy watched him yelling into his phone, a finger stuck in his other ear to muffle all the chaos from the soldiers and helicopters. While his uncle was on the phone, Lee went over his speech. As she watched him move his lips as he read, practice his gestures, she realized she didn't know how she felt about him anymore.

She didn't really want to know, frankly.

At first, it had all been so gosh darn exciting. Lee was incredibly handsome, powerful, and rich. He was a man who would not just provide for his family, he would take care of everything. He was the kind of man who didn't blink at spending over six hundred dollars on a four-hour meal for just the two of them. Back when she and Tommy were still together, she would try and explain that she wanted him to take her out, to make her feel special, and all he'd do was stare at her and blink uncertainly while he tried to figure out what she meant, as if it were some impenetrable calculus mystery that couldn't be solved.

Now Tommy was gone and although she felt bad sometimes, she didn't really want to see him again. He reminded her of a part of her life that she wanted to forget. She had closed the door on that chapter, and only wished to look forward. Like this quarantine thing. Soon it would be over, Lee would be seen as a hero, and their lives would only get better, filled with state dinners and long trips and getting her picture in the paper at charity functions.

Down the street, in the wash of the TV lights, she watched a rat crawl out of a storm drain. The animal was filthy, emaciated. She wondered if she should say something, let someone know, but hesitated because she didn't want to interrupt Lee's big moment. The rat scurried off into the shadows and she stopped worrying about it and wondered instead if they would be staying at a hotel tonight outside of the city or end up back at Lee's condo.

Kimmy turned her head away from yet another helicopter landing, shifted Grace again, and didn't see the second rat emerge.

Or the third.

Or the fourth.


Even with his right foot free, Tommy could not pull any of his other limbs loose or tear any of the other straps, all them each a full three inches of leather. He flailed even harder, kicking out with his bare right foot, and only managed to stub his little toe on the bench opposite. The pain almost made him cry.

It wasn't fair.

One leg. Nothing else. Just enough to tease him.

One goddamn leg.

The paramedics had left the windows cracked so he didn't die of a heat stroke. Still, it was terribly hot. Sweat streamed down his face, his chest, his arms. The moisture made the leather straps swell, which made things worse as they grabbed hold even tighter. The paramedics had kept him hydrated, but hadn't given him any food. He hadn't taken a piss in over nine hours. He was hoping that night would cool things off a little.

He caught a flash of something out of the corner of his eye, and turned his head to look through the back windows of the ambulance. At first, he thought it might be some kind of sticker on the window, maybe a dead leaf or something, because the image looked so out of place. After growing up next to Lake Michigan, he'd grown so accustomed to the flat, featureless expanse of water that seeing something large out there was like finding a tree growing out of the middle of the Dan Ryan Expressway.

There was a warship out there.

It wasn't one of the giant behemoths, of course, not like those huge aircraft carriers that lumber around the ocean, floating cities in their own right. Still, spotting it suddenly just offshore made it seem even bigger. It must have been five to six hundred feet long. It looked like it had one large cannon mounted on the forward decks, but that wasn't what took his attention. He blinked the sweat out of his eyes. It looked like there were not one, but two helicopters waiting on two separate landing pads on two levels at the stern.

Something Dr. Reischtal had said bubbled up in the back of his mind: "A proper laboratory is en route."

It all clicked into place. That warship must have some kind of lab on it, and now that it was here, Dr. Reischtal would be showing up at any minute to drag Tommy out there. He didn't want to think about what might happen to him once Dr. Reischtal laid him out on an operating table. He focused instead on the unyielding fact that he was out of time and out of luck.

In frustration, he kicked at the bench opposite, this time driving out with his heel, and drove his wheelchair back against the wall of the ambulance. The force of the kick was enough to push the back wheels off the floor an inch or so. He abruptly released the tension, and the wheelchair hit the floor with a creaking thud. He tried it again, extending his leg all the way, pushing the back wheels up the wall. This time, he guessed he must be five or six inches off the floor.

He relaxed his leg and crashed into the floor once again. The impact made the metal shriek. He rolled it forward. He couldn't tell if it was his imagination or if the chair actually felt wobblier. He tried it again, this time leaning slightly to his left, trying to put more pressure on a single wheel.

Again. And again.

He lost count after twentieth crash. The wheelchair started rattling and shaking loose every time he positioned himself for another drop. Somewhere around the fiftieth or sixtieth fall, the left wheel snapped off abruptly, dumping Tommy sideways on the floor.

He went berserk, kicking and arching his back, flopping around in one last burst of energy. Once unlocked, some of the metal bars simply slid apart, and he was able to bend the rest of it enough to break free. He still had both armrests strapped to his arms and a strip of metal along his left leg, but he was loose.

The first thing he did was to pull the catheter out. The second was to pull the needles connected to the IV units out of the back of his hand.

The third thing he tried was the back door.

It was unlocked.

# CHAPTER 67

Qween's cart was gone.

She'd left it here countless times back when the city was normal, filled to the brim with asshole businessmen, women in expensive suits and jogging shoes, bike messenger punks, bored cops, and other homeless scum who wouldn't blink at stealing a shopping cart. Back then, it had been the perfect place, tucked securely away behind a cluster of foul-smelling Dumpsters in a narrow alley perpetually shrouded in shadows a block from the post office. Nobody had ever messed with it.

Now, all of the Dumpsters had been pushed out in the center of Adams for no reason she could decipher. She poked around in them for a minute, making sure her cart wasn't still somehow stuck in the middle. It wasn't. It was gone.

She drew a hitching breath, let it out slow, rubbed her face. She hadn't cried in damn near twenty years, and she sure as shit wasn't going to start now. She tried not to think about some of the things that had been inside. Things she couldn't replace.

Faint laughter. She turned east, and saw two soldiers in the intersection of Adams and Clark. The streetlights had started buzzing, automatically switching on. In the spill of yellow light, Qween saw the soldiers kicking around a bundle of loose rags. Off to the side, lying sideways in the gutter, was a shopping cart.

Ice cold rage crackled up her back, coating her spine with frost. Her fingers drew back into fists. Fury fogged her brain, overpowering any sense of caution. She started down the street.

One of the soldiers bent over and picked up the rags daintily, using only his gloved forefinger like a hook. "Jesus. Makes you wonder how anybody could live like this." He wore a big, shit-eating grin that did little to hide his buckteeth. Like the boys in Tommy's neighborhood used to say, this guy could eat corn on the cob through a chain-link fence.

The other said, "No shit." He was smaller, with a face so narrow it could have passed for the triangular blade of a butcher knife. His sunglasses hung around his neck from a neoprene strap, no doubt necessary so the glasses wouldn't just slip right off the slim hatchet of a nose. "What gets me is why the fuck would anybody choose to be homeless in Chicago. I been here in the winter. It's fucking cold, man! You're homeless, why don't you just leave, you know? Head down to Florida or someplace warm."

Qween stomped into the light. "You dog dicks having fun?"

It scared them. They definitely weren't expecting to see anyone on the streets, much less a pissed-off homeless woman. Buck-teeth dropped the rags and went for his assault rifle. The rags hit the ground and split open, spilling yellowed envelopes. Most were full of handwritten letters, but one envelope contained a stack of twenty or thirty black and white photographs.

"Fuck's your problem, bitch?" he said.

The other one, the one that looked like the obstetrician had been a little too enthusiastic with the forceps during his birth, slipped his own machine gun off his shoulder. "Where'd you come from?" His eyes flickered to the darkness of Adams behind Qween.

"Y'all having fun with my stuff?" She glared at them.

They actually took a step backwards. Two armed men, and this old woman made them take a step back. It shook them, and once the fear had dissipated, once they realized there was no one behind her, their own anger took center stage.

Buck-teeth took three steps forward, as if to make up for his involuntary step backward. "My partner asked you a question, you dumb bitch. Where'd you come from?"

"Nobody's supposed to be left downtown," his partner said.

"That's mine," Qween said simply, hands on her hips.

"What? This pile of shit?" Buck-teeth ground his boot into the photographs.

Qween couldn't help herself. She stepped towards the soldier, reaching out in helpless despair to her photos. The soldier with the blade-like face stepped around behind her, brought the butt of his rifle around and drove it into the base of her skull. Qween went down to her knees.

"Teach you to scare me, you stupid cunt," he said.

"This is a fucking quarantine zone!" Buck-teeth yelled.

Qween struggled to stay erect, even on her knees. She knew that if she fell on her side, stomach, or back, these soldiers would stomp her to death. Their fear would demand nothing less. She forced her hands to grip the front of her thighs, anything to hold her upright.

"You're not supposed to be here," Buck-teeth said. "This is a restricted area. You know what that means? Huh? It means we can shoot you on sight, if we want to."

Qween exhaled, trying to clear her spinning head. "You got the balls, asswipe, then go ahead." Later, she would admit that probably wasn't the smartest thing to say, but at the time, she was too pissed off to think straight.

"Fuck you say?" Buck-teeth demanded, jamming the barrel

of his assault rifle into her temple, driving her head over to her left shoulder.

"I said"—Qween eye's found his face—"that your big, flapping, wet pussy puts mine to shame."

For a second, Buck-teeth wasn't sure he'd heard her correctly. His eyes met his partner's face, and those eyes, sunk into that blade-like face, looked everywhere but back at him. Buck-teeth finally realized the depth of the insult. His finger tightened on the trigger. "You think you're funny, bitch?"

"You fellas catch this prisoner all on your own?" came a voice behind him.

Two hazmat suits walked out of the darkness of Adams. One was skinny, but the second looked way too chubby to be some kind of hard-ass mercenary. Both carried assault rifles. Unlike Buck-teeth and his buddy, these two wore their helmets. It was impossible to see their faces.

Buck-teeth blinked uncertainly and smiled. It was a fearsome sight. Those teeth looked like they might just escape at any moment and go rampaging through the streets. "No problem here. Just interrogating a prisoner that got left behind."

"Yeah," his partner said. "She came outta nowhere."

"I see." The heavyset hazmat figure stopped ten feet away. "So you two thought it was okay to beat up some old woman."

"Hey." Buck-teeth shrugged. "She was asking for it. Stupid bitch must've been hiding."

"Well, shit." The thin hazmat figure strode forward, unslinging his own assault rifle. "Why didn't you say so?"

He settled his sights on the back of Qween's head, and without any warning, slid the barrel over and shot Buck-teeth in the throat in a short burst of gunfire. Before Buck-teeth's partner, could move, protest, anything, the thin figure shot him at point-blank range in the chest with another quick four-or-five-round eruption.

Sam pulled off his helmet and admired his assault rifle. "Goddamn. I'm gonna get me one of these."

The bodies of Buck-teeth and his partner folded in half, collapsing into the street.

Qween risked a look. She recognized the voices.

Sam looked up. "Hiya, Qween."

Ed shook his head, then slipped off his own helmet. He looked at the dead mercenaries and asked Qween, "You always go out of your way to piss people off?"

# CHAPTER 68

*8:43 PM*
*August 14*

Tommy's first instinct was to bolt from the ambulance and simply run, just pump his arms and legs and haul ass in any direction. He knew that wouldn't work, but maybe he could drop down by the shore, maybe slip into the water and try to escape that way. The urge to run was so strong he had the back door open and one bare foot on the ground before he realized he'd been spending so much time just trying to escape, he hadn't considered what he would do if he actually got loose.

He couldn't just run and hide. How would he find Grace?

He needed a plan. Fighting against every instinct shrieking inside of him, Tommy pulled his foot back and closed the door behind him. The first thing he checked was the ignition. Of course, the keys were gone. He still wasn't sure exactly how he was going to find Grace, but an idea was starting to sprout in the back of his mind. He tore through the inside of the ambulance, looking for anything he could use as a weapon.

The only thing halfway sharp he found was a basic scalpel. The blade wasn't more than an inch long. Tommy shook his head. It figured. The one time he needed something big, something with a bit of range where he could defend himself, and he managed to dig up one of the more useless blades for getting out of here. Just his luck that he would find the one thing that could have made it easier to cut his way out of the leather straps after he had already gotten out of the wheelchair. Instead, he'd put himself through the equivalent of a car crash.

Tommy told himself to stop being such a pussy.

He was loose and he had a blade. It would be enough.

He wrapped the IV tubes around his fist, tucked the scalpel into the front pocket of his hospital gown, and opened the back door again, slower this time. He leaned out and watched through the windows, but nobody was around.

He stepped out and shut the back door softly behind him. He couldn't escape the feeling that the warship not three hundred yards away was watching him. He tried to move slow and bored, acting like there was nothing out of the ordinary going on, like he was merely a doctor, or at the very least, a paramedic keeping an eye on the ambulance. The goddamn hospital gown tended to spoil the effect. No matter how tight he tried to pull it around his shoulders, it somehow still flopped open, leaving his ass hanging out in the wind.

As dusk fell, various lights began blinking to life, all over the ship.

He ignored it and slipped between two trailers. If he could find an empty trailer, he might be able to find some scrubs inside, anything to make him look like a medic, instead of a patient. Then he needed to find a computer, something that might be able to tell him if Kimmy and Grace were on one of the buses that he'd watched taking people into Soldier Field all afternoon. Then, with a decent disguise, and a whole lot of luck, he might be able to gain entry to the stadium and track down his daughter. He'd have the scalpel, just in case.

The first trailer's door was locked. The second had a ton of cables snaking underneath it, so it looked promising. It also had windows, open to take advantage of any breezes coming off the lake, and Tommy eased in close and listened. He could hear a voice, but it sounded tinny, fake somehow. And even stranger, it sounded like a voice he knew. Keeping his back flat against the trailer, he slowly leaned over and peered inside.

He heard other voices, closer, louder. He guessed there were at least two men inside, but he couldn't see them. One of them said something, something that made the other one laugh, but Tommy didn't listen. He was focused on the flat-screen TV on the table.

Lee was on the screen, sharply dressed as always, saying, ". . . could not unfortunately join us at the moment, but they will definitely be a part of our victory celebration later tonight." Lee paused for a moment. "I stand before you in the heart of my hometown, a city that has withstood its share of tragedies, from the Great Fire in 1871, the sinking of the East-land in 1915, the Our Lady of Angels school fire in 1958, and so many others. But this town, this city of broad shoulders, we have picked ourselves up by our bootstraps and marched onward into history."

One of the men inside the trailer said, "Laying it on a little thick, ain't he?"

"I can assure you that when this crisis is over, we will re-build what we have lost, we will honor those we have lost, and we will become stronger, and safer, than ever!" Lee paused, as if for applause. None came.

The camera pulled back, as if to explain the lack of an audience. Lee stood by himself behind a podium on a stage smack in the middle of Clark. City Hall was off to the left, the courthouse off to the right. Then, just before the camera slowly zoomed back in on Lee, so quickly Tommy wondered if he'd actually seen it or not, he spotted two figures standing back near the stage steps, as if waiting for their cue.

One was a strikingly beautiful young woman, wearing a

black evening gown. She was holding the hand of a young girl in a yellow dress. Lee hit a point in the speech, sounding like he was declaring triumph in a closely contested election, and beckoned the two to join him onstage. Lee put his arm around Kimmy's waist. He waved with his free hand for a moment, then bent down and hoisted Grace to his shoulder. She was smiling, but Tommy could see the confusion in her eyes as she faced the reporters and bright lights.

Tommy jerked his head back. He felt his insides clench. His heart sped up, booming away so loudly in his chest that he was worried that the men inside might hear it. He was certain that they would hear the gurgling of his empty stomach.

Kimmy and Grace weren't safe in Soldier Field. They were still downtown, in the midst of the soldiers, bugs, and the infected.

And even beyond that, Lee still had control of Kimmy and Grace.

The decision was easy. Simple.

He heard one of the men inside stand, and the trailer shifted slightly. The man said, "Fine, my turn to go check on the prick. But when Reischtal gets here, it's gonna be your job to help him. Guy's an asshole. Makes me nervous."

Tommy ran back to the ambulance. The new plan taking shape in his head wasn't much, but it was a start. He dropped to his stomach and wriggled under the ambulance. He unwrapped the IV tubing from his wrist, still not sure if he could use it or not. He might have been able to use it if the ambulance had been parked in gravel and he had a lot of time to bury it under dirt and gravel, but it was hard to hide the clear tube in the grass.

As he lay in the itching, late summer grass, the compulsion to bolt, to flee far, far away still seethed inside. He fought it, driving it down deep, the same way he fought the panic earlier that threatened to take over completely. He forced himself to focus on the sound of Grace's laughter. He knew he couldn't focus on just the memory of her face. It was too much. They'd find him, sooner or later, curled up under the ambulance, sobbing his eyes out. But something about her laughter tightened his guts, made him grit his teeth and promise the universe that not only would she be able to laugh again, all this would be nothing but a brief nightmare, whisked away by the morning sun; he would damn well be there and they would laugh together.

Footsteps in the grass. The boots of one of the paramedics came closer. Keys jingled. Tommy undulated, like some malformed snake, under the transmission system until he was directly under the driver's seat. He heard the driver's door open, saw the hazmat boots go up on tiptoe as the soldier leaned across the seat.

The soldier said, "Still with us, shitheel?"

Tommy braced his bare feet against the front tire, bent sideways at the waist, and with his left hand, he whipped out the end of the IV tubing, circling it around the paramedic's feet. He caught the end with his right, and slowly drew it tight around the man's ankles. He waited until the paramedic had leaned in just enough to realize that the prisoner was no longer in the back of the ambulance, then seized the man's ankles and yanked, flinging his upper torso backwards.

The force of the movement jerked the paramedic off his feet. The paramedic landed hard, flat on his back. It drove the breath straight out of his lungs. He gasped for a breath, but it was too late. Tommy pulled the man halfway under the ambulance, drawing the IV tubing tight around the ankles, snaring them together. The paramedic slapped at the side of the ambulance.

With his right arm, Tommy drove the scalpel deep inside the paramedic's upper left thigh. The one-inch blade sunk easily into the flesh. Tommy ripped it across the large muscles, slicing through the femoral artery.

Blood hit the undercarriage.

The paramedic went berserk, spasms wracking his back and legs. He folded in half, reaching down, tearing at Tommy's arms. Tommy jammed his left foot into the man's crotch and pulled the ankles tight against his chest and rode out the convulsions.

In less than thirty seconds it was over. The paramedic was dead.

Tommy dragged the entire body under the ambulance and went through the man's pockets. He found the ambulance keys and forgot everything else. He started to crawl away, then went back and unbuttoned the blue shirt, pulling it off the corpse. It took a while but Tommy kept at it, ripping the fabric at one point.

Once he had the shirt he slid into it under the ambulance, then scooted out and up and into the driver's seat. The keys worked; the engine sounded as if it had been waiting for him. He looked around, and even found a white lab coat that had been tossed on the passenger side floor. He put it on. The upper half was relatively clear, so he hoped it would look better if he was driving the ambulance.

He started the engine and pulled away, nice and easy, through a line of FEMA trailers; a few people were standing around, smoking. Tommy drove slowly, trying to pretend he knew where he was headed. He'd only looked at the route through the back windows and had only a vague sense of where to find the street back to Lake Shore Drive. Once he spotted the two white radio tower transmitters of Willis Tower off to his left though, amidst the absurdly cheerful lights of the skyline, he knew where to look for the right road.

If he got stopped, he planned on bluffing his way through it, saying something vague about an emergency. If somebody really got in his way, he might even try to use the lights and siren, if he could figure out how to turn them on.

He passed plenty of soldiers and medics, but nobody looked twice at the ambulance. The lights above Soldier Field were on, and it almost felt like a preseason game in the late summer. The lack of sound made Tommy wonder if everybody was in the parking lots underground. He'd taken Kimmy to a Bears game a few years earlier, and he'd wanted to make it a big deal, so he'd borrowed his parent's old Chevy, instead of taking the bus. Of course, the parking lot alone had cost him almost a week of wages, but he wanted to do it for Kimmy. They'd been amazed at how many levels had been built under the stadium. "Any deeper, and we're gonna start seeing dinosaurs," Tommy had said. This was back when Kimmy thought he was funny.

He drove between the stadium and the Field Museum, navigating through military trucks and Humvees. He saw a few other ambulances sitting around, so he tried not to panic when he rolled up to the barricade. Before he had a chance to try the siren and lights, a soldier in a hazmat suit was standing in front of the ambulance, motioning for Tommy to stop.

Tommy didn't have much of a choice. He was surrounded by entire platoons of soldiers, by those giant tank things, and he didn't think he'd make it ten feet if he tried to ram through the barricade.

He threw his elbow into the window frame, and leaned out, so the soldier wouldn't be able to see his bloody legs. "I gotta get through," Tommy said before the soldier could say anything. "There's been an accident."

"Nobody notified me," the soldier said. He unclipped his handheld device, checked it.

"Shit, you think they're worried about notifying everybody when there's an accident?"

"I haven't heard anything."

"Look, man, I don't know what to tell you. I'm just doing what I'm told. Said they needed me immediately. Something happened near the press conference."

"Who gave you the orders?"

"Dr. Reischtal," Tommy said without thinking.

"Who?"

"Jesus, pal. You want me to do your job for you? I gotta get fucking moving, you know?"

"Who gave the order?" the soldier asked again.

"I told you. Dr. Reischtal."

The soldier touched his throat mike. "Need a confirmation at the gate. Got an order from a Dr. Reischtal. Anybody under that name in the database?"

Tommy shook his head. "Fuck, dude. No rush. Might be the difference between life and death, you know?"

The soldier ignored Tommy. He listened intently. "Oh. No shit. Do you have that number? Can we call and confirm this?"

"Yes, yes, give him a call!" Tommy shouted. "In the meantime, let me go, so I can do my job. Jesus Christ, what, you think I'm gonna go in there and rob the banks or something?"

The soldier didn't know what to do. On one hand, he wanted to follow protocol, but on the other, he was expected to think on his feet. The name of Reischtal not only checked out, it elicited serious respect and no small amount of fear. If he held the ambulance driver up, and stopped him from getting to the scene of an accident in time to save lives, then he would be responsible. And if he let him go, what could one man in an ambulance do when downtown was full of solders? Who would want to try and break in to the Loop anyway? He should be worrying instead about waiting for clearance when the ambulance came back.

"Fine, fine. But in the meantime, I'll be contacting Dr. Reischtal."

"You do that, pal. But can you move, now?"

The soldier gestured at the driver of one of the CTA buses, who pulled forward just enough to let the ambulance slip through. Once he was tearing down Lake Shore Drive, the lights of the skyline twinkling through the trees, Tommy pumped his fist and grinned like a madman. He couldn't believe it. He felt like a genius for mentioning Dr. Reischtal. The fear that man cultivated was a goddamn two-edged sword.

He was a hundred yards away from the barricade when they started shooting at the ambulance.

# CHAPTER 69

There was still a chance, Dr. Menard told himself. Still a chance that the bug hadn't bitten him. And even if it had, there was still a chance that it didn't carry the virus. He didn't believe it, not really, but he still insisted that a chance was a chance, no matter how small. If he lost hope, then what?

He had almost convinced himself that he might not be infected when he felt more movement in the small of his back. He squirmed around, trying to slap back there and rip his lab coat away at the same time. More bugs fell off of his coat and onto his hands. He whipped off the coat and to his horror, saw that a dozen or more bugs were crawling over it.

He screamed then, an inarticulate howl of rage and despair. He slammed backwards into the driver's seat, trying to smash the bugs. The soft leather absorbed the impact, and the bugs didn't notice. Several of them crawled down into his pants, travelling down along the crease between his buttocks.

Dr. Menard shot up, jammed his right hand back there, and raked his fingernails up through his butt crack. He scraped up three or four of the bugs the way a snowplow might collect a family of dead possums, but it was over. The bugs had gotten into the bus. They were on the floor, under the seat, crawling across the dashboard, everywhere.

Dr. Menard's chance was gone.

He pulled the jump drive out of his pocket and stared at it. He'd fought his way through so much to get this information out to the public, only to have it end now. He had half a mind to get out and walk to the top of the stadium and throw the damn thing over the side. Maybe someday, someone would find it and give it to the proper authorities. He figured if he started up to the edge, they might shoot him before he got that far, but what else could he do?

He didn't even have a phone. And even if he could find one, it wouldn't help. The jump drive used a full-size USB connector, and Dr. Menard had never seen a phone with a port that large. He sat up straighter for a moment, reaching out to grab the steering wheel. Phones couldn't take a jump drive, but laptops . . .

He jumped out, ignoring the bugs that still were crawling on him. If he could just manage to find someone with a laptop, one that could connect to the Internet on its own, or maybe even the stadium had their own local Wi-Fi that he could tap into. He couldn't remember seeing any bags on the prison bus, so he ran around to other side of the closest bus and kicked open the doors.

Somebody growled from under the bus. People were waking up.

Dr. Menard jumped onboard. At first, the bus looked empty. He took another step, bent down, saw the sleepers. They were all either curled up on the seat or had fallen asleep hiding underneath the seats. A lot of them had bags. He started through the bus, testing the satchels and backpacks, weighing them, sizing them up for a laptop.

Dr. Menard had accepted the clear outcome of being bitten. He knew, on an immediate level, that he was infected and would likely die within a few days. Of course, he didn't truly understand the implications of his death, he hadn't had the time to sit and contemplate. He only understood that he had a few hours left to make a difference. If he could find a laptop with the right connections, the evidence, all the lists of names, pictures, and even video of the test subjects waking from the deep sleep could be transmitted, and even if he was gone, it could have a lasting impact. He had a catalog of every horrific act inside the hospital, with all kinds of helpful information like names, dates, lab work, and it would crucify those responsible.

He might be dying, but the information could live forever, if he could find the right laptop. He kept dragging bags out from the seats, until he came across one guy who had a laptop in a satchel still wrapped around his shoulders.

Dr. Menard felt the laptop inside, and ripped the strap over the guy's head. He unzipped it and pulled out the laptop.

The guy started to wake up. He stared at Dr. Menard, blinking furiously, trying to clear his head.

Dr. Menard opened the laptop and almost cried out in relief when he discovered it was already snapping out of its own sleep, powering up and ready. His forefinger slid across the trackpad, clicking on the Web browser. A few blank Web pages sprang out of the menu bar, still waiting for a signal.

"Please, please," Dr. Menard begged softly.

The owner of the laptop felt differently. He snarled, leapt forward, and slapped the laptop out of Dr. Menard's hands. They both went down, sprawling down the bus aisle. The movement and noise woke some of the others up. They groaned, whipping their heads back and forth, trying to claw their way out of a sea of bad dreams.

Frustration exploded in Dr. Menard. He drove his knee into the side of the man's face, knocking him into another seat. The occupant of the new seat moaned in pain. Dr. Menard grabbed at the laptop and scooted backwards. A quick glance at the screen told him the pages were loading. Slowly, but they were loading.

He had a signal.

He snapped the laptop shut and clutched it to his chest. Too many people were waking up on the bus. They were starting to keen and shriek as they swam up to consciousness, only to find unimaginable pain waiting for them at the surface. He stumbled back down the aisle, fighting his way through the outstretched arms until he fell down the steps to the cool grass outside.

He rolled over, and found the field was infested with the walking infected. They were up and moving, but they didn't understand what they were looking for, only that the loud noises and bright lights were unbearably painful, and they would hack and slash at anyone in their path. Dr. Menard folded his arms over the laptop and held it tight against his chest, then marched forward, eyes only on the driver's door of the prison bus.

He darted across the narrow space, climbed up into the driver's seat, and slammed the door behind him. He shot the bolts, locking himself inside. He took a moment to assess the infected lurching about the front of the bus, then put them out of his mind, opened the laptop, and fished around for the jump drive.

The Man was not happy. "You told us you could handle this, that if we evacuated the city, the situation would improve. But from the reports we're getting, it sounds as if things are getting worse."

"I promised no such thing," Dr. Reischtal said into his phone. No video conference this time—he stood outside one of the many FEMA trailers set up around Soldier Field, staring at the lake. He was not focusing on the president. Instead, he was looking forward to getting Tommy out to the medical lab out on the warship. "I merely gave you my opinion on how best to contain this pandemic."

"Let's not split hairs. Not with this much death. I need to know right now what is being done to stop this virus from spreading. As of right now, I have three major airports under lockdown. Those damn bugs have been discovered in luggage on flights from Chicago. Flights from Chicago have been quarantined, and are sitting on runways. We're running out of time. I will ask you again, what is the next step?"

"The next step has been taken, Mr. President." Dr. Reischtal didn't elaborate.

"And that would be . . . what, exactly?"

Dr. Reischtal responded with even less emotion that usual. "I have ordered a chemical agent to be dispersed throughout Chicago, once the soldiers have finished clearing out the rats."

"What kind of chemical agent?"

"Something that will clean Chicago."

"Listen, doctor, you either start giving me straight answers or I'll have my boys on you so fast it'll make your head spin. You want to be a smart-ass with me, you can disperse aspirin to convicts at San Quentin, you follow?"

"Very well. It is called two-four-five Trioxin."

"It will kill the bugs?"

"It will kill everything."

"The virus?"

"It will kill everything."

"Why the secrecy? Why didn't we just bomb the bugs in the first place?"

"Two-four-five Trioxin is perhaps the most lethal chemical weapon in our arsenal. It is not available to the Armed Forces."

"Why?"

"The effects are devastating and immediate. Nothing else we possess is capable of that much power. Kill rate is one hundred percent guaranteed. The only drawback, other than it will kill anything and everything in the dispersal zone without discrimination, is that the half-life is unfortunately, somewhat lengthy. If it becomes necessary to release the agent, Chicago will be uninhabitable for the next five to seven years."

"What? Are you joking? Who the hell gave you the clearance to use this shit?"

"With all due respect, sir, the president's authority is not enough to sanction the use of two-four-five Trioxin. That power lies solely with the head of the special pathogens branch of the CDC."

"You, in other words."

"At the moment, yes, sir."

The Man spoke to someone else on his end. "You getting this? Okay, okay. Find wherever they're keeping it; I want this shit confiscated, yesterday." He came back to the phone. "Okay, Dr. Reischtal. It's all over. The evacuation will continue, but I will be starting to pull the troops out. We need them in other areas. As for you, you're finished. I am officially removing you from this operation. Your replacement will be contacting you shortly."

"That's all well and good, sir, but I'm afraid you simply don't have the authority. I am the one in charge. That is final."

A soldier burst around the corner of the trailer and stood at attention next to Dr. Reischtal. He didn't want to interrupt the phone conversation, but the look on his face made it clear that this was an emergency.

Dr. Reischtal was aware of the soldier, but chose to ignore him for the moment. "If you check the laws concerning pandemics, you'll find that the CDC has a surprising amount of power, and I'm afraid this authority is absolute during times of national emergency."

The Man wasn't giving up without a fight. "No, doctor, you are the one that is mistaken. You have no right."

Dr. Reischtal held the phone to his chest. The Man was still yelling. He turned to the soldier. "Yes?"

"Sir, we have just received word that your patient is missing."

"My patient?"

"Yes, sir. Tommy Krazinsky."

Dr. Reischtal hit END CALL.

Huddled against the light post at Adams and Clark Street Ed and Sam and Qween decided they needed a place to hole up for a while, just to catch their breath. The majority of the soldiers seemed to be still working their way through the subways, but Clark was too well lit, so they crept back up to LaSalle and didn't have much trouble slinking through the shadows. Still, the helicopters were stabbing searchlights down on the dark streets, and Qween and the detectives knew they had to get inside somewhere.

Sam suggested the Chase Tower. Someplace above everything, away from all the shooting. Just down the street, a few blocks away. "Get up high. See if we can't see anything."

They made it without incident and found the front doors locked. Qween said, "I can get us in."

"One of your shortcuts?" Ed asked.

Qween said, "Sure," and heaved a newspaper vending machine through one of the windows. A strident alarm bleated out of the building and filled the street with its uncomfortable rhythm and pitch. After thirty seconds, Qween said, "Let's get to it."

The lobby was big and dark and silent. Lines of bank tellers' windows and half cubicles fought for space among large poster advertisements for the bank. The ceiling stretched up into the unknown, into the shadows. The whole place was empty.

They decided to take the elevator, just to get as far away from the alarm as possible. Sam hit the top button, and they got off on the fifty-ninth floor.

The elevator bank unfolded into a dining room, filled with spotless tables and chairs surrounded by a stunning view of downtown Chicago. The Chase Tower took up one full city block, bordered by Clark, Dearborn, Madison, and Monroe streets. The deep impression and its endless cement stairs were sunk into the south side, along with Chagall's *Four Seasons* mosaic. Except for a few buildings popping up that blocked their field of vision, like the big red CNN building, they could see most everything in all directions. They wandered around the perimeter, but still nothing much was happening on the streets.

Back near the elevators, they found a food prep area with a small TV on the counter. It was tuned to a sports channel. They switched around to find the news.

The anchor was saying, ". . . potentially graphic, so parents may want children to leave the room. This raw footage was uploaded less than an hour ago, and again, while we feel it needs to be seen, it could prove upsetting to sensitive viewers."

They switched to blurry, shaking video, obviously from a smartphone, as someone panned too quickly around an expensively furnished high-rise condo. It must have been shot earlier that day because the sun was shining and downtown Chicago could be seen through the windows. A woman's voice, tight and shrill, was saying, "And then we started finding them everywhere." She got closer to the leather couch and reached out to overturn one of the cushions.

It landed on the floor and reddish black bugs spilled out of the seams. The woman squealed and the phone went berserk as she stomped on the bugs. "Everywhere!" The footage spun back around, up the two steps from the sunken living room and into a huge white kitchen. "I will sue this landlord for everything!"

A boy, maybe ten, pointed up at the massive ventilation hood over the stove island. Bugs were crawling out of it by the dozens. Some fell out onto the black cast iron grates.

The woman leapt to turn the burners on. Flames licked the bugs. She hit the exhaust fan on the hood, which slowed the bugs' descent, but they still kept emerging. The video whipped across the floor. More bugs were crawling out of the heating and air-conditioning vents. Some squirmed out of an electrical socket. Her son had a can of Raid, and bent in front of the camera as he blasted them.

A bug trundled across his white T-shirt. His mom slapped it away. She started sobbing. She ripped the shirt off his back and held it up to the phone. Several more bugs crawled along the seam around the collar. Then she really shrieked and grabbed her son and ran for the door. There were a few more seconds of blurry footage before the network cut back to the anchor, who seemed to be at a loss for words. Maybe the teleprompter wasn't ready.

He shuffled his papers and cleared his throat. "At this time, we are unable to verify the status of the woman and her son that you have just watched in the video. We are assuming that they were evacuated, along with the rest of downtown Chicago, but we have recently lost contact with our field reporter on the scene. We have been following disturbing reports emerging from within the Soldier Field FEMA decontamination camp."

Ed switched the TV off. Nobody protested. Ed scratched at his back.

He wasn't the only one. Sam suddenly felt itching slither all over his body, and a hyperawareness of the bugs began to grow. Sam tried not to scratch anything, because once he started, he wouldn't be able to stop. Instead, he turned, let his breath out slowly, and started searching out crevices and shadows and under the toaster.

Wordlessly, they began to strip, examining every minute fold and stitch. Eventually, Sam turned his back, stripped bare, and gathered up the handful of clothes and stuffed them in the microwave. He stepped back and bent over, watching as his clothes rotated slowly. The zipper metal sparked, sending flashes bouncing around the inside of the microwave. "That's right," he said. "Ride the lightning, bitches."

Qween laughed. "You got the skinniest white ass I ever seen."

Sam was the first to take all his clothes off and cook the

hell out of them. Qween made them leave the room when she disrobed. When they came back, she was climbing back into her layers. The kitchen smelled like a wet dog that had been rolling in a dead moose.

Qween glared at Sam, daring him to say anything.

Sam raised his hands. "Not one fucking word, I promise. God knows I could, though. . . ."

Ed stepped out of his jeans and threw them in the microwave. "Wish you two would stop flirting and just kiss. Get it over with."

While Sam and Qween settled into a table along the southern windows, Ed found the light switches and turned most of them off. The lights of downtown snapped into life all around them. They opened the MREs the detectives had taken off the dead soldiers and ate without talking. Sam passed his flask around. For a while, it was rather peaceful, resting in the dim light, silently looking out over the city, with the gunfire, the bugs, the blood, far, far beneath them.

Sam squinted and sat up, peering through the window. He fumbled for his glasses, couldn't find them. Pointing down at Grant Park, he asked, "What's that?"

Ed and Qween followed his gaze. The headlights of a vehicle had just left Lake Shore Drive and were now tearing across the baseball diamonds at the southern end of the park. At least two Strykers appeared to be in pursuit. They were too far away to hear the chatter of gunfire, but they all saw the unmistakable flashes of heavy artillery.

Ed dug around in the pack and pulled out one of the soldiers' walkie-talkies. He couldn't figure out how to disengage the earpiece, so he stuck it in his own ear and listened for a minute. "Damn," he said. "It's Dr. Reischtal himself. He's pissed. Wants this dude taken alive. No more shooting." Sam started to ask a question, but Ed held up a finger, listening intently.

Ed met Sam's eyes. "They're after one of those rat guys from City Hall. Tommy Krazinsky."

# CHAPTER 70

**8:48 PM**
**August 14**

Dr. Reischtal stared down at the body on the grass. The paramedic's mouth was open, as if he was still protesting being slashed and bled out. A ripe, foul odor wafted up from his pants; his bowels had emptied in death. Maybe he was pissed about that too.

Dr. Reischtal fought to stop his teeth from grinding together. He could hear his dentist's admonishments. He was supposed to wear a special mouthpiece at night to stop the gradual demolition of his molars when he was asleep, and he certainly did not want to start wearing it when he was awake.

Tommy Krazinsky had escaped.

Patient 0.2. Gone.

Until he had been interrupted by the president's phone call, he had been watching that fool Shea attempting to hold a press conference in the middle of a quarantined city. While the current state of affairs was nowhere near as safe as the idiot kept pronouncing, as if saying it enough times would make it true, they were, at least, going according to schedule.

But now, now the situation jerked at his fingertips,

threatening to slip out of his grasp, like a pack of wild dogs going crazy on the scent of a bleeding pig. The urge to simply step back and burn everything boiled up inside of him, and he fought it, recognizing the feeling as panic. No. Someone with his control would not panic. Would not.

No matter what.

His voice was barely audible above the soft wind. "I expected this patient to be held until the laboratory was properly prepared. He is a confirmed bioterrorist and his escape is unacceptable."

The three soldiers surrounding the corpse nodded and grunted in affirmation.

Dr. Reischtal said, "Ready the choppers. I want him delivered, alive and relatively unharmed, in less than thirty minutes."

Sergeant Reaves said, "Sir, most of the choppers have withdrawn. We only have two Apaches left, and they will be necessary when the squads move out of the secure areas. We have no idea how many infected are still—"

Dr. Reischtal said slowly, deliberately, "My orders are quite clear, Sergeant. Please do not tell me you are suffering some kind of hearing disorder."

Sergeant Reaves nodded. "No, sir."

Dr. Reischtal went silent for a moment, thinking back to the press conference. He remembered who had been standing next to the fool. "I know his destination. He will be trying to reach the press conference, at Daley Plaza. He wants his daughter. Cut him off before he gets there. I want him brought back to me. Alive. Nothing else matters. His blood, his brain, may hold the key to this entire pandemic. Nothing else matters. Nothing."

"Understood, sir."

"I certainly hope so. I want both Apaches in the air. They can coordinate his location with the Strykers. Bring him back to me in one piece."

"Yes, sir."

Dr. Reischtal studied Sergeant Reaves in the bobbing glow

of the flashlights and the dim spill of the floodlights that had been erected over the FEMA trailers. He had just come from Soldier Field, watching for their old friend Dr. Menard. Three days of no sleep and constant vigilance had taken its toll on the man. Exhaustion had crinkled lines into his face like an old map, leaving dark hollows and dry, red eyes. "Please do not tell me you are second-guessing my command, Sergeant Reaves."

"No, sir."

"Then if you please, go catch that sonofabitch. Every moment we stand here exchanging carbon dioxide for oxygen, Mr. Krazinsky is pulling farther and farther away."

"Yes, sir."

When Sergeant Reaves turned to bark orders at the three soldiers waiting at attention at the head of the corpse, Dr. Reischtal saw the two little bugs, waiting patiently on Sergeant Reaves's back.

Dr. Reischtal did not hesitate, did not deliberate, did not think. He simply reacted. His hand flew down to his right hip, curled around the .45 Colt, pulled it out, raised it, settled the muzzle in the narrow groove at the back of Sergeant Reaves's head, right where the backbone disappeared into the skull, and fired.

The bullet spun through the very top of the spinal column, obliterating the connecting nerves, tumbled through Sergeant Reaves's mouth, churning his tongue into mush, and exploded through his upper front teeth, spraying blood over the waiting soldiers.

Sergeant Reaves slowly, hesitantly toppled over as if someone had given a sleeping man a gentle shove forward. The soldiers froze, their fatigues spattered in blood. Dr. Reischtal pivoted, raising his pistol slightly. Then he shot all three soldiers in the head. It couldn't be helped. If Sergeant Reaves was infected, then it was only a matter of time before the virus latched on to those around him.

When the initial blast of the four rounds had faded, leaving

Dr. Reischtal alone with five corpses tangled together before him, he holstered his pistol. Two other soldiers came running at the sound of gunshots. They gaped at the pile of bodies.

Dr. Reischtal said, "These men were infected. I want them burned immediately. And hazmat suits are now required for all personnel. The bugs are spreading beyond the confines of the city and the stadium."

"Yes, sir," one of the soldiers said. "We have reports that our squads are encountering severe resistance, mostly along the Blue Line subway system. We have lost contact with at least three squads. Based on their last transmissions, it appears that they were being overrun."

Dr. Reischtal nodded. "Tell the remaining squads to redouble their efforts. They must succeed. The future of mankind depends on it. Call my launch. I am now relocating the command center out to the ship."

"Yes, sir."

Dr. Reischtal clasped his hands and stared at the sky. There were no stars, not yet. But he had a feeling they would appear soon, triumphing over the light pollution. He shifted his gaze to the silent city.

There was no denying it now. The situation was officially out of control. The wild dogs had pulled loose, ripped free of their master.

He turned to assess Soldier Field and made his choice in less than three seconds. Again, once the decision had been made, there was no dithering, no second-guessing, no doubt. He would incinerate everything, burn the virus out of existence, wipe Chicago off the map. In a few years, they could start over, if they were so inclined.

He called Reynolds. "Are the trucks in place? Has everything been arranged?"

"No, sir. Three miles down the tunnel, we found a collapse. Looks like they brought it down on purpose. Recently too. We're digging it out. A couple of hours maybe. Your guy say anything about this?"

Dr. Reischtal ground his molars into each other and this time, he couldn't stop himself. Lee would suffer for his lies. "Call me when the trucks are ready." He hung up and walked down to the shore and stepped onto the launch that would ferry him out to the warship.

At least the trucks under Soldier Field were in place and armed.

As the boat skipped across the surface of the lake, he thought about calling and informing the president, but then another, more efficient idea blossomed. He considered the angles briefly, and decided the loss of his men would be acceptable. And only he and the truck drivers knew the truckers were even there, let alone what kind of death they carried.

Yes, he thought. Soldier Field first. Then, when they had the trucks in place under the Loop, in a few hours, then downtown.

As the warship grew closer and the single tower loomed overhead, he called a very specific number and waited for the security system to come online. The launch slowed and stopped at the stern of the Sachsen-class frigate. Collapsible stairs descended from the low deck.

Dr. Reischtal waited until he heard the recorded message, then climbed up to the deck. He gazed back across the moonlit waves at the bright lights of Soldier Field. He spoke his name, slowly and clearly into the mouthpiece, and answered the random question and ended with the date, then waited for the voice-recognition software to access the remotes under each truck. He heard the series of beeps, and knew that the steady yellow lights on the remote receivers were now flashing red.

He keyed in the code and hit SEND.

Dr. Menard flipped the jump drive over and over as he shoved it into the USB port on the laptop. His fingers trembled and he couldn't seem to get the drive to slip into the port. Finally it snapped into place, and a few seconds later, a new icon appeared on the desktop screen.

He steadied the laptop on the steering wheel, then opened the Internet browser, and had to type in the name of his university's email server three times before he got it right. Sweat dripped off his nose and hit the trackpad. His forefinger smeared it, and the cursor flitted wildly across the screen. "Goddamnit," he whispered. "Please, please work." He tried to dry it with his shirt, then tried again.

Someone banged on the bus door.

Dr. Menard flinched and saw a man in a reflective orange IDOT vest outside, lips pulled back in a feral snarl, eyes wild. Blood dripped from his hair. It looked like he had taken a gardening fork to his scalp. The man hit the door again, rattling the plastic windows.

Dr. Menard ignored him and concentrated on attaching the contents of the jump drive to an email. An empty sliding bar popped up, indicating the percentage of information that had been loaded. A blue bar began to eat up the remaining blackness of the gauge in lurching increments.

"C'mon, c'mon!" he shouted.

His voice attracted the attention of an older woman on the other side of the bus. She bounded up the steps on the passenger side and smashed her head into the plastic cocoon, leaving a streak of blood and makeup. She howled and scrabbled at the plastic, enraged at the movement inside, furious that she couldn't reach him. Her cries brought more of them, like bees swarming to their queen.

The blue band had filled up at least half of the bar.

The infected surrounded the bus and so many were attacking it in a mindless fury it began rock and shake as the suspension shuddered under the onslaught. If too many gathered in one area, they would set each other off in a new frenzy, attacking each other, anything to eliminate the immediate threat. They would use anything close at hand. A backpack, used to choke the other, or a shattered bottle, to slash and jab. Usually it was something big and heavy, and used as a club. Out at Soldier Field, they didn't have anything really big and heavy. One guy carried a gearshift off one of the older buses and used it to bash away at the bus door.

Dr. Menard didn't care. He held onto the laptop, eyes never leaving the screen. Seventy-five percent now.

Eighty percent.

Ninety percent.

Then, a flash. A curious floating sensation for the briefest moment, as if everything were suspended, like motes of dust in sunlight. A feeling of intense, horrible heat.

Then, nothing.

# CHAPTER 71

At first, Tommy didn't realize that the Strykers were shooting at him. The road in front of him didn't erupt in great geysers of smoke and the trees around him didn't explode in showers of sparks like in the movies. He heard a few dull thuds. That was all.

He raced down Lake Shore Drive, with Lake Michigan off to his right, and the ominous shadow of the warship growing out of the horizon like a tumor. After successfully negotiating his way through the barricade, he didn't want to think that anything could go wrong. So he ignored the tight, tickling feeling that crawled over his scalp and pushed the thoughts of the bullets singing above his head out of his mind. Then he saw the two Strykers in the rearview mirror, closing fast.

One of the back windows exploded and his passenger mirror disintegrated. Now, through the open back window, he could hear the bursts of automatic gunfire, even if he couldn't pinpoint the damage. He couldn't ignore the truth any longer.

Tommy yanked the wheel to the left and jumped the curb and tore across the baseball fields. He tried to keep an eye on his driver's side mirror and rearview mirror. He noticed that the

Strykers couldn't change direction as fast as the ambulance; they couldn't navigate as nimbly as he could. Of course, they could smash their way through obstructions like cars and sandbags, but when they had two or three cars caught up on the front, it slowed them down, at least until the pitiless front wedge ground the cars along the asphalt and pushed the crumpled vehicles aside.

The ambulance careened into Columbus, coming close to blowing a tire. Sparks flew as he swerved around the abandoned cars. He veered to his left at the last second and shot over the southern Metra railroad line on Balbo. He reckoned out in the open, it was just a matter of time before they eventually flanked him, trapping the ambulance between them. He'd never reach Grace.

He glanced at the mirror. The Strykers hadn't managed the turn yet, and hadn't started across the bridge over the Metra lines. He turned his attention back to the road in front, plotting a course through the low berms of sandbags strewn across Michigan Avenue. If he could just reach the blocks of buildings, he might be able to stay a few blocks ahead of them, twisting and turning, keeping the buildings between the ambulance and the Strykers. After the massive withdrawal of troops and equipment, the streets might be empty enough that he could keep running, and put a little distance between himself and his pursuers. He just hoped they didn't have anything that could blast through concrete.

He slalomed around the rows of sandbags on Michigan just as the first of the Strykers appeared on the crest of the Balbo Bridge. The windows of the Blackstone Hotel burst into dizzying cracks and shards rained across the sidewalk. It didn't matter. He was through the sandbags and stomped on the gas. The ambulance grumbled, but it shot forward.

Ahead, the next two blocks were clear. Once he hit State, he'd jog left and see if he couldn't disappear into the Printers' Row area.

A great circle of white light stabbed out of the night sky,

moving quickly, blowing away any and all shadows as it kept pace with the speeding ambulance. Another slash of bleached-bone luminosity appeared behind him. He leaned forward, craning his neck, and peered up through the windshield.

The tentative hope that had started flickering in his chest when he realized that he might just escape, sizzled and died as he saw quite clearly that he now had not one but two helicopters stalking him, with their immense spotlights burning a trail that a dead man could follow, leading the Strykers right to him.

Ed and Sam prepped for war.

They had the soldier's pack on the table, loading it with extra clips, boxes of ammunition, even a couple of grenades. Both had climbed back into the suits, figuring they would allow them to blend in with the rest of the soldiers.

Sam slung assault rifles over both shoulders and stuck his Glock back into his shoulder holster, and a Beretta in one of the hazmat pockets. He just wished he could carry more guns.

Qween was still sleeping. She had found a quiet corner to gather herself, curling up and sleeping for a few hours. At first, she listened. Tuned into the rhythms of the building. The quiet hum of the air system. How it swayed slightly in the winds. When she felt like she knew the building, and had gotten comfortable with the muted sounds of the fifty-ninth floor, she curled up on her right side, pulling her cloak over her shoulder and ear. Her breathing stretched, grew slower and slower.

She was the first to feel the shockwave coming.

Ed and Sam saw popping, flashing lights bubble up out of Soldier Field, far to the south, and as the mushroom cloud of smoke roiled up and out of the stadium, the ripples from the explosion burst through the downtown streets, leaving dust and smoke in their wake. The waves rattled the windows and everybody flinched, but the glass held. The entire building swayed in the wash of the blast.

Sam whispered, "Holy fuck me."

The smoke had an odd, shimmering quality, and they couldn't tell if the smoke itself had these speckles of color, or it was reflecting something underneath. It had a sickly rainbow glow, like the way an oil slick in a puddle will split light into a filthy prism.

"I think the CDC just cut their losses," Ed said.

Nobody wanted to mention Dr. Menard.


Tommy was slowing down to make the skidding left turn onto State Street when he thought he heard a sonic boom, as if some huge jumbo jet had just flown way too low over the city. The shockwave made the ambulance bounce a little, but it wasn't enough to throw him off course.

Tommy took a right instead onto State on two tires, heading north. He straightened it out and the ambulance rocked back down onto all four tires. The damn searchlights wavered and spun away as the Apache pilots fought the unfurling waves from Soldier Field.

Tommy hit the gas and shot north on State, weaving through the sandbags.

# CHAPTER 72

Lee wished he had a big MISSION ACCOMPLISHED banner, something bold and bright they could have hung above the doors on City Hall. Something that would tell people in no uncertain terms that Lee Shea was a man who got things done. Something he could turn and point to, something that would give his speech the big finish it needed. That would have been a shot he could see on the cover of *Time*.

He tried not to dwell on it. Phil had told him that giving the speech out in the middle of Clark would look fantastic on TV. He didn't need the banner. "It's a hell of an image," Phil had said. "You in the middle of the goddamn street, with City Hall all lit up behind you. Now's that's a fucking shot."

Phil had only written a ten-minute speech. They'd been planning on plenty of government officials wanting to share the spotlight, lined up to lap at the trough of success and show their face to the media. But nobody else had the balls to show up. Those assholes in the CDC. And the rest of the feds, shit, they'd pulled out at least half, maybe more, of the soldiers. And good riddance, as far as Lee was concerned. Every time you turned on the TV, all you got were those endless shots of the hazmat suits going underground, the soldiers standing around behind the sandbags, with blank expressions as they rode around on the top of those tank things.

In a way, Lee was glad nobody else had showed up to give any other speeches. He didn't have to share the spotlight with anyone. It made the whole thing that much more fucking dramatic. Like it was just him, the only politician who cared about his city, his people. His face would be on the front of newspapers. He had been building to this moment his whole life, practicing in front of the mirror, answering all those shouted questions amidst the dazzling flashes.

And let's face it, the only people who mattered at a press conference were the media. Especially the TV folks. Nobody read newspapers anymore. So when Lee decided it was time to get to the questions, he would start calling on them by name. He'd gotten to the end of Phil's speech a while ago, but since the spotlight was on Lee and Lee alone, he had simply kept going. The spirit of the situation had moved him, and he was giving the people what they wanted. His words would inspire the citizens of Chicago. His words would give them hope.

Phil, the asshole, had been walking behind the cameras, making increasingly violent gestures to wrap it up.

It figured. Here was Lee's chance to seize the moment, to spin the entire pandemic in his favor, and Phil wanted him to quit. Sometimes Lee wondered if Phil was a little jealous of his looks, of his success.

Kimmy was still standing next to Lee at the podium, still smiling, still keeping her brat under control, but he could tell she was getting tired of his speech. Bitch.

He was right in the middle of telling an utterly bullshit story about when he was a young boy on the family farm, and his grandfather was gently explaining the realities about the circle of life, when a deep BOOM reverberated through the streets and a sudden wind kicked up the dust and smoke almost as bad as all the choppers.

Lee stopped talking for a moment and wiped at his eyes, trying to dig the grit out of them. He couldn't help himself and patted his hair, just to make sure it hadn't been affected. Then, to camouflage the gesture, he touched his ear, as if he had a hidden receiver. "Ladies and gentlemen, please remain calm. It is unclear at this time what we have just experienced, but I am being told that it is nothing to worry about."

Phil was making angry slashing motions across his throat, but Lee ignored him and plunged ahead with his story. "As I was saying, my grandfather was a wise, wise man. He—"

Someone's phone rang. One of the reporters answered it. Her hand went to the round oval of her mouth. She looked to her fellow reporters and said, "Soldier Field just exploded."

Lee said into the microphone, "We have no confirmed reports at this time. I think we should all stay put until we receive some kind of confirmation or something. . . ."

But the media people weren't listening. Everyone was packing up, hoping to get to Grant Park and get a shot of the devastation.


The Apache pilots asked no questions. No matter how they felt about the explosion at Soldier Field, they had orders. Both of them regrouped in the turbulent skies above Chicago, then dove back down, using their FLIR systems to zero in on the ambulance. One of the gunners had everything lined up, both he and the pilot watching a bobbing, bright white vehicle in a high-res sea of green of the forward-looking infrared system. The images were projected directly into a monocular lens attached the pilots' helmets. Aiming was achieved by simply moving their heads as they followed the target. The crosshairs smoothly tracked the ambulance, bouncing a laser off the target to guide the Hellfire missiles.

The gunners wanted to simply unleash hell on Tommy Krazinsky, whoever the hell he was, carpet-bombing the streets with everything they had, but the pilots had been given strict instructions to merely locate the target, and nothing else. And nobody wanted to defy Dr. Reischtal's orders.

So they roared back down into the concrete and steel valleys, following the ninety-degree grid pattern of the streets and blocks, until they spotted the ambulance, and gave his location to the Strykers. "Target is fleeing up South Plymouth Court, on the east side of the library. Disable vehicle. Keep damage to target to an absolute minimum."

The Strykers responded, "Affirmative. Six, two, out."

As the Strykers rammed their way down parallel streets to cut Tommy off, both choppers noticed activity in the FLIR systems. A flailing mass of bodies spewed out of some of the buildings. The sea green screens flared with spastic, violent movement.

"That . . . that ain't our guys," one of the gunners said.

The pilots pulled back, and the rotors slapped against the humid, smoky air, dragging the choppers above the buildings to get a better view. All along the path of the ambulance, the streets were coming alive with lurching, running figures, as if Tommy was some kind of Pied Piper, calling to the infected.

"Strykers, six, two, be advised that we're catching a lot of civilian, ah . . . activity down there. Movement right now is confined to target's path."

The lead Stryker's reply was brief. "Fuck 'em. Estimate contact with target in less than ten seconds."

Tommy didn't see the Stryker come up on his passenger side out of the darkness of East Van Buren until it was too late to stop. He hit the gas instead, trying to outleap the Stryker the way a gazelle would strain in slow motion against the outstretched fury of a lioness's leap.

They had decided to ram the vehicle, instead of trying to shoot out the tires. If they missed and hit the driver, there was no telling how Dr. Reischtal might retaliate. He might even order one of the Apaches to take out the Strykers.

The ambulance almost made it through the trap unscathed. The edge of the Stryker's front wedge kissed the ambulance's back bumper, sending the lighter vehicle sideways across the intersection. The ambulance skidded into a line of parked cars, bounced a little, and came to rest backwards against the northwest traffic light.

The Stryker smashed through the El station stairs and crunched through hundred-year-old bricks in the dark building across the street. After a moment, the tires began to spin in reverse, as the driver tried to back out of the rubble.

That gave Tommy an idea and he jerked the gearshift into reverse and hit the gas.

He backed up until he hit Jackson, then spun around and took off. The searchlights followed. He took a left down Dearborn, bouncing over sandbags and taking off once he was clear. The ambulance's engine strained and whined like an old man trying to pass a kidney stone as Tommy pushed his foot to the floor.

Headlights flashed behind him, coming fast. Another goddamn Stryker.

Tommy was so busy watching the Stryker behind him that he missed the second one popping out of LaSalle to his right. The front wedge smashed into the passenger door and the center of gravity shifted inside the ambulance. He had one moment of clarity when he realized he was glad he was wearing his seat belt. The road spun and the air was suddenly full of crap from the floor and his seat threw him at the steering wheel. The ambulance jolted under him, around him, and whipped around like an unlicensed carnival roller coaster.

The ambulance rolled through the intersection and crashed, upside-down, on the far sidewalk. The Stryker behind him skidded and stopped in the middle of the intersection, while the one that had smashed the ambulance came to a shuddering halt ten yards down LaSalle. The hatch on the

Stryker to the rear popped open and a soldier appeared behind the .50 caliber machine gun.

Tommy blinked stars out of his eyes. He hoped they weren't shards of glass from the shattered windshield. It took him a moment to realize he was hanging upside down, held in place by his seat belt. He rolled his head, flexed his fingers, pulled his knees up, making sure that nothing was broken, and everything still worked.

His knee hurt like hell, but as far as he could tell, he was still in one piece. A pair of boots crunched through the broken safety glass outside his door. His door was wrenched open with a squeal of metal pain and a hazmat faceplate leaned down and peered at him.

"How ya doin', Tommy?"

The metallic voice sounded almost familiar, but Tommy couldn't place it. He slapped at the seat belt release button.

"Easy, easy does it."

From one of the Strykers, Tommy heard an amplified, no-nonsense voice say, "Step away from the vehicle, soldier. This man is a suspected terrorist. Step away. Now."

The man in the hazmat suit ignored the warning. He reached in, and hit the release button, catching Tommy when the belt gave way. His hands guided Tommy gently to the roof of the ambulance and unfolded him so he was lying halfway on the street. Behind the faceplate, Tommy caught a glimpse of a dark face and a grin.

"Relax. We got this."

"Last warning, soldier. We will open fire."

The man suddenly had a giant revolver in his gloved hand. He pivoted, brought the handgun up in one smooth motion, and fired.

The man visible in the hatch in the Stryker behind the ambulance flopped back as if he just needed a few minutes to study the sky. The driver was still very much alive inside, and he had control of the cannon. The Stryker's engine growled as the canon swiveled around with a mechanical purr, looking for the hazmat soldier.

Then an overweight black woman came out of nowhere, stepped up on the Stryker's tires, and dropped something down through the hatch where the dead machine gunner slumped. The cannon continued to rotate, until it was almost in line with the ambulance. A muffled boom came from inside the Stryker. It shook like a dog in the middle of a dream, and Tommy understood that the woman had dropped a grenade or something.

The second Stryker hadn't missed any of this, and it roared backwards. The top hatch swung open, and a soldier grabbed the .50 caliber. This gunner wasn't taking any chances, he was already firing, spitting bullets all over the place. He couldn't aim worth a damn while the Stryker was backing up, but it was clear to Tommy that once it stopped, they were all dead meat.

A dark CTA bus burst out of the darkness of LaSalle and smashed into the Stryker. Bullets sprayed into the night sky as the gunner snapped against the hatch with such violence it didn't appear that he had any bones at all, and was instead some invertebrate species as his body rolled in the whiplash with all the resistance of a wet towel.

The bus hit the Stryker hard enough that the back tires lifted off the ground a few inches. It dropped back, bounced once, and didn't move. The Stryker spun counterclockwise, blasting through a few sandbag berms.

The woman was now suddenly at that wreck, casually dropping a grenade inside. This time, the driver didn't try to use the canon. He may have been running for the hatch, he may have been trying to trap the blast with a shield or whatever was inside, but in the end, it didn't matter. There was another muffled whump, like a stifled sneeze, and it was done.

The boots left Tommy and ran for the bus. Tommy rolled over and watched the hazmat suit and the woman kick open the door. Tommy climbed to his knees. His ears were ringing and he couldn't quite nail a perfect balance yet, but he didn't think anything was broken. His fingers tingled now, where before there was only numbness. He cautiously rose to his feet and took a moment to orient himself.

When he felt he could walk without falling down, he lurched over to the closest Stryker. As he got closer, he found he could clench his fists and loosen his legs. He lifted the gunner's corpse, and pulled it out. There was nothing there he could use. He took a deep breath, and climbed down. The heat was still incredible. He squinted in the murk, found the driver. The man wore fatigues.

Tommy climbed out, and after some gasping to escape the heat, he dropped back down and went for a storage locker. He felt a couple of dense plastic squares, almost like baseball bases that a family might take to a picnic. He crawled out and rolled down the tank, stuck one square under each arm and went to the bus.

The driver was out now, coughing and holding his side, but pacing around like he was shaking off a bad dream, nothing more. Hazmat suit and the woman started arguing. Tommy walked up and saw that the man pacing around was the detective who had given Tommy his card. Sam something.

The detective started to speak, and coughed instead. His tongue and teeth were dark and shiny at the same time with blood. After a few tries, he said, "I'm fine, goddamnit. Knock that shit off."

Tommy said, "Thanks," then limped past them, heading north.

Ed called, "Kid, you okay?"

Tommy stopped and turned. "I have to get my daughter."

Dr. Reischtal watched the figures of white light start walking up Dearborn. Toward Washington and Daley Plaza. He pinned the microphone, a black bug with the foam head, a battery pack for the thorax, and a transponder antenna as the abdomen, to his new paper robe. He wore nothing underneath. After stripping out of the hazmat suit and his uniform and submitting himself not once, but twice, to the decontamination process, he had ordered his old clothing burned.

"Do not engage," he told the pilots. "Pull back and continue to monitor."

The sound of his voice was heard by a dozen satellites, who passed it back down, like electronic rain. A pair of headphones hung on the back wall of his unit, but he ignored those. Apart from the Apache pilots, he would only speak to a living human on the other side of the glass, through the exterior microphone, of course.

Dr. Reischtal was sealed in. *Tighter than a bug in a rug*, as his mother's maid was fond of saying.

He called it his unit. A sealed fortress, his own private citadel, secure inside a warship, no less. Austere, composed entirely of gleaming white plastic. Completely sterile, of course. It utilized its own air filtration unit, its own power, its own waste disposal, its own recyclable water supply. Next to the door that locked from the inside, a giant bubble of thick plastic faced a simple table and chair. A scanner sat on the table, so any hard copies could be digitally scanned and downloaded by the isolated computer inside. A wall of monitors covered one wall. Two monitors displayed the feed from the Apaches. The video from the cameras attached to several soldiers' helmets filled other screens. Several of these had gone dark.

The rest of the monitors were tuned to various television stations. Most had cut to aerial shots of the burning wreckage of Soldier Field. Although Dr. Reischtal was quite pleased with the level of destruction in the death of the stadium, he watched the last station that was still broadcasting the disintegrating press conference with interest. Lee, the fool, was dithering about, still trying to convince people he was in charge. No sign of Krazinsky, but Dr. Reischtal hadn't expected him to show his face yet. The station finally cut away to its own footage of the skeletal wreckage of Soldier Field, the sagging walls and twisted metal silhouetted by the raging fire inside.

He turned back to the Apache feeds. The four glowing figures crept north on Dearborn, keeping to the shadows near the buildings. They stopped, huddled together. He couldn't tell, but it looked as if they were trying to see something behind them. All four broke into a run.

Dr. Reischtal almost smiled. They had undoubtedly just become aware of the growing mob of infected five blocks to the south.

He pulled out his phone and dialed a recent number. "Shut your mouth and listen carefully."

# CHAPTER 73

Ed pulled at Tommy's arm. "Slow down, slow down. You go running in there, you're gonna get shot." Behind Ed, Qween slowed to a walk, sucking in air through her nose and letting it out in shallow hisses between clenched teeth. Sam brought up the rear, grunting softly every time his left foot hit the ground. He kept his right hand across his chest, holding the left side of his ribs. Every once in a while, he would turn his head and spit. The blood gleamed darkly under the streetlights.

They stood at the intersection of Dearborn and Washington. Daley Plaza was before them. A circle of lights had been arranged in the middle of the plaza. Semi trailers, Strykers, and M939 military trucks lined the streets. A block to the west, the lights of the press conference sent inky slashes of shadow up the sides of City Hall. No soldiers could be seen.

Ed said, "Easy, easy. Catch your breath, first. Let's think this through."

"We don't have time. Those people"—Tommy nodded back down Dearborn—"are gonna be here any minute."

Ed shook his head. "We got a couple of minutes. Maybe ten. From what we've seen, they're not the most organized."

Tommy wasn't convinced. "They go after noise. And light. But mostly noise. And those damn things"—he pointed to the two Apaches that kept circling overhead like a couple of hungry vultures riding the wind—"they're gonna piss 'em off and bring 'em right into our laps." He turned to assess City Hall. "Besides, I think the press conference is over. You hear anything from over there? They're gonna be moving out."

Ed watched the helicopters for a moment. "Yeah, you got a point. But let's not go running in there like a bunch of chickens with our heads cut off." He glanced at Sam. "How you doin', brother?"

"Right as fucking rain," Sam said, and discreetly wiped the blood from the corner of his mouth. "Kid's right. We gotta move."

Ed started to say something else, but Sam narrowed his eyes and gave his head an imperceptible shake. Ed gave it a moment more, meeting Sam's eyes, letting his partner know he didn't believe him, and finally said, "Let's move then. Slow and easy-peasy."

They stole along the southern sidewalk of Washington, using the various military vehicles and occasional CTA bus as cover. Darting from shadow to shadow, Tommy would drop to the sidewalk once in a while, scouting, trying to get a look at the press conference.

The last time, at least five rats stuck their heads over the curb and hissed at him.

He flinched and rolled away. He found his feet, kept moving. "They're still up there on the stage. Standing around. Like they're waiting for something."

Ed said, "Maybe they're going back on the air or something."

Halfway down the block, they slipped into the alcove, squeezed between the Cook County Administration Building and the Chicago Temple Building and huddled behind the Miro sculpture of Miss Chicago.

Ed whispered, "Here's the plan. I'll be the distraction."

"You mean bait," Qween said.

"Call it whatever you want," Ed said.

"I'm gonna be the bait," Sam said.

Ed started to say, "I need you—"

Sam cut him off. "No. I can't run. I can shoot, but I can't run. Let me walk up there and stand still. I'll get their attention. Trust me. You go around the other side. I'm done hiding." He used his thumb and forefinger to swipe at the corners of his mouth and met Ed's eyes.

Ed nodded. Slow. "Okay. Okay, if that's the way you want it, then okay." He pointed to the other side of the Stryker, "Sam goes out first, then. Me and Qween will sneak around to the west, hugging City Hall." He pointed at Tommy. "You wait a full minute, then cut across Washington here and circle around through the plaza. They'll see Sam right off, and he'll keep their attention. Me and Qween will get as close as we can. Soon as you hear us yelling, you slip in through the back and snatch your little girl. No matter what happens, you get her out."

Ed looked at each of them. "Any questions?"

Nobody had any.

Ed said, "Let's go," and nodded at Sam.

Sam strode off, still holding his ribs, but moving purposefully, back straight, eyes on the horizon. Ed and Qween flattened themselves against the glass walls of the Harris Bank, the first floor of the Chicago Temple building. Tommy peeled around to the east and ducked across Washington. He slid between a bus and a cab, both vehicles long since abandoned once they had been boxed in by a parked convoy of M939s. He froze.

The plaza was a full half of a city block in size, a vast speckled cement open prairie in a massive, dense forest of concrete and steel and glass. The absence of the Picasso sculpture made the emptiness worse. He felt like a mouse, about to dart across a moonlit field while hawks prowled the misty skies above. To his left, the lights still shone on a stage erected in the middle of Clark Street.

He could see figures grouped around a podium. One of them had to be Lee, with the dark head of hair and blue suit. Red tie. Yes, that was definitely Lee.

There was a woman next to him. Long hair. Tight black dress. Kimmy.

He didn't recognize the short, sour-faced man next to her, or the few behind Lee. He waited. Lee hoisted someone small to his hip. Tommy saw the white blouse and the way she held her head and how it canted her hair just so. He couldn't breathe.

It was Grace.

He had waited long enough. He scurried across the plaza, curving to the west, heading for the back of the stage. Twenty yards to go. He skirted around the fountain and stayed low by a broad cement planter for a couple of stunted trees. From there, he could be on them before they saw anything, and so when their attention was taken by Sam, then Ed and Qween, he would slip in behind and take Grace. He waited for Sam's signal.

It never came.

Instead, a solid slab of light thumped out of the sky and slammed him into stark relief against the flatness of the plaza.

Ahead, more lights speared him from a couple of Strykers along the western edge of the plaza. They'd been waiting there the entire time. Soldiers burst out of the light and rushed him, a vicious rugby scrum of guns, boots, and elbows. They surged over Tommy and he went down swinging. He caught a quick glimpse of more searchlights stabbing out of the sky, and then it was all over.

# CHAPTER 74

**9:05 PM**
**August 14**

Phil couldn't keep the grin off his face. It had worked just like Dr. Reischtal had said it would. Who knew that crazy CDC fucker could have been still useful? Not just useful, but necessary. If what he said was true, then they had to get out of the city as fast as possible. And they most certainly would need Dr. Reischtal's help.

Phil prided himself on always, one way or another, being ahead of the curve, on knowing more than the general public, and therefore, being in a position to take advantage. In the past, he had used this talent to gain traction in elections, to blackmail his enemies, and spot opportunities that would benefit him, often financially, later down the line. Now it would get him out of the city alive.

And not just that—his useless handsome nephew had found a scapegoat.

*Ladies and gentlemen of the jury, I give you the man who bombed Soldier Field.*

Tommy didn't look so scary. He looked crushed. He sagged in the soldiers' grip, blood trickling from his scalp down into his right eye. He'd puked earlier, when one of the soldiers had kicked him in the stomach. He looked like a man who was finished, someone who could barely walk. He'd been carrying a handgun and two unwrapped hazmat suits. The soldiers had tossed them onto the stage.

Phil wanted anybody and everybody to post pictures on the Internet. He had no idea how to do it himself, but he was nothing if he couldn't recognize the most effective way to communicate since the first written word. He wanted the world to know that this was the bombing suspect, and that later, the suspect would attempt to escape and be killed in the process.

"Daddy!" Grace screamed, and ripped out of her mother's clutch. That dumb whore. He'd told her to keep a tight hold on her daughter, and she'd listened about as well as his idiot nephew when he'd told Lee that Kimmy was nothing but trouble, and wouldn't help advance his career. "A single mother? Are you fucking kidding me?"

Phil was not a man burdened by sentimentality. Or gentleness. As Grace ran past, charging toward her father, Phil simply reached out and caught a fistful of her hair. He yanked her back, and her feet flew out from under her. She fell backwards, hanging in midair, hair snared in his fist. Her surprised, sharp scream echoed around the plaza.

Tommy drove an elbow into the nearest soldier's chest, and Phil heard the crack even fifteen feet away. The rest of the soldiers surrounding him responded with a flurry of blows. Some of them even used their rifle butts. Tommy's knees buckled and he went back down.

Kimmy rushed forward, but Phil stopped her with a single index finger, jammed up into her face. "Get the fuck back, you stupid bitch. You might be along for the ride, but you're nothing but scenery. And that's easy to replace. Remember that."

Lee, the dumbshit, couldn't resist taunting Tommy. Lee ambled over to the group of soldiers and squatted on his haunches in front of a barely conscious Tommy and said,

"Told ya, asshole. Told you I'd make you wish you'd never been born. Told you I'm the man here. All this over some dumb cooze that hates your guts."

Phil said, "Lee. Let's go." Fucking idiot didn't know to quit when he was ahead. Phil kept hold of Grace, because he knew damn well that this girl was the only thing that could control Tommy, and pulled out his phone with his other hand. Grace whimpered but stood carefully so he wouldn't tear any more hair out. He dialed Dr. Reischtal.

"We got him. Send in the chopper."

"He is alive, yes?"

"He's alive. A little banged up, and probably isn't in the mood to talk right now, but yeah, he's alive."

"And the others?"

Phil glanced back over his shoulder to where a group of four soldiers had the two detectives and the crazy homeless woman in the middle of Clark, hands on their heads. "We got 'em."

Dr. Reischtal was silent a touch too long and Phil thought that he had hung up. Dr. Reischtal said, "Ah yes. I can see. I can also see that hell is marching up the street, straight at you. You have less than ten minutes before every infected individual left in the city is pouring into that plaza. I want the two detectives and the woman dead. When it is done, I will let the helicopter know you are ready." He hung up.

Phil called one of the soldiers over. He knew his authority as an alderman with the soldiers carried about as much weight as a flustered nanny, so he started by saying, "Just talked to your boss, Dr. Reischtal. You know who I'm talking about, right?" The soldier nodded. "Good." Phil pointed at Tommy. "This fuck here, he's the one responsible for Soldier Field. Dr. Reischtal does not want him harmed. But those fuckers over there, they helped him. Execute them. Dr. Reischtal's orders."

The soldier cocked his head and gave Phil a look like he'd just stepped in dog shit and was trying to be polite about it.

He walked over to inform the soldiers guarding the three. They pushed the two detectives and the homeless woman around one of the military trucks and disappeared.

Phil still couldn't wipe his grin away. Everything was falling into place. First off, they now had a guaranteed safe passage out of the city, but they also had someone to blame everything on, and on top of everything else, he might get to watch soldiers blast the living shit out of a couple of detectives who had always been a pain in the ass.

A deep throbbing sound reached him and he looked up. A gigantic Sikorsky CH-53K Super Stallion appeared over the buildings to the east, the rotors slapping the air with a relentless, inhuman beat. The two Apaches slowed and hovered at a higher altitude, giving the larger helicopter all the room it needed as it settled into the plaza.

"Go, go!" Phil yelled into the storm of dust and vibration. The soldiers dragged Tommy across Clark, Lee took Kimmy under his arm, hustling her off the stage past the subway stairs, and Phil pulled Grace along by a fistful of hair. Once they passed the tree planters, they crouched along the sandbag wall and waited for a signal.

As the chopper landed, none of them heard the almost liquid pops under the street. White wisps began to curl out of the holes in the manhole covers and the grates of the storm drains along Washington across Clark. Thick gray smoke wafted out of the subway steps at the northeastern corner of Clark and Washington. More rats fled up the subway steps and cringed in the sudden light, then bolted into the shadows of Clark or Washington.

Sam didn't get on his knees like they wanted.

So they knocked his feet out from under him. He landed heavily on his side, tried to take a breath and something gave, so deep inside he felt it in his back. He doubled over, hacking red globules across the sidewalk.

Ed spoke slowly and relentlessly, taking his time getting on his knees. "Chicago PD, Detective Jones and Johnson, we're here under orders, you have our badges, we're just like you guys, radio it in, check it out, we're supposed to be here."

The lead soldier, an older merc with tired eyes, ignored Ed and repeated, "On your fucking knees. Head against the wall. Now."

Qween helped Sam onto his knees. The three pressed their foreheads against the rough-hewn rock of City Hall.

"Hands behind your head."

Ed wouldn't stop talking. "Just check with your superiors, we're on your side, you don't have to do this right away, give it a minute, just give it a minute."

The leader gave a call, a grunted "Hup," and the three soldiers stared at him for a moment. He glared back. They glanced at their weapons and readied them as quietly as possible. If they didn't like executing three civilians, too damn bad. The folks that signed the paychecks didn't give a shit if the soldiers liked their jobs or not. The three soldiers didn't dwell on it too much. This was the job.

Sam knew they were dead once they had been lined up and had prepared himself. He also knew that he was leaking blood, as if someone had popped open an old oil can, and now it was now taking its sweet time dribbling out of him. He'd been wearing his seat belt, but hitting that fucking Stryker had been like hitting one of the concrete slabs they'd erected around the Chicago Board of Trade after 9/11. He knew that unless he got to a hospital in the next five minutes, nobody was going to be able to plug the hole before he was empty.

A bullet in the head from the soldiers didn't concern him much. But the thought of bullets in his friends' heads did. So before the leader could get the second command out, Sam rose and spun, using the inertia of his twisting body for leverage as he unfurled his arm, reaching out with Qween's straight razor. The blade slashed up through the leader's face, catching him on the chin and slicing both lips in half, severing the entire right side of the nose, splitting the cheek and carving through the right eye.

At the same instant, Ed fought to get off his knees, twisting and trying desperately to pull his feet under him so he could lunge at the last soldier in the line. The two soldiers in the middle sensed this and turned to cut him down when the street rumbled. Sam thought the sudden vibration was coming from inside his own head, and ignored it. He got control of the leader's assault rifle, and fired. His aim was off and instead of killing both of the middle soldiers outright, the bullets tore through their legs, shattering bones and knees.

They went down, writhing and howling, where they met Qween. She couldn't quite rise to her feet yet, and went after them on her hands and knees. She got her hip on one of their shattered knees, and starting kicking out with her other leg, driving her heel into the shredded muscles and blood and jabbing the closest one in the chest with her elbow.

Sam ripped the rifle away from the leader, who couldn't resist and raised his hands to his face. He had to touch himself, see the damage. Blood ran down the fresh canyon like an ancient river. Sam did him a favor and shot him in the head.

Ed fought to rise, reaching out, clutching at empty space.

The last soldier had just enough time to pivot, raise his rifle, and fire. Three bullets stitched through Sam's chest. The third spiraled through the left ventricle, killing him instantly.

Then Ed was on the soldier, catching hold of the assault rifle, twisting it against the soldier's arms, jamming the barrel up into the soft flesh between the V of the jawbone, and pushed on the trigger finger. He emptied the clip. Nearly thirty rounds exploded up through the soldier's skull, obliterating the brain, transforming it into a fine red mist that hung in the air like steam over a hot dog stand.

Ed brought his foot down on the next soldier's head, driving his heel through the man's temple. He ripped that assault rifle away and unloaded it into the man in a blind tsunami of rage.

Qween rolled onto the last living soldier and drove her

thumb and forefinger into his eyes, brought them together in the soft meat behind the bridge of his nose, and pulled. The man's mouth flopped open, and he moaned. It was an alien, uncomprehending sound of pain and confusion. She shook his skull back and forth, the way a small dog will shake its master's sock. Eventually, the man stopped twitching and lay quiet.

Ed dropped the assault rifle. He stumbled past Qween, and knelt next to his partner. Sam was dead. Ed knew this immediately. He did not try to shake his friend. He did not try to speak, to try and reach the man. He laid his hand over Sam's chest, then patted it once.

He found another clip, reloaded, and stalked off, heading for the helicopter. Qween retrieved her razor and followed.

# CHAPTER 75

**9:09 PM**
**August 14**

They kept Tommy pinned to the ground, a boot on his head. When he'd been pushed to the sidewalk, he'd had a quick flash of everyone kneeling down behind the wall of sandbags. He couldn't be sure, but he thought that Grace and Phil were somewhere behind him, fifteen to twenty feet back down the wall. Kimmy too. Tommy tried to concentrate.

How many soldiers?

He couldn't remember. He tried to twist his head slightly, feeling the grit of the concrete grind into the side of his face, just to count the boots. The pressure on his skull was unrelenting. When the soldier felt him trying to move, the weight increased. Black stars bloomed and popped in front of his eyes.

Maybe a dozen soldiers. Maybe.

All he could really see was that the smoke was really pouring out of the subway tunnels now, obscuring everything in an acrid mist. He didn't think he could hear anything over the thunder of the helicopter, but he recognized the brief burst of shooting across the street, back toward City Hall.

"It's done!" Phil called out. "Let's go!"

More gunfire.

The soldiers paused. Maybe one of the prisoners wasn't quite dead, and that could explain the second round of shooting. They watched the trucks lined up along City Hall. For a moment, nothing moved but the smoke rising from underground. Then more gunfire, this time long and sustained. Someone was emptying a clip. Then, incredibly, even more firing.

Tommy rolled his eyes, trying to see how the soldiers were reacting. Several pairs of boots gathered, and he could hear them arguing. The crack from a single shot echoed across the plaza and was lost in the roar of the helicopter. Tommy barely heard it. But he felt the sudden release as the boot squashing his face against the sidewalk was suddenly gone. He twisted slightly and saw the soldier falling askew over the sandbag wall.

The soldiers around him opened up, sending a long, continuous barrage at the trucks across Clark. The gunfire even drowned out the Sikorsky for a quick second. Curved ammunition magazines hit the sidewalk around Tommy, bouncing and hollow. Fresh, full clips were slammed into place in the soldiers' rifles.

Several soldiers started back across Clark.

Tommy eased into a sitting position, when he felt a hot barrel against the back of his head. "Sit still, or I will kill you outright, I shit you not," a voice yelled above him.

Tommy froze.

Another burst of gunfire. This time it came from farther up Clark, halfway to Randolph. Another soldier fell. The rest responded, drenching the area with bullets. More clips hit the cement and more soldiers started drifting across the street.

Tommy glanced to his right. Only three soldiers crouched between him and his daughter. He could take them, but he wasn't sure he would survive. And if he couldn't get his daughter out of the city, then she would die as well. He curled his toes, flexed the muscles in his legs, and waited for a chance.

Five soldiers crept across Clark. Their rifles were up and ready, eyes alert, sweeping through the thickening smoke. Their boots were silent, hard rubber on pavement. A flickering flash of gunfire exploded from between two of the M939s. One of the soldiers went down. The rest answered immediately, squeezing triggers until the clips were empty.

Another single shot. Another soldier down.

More empty clips dropped. More full magazines were slapped into place.

More shooting. But this time, it came from a totally different direction.

A group of five or six soldiers erupted from the subway steps. They turned as one and fired back down into the subway. One of them suddenly noticed the giant Sikorsky, empty and waiting, in the middle of Daley Plaza. He punched the nearest soldier and pointed. They backed out of the stairs as one and bolted for the chopper.

Phil saw this and screamed, "Stop! Stop! That's ours!" He sat up on the berm, pulled the girl up by her hair and flung her over the other side. He ran after the soldiers, dragging Grace along. The Sikorsky could seat over thirty passengers, but Phil was afraid it would leave without him. When he got close to the blades he turned and screamed back at Tommy and the remaining soldiers, "Come on! Run!" His hand was starting to cramp on him, so he wound his other hand through Grace's hair and squeezed.

He flexed his first hand for a while, watching as two soldiers popped out and ran toward him. The soldiers fleeing from the subway started shouting at them. One of the soldiers from the Sikorsky shook his head and gestured at the circle of lights. The subway soldiers didn't like it, but they took up posts halfway between the spinning blades and the circle of lights.

The soldier in charge jogged over to Phil. "Where's the patient?"

Phil pointed back at Tommy, who was being pushed over the wall. For a minute, they had to drag him along, but only because he thought Grace was still back behind the berm. When he saw her with Phil near the chopper, he straightened up and walked on his own. The soldiers were content to follow him peacefully, keeping their guns aimed at the ground, as long as he was headed in the right direction.

The soldier nodded and jerked his head back at the chopper. Phil took that as a signal to get onboard, so he pulled Grace with him and climbed through the single door. Inside, an aisle ran up through the rows of seats, three on one side, two on the other. He dragged Grace up to the first row behind the cockpit and threw the girl into the seat nearest the window.

Phil stuck his head into the cockpit. "Soon as the patient is onboard, we're out of here, you got me?" He left before the pilot could answer and went back down the aisle and stood in the doorway. Tommy was making his way across the plaza, getting closer to the whipping blades, but still moving unbelievably slow.

"Hurry the fuck up!" Phil yelled. His words were lost in the wash of the rotors. No matter. Tommy would be inside the chopper within thirty seconds, and they would be safely in the air, leaving all the shooting and infection and death beneath them. They would deliver Tommy to Dr. Reischtal, and Phil and Lee could take their rightful place in the media as heroes of the pandemic.

Phil was just beginning to bask in the glow of the anticipated admiration, and yes, even awe, when the lights of the city disappeared, plunging Chicago into near total darkness.

\* \* \*

Every light surrounding the plaza winked out, and the only illumination left came from the blue flashing lights of the Sikorsky. The soldiers let loose with a few panicked bursts of gunfire, then stopped when they realized they couldn't see anything. The soldier closest to Tommy said, "Oh . . . you fucking, oh fuck . . ."

Tommy guessed one of the fires or explosions in the subways had fried one of the ComEd transformer stations. It had happened before, leaving most of the Loop without power for a summer afternoon. Beyond that, he ignored the darkness, focusing only on Grace, somewhere on that chopper. It was lit up like an angry, monochromatic Christmas tree, settled in the middle of Daley Plaza and none too happy about it.

As he got closer though, Tommy faced the stark realization that once he was onboard, it would be over. Once he was inside, they would continue to use Grace against him. He was back where he started, powerless while they threatened his daughter.

He ducked under the massive spinning blades, crept to the doorway, and stopped. He'd gotten far enough ahead of the soldiers that he could afford to sit and wait a moment.

Phil stuck his head out and saw Tommy just standing there. It drove Phil crazy. "Get inside, now!"

"No," Tommy said.

Phil pulled a snub-nosed .38 from his waistband. It looked like something an old-fashioned mobster would carry. Beyond five feet, it was about as accurate as a crumpled paper airplane. He'd be lucky to hit a tank if he was shooting from inside. Phil had waved away the teasing from his buddies at their dinners. "If I'm not up close enough to let this baby take care of a problem, then I deserve to die for being a dumb fuck."

He shook the pistol at Tommy. "Get in here!"

"Go ahead. Shoot me," Tommy said, knowing damn well that Phil wouldn't.

Phil smiled. "Not gonna shoot you, asshole. I'm gonna shoot your fucking daughter."

Lee came out of the darkness, struggling to pull away from the clutches of Kimmy. She was whimpering, begging for something. Lee ripped his arm out of her grasp. Lee had his own Glock out. He finally shoved it in her chest. "Stupid cunt, shut the fuck up."

"Thank Christ," Phil said and pointed at Tommy. "Get this cocksucker on board."

Lee put the Glock back in his shoulder holster, hopped out of the chopper, and came in low. Tommy tried to pivot, tried to get his arms up, tried to follow the bigger man's movements, but Tommy hadn't had anything solid to eat in nearly four days, hadn't gotten any decent sleep, and simply didn't know enough about bare-knuckle brawling to stop Lee.

Lee hit Tommy twice, an easy left-right combination that knocked Tommy to the ground. Tommy tried to push himself off the cement, but Lee kicked him in the ribs. And just like that, the fight was finished.

Lee grabbed the back of Tommy's scrubs and lifted him off the ground. Tommy struggled, but only managed to twist in Lee's grasp, and clung weakly to Lee's head and shoulders. He drew back one feeble fist, and Lee drove his own fist into Tommy's stomach. The air exploded out of Tommy's lungs and he collapsed in defeat, sliding his hands down Lee's chest as he crumpled in half. He huddled on the ground, tears spilling down through the dust and grit on his cheeks.

Lee threw Tommy inside the helicopter, then climbed on after him. Kimmy followed.

Tommy tried to crawl down the aisle to reach Grace. Somewhere, he could hear his daughter screaming, "Daddy! Daddy!" He kept crawling forward, head spinning, pain ricocheting through his body.

Shooting erupted outside.

# CHAPTER 76

It was the infected.

They came swarming out of the darkness, unheard over the throbbing rotors of the Sikorsky. The first soldiers saw them and started shooting immediately. The ear-shattering sound of the gunfire and the muzzle flashes drew the infected like moths to hot neon. They attacked with the speed of shadows, tearing the soldiers apart before the victims' eyes could adjust to the darkness.

Those inside the helicopter stared out through the few tiny windows, but couldn't see much beyond the incessant muzzle flashes as the fully automatic assault rifles ripped great swaths in the night, cutting down the infected by the dozens. But for every one that fell, another ten took their place. The soldiers tightened their perimeter, backing slowly to the Sikorsky, firing nonstop.

The infected got close enough that Lee could see them in the glow of the landing lights. He yelled up the cabin at Phil, "Oh, shit! They're everywhere!"

Phil opened the cockpit door again, and said, "Go! Go!"

Something smashed the door into Phil's head, stunning

him enough that he dropped to his knees. His revolver fell to the floor.

Tommy was on his hands and knees, but he wasn't helpless. He'd been waiting for his chance. So when Phil stuck his head in the cockpit door, Tommy launched himself at the door and drove his shoulder into it, slamming Phil's head in the doorframe. As Phil dropped, Tommy came up and turned to catch Grace, who had leapt out of her seat and wrapped her arms around her daddy's neck.

He rose to his feet and started back down the aisle.

Lee blocked his way. He smiled. "I'm gonna be there when that crazy fuck cuts into you. I want to watch the—"

Tommy didn't have the time. He shifted Grace to the side, still holding her with his left hand, and pulled Lee's Glock out of his waistband with his right. He'd slipped it out of Lee's shoulder holster when Lee had been lifting him outside of the chopper. After faking the extent of the blow so he could curl up and slip it into his pants, he'd let himself be thrown onboard, keeping the pistol pinned to his hip with his elbow.

As he brought it up, there was just enough time for the expression on Lee's face to crumble from a satisfied smirk to a narrowing of the eyes. He was reaching for his holster, as if to check if his handgun was still there, when Tommy shot him in the face at point-blank range.

Lee's head snapped back and he fell flat into the aisle. Kimmy screamed, wiping at the blood on her face.

"Run!" Tommy yelled at her, not stopping, still coming down the aisle, stepping on Lee's corpse. He heard movement behind him and started to turn, knowing that he was too slow, knowing that the bullet from Phil's revolver was in on its way. He couldn't believe Phil was upright so quickly.

But Phil was indeed standing up, wobbling and blinking through the pain. His nose had been smashed, and blood sheeted his upper lip, dribbling down over his mouth and pouring over his chin. "Mudderfugger," he wheezed and squeezed off a shot with his stubby .38.

Tommy flinched at the report, but the blast went wide.

Phil started forward, blowing bubbles of blood, intent on getting close enough so he couldn't miss. Tommy stumbled backwards, trying to shift Grace to the side so he could shield her with his own body. Phil fired again.

Tommy heard a harsh grunt and glanced over his shoulder at Kimmy. The slug had caught her in the neck. She dropped back into one of the flight crew's bench seats, raised her hand to her throat. She looked down in surprise at the blood on her fingers.

Tommy had the Glock up now, fired twice, and missed both times.

Phil dove sideways behind a row of seats.

Tommy turned back and ran, jumping through the open doorway.


Outside, the soldiers were still learning the hard way how noise and light drew the infected. The soldiers ignored Tommy and Grace completely, intent on shooting at the rushing swarm. More soldiers were now escaping from the subway and once they saw the chopper, they went sprinting for it across the plaza.

Metal scraped across metal. About fifteen yards down Washington, a manhole cover popped out of its groove and slid into the street. Soldiers immediately lunged out, crawling feverishly onto the street. Most were unarmed, having lost their weapons below. As soon as they found their feet, they broke out running in all directions. Some saw the chopper and broke for it.

Tommy stayed low and kept moving, holding Grace tight on his hip, running like a fullback weaving and dodging through the defensive linemen. He reached the sandbag wall on the western side of the plaza and dropped to his knees, crouching, covering Grace with his body. Her emotions had caught up to her and she started to cry. He put his lips against her ears and whispered, "Shhhh, shhhh. It's okay. Daddy's got you now. Daddy's got you. Shhh. Shhhh."

Behind him, the sound of the Sikorsky's rotors changed pitch. The pilots had finally decided enough was enough, and they were pulling out. The massive engines whined, and the tree-length blades sliced through the air, slow at first, then faster and faster as the last of the soldiers scrambled on board. More soldiers ran into Daley Plaza every second, bursting out of more manhole covers and the shadows surrounding Washington and Clark. But the CH-53K wasn't waiting. Lights flashed as the chopper lifted into the air like a constipated dragonfly, moving slowly, weaving slightly, having trouble putting distance between itself and the ground.

Some of the soldiers started shooting at the ascending helicopter. The panic had slipped into anger that quickly; if they couldn't get a lift out, if the chopper wouldn't wait for them, then fuck it, no one was getting out. At least two of the squads carried a rocket launcher and fired them. They missed two out of three times. The third time, the first rocket caught the helicopter right in the guts, and vaporized seven of the soldiers inside.

The CH-53K was blown sideways, tail up, nose at the rushing ground. The pilot fought against being blown head over heels, a death spasm for this helicopter. The blades, seventy-nine feet long, whipped through the air at eight hundred feet per second. The pilot brought the nose up but couldn't manage to stay in the middle of the street.

Phil spent the last seconds of his life trying to get out of his seat belt. He thought if he could just get out of the seat and move to the back of the helicopter he could survive the crash. He tried, but couldn't manage to compress the right buttons

SLEEP TIGHT

455

in his panic and stayed trapped in his seat. Not that it would have mattered in the end.

The pilot had almost leveled off when the blades smacked through the glass and concrete of one of the theater buildings to the east. One of the four blades caught fast on a steel beam in the building's fourteenth floor, and in less time then it takes to blink, the rest of the blades snapped into the beam and it was all over. The chopper whipped around as if it was slapping the building with its tail rotors. The fuel didn't catch until it was halfway down the building, tumbling and bouncing down the side of the wall of glass, and it finally exploded. The wreckage slammed into the sidewalk in front of a Starbucks, sending burning fuel across the street in a blazing sunflower display. The impact blew an angry huff of wind back through the streets.

Dr. Reischtal watched it all unfold on the two monitors fed by the Apaches. The Sikorsky's explosion blew out the infrared cameras and the images dissolved in a bright blast of green light.

Dr. Reischtal didn't move. He watched the chaos without expression.

A few seconds later, the heat died away, and he could once again see how the plaza had been overrun. It was impossible to discern the soldiers from the infected. He kept searching for a figure carrying a child. This individual was all that mattered now. He wanted, no *needed*, to see the figure surrounded and attacked, to watch the infected hack Tommy Krazinsky and his daughter into pieces, to witness the man and the girl being ripped limb from limb.

He couldn't find them.

Perhaps it was time to inform the president. Chicago was lost.

He dialed the number. Waited for the ring. Instead, there was just a dull click. Then nothing. He dialed it again. Same result. Dr. Reischtal left his phone face up on the table, stretched out his palms, curled his fingers into claws, then pulled them back to him, scraping his short fingernails across the plastic. The president was either too busy to answer, or was avoiding him.

Either way, it didn't change anything.

Chicago was still finished.

He called Evans.

"Just got through," Evans said. "Damn near there. Give us half an hour, forty-five minutes to get clear. I'll call you as soon as we're all topside."

Dr. Reischtal said, "Of course," and hung up. Evans had twelve trucks with him. They would provide the initial blast, sending death up through the underground caverns and subway tunnels. Three more tankers had been left in the massive parking garage under Millennium Park, at the north end of Grant Park. Six more had been spaced out along Lower Wacker, covering the north and west sides of the Loop.

If three trucks had been enough to utterly destroy Soldier Field, over twenty would vaporize most of downtown Chicago, and the tankers full of 2-4-5 Trioxin interspersed with the rest of the explosives would extinguish every form of carbon-based life within the blast radius.

Unlike Soldier Field, where only three trucks had to be synced, this would involve linking at least twenty-four trucks. It was time to begin. Dr. Reischtal dialed the number to start the arming process.


The fireball from the Sikorsky wreckage had drawn infected from all over the city. Most of them were infested with bedbugs. The bugs crawled through their hair, in and out of noses. Sometimes bugs would cluster in groups and feed, usually down around the corners of the mouth in a frozen, scaly scab of thirty or forty. Some of the freshly infected were still shambling around in a drunken haze. Not enough blood had been taken to steal consciousness and the victim could only fight to stay upright while coughing bugs out of their lungs and brushing them away from their eyeballs, surrendering the rest of their skin.

For the most part, the infected ignored Tommy and Grace, focusing instead on the fireball to the northeast. They flowed through the smoke across Daley Plaza, sometimes howling and gibbering with rage at the flickering light and erratic spurts of gunfire still chattering around the streets, as the soldiers fled in all directions.

Tommy watched a young blond woman, who might have been attractive once, stagger past. Her skin was blotchy and swollen. Bugs crawled up her neck. A pair of bloody panties was still clinging around one ankle. It didn't take much imagination to see how Tommy and Grace would be transformed, and how they would become a slave to the virus.

Tommy whispered to Grace, "We're gonna play a game, okay? We're gonna be as quiet as we can, okay? Remember that movie where the girl went sneaking around her house, 'cause she didn't want to get caught? That's us, baby. We're gonna be quiet, right?"

Grace nodded.

Tommy held her tight and breathed into her ear, "Good girl." He eased over the sandbags and moved slowly toward City Hall. As long as they were quiet and kept their distance, it didn't even appear that the infected even saw them. It didn't look like they could see much beyond their own agony anyway.

Tommy crouched next to the stage and looked for the square, heavy packets the soldiers had taken earlier. There, up near the podium. Tommy set Grace down and said, "Okay, little girl. You climb under there for just a minute and hide. I'm going up on top of this just for a minute and I can't crawl and carry you. I just gotta grab these two important things, and I'll be right back. You stay still. And quiet."

Grace nodded, putting her finger to her lips. Tommy

kissed her forehead and wriggled across the stage. He had one packet and was reaching for the second when he heard Grace scream.

In the street behind him, not ten feet from where Grace hid, one of the soldiers from the subways dropped to his knees and pulled out a knife out of his belt. He must have been freshly infected and the awful itching was upon him. Weeping, he twisted the blade across his skull, sawing it back and forth in a desperate effort to satiate the horrible sensation. His sobbing rose into a moan and he drove the knife blade into his armpit, scraping it back and forth.

She watched this, couldn't hold back the terror, and screamed.

Before Tommy knew what was even happening, one of the infected was already on his knees, crawling under the stage to reach Grace. She screamed even louder. The infected, a middle-aged man in a suit, stretched out and clawed at the girl. Bugs flitted across his face, wiggling in and out of his ears and collar. They covered his back and spilled out of his shoes.

Tommy scrabbled back across the stage, realizing that he wouldn't make it in time.

Suddenly, Qween was there, grabbing the man's ankles and dragging him away. She pulled him across the pavement, dropped his legs, and tried to catch her breath as he howled at her and rolled over. She kicked him in the head, avoiding the bugs that spilled off of him.

But she wasn't fast enough to avoid the bug that latched onto the back of her hand. And by the time she spotted it in the flickering light from the flames across the plaza, it was too late. The thing had already driven its proboscis into her skin and was drinking her blood when she smashed it with her thumb. She flicked it into the street.

She tucked the thoughts and panic away and let her eyes go soft. She knelt and peered under the stage at Grace. "Now,

now, baby girl, don't fret none. Miss Qween is here, and nothin's gonna hurt you."

Tommy rolled off the stage and met Qween's eyes. "Thank you."

Qween waved it away. "Hush."

Ed stepped close, assault rifle tight in his fists. "Didn't want to use the rifle," he whispered. "Too many—"

His words were drowned out by the roar of one of the Apaches as it came in low, driving a turbulent wind down Clark. It blasted them with the searchlight, and as Ed spun and looked back across the plaza, he could see every infected's head swivel and lock onto the light, as if it was a beacon where they could find relief and exorcise the crippling rage that scurried through their minds.

Ed fired up at the light, superior firepower be damned. The rifle spit empty shells across the stage and his crouching companions as he followed the light. "Run," he yelled, and fired again.

Tommy and Qween scrambled to their feet and ran to City Hall. Tommy had Grace on his hip again and carried the two square packets with his other hand. Ed followed, firing blindly over his shoulder. They pushed through the spinning doors and stumbled up the dark hallway.

Tommy and Qween stopped to rest, but Ed pushed them along. "No, no. Run! Run!"

Behind them, the doors exploded. The moratorium against killing Tommy was over, and the Apaches were itching to unleash a barrage of Hellfire missiles. The building shook as more missiles streaked down and transformed the east side of City Hall into smoking rubble.

Ed, Qween, and Tommy ran until they stood in the nexus of the four hallways, smack in the dead center of the building. Even before the smoke had cleared down the east hallway, they could hear the infected throwing themselves against the wreckage of the door, clawing their way through the chunks of concrete and the mangled remains of the spinning door.

More explosions.

Ed said, "They're gonna bring this whole building down around us if we don't figure out something fast."

Qween said, "Let's sneak out down there." She nodded at the south hallway. "Gotta be a truck or something, something that still has the keys inside, like Sam's bus. Fuck it. Drive that sucker to the lake."

Ed shook his head. "They've got infrared. Doesn't matter how dark it is out there. We wouldn't make it five feet."

"I got an idea. But it won't work for all of us." Tommy looked from Ed to Qween. "We go deep, into the tunnels," he said. "That was my idea from the beginning. That's why I grabbed these." He held up one of the packets and opened it. A hazmat suit, complete with a helmet and air filter, had been vacuum sealed inside. "These will keep the bugs out. But I've only got two."

Ed fingered the tears in his own hazmat suit. "Hell, we need four. Them bugs'll crawl right inside." He shook his head. "Maybe we can go a short distance. I can try and keep 'em off."

"That's how we gonna get out of here," Qween said. "We'll go down into the subway and come up on the other side of the street."

"We don't have enough suits," Tommy said.

Qween gave a tired smile. "It's okay. I ain't fitting in one a' them things anyhow." She held up her hand and the look on her face was enough to tell them that she was already bitten.

"We'll split up then," Ed said. "Me and Qween will take the subway and come out across the street. If they don't see us, then I'll call Arturo soon as we get a chance. If they spot us, we'll draw them off you."

Tommy shook his head. "Won't matter. I'm going deep. Gonna head down, go under the river, come up into the storm drains on the other side."

Ed thought a moment and nodded. "Fair enough. But don't waste time. I got a feeling that sonofabitch ain't gonna be satisfied by just watching those choppers shoot the shit out of City Hall. I bet he's got something else up his sleeve."

Tommy unfurled one of the hazmat suits and climbed inside. Ed and Qween helped Grace climb into hers. It was huge on her; her arms and legs barely reached the elbows and knees of the suit. "Doesn't matter," Tommy said. "Seal her in. Got an idea."

Once his own suit was completely sealed, he leaned over Grace and said, "Okay, little girl. Ready to go for a ride? Pull your arms and legs in and sit Indian style, okay?" Grace did. Tommy took the empty arms of her suit and lifted her onto his back, pulling the left arm over his shoulder and the right arm under his right armpit. Ed saw where he was going and tied the arms together across his chest, then pulled the empty legs around Tommy's hips and tied them.

"Good luck," Ed said.

As the Apaches continued to fire missiles into the building, the group descended into the darkness under Chicago.

# CHAPTER 77

*10:31 PM*
*August 14*

Dr. Reischtal's phone lay faceup on the table. The trucks had been synced. The voice recognition software had confirmed Dr. Reischtal's identity. The system was armed and ready for the signal. On his phone, the green SEND button blinked patiently.

He'd been waiting, hoping to see some sign, something, someone trying to escape from the wreckage of City Hall. The Apaches had fired over thirty Hellfire missiles into the doorway and first-floor windows, but the building still stood, a testimonial to the strength and tenacity of the stone structure.

One of the Apache pilots' voices crackled over the radio. "Still no sign, sir. Should we expand the sweep?"

Dr. Reischtal slumped back and didn't bother to answer. While his sense of professional responsibility had been bruised, as well as his pride if he was honest, he told himself it mattered little. One tiny signal, and it would be all over.

"Sir? Do you copy?"

Dr. Reischtal shut the radio off.

He looked at his phone.

Yes, the toll had been devastating. The ancient one had

almost succeeded with infecting the world and bringing with it a new age of darkness. But with God's grace, Dr. Reischtal was about to choke the life out of the evil, and send it back to hell by burning Chicago off the map.

He picked up his phone.

The door to the chamber on the other side of the plastic slammed open and Dr. Reischtal watched as the black detective and the homeless woman stared back at him.

"It's over," the detective said.

Dr. Reischtal agreed with him. Nodding, he hit SEND. "Yes. Now it is over."


Tommy found a discarded flamethrower and used the blue pilot light to find his way through the darkness. He had only encountered a few of the infected, and these were too sick to move much. They flinched and turned away from the light, forcing themselves tighter into cracks and under ledges.

Bugs covered everything.

Sometimes they crawled over Tommy and Grace and Tommy had to stop and wipe them off his faceplate. The hazmat suits worked, and kept the bugs out. Once in a while he would turn and see how Grace was doing. He couldn't hear her because she was too far away to use the little microphone in the air filter, but he could see her chubby fist giving him a thumbs-up in the flattened faceplate.

Tommy used his experience from working for Streets and Sans, and tried to remember everything that Don had taught him about the labyrinth of tunnels and cracks and abandoned lines under Chicago. He worked his way through the darkness, flicking the trigger on the flamethrower to make sure the tunnels were clear. In some ways, it was almost easier than if the city was up and running. Back then, they would have had to work hard to avoid the rushing trains and electrified third rail. Now, Tommy could walk straight up the center of the tracks.

He passed the signs of the battles. Huge piles of dead rats. Misty pockets of pesticides, where the dead bugs created a swamp nearly two feet deep. Bodies of soldiers. Bodies of subway passengers, caught by the rats or bugs before the evacuation. The bodies of the infected, who had crawled down into the musty gloom to escape the noise and light from above.

He untied Grace and cradled her as he slipped through a crack that took him down nearly twenty feet. This particular tunnel had not been used in years, and the tracks were covered in dust. No bodies of humans, but plenty of dead rats. And always, always, the bugs. They swarmed over Tommy and Grace, sensing heat and blood inside. Tommy moved slow, careful not to snag their suits on anything sharp.

He retied Grace on his back and studied the tunnel before him. It split in two, and Tommy's gaze went back and forth between the two dark channels. "Goddamnit." His metallic whisper echoed around the chamber. One of the tunnels eventually hooked up with north branch of the Blue Line at Clinton. The other dead-ended back in the massive cavern where Lee had been dumping all the illegal trash.

He couldn't remember which tunnel was which.

The blackened railroad ties under his feet shivered, and he heard a distant, deep rumble. The cracking roar grew louder. Dust sifted off the walls and filled the air. The ground started to shake in earnest, as if Chicago was suffering an earthquake.

There was no time left.

He picked the left tunnel and started running.


When Dr. Reischtal hit SEND, they heard a growl of thunder somewhere far off on the horizon. But that was all. A few minutes later, there was a gentle rocking as the warship rode the lazy swells that had been pushed into the lake from the blast.

Ed ran his palm over the smooth, transparent plastic and

ignored Dr. Reischtal. Qween clutched her bundle of rags, sat at the table, and just watched the man inside the sterile room.

Dr. Reischtal was hitting buttons, making phone calls, but no one was answering. Ed wasn't surprised.

Earlier, they'd come up out of the subway across Clark and quietly made their way east to the lake. Ed had called Arturo. Arturo sent a police launch for them and told Ed that somebody in the upper levels of the federal government, somebody with some juice, maybe even somebody in the joint chiefs of staff wanted the mess in Chicago over. They couldn't trust Dr. Reischtal anymore and they were more than willing to let someone else do their dirty work for them.

Whoever it was had called ahead. No one on the boat stopped them. The soldiers stood silent and still and watched as Ed helped Qween along. One soldier had escorted them down to Dr. Reischtal's safe room, then stood aside while they went in.

Dr. Reischtal said, "I know your names. As before, I will find you. I will finish you."

Ed didn't say anything. He studied the bubble of plastic, feeling for any cracks, any stress fractures. He settled on the curve along the upper right corner, then hefted the fire axe he'd picked up on the way down into the bowels of the ship.

Dr. Reischtal almost laughed. "You do realize that this material is virtually indestructible. This warship could sink to the bottom of Lake Michigan and I would still be sitting comfortably inside when the divers came."

Ed peeled his hazmat suit down to his waist, hefted the axe and swung it sideways in the cramped room, as if he was swinging for a high fastball. The blade bounced off the plastic with the sound of a boat propeller hitting a frozen pond. Ed looked like he expected nothing less. He pulled the axe back and swung again.

And again.

Dr. Reischtal said, "Even if you manage to crack it, it will take you days to create a hole large enough to fit inside. And I have no intentions of leaving. I have enough rations to last weeks, if necessary. When the authorities do show up, I will make you wish you had died back in that city."

Ed never stopped. He kept swinging, smashing the axe blade into the same spot, over and over. After nearly half an hour, sweat was pouring off of him and he was breathing in short, whistling bursts. He swung again, and this time, it sounded slightly different.

A tiny sliver of plastic landed on the table in front of Qween. She picked it up and sleepily inspected it. She smiled. Ed stepped up the pace, swinging even harder. When the blade struck, it now sent up a flurry of plastic shards.

Before long, the blade broke through, puncturing the surface.

"Not so airtight now, are you, motherfucker?" Qween asked.

Dr. Reischtal didn't answer. He tried his phone again, but it wouldn't function at all.

Ed didn't stop. He worked at the hole, created a jagged rupture nearly a foot in diameter. He stepped back, gasping, and dropped into one of the chairs. The axe clattered to the floor. Then, as if remembering something else, he picked the axe back up, walked over to the locked door that led into Dr. Reischtal's safe room, and wedged the axe handle up under the door handle. He kicked it tight, then went back and sat down.

Qween rose with all the regal elegance her name implied, and approached the hole. She still carried her bundle. She gave Dr. Reischtal another chilling smile, untied the bundle, and pulled out a rat by the tail.

Hundreds of bugs wriggled through the coarse hair.

The rat blinked, dazed, trying to shake off the deep sleep. She gently pushed it through the uneven hole and dropped it inside the once sterile room.

As Dr. Reischtal gave a hoarse cry, she turned to Ed and leaned on the table. "I need to breathe some real air."

He stood and took her arm. They left Dr. Reischtal scrabbling around, stomping at the bugs that were flowing off the rat. He slapped his phone down, squashing four or five at a time. But they kept coming, covering the floor. He climbed up on his chair, then to his table. All of the monitors had gone dark.

As they were leaving, Ed turned out the lights, leaving Dr. Reischtal alone with the bugs.

Dr. Reischtal still had lights, of course, but the darkness beyond the plastic bubble filled him with a horror he hadn't felt since his parents had used to lock him in the basement closet.

For a few brief moments, he thought he might actually be able to kill all of the bugs, until he spotted one nestling into the cleft between his toes. He snaked a finger down there, squashing it. His finger came back up with just the hint of a smear of blood. It was enough.

And while he stared at the fresh blood on his index finger, more bugs swarmed his bare feet and ankles, and started up his legs. He knew it was over and knelt back down on the floor, clasped his hands in front of his chest, and closed his eyes.

If he could only see the stars.


Ed and Qween made their way to the bow, faces lit by the glow of the fires in the Loop. The skyline was so different, as if a child had come along and swept his building blocks away, leaving some stacks barely standing, dashing others to the ground.

The sky over the lake was alive with helicopters.

"I'm awful damn tired," Qween said. "Gonna rest now, I think."

"You want help?" Ed asked without looking at her.

"You got a good heart for a cop, Ed Jones. And I thank you. I truly do. This is my job. Not yours."

Ed nodded, not trusting himself to speak. He stood abruptly, pulling his .357 out of its holster. He held it by the barrel and offered it to her, handle first.

She took a deep breath, then finally took it. "Now go. Find your woman. Take care of her. And yourself." She met his eyes, shiny with unspilled tears. "Gonna take me a nap."

He kissed her forehead and left.

She watched Chicago burn for a while, felt her eyelids grow heavier and heavier. She considered the long sleep ahead of her and what awaited when she finally awoke. She could feel the strength slowly leaving her bones, replaced by something cold and sluggish.

She thought about her home. Gone now.

She opened her mouth and put the barrel of Ed's .357 inside. As she watched the distant glow of the shattered Chicago skyline, she tilted the handgun until she felt the tip of the barrel tight against the roof of her mouth. She took one more deep breath and let it out slow, aware of the humidity in the air, the slow roll of the warship in the new waves spreading out across the lake, the coolness of the bench under her, the faint spattering of stars above, the rough checkerboard pattern of the handgun's grip in her hand.

Then she squeezed the trigger.

And slept.

Ed got back in the police launch and heard the single gunshot.

He sat heavily in the stern. He kicked off the hazmat suit and threw it in the lake. He stuck his hand in his back pocket and pulled Sam's flask out. He unscrewed the lid, avoiding the surreptitious glances from the two cops at the controls.

"You wanna go back?" one of them asked.

Ed shook his head. "No. It's gone. How much gas we got?"

The cop checked. "Full tank."

Ed took another shot from Sam's flask, felt the burning as it trickled down his throat. "East. Michigan."

The cops looked back at the ruined city. One threw the line back to the soldiers on the warship. His partner hit the throttle, spun the wheel, and they headed east.

Ed screwed the cap back on the flask and tucked it safely away. As they sped across the lake, he leaned back and watched the sky.

A harsh, foul-smelling wind swirled down Clinton, a narrow side street west of the Loop. Tiny pink particles floated in the air currents, little messengers of death for anything that used oxygen. Flowers wilted. Leaves fell from trees.

Down in the middle of the empty street, a manhole cover moved slightly. It rose up, then fell back. It was lifted again from underneath, and this time, it was pushed up hard enough to slip out of its circular edging, and shoved across the pavement. A figure in a hazmat suit climbed slowly out, then lifted another suit with a smaller figure curled inside.

The hazmat suit staggered along, carrying the second suit, slung over its shoulder like hobo luggage. It bent over, peering into parked cars. It came to a car, a late-model gray sedan, double parked, blocking the right lane. The door was unlocked. The keys were in the ignition.

The hazmat figure looked at the pink dust on his suit, then back at the peculiar rainbow smoke rising from the manhole. Beyond the manhole, back toward what was left of the Loop, a shimmering glow filled the sky.

Tommy lifted Grace, put her in the passenger seat, and strapped her in. He held the faceplate over her head and asked, "You good?"

She smiled as if sitting in this strange car, encased in an adult's hazmat suit was the most natural thing in the world, and gave him another thumbs-up. He smiled back, unable to contain his joy. He had his daughter.

He twisted the key in the ignition, expecting to hear the monotonous clicking of a dead battery. But it had only been four days, after all. The engine turned over almost immediately. He turned on the headlights, put the car into drive, and they pulled away.